MW00423162

NATHAN M. HURST

Clarion

Copyright © 2018 by Nathan M. Hurst

All rights reserved.

First Edition: March 2018

This book is a work of fiction. Names, characters, places and incidents are products of the author's imagination. Any resemblance to actual events, locales, or persons, living or dead, is entirely coincidental. No part of this publication can be reproduced or transmitted in any form or by any means, without permission in writing from the author.

ISBN: 9780993582332 (e-book)
ISBN: 9780993582325 (paperback)

Published by Nathan M. Hurst
www.nathanmhurst.com

Copyediting: Fiona Viney

Cover Art: Sparth
www.sparth.com

Formatting: Nathan M. Hurst

To Mum, Dad, Simon and Aryn.

ACKNOWLEDGMENTS

As always, a huge thank you to Fiona Viney for her keen edits, and to Stu Viney for his constructive beta views. To my wife Jo, for her constant positive support and understanding, even as half-formed ideas leave my brain mid-sentence. Cool cover art as always by the amazing Nicolas Bouvier (Sparth). To the many behind-the-scenes people who don't even know they are helping. Thanks.

And thank the maker for good coffee.

Clarion

PROLOGUE

Waking was not always the best option in life. From the comfortable oblivion that had been his slumber, he found his eyes complaining about an intense brightness searing through his eyelids, a pink and orange which also felt like it was melting his face with the heat of it. He tried to raise his hands but found he couldn't move them: restrained at the wrists. He tried several more times with increasing levels of force and anxiety. His feet seemed to be equally restrained and there was also a wide band around his chest, which clamped him tight to the couch he was laying on. Someone didn't want him moving.

Slowly opening his eyes a crack to try and get an idea of his situation, a lance of white light worked across them. Squinting into the brightness, he tried to look around for somewhere in the room that might have a light source less intense than a supernova, but it seemed like he was surrounded. He was surprised that he could move his head. With the rest of his body restrained, he wondered why they had left his head free to look around.

Memories started to come back to him. The last thing he remembered was being carried through the hatch of a maintenance airlock, manhandled by a security team down to the brig. But this wasn't the brig.

They had been sneaky and duped him; he should have listened to his instincts but he was just too curious to let it go. When a new nav trace had appeared in his bio-comms, he had instantly believed it to be a glitch, but when it started moving with him and tempting

1

him to take a different path away from the safety of the others and his base camp he got curious. It had crossed his mind that it might be a trap, but how could they have found them? There was no indication, they had not given themselves away; they had been very careful. So very careful. The lure had been too much for his curiosity to handle, and he had stepped off the task he was doing to follow the new nav track.

Going a little further than he had wanted, the track had come to a sudden end in what appeared to be the middle of nowhere. He could see nothing in any direction in between the double skin of the hull. He had been running dark, as was the current team protocol, so seeing nothing was pretty normal, but he had then realised he was way off course. If his team had needed to find him or mount a rescue, he wouldn't have been on any of the tracks he was meant to have been travelling; he would have been truly lost. He had been seriously thinking of breaking protocol and putting his torch on to light the area and get some very much needed information on his surroundings. Mentally, he had kicked himself for being so nosey. Had he really needed to take this track? No. He should have just stayed the course and reported it. They may have been able to do something together later; better than wandering off on your own. He had turned to head back.

That's when they had stunned him and locked out his suit. When he had been contacted by the person he now knew to be St John, *Endeavour's* head of security, St John had been acting a part, colluding with him to warn him of danger. But it was more a probe for information and a delaying tactic to allow the security team time to get to him before he could do anything to escape.

It had worked. He was furious with himself and had stayed tight-lipped and unbending in the face of all their questioning. They had beaten him, they had drugged him, they had questioned him relentlessly without the chance for rest or sleep. He had fallen back on his training and told them little bits here and there to keep himself alive, nothing more, and nothing more than they already knew. He smiled at himself. He took his successes where he could.

They had reminded him that his resistance was irrelevant, as if they didn't get what they wanted they could simply clone him and start again. It would seem like an eternity of torture. This was inconceivable, but he knew they didn't have the time for that—it was a bluff. They couldn't wait twenty years for a clone to mature in order to continue an investigation they needed answers to now. A bluff. But within moments of their bluff he had been drugged and put to sleep.

Getting a sense of his surroundings was difficult: the light was too intense, too bright. Even squinting as he was, his eyes were watering with the effort and heat, in itself adding to the problem. He simply couldn't see anything to his front; it was like looking into the sun. To his right he could see a little, although it was completely washed of all colour, everything taking on a stark whiteness that seemed sterile. He could just about make out the body of another, reclined and asleep. Raising his head and fighting the restraints, he managed to see over the body to find that they were not alone. Looking to his left, he found the same: a line of people reclined and asleep in the face of this terrible brightness. Nothing was making sense. Who were all these people and why were they here? Why was he here? Didn't they need to finish their questioning?

A jab to his wrist from the restraining cuff made him grimace and yell out; it was both unexpected and extremely painful. He felt liquid being pumped into his vein and a heat start to spread through him as the injected substance made its way slowly, inevitably, around his body, each heartbeat pushing the heat further and further on in waves. With the temperature from the blinding lights and now this increase of his core temperature due to the injected substance, he started to become almost delirious. The world around him was becoming more and more distant, and his ability to concentrate and follow any thoughts or ideas to a meaningful conclusion fell to be almost zero. It was worse than being drunk; his mind being this addled left him numb and without focus or reason, his sense of self drifting and out of reach.

Looking to the side, he tried to concentrate on something he could see, to give himself something to grip onto in the physical world. The person next to him was still laying inert, eyes closed, but now with a heavy sheen of sweat over his naked form. Whatever had been administered to him had clearly also been given to all the others. Within a few moments the skin on the body started to quiver, like the muscles were in spasm just below the surface. Shortly after this, the picture became streaked with black as the skin began to lose cohesion. Within seconds, the body next to him liquefied completely, splashing to the grated floor and leaving nothing—not even the more solid skeletal structure of the body remained. It all slid from the couch in a dark, black river of death. His eyes were wide and burning dry in the deathly environment. Snapping his head around to look to his left, there were already many couches now empty, only a residue of black to indicate where a body had once been. There were fewer and fewer in the room. His heart was racing and a noise filled his head, resonating around the room. He realised he was screaming, for himself and for the dead. His throat ruptured and sprayed black blood down his chest, the scream now replaced by a quiet rasping sound. He flopped back on the couch exhausted; suddenly overcome by a complete lack of energy, his fight went away.

The temperature in his body seemed to reverse as a paralysis took hold. In his last moments, his eyes flooded with tears just before he passed into unconsciousness. It came as a relief.

RIVERS

Leaving the lake and the remains of the shuttle had been really hard. She knew they had to keep moving, she knew they couldn't hang around, but she still had the feeling they could have done more. Larsen had told her to put it down to survivors' guilt but that didn't help much. That was cold hard logic in the face of a traumatic emotional response; one didn't counteract the other, no matter how much she understood the science. She had kept trying to reach anyone on the shuttle with her bio-comms as they walked further into the forest, in the hope that someone might respond. They had been out cold for twenty minutes, why couldn't others be unconscious for longer? It was possible. They could only now be making their way to the surface and freedom. But the more she thought on it as they walked, the more she believed it was unlikely. They had been really lucky. If the water level had been another 20 centimetres higher, Larsen would have not survived, another metre higher and she would also be dead. It made her ill thinking about it. She tried to reach out to the shuttle again.

Larsen was striding out ahead—not far, maybe four or five metres—periodically checking over his shoulder to make sure she was still there. They had changed their clothes almost as soon as they reached the tree line and had a small amount of cover. Wearing their wet clothes for much longer in this cool climate would have caused them more problems—exposure, hypothermia—all avoidable for five minutes effort. Add to the new clothes a brisk climb up the valley side to the ridge line and she had

5

warmed up pretty quickly. If anything, she was now a little hot and out of breath. She could use a rest.

"Hold up, Larsen."

He stopped and turned to her, his face one of concern and exhaustion. If she looked anything like he did, they could both use the rest.

"You okay?" he asked in a straightforward tone. She considered the context of his question and responded in relation to their current localised situation and not the wider catastrophe she knew they were both well aware of.

"Yeah. We've been walking for two hours without a rest. I think we could both do with a break."

His head slumped to his chest, like his body had just given him the message that he was also exhausted and in need of a few minutes to recover. He nodded.

"Okay. But not long. We need to get to the ridge line before dark. If anyone from the fleet is looking for us, I need our beacon to have the best chance at being heard."

"Ten minutes."

"Sure." He walked to the base of the nearest tree and sat down, using the tree to lean against. She walked over to the same tree and sat next to him.

She took her backpack, placed it in front of herself, pulled open the drawstring and started rummaging through the contents. "So, we have rations for about five days. We have mobile shelter, we have two days water. I don't think water is going to be a problem, the lake must be getting its supply from somewhere, failing that we always have the lake. Food, that's going to be tricky. We can't eat pine needles and there is no readily apparent food source, we have no idea what flora or fauna there is around here, second to that, even if we did find it we'd have to catch it."

"Snares." Larsen mumbled, head back against the trees trunk, eyes closed.

"Well, yes, but problematic if we're on the move. And even if we caught something, would it be poisonous?"

"I thought you said you needed a rest?" he asked with a smirk. "I don't see much evidence of you being tired."

"I'm still pumped after that landing."

"What landing? That was a crash! Actually, it was more than that. We got our asses shot out of the sky." He looked up through the tree canopy, as the mention of the Xannix ships had reminded him of the pursuit. Shaking his head, he looked towards her.

"What?" she said, feeling like there was a question in the air which she hadn't understood.

"Don't you find it odd?"

"Odd, how?"

"Well, we got chased down from orbit, shot out of the sky, then nothing. Where is the follow up? Where is the ground team searching for survivors or to drag the shuttle from the lake for investigation? You would have thought there would be some activity."

She nodded in agreement and searched the trees, looking back down the valley towards the lake. "How do you know they haven't?"

"Well-" he stopped mid thought. "Hell."

"I don't see why not. They've been pretty good at hiding and camouflage; why wouldn't that apply here?"

Larsen was thinking, he was now also searching the trees for signs of movement or anything to give away a search party moving with stealth through the trees.

"I'm not sure. Yes, they seem to be able to cloak their ships, and their own planet to a degree, but I've seen no evidence of that for the Xannix themselves, no personal cloaking. At least they didn't in all the contacts we had aboard the *Intrepid*."

She nodded at his assertions as he continued, "That's not to say that they're not really good at fieldcraft. This is their turf after all; they have home advantage."

"Thanks. And I was just beginning to feel better about the situation."

He smiled, put his head back to the tree and closed his eyes again.

"You're welcome."

With no warning, a storm of noise like a screeching daemon hoard raged around them, and a large craft flew at speed and at very low level over their heads down towards the crash site, the sound of its approach shielded by the ridge. Dust and grit was thrown up all around them as the ground and air shook violently. The noise ebbed slightly as the craft tracked down the valley to the lake, but the dust hung in the air like a choking smog. Larsen was already moving.

Grabbing her by the arm to help her up, he bounded off up the valley to the ridge line like a gazelle. She slung the backpack over her shoulder and followed at a run. She had no idea where they were going, but at that moment hanging around seemed to be a bad idea. At a sprint, they reached the crest of the ridge and continued over the top, momentarily taking shelter behind one of the larger trees just long enough to dump their kit. Larsen reached into his pack and retrieved a scope, standard issue for each emergency pack, quite powerful at x80 magnification. He crawled on his belly back to the ridge line and started scanning the lake below. A moment later she was at his side with her own scope.

"See anything?" she asked, before taking a look through the scope. The tree density along the ridge was not high, so the view to the lake was quite uninterrupted. As she put her eye to the scope, she realised what an idiot question it had been: the craft that had arrived moments earlier took up her entire view, and she had to wind the magnification down to get a better, more measured, picture.

"Straight ahead," Larsen responded, seeming not to notice her obvious oversight. "I can't make out what they're doing yet, probably scanning the shuttle wreck."

The craft was hovering about twenty metres above the lake and 200 metres out from the shore, when suddenly it belched a fireball of white light from its belly which disappeared into the water and caused the surface to bubble, hiss and boil under the immense energy of the blast. The speed of the fireball, however, was not fast and she could see it illuminate the depths as it descended towards the shuttle. Once it had reached the lake bed, the ball of light seemed to pause for a few moments. The craft, anticipating what was coming next, tilted its nose up and moved back from the glowing light beneath the surface. With a thunderous explosion, water and debris erupted into the air in a huge column of fire and water. Her heart thumped in her chest, though whether it was due to the explosive overpressure or her own emotion at the insult she felt to the last resting place of Horus One and her crew, she couldn't tell. She bit her lip in anger.

"Well, they seem to be consistent," Larsen observed. It didn't help. "The question is, will they pick up our trail?"

"How can they not? We have to get going."

"Wait." He put out a hand. "They have just landed a search

party on the shoreline. I count five. Time to go."

They returned to the tree and retrieved their backpacks, then headed at pace off down the opposite side of the valley, moving in a direct line away from the lake to put as much distance between them and their pursuers as possible. She could see the worry in Larsen's face; this had just become a deadly game of cat and mouse, and she didn't think either of them liked being the mouse.

"I sure wish Silvers was here." Larsen said.

"I wouldn't wish anyone here."

"Well, there is that. But he'd have this situation under control in about five minutes. What would he do?" Larsen was thinking out loud and his thought process was leading him down a violently defensive path.

"Couldn't we just keep running?"

"We could, but as you pointed out, we've got about five days. Any hope of rescue only comes from above and I think we both know that's going to be a problem for everyone. They will have their own fight keeping the Xannix at bay as soon as they pass through the satellite net."

"Have we tried getting a message out?"

"Carroll did as we came down; after that, no. I've been worried about giving our position away. I'm even more worried about it now, with that Xannix team back there. When we send the call, we need to be in the clear."

"That could be a long wait." She thought for a moment, then had an idea. "We've got two beacons, right? One in your pack, one in mine."

"Yes."

"How about we set one down here, transmitting our distress call, while heading out with the other. It won't matter if the Xannix find it; at least the signal will have reached the fleet. We can save the other one until we need it."

"Sounds good. But there are a couple of things to consider. What if the fleet is outside the jamming net? They'll never receive our signal. I think it best to keep going for now until we see signs that the fleet are in orbit, then send the signal."

She realised there was a cold truth to Larsen's comments. They were on their own for the moment, the fleet were too far out, and they needed to wait for them to be within range to receive their call and, more importantly, not to have their signal jammed by the

Xannix.

"Okay, so we keep going for now. How far behind us were they when we landed?"

"Crashed. About four hours I think. Not that long. But depending on how good those Xannix trackers are, we may not make it to four hours."

"Wow. Optimism."

"Yeah. Well, I thought you'd appreciate the facts."

They continued on down the valley at pace brushing away branches carefully and walking clearly round bushes where they could, so as not to leave any signs of their travel. She felt that they had got lucky with the ground conditions, which were cold and hard; hopefully, this would leave the Xannix little or no footprints to follow. They would need to think about everything they did, from toilet breaks to eating and drinking. As crazy as it sounded they would need to hide everything, leave nothing behind. She was quite sure neither of them had been trained for this situation—it certainly hadn't been part of the Science Officers training course, and she was pretty sure it wasn't on the Engineering curriculum either—but they had been taught what to do in event of a crash landing, which is exactly where she found herself now. She didn't see it at the time, but it had been time well spent. Although, in the scenarios they had trained under, no one was hunting them down. It was all about finding water, food and shelter and staying in one place while a rescue team came to pick you up. Surviving on the go was turning into something completely different and taking away many of their options; it was becoming tougher to fulfil their primary needs for water, food and shelter. They were fundamentally working on instinct, which she knew was fallible.

*

Larsen had insisted on pitching the shelter and as he was an engineer she decided to let him. He was quick at it, too—the shelter was built and inviting within minutes. She found herself smiling just thinking about getting a few hours' sleep. They had been at pace all day, power walking their way through forest and across rivers; she really needed the rest.

With nothing much to do but walk, her mind had been wandering and questioning their surroundings as they went. She had been surprised at a couple of observations. First, there appeared to be a real regularity to the spacing and type of tree in the forest. The more she thought about it the more she believed that the forest was planted and cultivated rather than naturally evolved and developed. Pacing and counting, there were roughly ten paces between each trunk and looking left and right of her path trees were quite definitely in rows which undulated slightly, or curved away into the distance, so they were never dead straight. Someone had gone to great lengths to create patterns in the trees' planting. Second, it was quiet. Deathly quiet. Like the forest was abandoned and nothing lived there; not birds, not insects, not mammals. There were not even any signs of life that you might usually expect, like nests, or the odd entrance to a den or sett. Where was all the wildlife?

They had pitched their shelter on a slope looking back the way they had come, which would give them a great view of anything coming up towards them from the direction of the lake. They had taken a couple of sharp turns in their path and backtracked on themselves a couple of times to create false tracks but they were unsure how successful they were being. Maybe the fact they hadn't made contact with a Xannix yet was a sign that they were doing the right things at the right time. Maybe.

Larsen had taken first watch and let her sleep, but it was more rest than sleep and the shelter did little to keep out the cold. Her mind kept spinning and running over the crash again and again. At moments when her mind gave her the chance to think about something else, it was generally about being chased down by a pack of rabid dogs. Sleep would not come.

When it was her watch she found the unnatural quiet extremely disconcerting. Forests, as far as she remembered, were places of constant movement and sound—the movement of the wind through the canopy or the cries and calls of birds and small mammals as they made their way through the night. The absence of these things made the forest feel dead and somehow more sinister, like its heart was missing. What she did notice was the cold, a creeping cold that chilled her to her core, right through to her bones. Her teeth chattered involuntarily as she sat in a ball, curled up with arms wrapped around her knees, head resting on top, looking out into the darkness. The night was dark, and incredibly black. She knew Xannix had a couple of moons but she guessed neither were currently this side of the planet to reflect any light down to her. It made looking for movement and lurkers a real problem, as there was simply no visibility; her ears became the primary warning system, listening out for the slightest sound.

Larsen was a fidget. He was having a fitful sleep but at least he appeared to be getting some. On the odd occasion he had started snoring she would give him a gentle nudge with her boot to stop him. Eventually he took the hint and rolled to his side: no more snoring.

It occurred to her, through her silent musings, that she didn't know how long the Xannix night was. She probably should know, as it was bound to have been in a lecture she had attended, but right now it slipped her mind. She guessed it would be similar to Earth—it was an Earth analogue, after all. So, twenty four hours-ish. She would wake Larsen in another hour for his next shift. Maybe she would sleep then.

She found her backpack and took out her rescue beacon. It was a rugged bit of kit and easy to operate. She could encode it with her identifier, or not, depending on the situation, then flick the red button on the bottom to begin transmission. Simple as that. It would then sit there happily pinging away, calling out into the ether for help, for someone to come and rescue them. Holding it made it a temptation, rolling it around in her hands, viewing it from every angle, mulling over whether or not to press the button and make the call. The fleet would be in orbit by now. She looked up to the night sky, her eyes searching for any sign of orbiting ships; nothing apparent, she looked back to the emergency beacon and sighed.

Putting it back in her pack, she thought she saw something move out the corner of her eye. It made her freeze, as her heart rate accelerated and breath stopped. There was no sound that she could hear other than the tremendous thumping of her pulse through her ears. Slowly, she turned her head. As she turned she saw a grey shadowy humanoid character walking up the valley towards its crest and passing them, about ten metres from their position. Looking straight at the ghostly apparition and focusing, it seemed to disappear, then, as it moved further up the slope, she saw it again in her peripheral vision. A moment later there was a second one, further down the valley and walking to follow the first. Both had been carrying packs and what appeared to be some sort of weapon, although she couldn't make out any fine detail, as it was just too dark.

As the fifth one moved past and out of sight, she waited another half an hour, still frozen and unmoving in the dark, before she dared to wake Larsen. She put her hand over his mouth and he was instantly awake; she felt his whole body flex, though in the shelter she saw nothing. He was quiet and still--she wanted to send him a bio-comm message to calm him but she didn't know whether the signal could be intercepted to give them away. She just moved very close to his ear and whispered, "Xannix passed 30 minutes ago. We have to go." He said nothing in response but she felt his head nod against her hand in agreement.

They left the shelter, didn't even decamp. There was little point, they had another and they needed to be quiet, breaking down the camp would have used time they didn't have and made noise they didn't need. Larsen made the decision to head north and perpendicular to the course the Xannix appeared to be taking. Heading off along the contour of the valley at a dead slow felt really counter-intuitive to her, but they couldn't see a thing and didn't want to end up tripping on tree roots, or falling into a ravine; both outcomes would give their position away. Slow and sure would get them away.

CLAYTON

As official liaison to the Xannix, Dr Spencer's first official duty had been to dispense him a warning. It had been delivered with steady nerve. *Endeavour* had breached protocols by allowing a vessel to enter 'close space proximity' to Xannix. The fleet had also been charged with the murder of Captain Yannix and his pilot, Lieutenant Aldaa, as they had departed the *Endeavour* on their way back to the scout ship *Spixer*. They had been warned and now they were going to be boarded and he was to relinquish command of the *Endeavour* to the Xannix acting captain, Polder. Spencer had followed up almost immediately via a bio-comm message on his personal channel. He opened it.

'Sir, what's going on? They are calling us a hostile species, which, as a cultural reference, means that they are going to put in place measures to eradicate us.'

'That doesn't sound very friendly.'

'No sir, it does not.' There was a slight pause, then Spencer continued. 'Sir, could I ask what you intend? You've not changed course. I suspect you fully intend to stay the course to Xannix.'

The doctor was right but the Xannix needed to be kept guessing.

'We are still looking at our options. The terrorist who caused the incident with the shuttle has been neutralised. As I understand it, the shuttle which entered Xannix space was unarmed.'

'Sir, they don't see it that way.'

'According to Earth law, we are defending ourselves, Dr

Spencer. We have been defending ourselves since the moment we arrived in this system. We will continue to defend ourselves.'

'I understand. But, I should point out, sir, that you are dealing with a highly neurotic species. The fact that they have built a satellite net around their planet to hide themselves from others should highlight that point. Whether you believe our fleet to be on the defensive or not, just being here is incitement enough for them.'

He took a moment to look around the bridge while he thought of his next response. The main screen was showing the *Spixer* moving slowly towards an airlock to begin docking procedures. There were people shouting orders and working vigorously to put in place some sort of defence of that airlock. One thing he did note: the *Spixer* and the Xannix hadn't cloaked their ship. Maybe they had discovered how Dawn had been able to track them; Spencer's bio-comms must have given him away by now. He punched a few buttons on his own console and viewed the corridor to the airlock. It was lined with security personnel and a few reassigned Rem-Teks, with some notable modifications and uncharacteristic armament.

As with most leaps of logic and design, the modifications to the Rem-Teks had come about due to the lack of available security staff aboard the *Intrepid*. The crew were still in stasis and those of Havers' team able to defend their position were few in number, as the team's original task was to fix a communications array, not to tactically defend it from boarders. Havers' team was therefore mostly comprised of engineers and technical staff; the number of security personnel he had could be counted on his fingers. The changes to the Rem-Tek design were required to circumvent the command core, which stopped any form of weaponry from being used by the automated machine. Now remote control of the Rem-Tek put a human at the decision-making centre of all aggressive actions, be they offensive or defensive. With some added armour to defend the power cell, the Rem-Tek had been reassigned to the roll of primary encounter security. Clayton believed that they used to call that particular type of asset 'cannon fodder'. Either way he was pleased, as it meant, hopefully, lower crew casualties.

'Spencer, please tell your—our—Xannix friends to cease their boarding action. We do not want any further loss of life.'

'I'll relay the message, sir, but I think they are pretty intent.'

'I'd prefer to avoid another incident. They are racking up at the moment and we could all do without them.'

'Yes, sir.'

'Clayton, out.'

Clayton turned to Roux who appeared to be in conversation with Commander Fellows, the acting head of security. "What's the status on Fellows' team at the airlock."

"All set," Roux replied.

"Helm, continue course and let me know when we're through the Xannix satellite network."

"Yes, sir."

He continued to watch the events unfold, each second critical and each link in his command chain doing their job like a cog in a very well-oiled machine. Watching his console, he brought up the vid-comms for the security team. He felt like he had done this once too often since coming out of stasis, but this was his chance to do two things. Firstly, rescue Spencer. However much Spencer felt he was having an adventurous, up-close-and-personal experience with the Xannix, he needed to get Spencer back. He had become a valuable commodity, someone who could speak the language and understood certain elements of the culture. That knowledge would be critical in the coming days and he wanted to get Spencer back on board the *Endeavour* before the risk to his life became any greater. Secondly, he wanted a chance to look around the Xannix ship himself, and for his science and engineering teams to get a few minutes first-hand investigation and analysis. He needed to find out as much as he could about the people he might need to go to war with. It was the hard way, but too much seemed to be going wrong to hope that the easy diplomatic way was even an option.

Scanning the list of vid-comm links and images, he recognised a couple of names: Lieutenant Reeve and Sergeant Silvers. These two had been through a lot over the last few days and had managed to get themselves mixed up in the centre of almost every encounter with the Xannix. It was good to have the experience on the team; they would be giving the others around them a level of confidence and focus that they themselves wouldn't have had that first time on the *Intrepid*. He imagined that Fellows had placed them there by design for that very purpose. You could not underestimate the need for confidence and character in the line-up for any action. He silently wished them luck.

Helm flashed him a message: two minutes to the satellite boundary. Time was not standing still; events would soon cascade into chaos. He would just need to concentrate on the big picture and trust in his team to make sure the detail was taken care of. The *Spixer* docked. The trouble he had been expecting took no time at all to arrive. It was instant. The external airlock door was breached immediately by something he could only think to be a thermite charge arranged in a circular pattern, a sharp circular flash of light and the door was cut through, falling with a harsh metallic crash to the floor. A tubular sleeved umbilical probe made a swift entrance from the blackness of the Xannix craft and lanced the inner door with a similar thermite blade. This time a single point of light and sparks flared into the corridor where the Rem-Teks and security team were prepared for the coming confrontation, taking cover as best they could behind the Rem-Tek shielding and each other.

Expectation can be misleading. While he could sense the tension in the team and that urge to launch themselves at their foe, they found themselves paused in time. The lance that had penetrated the inner door extended into the corridor half a metre then scanned across the space from left to right, all the observers hit with a white and orange oscillating beam which in itself appeared to do nothing to any of those it touched. As the beam passed by each of them it left a rotating disc of light about ten centimetres from their chest. The confusion was obvious as each seemed to look at the other with a question in their eyes. The probe withdrew.

Movement. The lights within the airlock failed and the darkness crept a little closer followed by movement and torch light as the Xannix approached and set up the other side. Clayton knew it was only a matter of seconds before the inner airlock breached and both sides would become embroiled. He concentrated on listening to the conversation between Fellows and Reeve.

"They're just sitting there."

"Ready the Rem-Teks," Fellows told her. "We need a quick take-down and advance."

"Roger that. Silvers, what are they doing?"

"Can't tell, LT. Too dark in there."

"Get up behind that Rem-Tek. See if you can get a better look."

He saw Silvers' vid-comm image show a swift move across the

corridor to the forward Rem-Tek. Taking cover behind it and peering through the gap between its shoulder, neck and head he got a much clearer look.

"Switching to low light." With the low light optics activated, the darkness was pushed aside; there was a Xannix face right in the inner door viewer, eyes focussed directly at the camera, at Silvers.

"I think I've been made," Silvers reported. "They're right there, just looking at me."

"I don't like the sound of this. Silvers get back in position."

Before he turned, Silvers took one last look at the Xannix in the window. It seemed to be pulling a weird face, which he could almost have translated as a smile but not quite.

Silvers joined the formation next to Reeve and took up the best defensive position he could in the open space of the corridor. Reeve and Silvers exchanged a look, as if to say 'Here we go again.'

Without warning, the lights in the corridor failed, plunging the corridor into total darkness. Each of the security team was now only visible to him from the personal transponder overlay on his display. Slowly, more lights pricked the darkness to join the strange chest-height alien glow, as some turned on their head-mounted torches, some their low light optics.

Then chaos came. The airlock door was open before any of the defenders realised. Fellows barked orders over the comm and carbine fire erupted all around. From Rem-Teks at the forefront, Clayton could only see fast-moving shadows and strobing lights, as they tried to turn and track the movements of their targets. From the background noise, he heard something stirring. To begin with it was a low rumbling noise but, as it went on, the pitch and intensity grew; considering the current situation he didn't believe that it meant anything good. He cut in on the comm.

"Fellows, can you hear that noise? Can you identify it?"

Fellows came back instantly: "I can hear it but we have no idea what it is. Can't pinpoint it."

"Well, it's not us. What are they up to?" said Reeve.

"Your guess is as good as mine, sir," replied Silvers.

The crescendo built to a deafening pitch. Some of the security team had collapsed to the ground, holding their ears in pain, and some had started to back off towards the next corridor intersection. There was shouting and screaming, but it was being drowned out by the overwhelming noise. The cohesion of the group was breaking down. Then, in an instant, there was a volley of thin needle beams of light which tracked to each of the defending team in sequence, there was instant silence and Clayton's command console lit up. The whole screen was a deathly red. The entire team terminated in less than a second.

Fellows was on the comm within moments, implementing his contingency plan, giving him updates and informing him of readiness at the agreed second line. He wasn't really listening, his mind was now side-tracked and thinking about the incident he had just witnessed. They had just killed twenty of his people out of hand and were now most likely on their way to the bridge. He had tried reason, he had tried negotiation, but this species was needlessly violent and aggressive.

"Roux, you have the bridge. I'll be with Dawn if I'm needed. You are to repel boarders and take that ship."

"Yes, sir. I'll find a way."

*

Dawn was already waiting for him as he strode into the briefing room at the rear of the bridge, arms folded and a stern look on her face. "They've reached the second line already. It makes you wonder who has been playing whom."

"Indeed," he replied, "but I'm not worried about them. We have more than enough resources to deal with them now, regardless of the tech they've brought with them. What worries me now is what's on the other side of that satellite network." He stopped and leant against the handrail that circled the central holoprojector and tactical display. Looking intently at the display he saw that Dawn was projecting the plotted location of all the Xannix invaders and the defending security forces headed up by Fellows. It was like looking at the map of an ants' nest with dots scuttling here and there as the battle proceeded, advantage being pushed and pulled, but—to give Fellows credit—his plan seemed to be working.

Just as he was about to turn to Dawn, something caught his eye: two tiny green dots at the airlock. All the action and the major Xannix force was now split out and moving towards the bridge as anticipated but there were two green dots—two of Fellows' team still active outside the airlock.

"Sneaky bastard," he mumbled to himself.

"Who?" asked Dawn, clearly bemused by his train of thought.

"Fellows, that's who." He turned to her with a smirk on his face. "Remind me to commend him at the end of all this. From this moment on, he's the new head of security."

He continued to smile while he looked at the tactical projection for a few more moments then returned his attention to her, shaking his head and rubbing the back of his neck.

"So, the other side of the satellite net."

"Yes."

"Are we ready?"

"Yes. Protocols have been implemented. Obi and Ellie report the status of their systems to be online and ready, as are ours."

"Good."

He started pacing around the central projector, lost in thought. This was as far from the 'optimal plan' envisaged before they had left Earth; this was a last resort. The previous captain of the *Spixer*, Yannix, had mentioned a second planet ten years distant which they could get to. They had provisions enough and could simply alter course, but the Xannix, for all their caution and paranoia, seemed intent on violence at the slightest opportunity. Even if they did alter course and head for this planet, in the fullness of time, how would the Xannix respond to having a human colony on their galactic doorstep? If they responded in a similar fashion to the reception they had received in the last few days, there would be problems within years.

Diplomacy was failing, which he blamed on the terrorist action inflaming an already difficult situation. GAIA, La Guerre à l'Intelligence Artificielle, originally a French-based terrorist group who eventually managed to catch the global conscience as the political and economic situation on Earth deteriorated during the Great Decline. They had infiltrated the construction crews and management teams working on the OWEC shipyards, initially without much opposition but security was soon stepped up to compensate. The Outer Worlds Exploration Corporation put in place intense screening—any new employee no matter how menial the task, went through an intensive investigation—but still at times it was not enough. He could remember at least five attempts to disrupt the build of the *Endeavour* alone. It was no surprise to him that Dawn discovered a GAIA faction member hidden amongst the crew; there were likely more.

Travis was now gone. They had all the information they needed on his operation right now and if they needed more in the future, well, they still had his wave in stasis, so they had options on interrogation. In the short term, the fact that Travis appeared to be working in isolation and without assistance was some minor comfort. Although it was wise to be vigilant in this matter, they had caught one team, and there was no evidence to suggest there was another. However, that was not to say that there couldn't be another, perhaps a sleeper in the fleet somewhere who had bigger problems at the moment and had not made their move. Yes, it was definitely better to keep his eyes and ears open.

"Inform the senior team to prepare for Angelfall."

There was a moment's pause before Dawn responded.

"Confirmed."

An incoming message icon flashed within his bio-comms display and demanded his attention. It was Roux. 'One minute to the satellite boundary.' He acknowledged the message, straightened up and made his way with a resolute determination to the bridge. The Xannix had forced his hand. The whirlwind to come was on them.

SILVERS

The noise of the carbine fire was deafening but it was something a soldier got used to: the rapid staccato, the repeated kick to his shoulder as the recoil of the weapon obeyed some fundamental law of physics. The short aimed bursts found their target and dropped a Xannix here and there. He was unsure how many of them there were, they just seemed to keep coming. Reeve, to his side, was doing similar but seemed to be having an intermittent conversation with Fellows at the same time. The darkness and noise, combined with muzzle flashes, torch light and beam weapons darting around the corridor made for mass confusion.

"Push up!" Reeve yelled in his ear.

"To where?" he yelled back. There was nowhere to go.

"We need to get to the ship. Get up behind one of those Rem-Teks."

"I don't like this plan. It's a crazy plan."

"Noted."

They pushed forward, sliding along the corridor wall, working past a couple of others busy defending the corridor. It was at that point he heard a weird noise, an underlying tone to the rest of the cacophony, undulating and gaining in pitch and intensity, like it was searching for something, buzzing around like a bee searching for nectar. A really big bee, he thought to himself. As they moved up, the noise got stronger and he could see it was getting to a couple of the team in the corridor, the guy in front of him shaking his head and blinking hard as if to clear his vision. Then the pinching in his ears started. Whatever pitch the sound had reached, it was now at just the point to affect him, pinching and buzzing at his eardrum, he tried hard to concentrate through the distraction but it was hard to do as his chest had now begun to vibrate, it was like his ribcage had hit some resonance and the focus was centred in line with the floating disc of light the Xannix had tagged them all with at the beginning of the encounter.

Something in him registered. Connecting the disc with the sound and the sense that it was *danger close*. The volume then began to rise sharply and spike, that was his cue. He turned sharply and found Reeve right beside him, she was holding her head in both hands, carbine hanging from her webbing sling, probably screaming, though he couldn't discern the sound from the rest of the noise bursting his ear drums. He hooked his arm under her armpit and lifted hard while at the same time spinning and diving the last couple of meters for the cover of the Rem-Tek. They hit the floor hard. Silence.

*

He opened his eyes but nothing registered. It was still dark, the corridor lights had not come on again. Trying to move, his head swam, there was a stabbing pain to his left ear and his right ear was whistling constantly. Lifting an exploratory hand to the left side of his head he felt a sticky slickness that told him all he needed to know. He grimaced, more out of annoyance and frustration than anything else. The pain was pain—he'd experienced a lot of that over time; the fact he'd potentially lost the hearing in one ear, well that was a tactical disadvantage and right now he needed every advantage he could keep hold of.

Sitting up he felt across to where he had slammed Reeve into the deck. As he put his hand out he felt something soft and yielding. A message flashed into his bio-comm view: 'Do you want to lose that hand, soldier?'

He instantly withdrew his hand. 'You're alive then.'

There was no response, although she grabbed his hand, then shoulder to help herself up. They both took a moment to assess their surroundings.

'You okay?' she asked.

'I've been better.' Her torch focused on him then the side of his head.

'That looks pretty bad.'

'I'll get it looked at, if I live,' he joked.

'You're all hero, Silvers,' she said, but he knew sarcasm was written large all over the comment.

Instinctively, they both began to run the register across the rest of the team. It stopped them both in their tracks. She was then suddenly distracted and raised her hand to him to be silent, her face suddenly one of anger and concentration, probably in communication with Fellows. The whole team, all those in the corridor, dead. In an instant. He remembered hitting the ground hard with Reeve and nothing more. His face hard against the ground behind the Rem-Tek.

He took a moment to examine the Rem-Tek. It was pretty chewed up. The armour was scorched and black in sections, a couple of its limbs were missing and the head was slumped forward with loss of power and nothing to control it. The section which interested him most was in the lower section just above the wheels and caterpillar tracks of the drive module, two large holes each the size of his fist. Crouching down to get a better look he tracked the hole back to the door with his torch, the angle wasn't quite true, possibly on an arc. Extrapolating the trajectory past the Rem-Tek he found the spot where Reeve and he had been laying.

'We were lucky,' he sent Reeve. 'The Rem-Tek took our kill shot.'

Reeve was at his side and looking at the same evidence; Fellows would also be going over the data.

'Let's make that luck count,' she said. He knew what she meant. It was still a crazy plan.

'No time like the present. After you...' He motioned towards the airlock with an outstretched hand and a slight tilt of the head. She didn't need any further invitation; raising her carbine to her shoulder and aiming down the entrance of the Xannix craft, she entered the airlock.

They stepped carefully through the airlock, feet padding either side of fallen Xannix and discarded equipment. Both doors were open, which concerned him straight away, and there was a tripod weapon set up in the centre of the small camber, an umbilical connecting it to a pack on the floor. Maybe ammunition, but more likely a power cell. He touched the airlock console to close the inner door; it did so, although there was still a small hole at its centre where the probe had entered the interior. Perhaps it would slow the loss of air and give a little more time to anyone close at the time. Better than a massive explosive decompression if the Xannix ship decided to just up and leave, removing the atmosphere seal as it went. It would need a patch fix, but right now they had other things to attend to.

Stepping up behind Reeve, he looked round her into the darkness of the ship and tapped her on the shoulder; she nodded and they headed in. At this point it was all training: they advanced into the ship in a two-man cover formation, checking angles and exits for danger and targets as they went. The problem was they were now working blind. They had no schematic for the craft, so could only guess at where the sections of the ship might be, but they had a pretty good idea where the bridge was, as that was where Spencer was, his bio-comm still active and giving his position with a solid signal. They zig-zagged their way through the corridors towards him.

Switching their weapons to silent operation, they had made their way past a couple of corridor junctions before they encountered their first guard. Reeve didn't even hesitate. The shot was a quiet cough, and the Xannix slumped to the floor without even registering their presence. Moving up, they were no longer using non-verbal bio-comms, having both fallen back on their old military training and hand signals. Reeve held up a fist, indicating that they should stop their advance.

Corridor lights through the ship appeared normal, but what was *not* normal, as far as he was concerned, was the lack of Xannix. Where were they? He could only think that they had played a blitz, and the last of the crew were now trying to advance on the *Endeavour*. It was a risky tactic, as it left them completely exposed. He and Reeve would need to capitalise on it. He checked his bio-comm display: Spencer was only twelve metres away.

Reeve slid close to the edge of the corner of the corridor and quickly took a practised and fleeting glance round the corner. She held up two fingers. Two targets, he would go left she would go right. On her movement, they both took up firing positions in the centre of the corridor aiming towards the bridge and the guards. He stood high, Reeve knelt low, and their shots synchronised to a single mute sound as their bullets sped their way to their targets.

With wet blue spray covering the wall behind them, the Xannix figures slumped—one sliding down the wall to the floor, the other to its knees and down—both still and lifeless.

They advanced to the door at the end of his nav track, the final way point only a couple of meters the other side. The next question was how to open it. There was no obvious control or means by which to operate the door. He exchanged a brief puzzled look with Reeve. 'Now what?'

She looked at the door again as he started padding round the door jamb and wall for any obvious lumps or bumps which would give away the location of a controller.

'Stand back,' she ordered. 'Take position to my left.'

He moved with haste and aimed himself towards the door. 'All set.'

'Spencer is centre right. Do not hit him.'

'Man on the inside, hey?' Always good to have a man on the inside to open doors, he thought.

'Three targets. Two left, one above the door. Zero g.'

'Copy.'

She nodded. A second later the door opened, sliding sideways into the wall, revealing a dark interior with a few lights twinkling in differing colours and intensity. From his position he could see a single shadowy humanoid outline laying inset into the wall of the internal sphere; the moment the door opened, it scrunched into a ball then leapt for the door, coming straight at him. The flood of light from the doorway illuminated the face of the moving body, and, in the heartbeat before he pulled the trigger on the carbine, he recognised Spencer's face. He exhaled sharply and moved his aim.

Spencer came through the door head first and high, at about a metre and a half from the deck. As the gravity of the corridor took hold, he fell head first, rather unceremoniously and awkwardly, to the floor. There was a sharp yelp as his head hit the floor with a loud crack, his momentum carrying him forward and over to land face up.

"Hi," Spencer said, looking up with a grimace. Then he was up and off down the corridor at a sprint.

"Wait!" Reeve shouted after him, but he was gone, skipping over the dead guards and around the corner at the junction.

Before they had a chance to enter the Xannix bridge, the door closed again. With that route cut off to them and Spencer running for the *Endeavour*, Reeve had clearly reassessed the situation. He thought Spencer had the right idea, and they both took off at a sprint after him. If the Xannix decided to manoeuvre away from the *Endeavour* with the airlock in the state it was, there would be trouble for them. They needed to get back fast.

Spencer was already waiting for them at the open airlock when they got there. They passed him at speed then took positions behind the Rem-Tek for cover and aimed back into the *Spixer* to defend against possible pursuers. The inner airlock door closed but it would still be of little use with the breach hole through it.

"We should plug that breach," Silvers stated.

"No time," responded Reeve, as she watched Spencer, who was already moving at a rate away from them down the corridor. The guy was like a gazelle.

"What about the word 'wait' does that guy not understand?" he asked Reeve.

"He probably just wants to live another few minutes."

"That long?"

They gave chase down the corridor after him. Reeve was shouting again, probably talking to Fellows on comms. From the short update, it sounded like the invading Xannix had been contained. They caught up to Spencer who was now clearly flagging after the initial hard effort to escape. As Reeve passed him, she shouted over her shoulder at the two of them: "This way!"

He decided to stay on Spencer's shoulder as they ran, to give him some encouragement and make sure he didn't get himself into any more trouble. They followed Reeve to the next junction then took a right; the bulkhead was ten metres away.

As they reached the corner, a terrible tearing sound reverberated through and around them, then the atmosphere began to bleed from the ship. He felt a small breeze against his face to begin with, but it soon built. They reached the bulkhead door and it slid open as Reeve triggered the control; the loss of atmosphere had become a gale and he had to push Spencer against it to get them both through the door.

"Come on! Come on!" Reeve shouted over the noise of the venting air. He pushed Spencer to the floor and jumped the last to clear the door. Reeve activated the bulkhead control and the door slammed across with urgency. Silence broke out instantly as the pressure settled back to one atmosphere and his ears popped.

Spencer was laughing hysterically. It was the sound of the saved man escaping the clutches of impending doom; a release of all the anxiety and hardship. He found himself smiling. Through all this madness, it was like being back in mountain rescue. Score one for the good guys.

OBADIAH

Receiving the message from Dawn had brought mixed emotions. Being an AI could be confusing at times, pulling apart the man from the machine. He always considered it just another state of being. He had a flesh and blood body before, now his body was a galaxy cruising super ship carrying thousands of people to their new life. The irony of that was that it was a life he would never have. Once they were in orbit around the planet, that would be where he lived out eternity, taking on the roles of orbital defence platform, fabrication station and habitat. They as yet had no idea how long an AI could live, but his assessment was that he would have to terminate himself way before he went mad. He knew all too well the repercussions if he allowed that to occur. The documented account of the AI on Aarongate station was case in point, terminating all the people in a section of the station just to find out if they could do it and what it was like to have that kind of power. The trick was knowing. He had put a few check programs in place to monitor his state. Hopefully, they would give him the alert he needed early enough to do something about it.

But there was always the danger of going before your time. In that regard, being an AI was no different. They had reached the planet and it had been populated. How inconvenient. They had been travelling for decades with a nice simple colonisation in mind and these interminable Xannix had been inconsiderate enough to have evolved there first, growing into a race exhibiting neurotic and violent traits. What was interesting to him, among other things, was the 'why'. They were the apex species on their planet but something had made them jittery and aggressive. Up to this point, it was just lucky that humanity had been able to defend against this behaviour, being the creative, adaptive beast it had become. The result of their evolution was what might just cause his early demise. If what he assumed to be the other side of the satellite net was as he expected, this was going to be a tough battle.

So, Clayton had initiated preparation of Angelfall. That decision wouldn't have been taken without some considerable thought, and the justification would only have been the perceived complete failure of the mission, such that there was no way to cohabit, negotiate, or discuss alternatives with the indigenous species.

He had suspected that they might move to this conclusion, as he had received Xannix DNA material some hours ago from the *Intrepid* and there would only be one reason for that. He would need to start incubating and producing the Xannix pathogen. It wouldn't take too long, as there were plenty of clones in the system, and therefore no shortage of biological material for the pathogen deployment. The thing that worried him was that they had got to this decision so quickly.

Even with the events that had occurred within the fleet, the Xannix boarding the *Intrepid* and the *Endeavour*, skipping round him each time, he felt that a single alien ship's actions were not justification enough to eradicate an entire world. Especially as he had also learned that the Xannix had offered another local space planet as an alternative world for colonisation. He was reserving judgement on the affair. He would prepare, no point being unprepared, especially if he wasn't in command of all the facts, but he wasn't going to commit genocide without there being no other alternative. That was what the protocols were designed for, so that was what he would hold to.

Watching the *Endeavour* over the relatively small spacial distance of ten thousand kilometres, he could see the *Spixer*, the Xannix scout ship, docked to the starboard side and forward of the central habitat section. It had docked about forty minutes before and was just now disengaging. From the streaming vids he'd been receiving from Dawn, he could see the trouble going on inside and the failure of the airlock. Three of the security team had just made it to safety before the airlock had failed catastrophically and vented the local corridor atmosphere into space. They had managed to contain the boarding party, even keeping a couple alive, who were now residing comfortably in the *Endeavour's* brig.

The Xannix had fought a brave but ultimately foolhardy action. They had used some interesting technology but had knowingly made an attempt to gain access to the bridge and Captain Clayton with a team of twenty, half of which had not even made it out of the first corridor, regardless of the fact that they had wiped out the initial encounter team and first line of defence with an exotic weapon. However, the Xannix had history, albeit a very short history, of playing games and having an ulterior motive to almost everything they did. He was sure that the true purpose of the boarding was nothing to do with getting to the bridge but that left the question: what *was* the purpose? No doubt, Clayton had people working on it.

The immediate issue was the *Spixer*: it was manoeuvring away from the *Endeavour* and they were only moments away from the satellite boundary. He saw the answer to his question in a flicker, like fireflies, across the side of *Endeavour*, as the point defence cannons sparkled and twinkled, releasing thousands of rounds per second into the Xannix vessel. Thousands of tiny, high-velocity rounds tore their way through the *Spixer* and raked the drive units towards its rear, removing sections of hull and causing small detonations to the interior. He knew that Clayton would be keen to avoid the devastating close range disintegration which occurred to the *Spixer's* shuttle and caused so much damage to the *Endeavour* itself. Clayton would be aiming to disable his target and make sure it would be out of any upcoming fight. He got his wish.

As engines failed and the *Spixer* began to tumble slowly on several axes the *Endeavour's* point defence system ceased fire. The quick and accurate attack had maimed the beast which was now limping away to lick its wounds. He watched the ailing ship closely, looking for signs of recovery, but in the immediate aftermath there seemed to be no change in condition. A couple of minutes after the initial engagement, the *Endeavour* was clear and through the satellite net heading for Xannix but the *Spixer* was not finished, he noticed a spherical section of the *Spixer* disengage from the belly of the vessel, possibly a lifeboat, but at this distance it was difficult to tell precisely. Once the sphere was clear of its tumbling mother, it seemed to morph and change shape in sections, engine pods spinning into existence and the front elongating to a blade. With the transformation complete the engines sparked to life and the craft accelerated at 4 g to pursue the *Endeavour*.

Packaging up the images he had just seen, he sent them to Dawn and Ellie. They were probably well aware but assumption was always dangerous at a time like this. Better they had the information and didn't need it than need it and not have it.

Back to the task at hand. "Ten seconds to satellite boundary," he informed Captain Straud.

"Thank you, Obi."

He was pleased Elizabeth Straud had been assigned to the *UTS Indianapolis*. She was a great commanding figure: positive, always calm under pressure and with a very polite manner. Even when she was tearing strips off you for some misdemeanour, it was polite, factual and professional. She led the crew through example, pure and simple.

Monitoring the crew was part of his remit. He watched each of the crew, looking for signs of stress and fatigue, to ensure the smooth running and optimum performance of the ship. In practice it never quite worked that way. Understandably, some of the crew liked their privacy and didn't like the idea of some all-knowing omniscient presence poking around their private time, so he had limited his actions, as had the other AIs, to duty time only. When they were on shift, he could give them a good scan and workup, he could gain all the information he needed at that point anyway with no need to intrude. Everyone was happy.

At this moment, Straud's usually calm demeanour was cracking slightly: her heart rate was elevated and her adrenaline levels were higher than normal. Considering the circumstances, he didn't find this the slightest bit odd. Even he was feeling anxious over what he couldn't see on the far side of the satellite net.

They passed through the boundary in moments, and a few seconds later the *Intrepid* was also through, each tracking towards their designated way point. He instantly felt overwhelmed by the change. The *Indianapolis* was awash with electromagnetic communications, bands across the spectrum, chatter from the surface and around the perimeter of the satellite network, most encrypted, some not. He concentrated on the most dense communication hubs and tried to map the network for patterns, both in transmission and in reception. The fundamental problem was the language. Even if he could crack the digital code—however he did it: cryptanalysis, brute force—it didn't matter if he couldn't understand the plain text anyway. He needed a Rosetta Stone. He needed that kind of breakthrough again, and fast.

Instantly he thought of Spencer. Dr Spencer had been working on the *Intrepid* with the Xannix scout ship captain. The Xannix had reportedly a highly evolved sense of language and their capacity to pick up and understand the basic structure and meaning of their language in a few short hours was proof of that. Whether it was a natural ability or a technologically assisted one was an open question, but the result was undeniable, their captain had been speaking English with near fluency by the end of his negotiations with Captain Clayton on the *Endeavour*, only a few hours ago.

Spencer had ultimately been how they had tracked the cloaked Xannix ship. His bio-comms pinging his location back to the *Endeavour*, a simple passive signal which the Xannix either didn't deem important or missed completely. Either way, they didn't block it and an accurate trace of the *Spixer* was achieved.

Either through purposeful action or accident, he was unsure of the events, Spencer had been abducted by the Xannix. The next they had heard of him was that he was acting as the Xannix liaison to the fleet, the most noticeable point being he was able to speak the Xannix language flawlessly. This indicated a tech solution to the accelerated language learning. Maybe, in time, they would get the opportunity to research that tech and utilise it themselves; it could be a great positive tool in the negotiations with the Xannix, which he still believed possible.

Whatever he did, he would need to act fast. He felt an impending sense of doom about the mission's current trajectory. The more he thought on the matter, the more he believed implementing Angelfall was wrong. He knew the reasoning, he had obviously been read into the protocols around it and understood its purpose, but he believed the interpretation of this original purpose was being misread, or perhaps warped to a more misguided understanding. He would need to find out immediately; he opened a forum with Dawn and Ellie.

*

With his transition to AI, the major intriguing difference he found between life before and life after was the level to which he could multi-task In fact, he was simultaneously in many places: on the bridge, main engineering, hydroponics, medical. Now, an instance of himself was in private forum with the other fleet AIs, Dawn and Ellie. The construct they always used to meet took the form of a private library, with shelves of old leather bound books, three old leather buttoned high back armchairs circling a low coffee table and sitting on a deep crimson Persian rug, all bathed in the warm orange light of a log fire. It was a construct of Dawn's design and modelled on her father's stately home back in the UK, most likely a place she held dear and reminded her of better times and a good place to discuss important matters. It was all a fiction of course—they could equally be sitting on a beach or in a sterile white room—but he felt that the homely touch and the intimacy were actually quite conducive to frank and open discussions. It was also, for want of a better word, cosy.

They each had their usual chair. Dawn preferred the chair nearest the fire, again an illusion, as there was no physical heat, but it kept her happy and as an AI you took these emotionally warm moments where you could. Ellie always took the chair to Dawn's left which gave her a good view of the fire place and the chaotic dance of the yellow and orange flames. He took the remaining chair to Dawn's right which gave him the window vista. Whether by chance or by design, the panorama outside was of rolling hills and majestic and sympathetic forests akin to those of Capability Brown, which were stunning in any season, but his personal favourite was spring, when all the vibrant lime greens burst into verdant existence and reminded him that he was still alive. He knew his past could have taken such a different turn.

His story was slightly different to most AIs, in as much as most chose to become AIs after an unrecoverable and ultimately mortal physical trauma. As far as he could see, these circumstances left them no real option at all, if you wanted to live you took option A, option B was only darkness and death. No choice. He had a choice. He had been alive for many years, initially living a productive life as a propulsion engineer for OWEC, but in his mid-thirties and married to his work he began to suffer the early signs of the illness to come. Motor neuron disease slowly deconstructed who he was to the outside world and his ability to interact with it. It was a horrible disease and one which he railed against with all his will and remaining physical strength. Over several years he declined to such a state that he was entombed within his own body, his bio-comm interface the only outlet which gave him real communication with his carers and medical staff. He came to think of his body as his own biological prison cell and spent hours looking out of a similar window to the one he found in Dawn's construct.

He was in the hospital for five years before he found a small tantalising trace of information on the local network. A little known research project was looking for candidates for a life extending procedure. The candidates needed to fit a rigorous set of requirements, which reading between the lines meant that they needed to be within weeks of death and with no chance of being saved from their fate by any traditional medical methods. It piqued his interest and he began searching for further information on the project. Tiny scraps here and there pieced themselves together. The operation appeared to be very low key but not quite secret; someone wanted to keep this quiet. He considered this and rationalised it as a doctor who wanted to keep a very speculative cure to himself until he had more information. It was exactly what he would do—build a prototype then make a decision on whether it was worth shouting about to the wider community.

Eventually, he managed to scrape enough information together to identify the lab where the work was being carried out. He looked up the lab's head researcher; it was a doctor by the name of Clayton. As soon as he found Clayton's comm details he pinged him a prepared message. He waited.

To his surprise he received a return message the same day and not from Clayton but from his daughter, Dawn. The Famillian Institute would be very interested to interview him in relation to the project and could he spare the time to see them? He laughed for what seemed like an hour before he could get himself under control again, the only outward sign of his mirth being the tears which rolled down his cheeks and the odd involuntary facial spasm. He was overjoyed, and returned the message telling them they could see him any time they chose, either in person at his bedside or over vid-comm.

It was not a hard sell. Clayton and Dawn had been working on their own past experience as to what would make a good candidate for the programme, they had not considered those like him who would be more than willing to volunteer for the chance for a second life and, more importantly, as he pointed out to them, for the opportunity to become productive within society again and to be lifted from the isolation which he and the others felt.

He looked at Dawn, sitting across from him in the virtual forum of the old study, her appearance that of woman in her late twenties, short cropped hair and keen brown eyes which gave the observer a glimpse of the intelligence behind them. Whenever he was with her he always smiled. It was involuntary on his part, as she always reminded him of that moment back in the hospital, and the message from her which changed his life and was the beginning of his greatest adventure. It was a good memory.

"I've asked for this meeting, Dawn, in light of the unfolding events and your message calling for the preparation of Angelfall."

"Have you begun?" she asked, blunt and to the point.

"Yes. Yes, I have. But my question over its application so soon into our contact with the Xannix is a valid one which I need answered. This protocol is a measure of last resort. Are you saying that by implementing it now there is no chance for any diplomatic negotiated solution?"

"We don't believe there is. We have tried once and the outcome of that seems to have sparked a conflict."

"Once? What did you discuss? I don't see that the meeting records have been made public," he asked pointedly.

"No, they haven't. It was a condition of the visiting Xannix captain that it not be recorded in any way."

He thought that convenient. "So, what happened?"

"I'm sure you saw the events occur from the shuttle bay. A GAIA faction sympathiser detonated a bomb which initially disabled the shuttle, but which destabilised the fuel core and resulted in an explosion which caused significant damage to the *Endeavour.*"

"Yes, Dawn, we both saw that, but what we don't know is what was said in the meeting with the Xannix. Could you elaborate?"

Ellie seemed very happy to let them both talk this through. She had not said a word but she was listening to everything, scrutinising and analysing.

"As mentioned, I was unable to keep records of the conversation, so there is little I can say. I can only divulge information I've gleaned since, from conversations with those that attended."

"Who?"

"After the recent events, Clayton is the only surviving person who attended the meeting." There was silence while this information was absorbed. Ellie and he exchanged worried looks. "So what can you tell us?" he asked. "Clayton has spoken to me about their desire for us to go elsewhere. They see our arrival as aggressive and our breaching of borders an act of war. This information was passed to us late, too late to act on, and by the time we were in a position to act the Xannix had already begun their military action against us." Dawn shifted in her chair, moving to a more open and honest body language. "We have tried opening up further channels of communication without success."

He was unsure of her intent but felt there was something off in her description of events.

"So why did the *Spixer* need to be disabled?"

"We had no response from the ship once we had regained Dr Spencer and dealt with the invaders. We could not risk a ship that close being able to bring weapons to bear."

"One moment. Dr Spencer is with you?" he asked with a little surprise.

"Yes," Dawn replied. "We were able to get a small two man team aboard the *Spixer* to rescue him while the Xannix were otherwise engaged in their attempt to take the *Endeavour's* bridge."

He shook his head. "Well, that's good news. How is he? Not too shaken up by his time with the Xannix."

"Far from it. He's being extremely helpful. For whatever reason, they appear to have given him open access to their ship and personnel. In fact, it seems their actions, though aggressive to the wider human populous were quite open and friendly to him as an individual."

"Maybe it's not him they object to," he said with a raised eyebrow.

"I don't see what they were objecting to on the *Intrepid*, they fired on our team and killed many with no provocation."

"That you know of," Ellie interrupted. It was the first words she had spoken in the meeting. Dawn looked at her sharply. "You have to understand they are not like us; their culture, their whole species acts and thinks differently. Their priorities are very focussed and their allegiances are not like our own. We can tell they are hugely territorial but what we haven't yet understood is how they interact socially."

He nodded. "It's likely this is why they are not speaking to us. We must learn how to engage them and open up those channels of conversation."

"That is all well and good, but we haven't got long to achieve this." They all knew what she meant by this. While they were in this forum discussing how to proceed and how best to avoid the full deployment of mass effect weapons, there was a raging battle going on outside and, as if to punctuate the point, Ellie's image crackled with static as something interfered with her transmission from the *Intrepid.*

"Agreed. Might I suggest we employ Dr Spencer in this task as quickly as possible."

"I will request his assistance immediately," Dawn agreed with a nod. "In the meantime, continue as scheduled while we work towards an alternate, less extreme resolution." They all seemed in agreement. "It is a final sanction but we need to be ready. The survival of humanity is in our hands and I'm not going to let them down at the last hurdle."

The connection to the forum closed and he found himself alone in the room, the fire crackling in the background as he stared through the window, across the fields, lost in thought. A herd of deer passed from one forest enclosure to another, a majestic stag leading his charges to the safety of the shade and shadows beyond. As he watched, the dominant male of the herd stopped as if startled and looked directly at him, their eyes locked. "No," he said to the room, to the stag, "I didn't believe her either."

SILVERS

Fellows had been insistent—they were to take Dr Spencer to the bridge briefing room where they were to meet Clayton, Dawn and himself for a debrief. They were both now reassigned as Spencer's personal body guard, about which Reeve's complaints and objections went largely unheard. She felt that there were bigger tasks ahead than baby-sitting a wayward medical practitioner, but grumbling was cut short as the first blast rocked the ship.

As they reached the bridge, the scene was one of pandemonium. A couple of bridge officers barged past them as they walked through the door, others were shouting and barking orders to their section heads elsewhere in the ship. The main screen was showing a view of the planet Xannix below, beautifully green and blue with swirls of cloud across continents. For a moment, he mistook it for Earth and wondered how they might have travelled full circle, but the other large tracked items in the view shook him back to reality. The Xannix ships moving to intercept them were of a size magnitudes larger than the scout craft they had been aboard earlier; they looked more like destroyer-sized vessels, bristling with weapons and built for speed. Numbers ticked over by their side, indicating speed and distance, but he didn't need those to know they were getting a lot closer very quickly.

Fellows met them in the walkway to the bridge briefing room and shook Reeve's hand excitedly.

"Good work with the rescue, Reeve. You too Silvers. For a moment there, I thought we'd blown it."

"Literally," he said with a smirk.

"Dr Spencer, it's good to meet you." More handshaking. "Please come this way."

He led them through to the briefing room and found Dawn already standing at the projector, looking at the 3D battle progress in digitised form in front of her. It always puzzled him how much AIs kept their human characteristics and mannerisms when there was no need to: the battle she was watching was no doubt being compiled and rendered by her own systems, which she in turn was experiencing directly as part of her symbiotic integration with the ship; watching it unfold on a 3D projection seemed pointless.

Following them down the walkway at a trot was Clayton. He had left command of the battle to Roux but the urgency of all things demanded that he keep the briefing short. "Ladies and Gentlemen, however much I'd like to take some time on the details of the rescue—and, may I just add, welcome back Dr Spencer—" he flashed a quick and sincere smile to Spencer, who nodded his appreciation in return, "the Xannix are pressing us and we need to make some major decisions quickly."

Clayton pressed some buttons across the terminal on the lectern and the central holo-projector cleared the visual of the battle outside and began to play a sequence of pre-defined fleet manoeuvres, including the three capital ships and their shuttles. Once he had confirmed the display was running, Clayton turned back to the assembled.

"The time for secrets has passed. Due to the nature and level of your work, you are now being read into the Sol protocol. What you are watching is the protocol's deployment phase, which we may be forced to implement, if we don't find an alternative way to come to some agreement with the Xannix." Clayton paused but appeared to be taking a measure of the room. "It is a dispersal formation for the fleet, which enables the primary ships to introduce an aerial pathogen into the upper atmosphere of the target planet. The simple aim of this process is to remove the apex species from the planet, in this case the Xannix."

Everyone had a better poker face than Spencer, he went pale and his jaw fell slack in shock. Unable to recover to speak, Reeve took the lead.

"How long do we have to find an alternate solution?" He noticed Reeve had included herself in the resolution. He felt a burning need to do the same. There were many questions flying round his head, and high among them was how Clayton had readied the pathogen in such short order. How did this peaceful mission to a far-away world suddenly obtain biological weapons and who knew about this and when? He certainly didn't sign up to genocide when he joined OWEC.

"The fundamental problem is that the Xannix won't speak to us."

"Or can't," he found himself saying out loud.

"Indeed," replied Clayton. "But whatever the reason, we need to get through to them. We have limited options and this really is our final battle. If they get the better of us here then we, as a species, are lost. I can't put it any clearer than that." He turned to Spencer. "Now, Dr Spencer. What is it that you need to make contact with the Xannix? Who do we need to contact? What's their cultural hierarchy?"

It took some time for Spencer to realise he was being spoken to. His eyes were reeling as if he'd been punched, and his skin was still a pallid grey. He stammered to life: "You, you need their Prime, their Setak'da. The word translates to Ruler of All Worlds." Looking around for support, Reeve urged him on.

"We need their Prime? Does this Setak'da have a name? A location?"

"Yes. Setak'da Celicia," he offered.

"Celicia?" repeated Fellows, lost in his own thoughts.

"Yes," confirmed Spencer.

He could tell Clayton was really inquisitive and wanted to know far more, but events were getting on top of them. "Fascinating, Dr Spencer. Truly. But for now, where might we find this Setak'da Celicia?"

"Their planetary capital is located…," he paused while he went to the projection which was now showing the planet and all the cities and population centres as a network of contrast orange on a blue sphere, "there," he said pointing at a city in the far north of the world. "The central building of this city is a very sacred site to these people and one which their Setak'da oversees." The projection zoomed in and altered to show a graphic of the central building complex, rotating in space to display as much detail as was available at this time.

"We'll start there," Clayton announced. "Dr Spencer, please

concentrate all your efforts on making contact with the Xannix Setak'da and inform them that we wish to cease hostilities and talk."

"Of course, sir."

"You may use any of the ships resources to do so, though I suggest you contact Commander Alderson in Communications. Work fast, Dr Spencer, work fast," and with that he nodded to Commander Fellows and they both headed back to the bridge.

He exhaled loudly and slumped in his chair.

"You can say that again," said Reeve.

"We've just turned up and we're in an instant battle with the native population and about to wipe them out? When was this ever part of the plan? I don't know about you but I didn't sign up for this," he said with some resignation.

"Nor me," added Spencer. Reeve just stared grimly at the now closed briefing room door, a cloud of thoughts running like a wildfire through her mind.

*

Commander Tim Alderson was a tall man and Silvers imagined that he spent as much time sitting down as possible. There were few places on a starship which did not cause the man risk, as most of the bulkheads and door jambs were set to just about the right height to give him a regular headache. As Alderson looked up from his crash couch and workstation to greet them, Silvers saw a red mark to his left temple, a line from his hair line poking out like an accusing finger at the face of the man who was not looking where he was going when the wound was inflicted. He had to hide a smirk at his own observations.

"Dr Spencer," Alderson began, "I was told to expect you. I've given you and your team some workspace in the next compartment. All terminals are linked in to the primary communications system. Any band, any power setting, any direction; you name it, I've been asked to oblige."

There was a constant low level murmuring as people went about their work, relaying messages and orders. It certainly wasn't as animated as the bridge, but there was still a constant background noise. Being communications, he thought it would be louder, but assumptions were always the wrong side of right. The main communications room was set out with two long lines of crash couches, one running down each wall; about twenty people worked in this section. Reeve headed off without any further invitation down the walkway between the comms couches and through to the next room.

"Thanks," Spencer threw out apologetically, as he rushed off after Reeve.

The next room was much the same, with a similar number of couches and three at the far end vacant and ready for them to begin work. Reeve and Spencer were already seated and working by the time he walked through to join them; they had a purpose and no time in which to do it. He understood but was unsure how he could assist. He took the final seat next to Spencer.

"Okay, Doc. What do you want me to do?"

Not even looking up, Spencer was already scanning through frequencies and communications which the Comms team were processing. "First thing I noticed about the Xannix when I was aboard the *Spixer* bridge was the audio communications is limited. Between themselves they utilise a fluctuating skin tone as much as the verbal spoken word to impart additional emotion and meaning to whatever they are saying. My initial guess would be that we are only working on half the information available to us."

"So— in English?"

"Look for patterns. Communications with visual components not originating from within the fleet."

"Visual comms, with non-fleet comms tags."

"Yes."

"I can do that," he said, a little sarcasm to his tone. As he said it, the peace of their surroundings was interrupted by an overbearing rumbling noise which reverberated all around them, through every beam and surface of the ship.

"What was that?" Spencer asked, as they all looked up and around at the walls and ceiling, trying to pinpoint the epicentre of the sound.

"Work faster," Reeve said with a sudden renewed urgency.

"Whatever it was, it didn't sound good," he said.

They worked at pace and quickly shuffled through possible data matches and collected them for analysis; whenever he found something fitting the description he pushed it Spencer's way. It felt like they had been working for hours, but in reality it had probably only been about twenty minutes when he noticed something flashing on the terminal screen to his right. He had a quick glance—flashing lights were always a draw. Although not his screen, the comms officer working that terminal instantly brought it to the fore and marked it as high priority. As far as he could work out it was a signal coming from the surface, an emergency beacon? Who would be setting off an emergency beacon on the surface?

Another deafening sound reverberated through the ship, this time sounding more intense, much closer. Outside the ship, the Xannix were clearly getting more determined to stop them, and whatever bombardment or weapons they were using, the odd shot was getting through. He considered what weaponry they might be using, as the damage being inflicted sounded very much like missile strikes. He knew they had beam weapon technology, certainly at a personal level, but whether they had been able to scale that up for use on starships was the question. The answer at the moment seemed to be 'no', but, if they had, they would be pretty much helpless, as their defences were almost entirely geared towards high velocity strikes. Particle beam weapons would make short work of them. He hoped they didn't have particle beam weapons.

"What's the priority signal?" he asked the comms officer. He got a hand gesture which indicated that he should wait a moment, which he did. The comms officer stopped, then made a short nod in confirmation of some incoming data, then turned to him.

"Emergency beacon from the planet surface."

"How could that be? Who did we send to the surface?"

"It was an advance party. The shuttle was meant to recon past the satellite boundary and report back. I guess it didn't get the chance to report back. There are two survivors as far as we can tell." He turned back to the screen to pick up additional information. "Here: Lieutenant Larsen and Science Officer Rivers."

His eyes went wide. Larsen? What was he doing roaming around on the planet surface? He knew the guy had a propensity to get himself in trouble, but this was taking it to the extreme.

"Damn."

"Sorry, do you know them?"

"Yes. What's being done?"

The comms officer looked quite apologetic. "At the moment there is nothing we can do," he said with a shrug. "We've marked their location and are trying to track them for pick up at the earliest opportunity."

"Do we know anything about their situation? What's their position?" He scanned the screen for coordinates. They looked to be in the northern hemisphere in a mountainous region with an arcology or city complex about two hundred kilometres further east. He turned back to his own screen and punched in the coordinates, beginning to scan for evidence of their trail and where they might be headed. If he knew Larsen, he would be forging ahead regardless, staying alive, but ultimately there was no exit other than to get back to the fleet. And, even then, the aim of the fleet was to make a landing, so there was also an argument for staying put and being a pathfinder for the mission. Either way, his friend would not be armed, nor was he able to broadcast to the fleet without being detected. He had taken a huge risk setting off the emergency beacon, as now it wasn't only them who knew where they were.

"Sir, take a look." He pushed the data to Reeve who was still busy searching through comms traffic.

"What is this?"

"Emergency beacon broadcast from the surface. It's Larsen and Rivers."

"How did they get down there?"

"I don't know, but no one is doing anything about it."

Reeve stopped what she was doing and looked at him past Spencer, who was busy focussing on the search data, wrapped up in his own concentration. He had clearly not heard a word of what they were saying.

"What are you thinking, Silvers? I hope it's not some fool rescue. We've already done one of those today," she pointed a nod at Spencer, "and I don't know whether you've noticed but we're in the middle of a battle with the Xannix."

He grimaced as the facts took hold. "Yes, yes we are," he paused as an idea started to formulate. "But. But, we've been asked to make contact with the Xannix. We can do that best from the surface."

"What, by being captured?"

"Didn't do me any harm," said Spencer. He had been listening after all.

"What do you say, Doc? Want to go rescue some people?"

Reeve looked at him with scorn.

"No one is going anywhere. Silvers, you need to focus on the priority, which is to stop the annihilation of the Xannix—and potentially even ourselves, if this battle continues. Whatever you have to do to work it out, do it. But get back to your task. We need to open a channel to the Xannix." It was forceful and impassioned, but fundamentally he believed it was coming from the wrong direction.

"Lieutenant, we've got to do something. They're as good as dead if you leave them to the locals. I've seen nothing good come from any contact with the Xannix and I don't see why that is going to change once they catch up to Larsen. You're letting them die."

"Outside," she snapped through gritted teeth.

They all got up, "Not you," she pointed sternly at Spencer. "You're on point with comms. Get us linked to the Xannix." Spencer said nothing but sat back down and got back to work, slightly flushed at the outburst and being caught in Reeve's glare.

He and Reeve stormed past the comms team and past Alderson back out into the corridor. If you need to vent, the best place is out of the way. He could tell Reeve was winding up for a fight and he was ready for it; this whole situation had everyone's priorities out of kilter and someone had to do something to sort it out, or at least redress some of the karma.

As soon as they got out of immediate earshot, she faced off to him and poked him hard in the chest. "You need to get straight, soldier. Our highest priority is saving the fleet, and that means calling off the Xannix. If we can do that, then there are other things to worry about, but if you're dead, you can't do any of that. Got it?"

"Someone has to do something. We have to reach out somehow. I signed up to save life, especially when I have the means to help. What are you going to do? Neatly follow orders? Every moment's delay is a moment in which more people die. Getting Spencer to the surface is going to be the best chance we have. He will be face-to-face; they'll have to talk to him."

"And I suppose you can run off and rescue your friends at the same time?"

"If the opportunity arises, yes."

"It doesn't work like that. We have to think of the fleet goals."

"Says who?"

"Clayton, for one. You can't save everyone, Slivers."

"I can bloody well try."

They stood staring at each other—eyes wide, blood up and both in a rage—when Spencer opened the comms room door and poked his head into the corridor. Apologetically, he asked, "Do you two lovebirds need a moment more?"

"What is it?" Reeve asked, with barely restrained aggression, her rage still spiking.

"I've found them," he announced, then before either of them could answer he headed back into the comms room.

"Did he say, he'd found them?" he asked.

"Yes, yes he did."

They both stood staring back to the comms room door.

LARSEN

Running was becoming somewhat of an occupation. Deciding that it was time to set off the first of the rescue beacons, he had rigged one to delay transmission by an hour. He hoped that would give them enough time to get clear of the area and cover their tracks. It had worked, as far as he could tell. It had enabled them to get to the far side of the valley and to a small rocky overhang under which they could conceal themselves and view proceedings.

"It's not going to go off," Rivers whispered.

"Patience. It's not up to the hour yet."

"It is, by my calculation." She was shuffling as she sat, her nerves apparent.

"Well, we can't go back and check it. Going back is the last thing we should do. I think we should head north. Just keep heading north."

"Why north?" she asked.

"The last mapped image of the planet I saw before we crashed showed the north of this place as sparsely populated, whereas east and west both had large population centres. So, north. I want to stay away from as many Xannix as possible and give the fleet the best chance of picking us up."

Rivers stared into the distance. "Sounds reasonable." She paused and sighed. "So, how long do we leave it before we head out?"

"Another ten minutes?"

As he spoke, a ping came up in his bio-comm: an emergency

beacon; his emergency beacon. It had worked. He looked at Rivers, both sharing a moment of relief. Someone in the fleet would now know they were down there, and they would send help.

"Now the fun starts," he said to Rivers. They both turned to the valley to watch for Xannix activity.

It didn't take long. Within five minutes they heard the familiar sound of the search craft engines begin to bounce around the valley walls, and a moment or two later they saw it in the distance coming up the valley at low level from the south. It was moving at pace and kicking up water from the river; he estimated it to only be about five metres from the surface. Sweeping up and over in a wide arc it tightened its turn and came to an almost perfect stop immediately over the beacon. They had placed it high up on the far valley wall near the ridge to give it the best chance of signalling the fleet, but it had also been wide open to the Xannix hunting party, and they had responded quickly—much quicker than he had anticipated.

"Is that the same search team?" Rivers asked. "It looks like it might be."

"Yes," he replied, still focused across the wide expanse, peering through his scope. "The markings on the craft are the same as we saw last time."

"Well, what does that tell us?" she pondered to herself.

"It means they are not flooding the area with people trying to flush us out. Maybe they are trying to keep things quiet."

"Possible. If you're the government of a populous as skittish as they seem to be, I'd not want to panic the masses either."

Xannix were dropping from the hovering search craft. "Time to leave. I think we know how it works from here."

They moved quickly out of cover, heading swiftly over the ridge, and began the descent into the next valley using the same tactic as before: moving in a straight line away from the hunting Xannix to put as much distance between them as they could. Taking a winding road only slowed their own progress, especially as those tracking them had a pursuit craft which could cover the distance that they covered over a day within a matter of minutes. In all, he began to think the odds were stacked against them.

Having jogged their way to the valley floor, he was looking towards the crest of the next ridge and trying to plot their best course when he received a message to his queue. He opened it thinking it was Rivers and was about to have a word about breaking transmission silence when he realised it was not from her but Silvers. He almost lost his balance and tripped, being completely stunned and distracted, and Rivers caught him.

"You okay?" she asked.

"I didn't think we would get contact from the fleet this quickly."

"They've contacted you already?" she looked puzzled. "And why just you? Wouldn't they transmit to all of the survivors?"

"Yeah, something is off," he said, opening the message.

The face of Silvers popped into his view. He was leaning in closely to the camera and speaking quietly. "Hey Larsen, what you doing down there?" he flashed a quick smile. "Anyway, here's the thing. Looks like the battle up here is taking all the resource out of planning your rescue, so the brass says you're stuck down there for a while. Still, looks like you have company, so I'm sure you're having a party and are not worried about all the *crazy* back home." Another smile. "But I wanted to let you know, there are people here about to do something stupid and attempt a rescue. And by people I mean me. So hang in there, we'll be there with coffee and doughnuts before you know it."

Silvers leaned back in his couch as if about to end the message then seemed to remember something and moved quickly back to the camera. "Oh, almost forgot. Don't respond to this message. You'll give your position away if you do. We're tracking you and we'll send you updates as we can. Those guys over the next valley are working in circles to find your trail. Keep going and we'll update you as we can with their location. Ciao." The vid ended.

Another message dropped. This one connected them to a live vid stream of the mapped area with a red locator beacon which had the label 'Bad Guys' floating above it. Silvers' idea of a joke. There was also a locator for their own position—labelled 'Good Guys', obviously.

He knew he liked Silvers for a reason. They guy had just saved their necks. Well, as much as he could with what was available to him. Knowing the exact position of the Xannix pursuit team was intelligence they were in desperate need of right now. Just knowing they weren't about to get jumped or walk into a trap was one less thing to worry about.

"Well?" asked Rivers, desperate to know what was going on.

"Well," he started. "There's good news and there's bad news."

"There always is," she said. "Come on, out with it."

"Okay, well. I can't send you what I received, as the transmission might give us away but," she looked at him, an eyebrow raised, still waiting. "But it was a friend on the *Endeavour*, he says they're in a battle up there at the moment so they can't send anyone right now."

"Great," she said with sarcasm.

"Although, he is going to try and find a way to help. Sounds like he's working on something."

"What? Did he give any indications?"

"Not really. But he did send me something which will help us. He sent a map which tracks the Xannix and shows us their location at all times."

"Actually, that is really useful."

"Yeah."

"So, what next?"

"Simple: we keep moving and stay invisible." He looked up at the ridge and decided on a route. "Let's go."

*

In the tree line, the sunlight flashed and flickered, the clear blue skies dotted by the odd flying animal; it was the first sign of wildlife he had seen on this planet, as the forest they had been walking through was oddly eerie for the lack of fauna. No little birds flitting between branches, no chirping or tweeting which was common to the forests he had walked through as a child. But now, high in the sky and circling were two or three birdlike creatures gliding on the thermals and updraft from the valley. They had both taken a moment to look closer at the creatures using their scopes. They were high, so it didn't give them much more information, but they were certainly feathered and had longer bodies than the birds they recognised on Earth, extended torsos with longer legs which dragged out behind them as they flew. He thought they looked a bit like long-legged parrots, their plumage colourful and bright in the sun.

They had been following the valley to its mouth where the ground flattened out into a wide lush meadow, dotted with small white, purple and yellow flowers. He wondered why flowers would be needed by plants as he had not seen, heard nor been bothered by a single insect since they had arrived. Maybe they just looked like flowers but performed some other purpose. He concluded that he didn't really know enough botany to make an educated guess, and it was probably best left to the scientists when they arrived.

At the edge of the meadow, he stopped. Rivers, who had been following a few metres behind, stepped up to join him.

"Well, where to now? If we head out further north, we'll be in the open, and I can't see over the rise of the meadow. What's the map say?"

"Looks clear for miles; nothing but open plains and meadow."

"Where are the Xannix?" she asked.

Consulting the map in his bio-comm display he saw the 'Bad Guys' marker wandering off into the valleys to the south; they seem to have lost them for the time being. "South and nowhere near our position. Looks like they are about fifty to sixty Ks away at the moment and moving further away."

He didn't like it. It wasn't that he thought that they should be better and have caught them way before now—maybe they were just lucky? Certainly, the map and location updates from Silvers was a gift, but he still thought that a highly technological species like the Xannix would be able to pick them up within minutes. Didn't they have satellite tracking or defence platforms in orbit which could get them locked down in moments? It was another indication as to the difference between them: their thinking was clearly working to overcome the same real world problems but their solutions and problem-solving process wasn't using any form of methodology he would consider.

"Ah, ouch!" Rivers stepped back holding her hand. Shaking it a few times to relieve the shock and pain, she held it out to inspect. It had a small prick of blood pooling in her palm and a red rash had started to affect the skin already.

"What did you touch?" he asked quickly, and looked over to where she had been standing.

"I think it was one of the grasses there." She nodded at the spot in front of her. Carefully, he stepped closer, making sure he didn't touch anything himself. After a short search he found a white flower which now had a drop of blood at its centre, glinting in the sunlight. He'd not noticed before but each of the flower heads appeared to have a thin spine protruding from the middle and the centre didn't contain nectar and pollen carrying structures but a well which seemed designed to drain liquid.

Stepping back to her, he took the palm in his hand to inspect the wound. It wasn't anything more than a small puncture mark but the rash was spreading fast, covering most of her lower arm.

"Larsen, I don't feel so good."

Whether from the shock or by some poison from the plant, she started to topple. As she collapsed, he caught her and moved her back to the tree line, gently seating her against one of the tree trunks and urgently pulling the first aid kit from his pack. Throwing unwanted items aside, he found the spray canister he needed and began to apply it. A blue flexible coating applied itself to Rivers' hand to seal the skin and provide an antiseptic shield, the contrasting blue against the bright red of her hand making her body's reaction even more alarming. He didn't know how long she had or what the effect of the poison might be in the long run, but right then things didn't look good. He had to do something. Something was always better than nothing.

A second canister was applied to her wrist and activated, pumping a pain killer through the skin to the blood stream. It would take away and relieve the local pain for a while and maybe give her some time to sleep while he figured out what to do next.

Looking around, there was nothing, and the reality of the situation hit him hard: they were totally cut off and alone. The only person whom Rivers had to rely on was him. There was no one else.

Options, he needed options. There was nothing immediately apparent from the forest and he sure as hell couldn't head out into the meadows, it was full of the little white flowered plants which had just taken down Rivers. He would be flat on the floor beside her before he had taken ten paces into the long grass. The only way forward was back, back into the forest or along the tree line and possibly into the next valley.

He referenced the bio-comm map, this time not for the Xannix patrol craft but for somewhere, anywhere which might be a shelter for them, somewhere to recover and hold up for a while, so he could tend Rivers and think about what to do next. He needed a plan. Scanning the local area brought up nothing, but further west there was another valley which appeared to have a small Xannix structure near its mouth to the meadows. Doing some quick maths he calculated he could walk it in about two hours, then kicked himself, he would need to carry Rivers too so that would almost double the time. He needed an alternative. They could probably move faster if he could put together a stretcher of sorts, maybe a drag sled similar to the old North American travois. After a few minutes of searching, he found a couple of fallen branches of roughly equal length and a couple a little shorter. Taking his blade, he cut some cord from his supplies and bound the branches into a large triangular 8 shape, then slung and strapped their shelter material between the central space. Stepping back to admire his work, he wiped his brow. The sun was getting high in the sky; they should make a move.

He tested the stretcher for strength by putting both their backpacks in it, slinging the yolk of the stretcher over his shoulders and dragging them up and down. It appeared to hold well. He tightened the bindings to one joint and went to get Rivers. Checking her over, he rolled up her sleeve and found the rash to have spread further. She had also started a fever in reaction to the poison in her circulation. It would be no use him panicking over the situation, but he could feel himself close to the edge. There had been too much loss of life since they arrived in the Xannix system and he had not been able to stop any of it, but this felt far more personal. Rivers was the only other human on this planet and, right now, if she couldn't count on him, then who?

Picking her up in both arms, he carried her and placed her gently into the stretcher. Slinging the backpacks around the yolk of the stretcher, he picked up the other end of the travois and pushed against the crossbar. After some initial resistance, the stretcher moved heavily across the ground, a distinctive track ploughed in the earth behind them. There was little he could do about that; there was no more time and they had to get to that shelter. Maybe he could find help or a way of contacting the fleet. Anything. But he was resolved: he was not going to let Rivers die.

*

Hiding behind some unidentifiable shrubs, he spent ten minutes recovering from the last couple of hours, which had been hot, hard work. Muscles ached and complained all over his body, and his hands were raw from the effort of pushing the travois; he was sure if he looked close enough at the yolk he would find most of the skin from his hands as a thin coating to the wood.

Panting and sweating hard, he observed the structure before him. The main body of the building was circular and made of the local forest timber, with a couple of squarer-looking protrusions which allowed for access to the central body. A few towers dotted the premises like chimneys but what their purpose was he couldn't tell. It was an odd mix of natural materials and Xannix technologies that seemed in complete harmony, every element looking as if it was in the perfect place for both structural and aesthetic purpose.

There appeared to be no signs of life, although there were well-trodden tracks into the forest. He did note the vista into the meadows was unbroken. Clearly, grass was dangerous on this planet and somewhere you didn't go.

He wanted to be sure the property was empty and wait longer, but he was now really very concerned about Rivers' condition and his hope was there might be some medical equipment inside which she desperately needed.

Breaking cover, he held Rivers in a carry across his shoulders and made his way at best speed the last few metres to one of the access ways. Once inside the cover of the entrance, he found there to be a closed doorway ahead, but, just as he began to curse and think of ways to open it, the control to the door flashed a sequence of lights and a beam scanned them both from the centre of the door. It opened immediately and without prompting. He darted through the door before it had time to close on them and change its mind. Some part of his mind nagged him as he entered—'Trap,' it said—but the part of his mind screaming at him to save Rivers won out. There was no decision to be made.

Moving further into the building, it had all the oddly familiar trappings of a comfortable home, a cooking area, a fireplace, floor coverings of a couple of different muted and faded coloured patterns and a reasonably large bed to the left of the room. He immediately moved to the bed and gently lay Rivers down, making her as comfortable as he could, then turning to the room he went hunting for medical supplies.

He quickly realised he had no idea what to look for; even if the Xannix had a specific sign, logo or written identifier for any medical supplies, he wouldn't know it even if he was staring right at it. Rather than just tip the place upside down looking for something he probably couldn't identify anyway, he thought it best to apply some logic. Where would he keep his medical kit if he had a house? Bathroom? Kitchen? The kitchen was obvious and positioned opposite to the bed across the room. It was a little low tech, but for most of what he saw there he could guess as to its function. A bathroom or wash room was not apparent. He started with the kitchen. Pots, more pots, a basin, some clear-sided containers displaying ground and chopped vegetation. He worked his way across the work surface and through the shelves and recesses. Nothing leapt to his attention indicating life-saving lotions and medication.

As he reached the end of the kitchen, he noticed a heavy hanging drape supported by a rather ornately carved pole and fixings. He carefully pulled back the drape to find a short sloped tunnel ascending to a second floor, handholds and undulations in the floor and ceiling reminded him of stairs leading to a landing space and an archway to another room off to the right, he climbed to the landing in four bounds. It was less a bathroom, more a room with an open shower and what appeared to be a shower head in the ceiling and a similar shaped podium to the floor. There were some more recesses and a couple of items which looked to be ornaments or art of some description; he certainly couldn't imagine a use for them. He was starting to feel the search was hopeless—he couldn't find what he didn't know.

Sunlight beamed through the window across the hall from the archway leading back to the stairs, or, more accurately now, the light from the Xannix star. Scientists back home had named it the Hayford star; it was yet another reminder to him that he was the visitor here. Captivated momentarily by the light, he strolled over to the window, lost in thought. He closed his eyes and leant against the window frame, hanging his head. The rays from the Xannix star were warm and no different to those of home, but he had no time to stand and enjoy the warmth, he had to continue his search. Opening his eyes again he found that his view was directed towards the track leading up from the forest. More than that, there was now a vehicle parked there, with no wheels that he could see, a cabin and an open framed rear which was loaded with various shapes of container of differing colours. His eyes grew wide; the vehicle hadn't been there when they arrived.

Launching himself at the stairs again, he almost slid to the bottom. Falling through the drape, he spun to face the room, slightly disoriented. He wasn't going to let anything happen to Rivers; he had promised her they would get through this and no Xannix was going to change that. Looking across to the bed, Rivers was there unconscious and unknowing, but there was a large Xannix figure kneeling at her side, hand on her head. Emotion overtook him and an enraged howl escaped his throat as he flew at the Xannix. Base instincts overriding his logical thought, he completely forgot his sidearm as he launched himself bodily at the thing threatening Rivers.

The Xannix was quicker: in a fluid motion and a flurry of robes it moved up and forward, spinning and reversing his view back to Larsen. A quarterstaff appeared from nowhere, and aimed with accuracy and force it struck him cleanly on the temple. The world disappeared.

RIVERS

Gravitons. It was her favourite game as a child; she used to play it with her brother all the time, while her mother pottered around, cooked or worked. They would all be in the main room of their assigned dwelling, and her VR goggles would be linked to Jack's as they both teamed up to face down the powers of evil and the hordes of the Dark Lord Django. Their characters could warp and bend the laws of gravity, and—as they built up their characters' powers—they found they could boost their abilities by playing off each other. Networked to the gHub, they could then pit their skills against any player in the world that cared to try.

She found that the pair of them were unbeatable. Yes, they had their weaknesses, but problem-solving was what they did. Any puzzle room they had found themselves in, they had always found a way out. In a way, she began to think that she could see a pattern in the way the programmers were thinking. The VR was good, but there were also certain themes that she saw repeating—like, under particular situations, the AI character would always cut and run, and at other times they would become locked with indecision, making them easy to finish off; you just had to engineer that situation to occur and, with Jack working with her, that was becoming easier and more inventive.

"You two should take a break; you've been at that all day. It's almost tea time," her mother was saying.

"Mu-um!" Jack complained.

"Come and have something to eat."

"I can eat it here," insisted Jack. She was about to add her voice to the chorus when there was a chime at the door.

"Are we expecting anybody?" their mother asked.

They shook their heads. Jack didn't even bother taking his VR rig off, but she decided to join her mother, her inquisitive nature getting the better of her. Who was it? Her mind was going through the potential candidates: there was no school today, it was too late for friends to be out and it was supper time. Her mother opened the door and her twelve-year-old self stood close by, confident and nosey. There was a tall man outside in the summer evening; he had blond wispy hair, a bright and breezy manner with a relaxed smile. He looked dusty after a drive. The drive to the stacks could be quite a dust storm on a dry day.

"Hello," he said, "is this the Rivers' residence?"

"Yes. Yes, it is. Can I help you?" asked her mum.

"I hope so. I'm Bill Copeland and I work for OWEC, the Outer..."

"Outer Worlds Exploration Corporation; yes I know who they are. I watch the casts. What can I do for you, Mr Copeland?" she asked, staying formal.

He smiled at the remark but stayed professional. "May I come in? I have a proposition for you."

Opening the door further, her mum stood aside to let him past. Turning back to the waiting car, he waved, and another couple of OWEC people got out to join him. Lifting the boot of the car, they carried a metal crate with them into the house. She thought it looked heavy, but as the two reached the door they seemed to manoeuvre it through with ease and placed it in the centre of the room in front of the sofa. The woman in her thirties, the man younger, maybe late twenties, opened the case and revealed a range of medical and scanning equipment. She had heard of these people from her friends; more folklore than fact, as no one had ever had a visit—apart from the Duncan family on the far side of the stacks a couple of years before. Shortly after, they had disappeared. No one saw them leave, and no one knew where they went. OWEC had just vanished them. Gone.

"So, Mr Copeland. What's this all about, and what's all this equipment?"

"Mrs Rivers, I'll get straight to the point. Your children are talented; *gifted*, you might say." Another smile. "We would like to run some final non-invasive tests, which we will use to determine our offer to you and your family."

Always quick to pick up on the detail, her mother questioned a couple of points straight away: "What do you mean by final tests? When else have you been testing them?"

"Oh, there are a few games we pitch out to the gHub to filter out the masses. Most kids these days play them as a matter of course, and we can learn a lot about their cognitive reasoning and ability to extrapolate data or think creatively. We've been watching your son and daughter for some time now and have been quite impressed. With your permission, we would like to complete those tests."

"What tests?"

"The final tests are purely physical. DNA samples and brain wave analysis. All procedures are non-invasive and incur no pain."

The other two OWEC employees stood silently by the equipment and said nothing, watching her, and waiting for her mother's response.

"You mentioned an offer?" Jack said, as he continued his game, multitasking the situation.

"Yes, I did. Basically, if your scan is agreeable and suits our needs we will be able to relocate you and your family to new accommodation in the countryside, out of the stacks and into something a little more…roomy." He gestured around the two room apartment to emphasise his point. It was an easy sell and he knew it.

"And all we have to do is what?" she asked. Her father had always told her that if it was too good to be true, it most likely was. This was a ridiculous offer. A new house in the countryside; a new life outside of the stacks for what amounted to nothing more than wearing a strange-looking head piece for a few minutes.

"What's the catch?" asked her mum.

"I can honestly say there isn't one. We need bright, intelligent stars for our programme and your children, with the right tuition from the best scholars this world has to offer, will offer the whole of humanity a life in the future. Isn't that what every parent wants for their children? A better future?"

She could tell her mother was torn. She did want those things for her children, but at a real base level her mother didn't like this; she didn't trust this man, and she didn't trust OWEC. There were too many stories and disasters which were the direct or indirect responsibility of OWEC; the news casts were full of negative chatter every day. She could only think that there must be an unwritten rule that it was the remit of the news channels to pump out horror and depression. She never knew why the grown-ups watched so much of it; it just painted a picture of negativity and war. Was that all humanity was? She couldn't believe that. Even as a child, she knew what she didn't want the future to look like, and mostly it was exactly the opposite to the world the news casts put a lens to.

Scrunching up her face and holding her breath while she made the difficult, or not so difficult, decision, her mother finally exhaled sharply and said, "Okay. Yes. What do we do next?"

"Wonderful," said Copeland. "Let's get started."

The two assistants moved to the case and extended a low-level chair to a reclined position. "Who would like to go first?" Copeland asked the children, looking backwards and forwards between the two. Jack and her exchanged looks but, being the older sister, she felt she should step forward—it was the right thing to do, and she didn't want anything happening to Jack; he was her little brother. She sat spinning her legs to the length of the chair and then lay back. It was probably meant to relax those using the scanner, but she didn't feel relaxed; in fact, she felt far from relaxed. With assurances from Bill and her mother, she closed her eyes and tried to let every muscle in her body become loose.

She felt a soft squeeze around her arm and something press gently to her head, with some heavier pressure at five or six points around her forehead. There was a click and further pressure, as a band must have been locked in place around her crown. The female technician spoke for the first time: "All set. Now just relax and we'll be finished in a moment."

Low humming and strange oscillating vibrations could be felt through the head gear; not direct noise to her ears but second-hand information via the skull. She then felt the pressure around her arm increase and her lower arm go a little numb. It was a peculiar sensation followed by a sharp prickling. She opened her eyes and looked down. "I thought you said this procedure was non-invasive?" she heard her mother say.

"It is, Mrs Rivers: this is vacuum extraction; no pain will be felt and no lasting damage. It might leave a little bruise on the skin for a few days, nothing more."

The cuff around her arm was tight fitting and mechanical, with a couple of tubes running to the machine behind her and a small vial plugged into the side, which she could see filling, drop by drop, with her blood.

"He's right mum; doesn't hurt a bit."

"I'm still not happy about it."

"It will all be over in a moment," said the female technician.

Relaxing back into the chair, she was putting on the best brave face she could for her brother; he would be next, and the dreams and thoughts of a better place than the stacks was something she was really excited about. It would change her life, all their lives. Clean air and green fields—things she had only ever seen on the vids or the casts or online. It would be the best place in the world to grow up. She found herself grinning just thinking about it; it would be magical.

"All done," came a voice, this time the male technician.

"Excellent, now if I could ask you to change places with your sister," Bill asked Jack, guiding him with an open palm and helping him into the chair as she vacated it.

The same procedure was applied to Jack, with little fuss or effort; it all seemed so easy. She stood watching the machine working, scanning Jack's brain patterns and taking a little blood from his arm. She rubbed her own arm where the blood had been taken. It was a little more than a bruise, about a centimetre in diameter, and the spot stood proudly on her arm as dark and purple as the night sky. It only ached a little, and she rubbed the spot to ease the ache more out of reflex than real need.

That night, she slept soundly and dreamt of the better life they would all have: the new house, her new bedroom, which would of course overlook the biggest grassland and forest full of the most wonderful creatures, and she would be able to see the stars. She always dreamt about the stars, something that living in the stacks denied her. The light from the city, even at night, was just too bright and washed out any chance of seeing a single star. She knew they were there— she had seen, read and watched enough to know that—but there was never anything like seeing the expanse and endless wonder with your own eyes. It was her drive and she would achieve it, one day. This was a real opportunity. This was her chance.

*

"Hey, sis!" Jack called out across the courtyard. They had been at the Formillun Institute since a couple of months after that day Mr Copeland came to visit; she had been twelve, and Jack only ten. She had just turned twenty-five; it was her year to graduate. Since joining the institute, she had been schooled in advanced mathematics, astrophysics, astrogation and engineering, but what she excelled in and loved was astronomy. She knew every constellation and could name all the stars and nebula that comprised them, but what she couldn't wait to find out was what it was like to go there, to watch the formations move and shift around her, so that when she got to Hayford b she would have a whole new sky to map and ponder.

She was on her way to her graduation and was dressed the part. Standing proud and tall with her friends, she was one of two hundred and thirty-three graduating that year. She felt privileged: with the planet's current population running at twenty billion, she was representing a large chunk of humanity. There would be more to come, but the odds of getting a position on a colony ship were infinitesimally small. There was no way she would have been able to foresee it or that Jack would also have made it through the system. They were pretty unique as brother and sister at the institute; there was only one other pair, and they were identical twins.

Turning to greet her brother, she grinned like a child at her birthday party, everyone praising her and giving her presents—it was the happiest day of her life. She was achieving everything she set out to achieve, and that in itself was something to feel lucky about; she knew too many people who had burnt out, faded or simply failed to reach the high level the institute set for all its students.

"Hey, Jack!" They hugged. "Glad you could make it."

"I told them it was your graduation today. I received special dispensation from my studies. How cool is that? I've got the whole day off. So, what are we going to do after?"

"Are you kidding? I'm going to find the nearest bar and drink myself under it!" They laughed.

"Not if I beat you to it," he replied.

"Oh, yeah. I forgot what a lightweight you are."

"I'm so glad my big sister has grown up and moved past all her infantile comments. I'll have you know, I can now drink a full two pints without falling over." They laughed again.

Happiness faded a little the moment she realised there would be two people missing from their family reunion. Her mother and father had died only a couple of years ago in a tragic helojet crash on the outskirts of the London arcology on their way to visit them for the summer break. It had been a tragedy, not only for them but also for several of those at the school, as the helojet was a connecting flight for many of the European hubs and many families were making the twice yearly trek to see their children and catch up on their lives. It was the sad reality of the OWEC programme that the children needed to be completely submerged in the learning and life they would ultimately lead, so there was always sacrifice. That sacrifice, for most, was personal contact with their families. A student could leave at any time, as there was no enforcement policy, but the simple fact was that to attain a place was so unique and the families so rewarded in terms of other enhancements and benefits that the students felt obliged, not only to the cause but also to keep their families from being returned to the stacks and outer wastelands. No one left unless they were compelled by poor attainment. Achieving a place at the Formillun Institute rewarded the family with a life in the nearest arcology with the richest and wealthiest. You didn't let something like that go.

"I wish mum and dad could have seen this," she said, hugging him even closer.

"I know," he said with equal sorrow. "But, hey, enough. It's your day, big sis. I'm here to make sure you enjoy it."

As they pulled apart and she could see his big cheesy grin and blue eyes, fringe flopping across his forehead and drifting in the breeze, she was startled by his eyes. They suddenly weren't his. Well, they were, but not human; these were more feline. No—more like those of a goat with elongated pupils. Finally, his eyes became full dark orbs, jet black and menacing. She tried to pull away but he gripped harder around her upper arms.

"Don't be afraid," he said. But he didn't say it. His lips didn't move; the words came from somewhere else. No, not somewhere but all around, like it was in her head, like his voice was her alter ego, her other self, the voice she communed with when thinking and in moments of reflection. She shook harder and twisted in his grip but there was no escape; his features looked compassionate and understanding but the eyes were not her brother's. The voice was shifting and modulating and becoming otherly.

"Let go of me!" she yelled at him. "What are you doing?!"

Beginning to feel faint, she started to black out, the world beginning to tunnel into a small circle in front of her, but her brother shook her: "Focus on me. Look at me. Stay with me." She wondered what he meant, although she did feel sleepy. It must have been the excitement of the day, she thought to herself. I should take a rest. "Please, stay with me."

There was a flash of white across her vision, like someone had let off a flare in her face. Intensely bright and almost blinding, when she opened her eyes again to shout at her weird brother the scene had changed completely. Taking up almost all her vision was a creature with those same jet black eyes; the features were unrecognisable. The large hands were clamped to her upper arms, holding her to the bed and restraining her, and a second pair of arms seemed to be tending her and operating some device, which was fixed in some way to her right temple and cradled part of her forehead. She had woken and had gone rigid, paralysed by the shock at being in such close proximity to danger, to the misunderstood and unexplained. The Xannix made a contorted shape with his face; not like anything she would consider relaxing, but maybe it was a smile—she hoped it was a smile.

Identifying that she was now conscious, he took one last look at the device on her head then removed it. He then moved to stand from the bed and released his grip from her arms. Immediately, she flew to the wall and curled into a defensive posture, eyeing him warily.

"It's okay. You'll be fine, although your arm may be a little sore for a couple of days."

Two things struck her immediately. First, she could understand what he was saying; she wasn't sure how and probably shouldn't care for the moment, but it was communication, simple and direct. Second, was that her arm was feeling a hell of a lot better; there was some residual feeling like pins and needles, but other than that the alarming swelling and redness that had spread through her hand and lower arm was gone, a little scab at the centre of her hand the only physical indication of the incident.

Then she saw Larsen spread out on the floor, a wicked-looking bruise visible across the side of his head. She leapt from the bed and to his side, checking him for signs of life and looking for a pulse.

"He's okay. Just needs to sleep it off. He'll be fine."

Rivers felt breath on her hand then Larsen began snoring; she was relieved and surprised at the same time. Only Larsen could get himself knocked cold and find it the ideal opportunity to catch up on some sleep. She started to laugh in spite of herself.

"Let him sleep, little one," said the Xannix. "Here, you must eat. I'll prepare something."

Moving off to the kitchen area, the Xannix called over his shoulder, "Hot food, yes? I think Hetfol broth should do the trick." He started pulling containers from recesses and from shelves and putting the contents into a large cooking pot. "What's your name?" he asked.

"Rivers, and this idiot is Larsen."

"He's a quick one. Almost got me—I must be getting old."

"How old are you?" she asked, as inquisitive as ever. She was still wary, but this Xannix was being very kind and welcoming, quite counter to the recent dealings she had had with his species. The Xannix stopped and looked to the ceiling while considering the question.

"Eighty five cycles this cycle," he responded, the calculation made. "To be honest, it's not something I tend to think of; once you get past a certain age, it doesn't really matter. It's just another cycle."

Picking up the pot, he moved to the fireplace and began pouring the contents of the bowl into the cauldron suspended there. It didn't look appetising, but she had to admit it smelt good. She would reserve judgement.

"So, shall I ask you or are you going to ask me?"

"Sorry?" she asked, confused. "I don't understand."

"Yes, this is true, but there is a lot of misunderstanding going on at the moment." He padded a few buttons to the side of the fireplace and the flames jumped another couple of centimetres, dancing and caressing the base of the cauldron as it began to cook the food. He turned to look at her and inclined his head. "But you and your friend here, what do you think?"

"I don't know what to think; we're just trying to survive."

"We are all doing that. What are you looking for?" he asked.

She thought about it for a moment; it was an easy question and an equally easy answer: they wanted a home. She wanted a home and humanity wanted a home. Somewhere to be, raise kids and enjoy life. Wasn't that all anyone wanted? Well, probably not everyone, but the majority. It seemed somehow ridiculous, like the answer given by a child who wanted the other kid's toy because they had just broken their own. It wasn't a good enough answer.

"We have destroyed our own home," she said with a sigh. "Our planet was plundered to a point where it was no longer viable. We grew too many, and our population was too great to support. So, we departed for a new home. We came here."

The Xannix nodded. "It happens to young cultures. It is a growing process. You will learn."

She was more confused now than before. The Xannix was clearly old, but just how old was eighty five cycles? And what cultures?

"You speak of cultures, on this planet?"

"Yes," he replied as he sat on the floor to the side of a large square of flat wood in the centre of the room which she realised must be the table, there were no associated chairs or other forms of seating, just the rugs on the floor and this large slab of polished wood. "We are an old culture."

"An old world?"

"You could say that, yes. Soon there will be nothing and we will have played our last."

"How could you say that?" She thought of the scans they had completed of the planet when they passed through the satellite network: the planet was covered in cities and the population was considerable, enough to continue a species into the future. Unless there was something more fundamental going on? "All the evidence we've seen so far shows a thriving planet. Cities and population centres of all sizes, and activity between them. You are far from your last day."

He just smiled, that weird strained grin.

"So, what do you intend? There is a battle up there already and you've only just arrived. That doesn't feel like peaceful intent to me. I'd like to know what you intend. Your leader has already been given an alternate to Xannix. There is an alternate planet nearby, and yet he persists with this one. It is odd, don't you think? To be given the choice to avoid conflict and instead choose to engage in it. Our species has spent many cycles keeping ourselves private and now you arrive and wish to take what is not yours?"

She felt confused; what was he talking about now? How could he know about conversations with Clayton? Larsen began to stir, and his arm flopped across his face as he rolled over, waking him fully. She could see a moment of disorientation, then, as the memory of events returned to him, he sat up with urgency and a look of panic across his face.

"It's okay," she said. "We're okay," she said again, as he grabbed her hand and checked it over, flipping it from front to back. "I had a little help from you and our new friend-" She realised she didn't know his name "Sorry. In all the excitement, we've not properly introduced ourselves. I'm Jill Rivers and this is Lieutenant Larsen."

"Luc," interrupted Larsen. "It's Luc," a slight apologetic sideways smile on his lips.

She realised that they had not really been personally introduced either; things were happening fast and simple pleasantries were slipping. "Nice to meet you, Luc," she said, "and how about you?" she asked the Xannix. "What do they call you?"

The Xannix shifted as he sat, making a gesture with his upper arms, "Aldaan, and I'm happy to be your host."

*

They had finished eating and still sat around the low, square table, each sat astride a rolled cushion, which she found actually quite comfortable. The Hetfol broth was the best thing she had tasted since she had been revived from stasis and, although she didn't recognise any of the ingredients, she was so hungry that she easily accepted second and third helpings when they were offered. It was so close to a herb-infused chicken broth that she had no cause to complain and the fact that it was recognisable to her pallet made it all the more enjoyable.

"What is this 'Hetfol'?" asked Larsen. He seemed relaxed, but still slightly wary of Aldaan. She had to concede that the lump to his temple was sizeable, and thought Larsen must be suffering one almighty headache.

"It's a local root plant. It is readily available across the planet. A very easy food to find. I often eat it when I am here."

They both nodded. "And you are here often?"

Aldaan inclined his head. "Not as much as I'd like. It was where I grew up. I have a real fondness for the forest and the lakes in this area."

With all the new information, she found herself distracted. Her mind wandered back to the earlier conversation.

"I'm having problems trying to translate your cycles into our time-frame," she said. "How do you measure a cycle?"

"It is the time between the emergence of one Setak'da and the next," he said, with what could have been a hint of amazement to his voice, as if this was such basic knowledge they should have somehow known innately.

"And the Setak'da you talk about, what is that?"

"Not 'what'—'who'."

"It's a Xannix?" asked Larsen in confusion. She continued the question for him.

"So, there have been 85 Xannix Setak'da during your lifetime?"

"Yes," he said nodding his head appearing to mirror their own body language as he spoke.

"So, they are appointed?"

"No, no, no," Aldaan said, shaking his head vigorously. "Not appointed, revealed," he stated, with a big gesture utilising all his arms. She and Larsen must have still looked totally perplexed because he paused while looking at them, motioned again then slumped with disappointment. It must have been worse than teaching the young of his world; they were unknowing and reasoned enough to know it. "The Setak'da blesses a few of us with her presence every generation. She takes command of us and guides us to her divine purpose to the benefit of all Xannix. Sometimes, there are more than one Setak'da in existence at a time, but that is rare. At this moment in time there is only one Setak'da and she is named Celicia."

"Is the Setak'da always female?" she asked.

"No, the Setak'da takes whatever form is necessary to guide us forward as a people."

"So you don't take your cycles measured against a reasonable constant, like the orbit of your planet or atomic frequencies, but from a variable re-emergence of a Setak'da, which could happen at pretty much any time?" Larsen asked.

Aldaan considered this for a moment, "Yes."

"How does anything function?"

"Very well. What do you use?"

"We use the second as a base measure of time, which is the atomic oscillation of caesium-133." Larsen said in a mechanical tone, as if recalling from a memory learnt by rote as a child.

"That seems rather a random selection; lots of things oscillate, so why not something else?"

"Well, at least it's a fixed form of time measurement."

"But time isn't fixed," Aldaan stated, "Why would you fix a measure to it?"

"It's only your perception of it that changes, not time itself."

She could see Aldaan's comments beginning to mess with Larsen's calm, as he stared back and fidgeted in place. A change of subject would probably be useful.

"So, Aldaan. What do you do on this planet?"

"Do?" He shifted and looked intently at her, as if weighing up his answer. "I'm an archivist. I work to remember and store the historical data for the planet, as do many. There is much to be remembered and it is important for the future generations to know all that is important for their growth and enlightenment.

"And you?" he asked in response, "What is your purpose amongst your people?"

"I'm a scientist, mainly working in astronomy, astrogation and engineering. Lieutenant Larsen, he's an engineer."

"So, neither of you are military?" Aldaan asked.

"No, not military."

Larsen clearly had something on his mind and was looking distracted. She wondered if he was getting some update from his bio-comm which he didn't like. Maybe the Xannix search team was getting closer. She couldn't tell, and Larsen wasn't saying.

"So," Larsen interrupted. "What's next? Do you hand us over to the authorities or are we free to go on our way?"

Aldaan made another strange face, which she could only translate as one of surprise. "I am not your keeper, Lieutenant Larsen; I am your host. You are free to go as you please, but I would warn you that, being new to this planet, you are likely to run into trouble again." He pointed at her hand. Larsen nodded in agreement. He had to concede that point, not only that, she thought, but also: where should they go?.

They sat in silence for a moment, each of them lost in their own thoughts, trying to figure out the best plan of action.

"Might I suggest," Aldaan continued, "that I be your guide? As an archivist, this will be a perfect opportunity to document your exploits, and I will be able to assist in steering you away from some of this world's dangers."

She looked at Larsen, and there was another long pause while they both weighed up the offer and considered the options. "His offer does sound appealing, but that depends on what you have in mind. I, for one, don't see much point in leaving the safety of this habitat straight away."

"Yes, that had occurred to me. Aldaan, do you have communications equipment in this building?"

"Yes, I do. But I don't know how much use it would be to you; it's not designed for orbital transmission. I don't think it has the range."

"I'm more concerned about communication to the team flying around trying to catch us. I'm sure you can understand, but I'm a little distrusting of the Xannix at the moment. Ever since our first contact with your species on our own ship, you've been shooting at us. You are the first Xannix I've met that appears to have any peaceful intent."

"I'm sorry to hear this. I can assure you we are mostly a peaceful species. But our world history is one of persecution, so we have since hidden ourselves away. That our Overseers are over cautious is born from bitter experience."

"And this bitter experience has caused another conflict. This is not how our first contact was meant to play out. Can we not talk?"

"We are talking, but I am aware from the archives that our first negotiations were a failure. Our team was killed as they returned to their vessel," Aldaan said, with a disappointed tone. Larsen looked shocked. This must have all happened while they were in transit to Xannix and being pursued by the interceptors. It was no surprise they had been shot down.

"This is all getting out of hand," she said. "Can we not stop it?"

"The only one who can stop the aggression is the Setak'da," Aldaan stated. "Unless you have her approval, the Overseers will not cease in their efforts."

"Then that's the plan."

"We have a plan now?" she asked. "I thought staying here was the safest option."

"Plans change," Larsen said, frankly. "And, anyway, someone has to stop all this lunacy." He turned back to Aldaan with a serious determination. "Aldaan, will you help us stop the conflict?"

Aldaan didn't even pause to consider the answer: he had already made his decision. "Yes, Lieutenant Larsen. I'll inform the archives."

DAWN

She had all the archived records detailing every battle in the last four hundred years of human history—naval battles, land battles, a couple of near orbit encounters between OWEC and anti-world government factions—and each was part of her Volatile Encounter Resolution Simulator, more simply known as VERS to the crew. The current VERS status indicated a positive outcome for the human fleet based on current Xannix strength and tactics, although there would be heavy damage to the *Endeavour*, as the main thrust of the attacks were targeted at her. The *Endeavour* had likely been singled out as the flagship through some means; as the hub of communications, the Xannix may well have extrapolated her as the head of the command structure. They were right of course, but it was going to do them little good.

Xannix ships of various shapes and sizes swarmed around the fleet, but didn't have the penetration to get close enough to do any real purposeful damage. A couple of craft had tried but the defensive cover from the point defence system was lacing the local space with so much high-velocity munition and debris that the smaller Xannix ships were being hampered in their efforts. Several had ended in balls of plasma before being able to properly engage the fight.

Between them, the AIs were coordinating the arcs and angles of global fire, anticipating the Xannix manoeuvres and herding them where they could into traps. She had noticed that the Xannix tended to swarm just before an aggressive push, which gave them away. Wondering why any tactic that flagged your intention was of any purpose, she continued to aggressively pursue each and every ship.

Plasma and fire punctuated the space around them, as the fleet manoeuvred into orbit. They would initially take up a high-orbit position and assess the planet while simultaneously degrading and eliminating the forces applied against them; then, if there was no further contact from the Xannix populous, they would have no choice but to implement the final stages of Angelfall. She saw no other alternative: the Xannix were violent and had yet to show themselves as peaceful in any way. Every encounter had ended in death and destruction; humanity would need peace to thrive and there would be no peace with the Xannix in it.

Another swarm of craft began to form between the *Intrepid* and the planet. There was little the *Endeavour* could do to assist, as they were too far away, but she sent a warning to Ellie anyway. Ellie acknowledged and began to lay down a barrage of defensive fire to suppress the move.

Obadiah sent a communication request: "What can I do for you Obi?"

"I don't know if you've noticed, but there is movement from the CJN." The Communications Jamming Network was the satellite array on the boundary of Xannix space, and it had obfuscated the world and made the Xannix essentially invisible to the distant observer.

"What is moving in the CJN? Is it a ship?" she asked.

"No, you don't understand. The CJN is moving."

"Moving? Moving how?" She looked out to the satellite network and the scanners of the *Endeavour* gave her an instant representation of the CJN in granular detail; Obadiah was correct, the network was moving. Now, that was something neither she nor the VERS had anticipated.

The satellites of the CJN were accelerating towards the planet, and the effect was like a fisherman's net closing in on the fish within: they were trapped.

"How long?" she asked pointlessly—she had the information from her integrated AI self as soon as she asked the question—but Obadiah replied anyway.

"It's not moving that fast. Each satellite is small and will have limited propulsion. I estimate a little over four hours."

"But what is it likely to do when it gets here?"

"Most likely they are either fitted with some explosive device or they are armament platforms of some description."

"Which didn't fire on us as we passed through?" she asked.

"Well, that would give away their purpose early and probably not have the desired effect. You don't spring the trap until the right moment."

"Four hours is not enough time to deploy the Angelfall weapon, but we could take out their communications with a beam weapon—that might slow them down and give us some more time."

"Dawn, you are talking about escalating this even further."

"They have already escalated this by springing their trap. We are only defending ourselves."

"Have we no other options? How are our communication efforts coming along? We urgently need that dialogue." The conversational tone was still cordial, but there was strain there. Obadiah was pressing her on a negotiated peace, but there was no way that could happen under the current situation.

"They aren't. Communication has not been made. I will ask for an update from the team responsible."

"Try harder, Dawn." He cut off the communication link.

Who did he think he was? Her anger spiked; she felt like a petulant child having her wrist slapped, but there was little she could do other than those things she was already doing. It was frustrating and, more than that, it was disrespectful. After all the kindness she and her father had shown him, to be reprimanding her for poor results was laughable. She would deal with it later.

She searched the ship for Dr Spencer and his team, finding them in the midsection shuttle bay speaking to a pilot and crew. She opened a link to Dr Spencer.

"Dr Spencer, how are your efforts to contact the Xannix coming along?" Dr Spencer stood momentarily, as if he had been startled, his back rigid and arms by his side as if standing to attention. Relaxing, he found his composure and managed a response, albeit stilted and excited.

"Dawn. Hello. We have had no luck with our communication efforts so far. The Xannix seem either to not want to or are unable to respond on the frequencies or channels we are using. We are resorting to a direct contact method."

"Could you elaborate?"

"We are going to go to the surface and try to gain an audience with the Xannix Setak'da."

"What's a Setak'da?" she asked.

"As far as we understand, it is their global president," he answered, with a slight frown on his face as he tried to make the comparison.

"Do you think that making contact with this Setak'da is possible?"

"Unknown. But we have to try something."

"This is a very extreme measure; the probability of it succeeding is small."

"But possible. I have had contact with the Xannix and they can be reached. We just need to know how, and currently they seem not to want to speak with us."

"Understandable, considering the current situation, don't you think?" she asked.

"Yes, I agree. But we can't stop trying and I think the best way to do this is face to face on the planet surface."

He seemed convinced. It was a highly risky move and one which, if his calculation was wrong, would undoubtedly get him and his team killed. She could see from the ongoing conversation between Reeve and the pilot that he was unconvinced; taking the shuttle out in the middle of a battle would be like committing instant suicide.

From her point of view though, it would be an instant and final indication she could use against Obadiah to convince him of his over-idealistic stance on peace with this species. The Xannix were trouble and needed to be dealt with; she would need to play tough.

"Okay, Dr Spencer. Tell the pilot I will clear a flight corridor to the surface."

"Thank you. I'll keep you informed."

She closed the communication and started to plot a course to the largest population centre on the planet. It was undoubtedly where the Setak'da would be, as the premier of any state always located themselves amongst the largest population centre.

SILVERS

The pilot had changed his mind the instant that Spencer had stopped reporting the situation to Dawn; clearly an instruction had been relayed to the pilot and his objection to flying into a hot zone became no objection at all. Dawn had promised them safe passage to the surface, and Commander Roux had confirmed they were manoeuvring the *Endeavour* into low orbit to cover their descent. It looked like progress.

Dropping through the upper atmosphere always worried him. There were lots of things that could go wrong with a descent, but it was mostly about the speed and angle of the descent at that critical re-entry point where the atmosphere of the planet took hold and aerodynamic drag began to grab and batter the frame like daemonic grasping claws. The buffeting and shaking made him curse and grip the couch arm rests. He had asked himself on many occasions why he was worried about a simple shuttle drop when there were so many other dangers in space and he had come to a couple of conclusions. Firstly, that of all the things that could go wrong he may as well fixate on something as his likely nemesis, and, secondly, he couldn't think of a worse way to go. If the shuttle came in at too high an angle, they would take up the attitude of a fireball for the ten minutes it would take them to get to the surface, or, if the shuttle re-entry angle was too shallow, they would skim like a pebble on a pond and have to try again if they had enough fuel, otherwise it was a long journey into the void of space until their air ran out. The angle and speed of re-entry had to be just right, calculated and obvious, certain. All this predictable manoeuvring made them a sitting duck to any Xannix ship or ground defence position that happened to be scanning them. Although he had mentioned it briefly, he hadn't really understood everyone else's complete lack of understanding or ambivalence to the situation. He gripped the arm rests tighter, his knuckles white.

"Relax, Silvers," said Reeve, "we'll be on the ground in a few minutes."

"That," he said with a deep breath, "is a certainty. It's the state we are in when that happens that worries me." He was trying to make a joke of it, but not quite. He grimaced at another buffeting, which shook the cabin vertically. They all rattled in their couches and Reeve let out a laugh. "I just don't want to be too crispy when I get to the surface. Is that too much to ask?"

"Ah, it's a rollercoaster, Silvers. Just enjoy the ride."

He looked over to Spencer who was listening to the conversation and grinning like a Cheshire cat. "I suppose you're enjoying this too?"

"Nope, not much," Spencer admitted.

"Then, why are you grinning like an idiot?"

"You have some entertaining phobias," he responded.

"It's not a phobia. A phobia is an irrational fear. Being scared of crashing into a planet at hundreds of metres per second is a completely rational fear. There's nothing irrational about it. I thought you'd know that, doc?"

"Yes, well. It's still funny. And you're keeping my mind off the situation, so that's good for me."

"Doc, you're all heart."

Lieutenant Paul Jacobs interrupted their conversation. He addressed Reeve, but it was on an open channel. "Lieutenant Reeve, we are now through the upper atmosphere and setting course for the LZ coordinates. We should be on the ground in eight minutes."

"Thank you, Jacobs. Keep an eye out for trouble. Let us know when we're two minutes out."

"Roger."

Now they were through the worst, he decided to try and take his mind off things by plugging into the shuttle's external cameras. Instantly, he was enveloped in white wispy clouds, the altostratus in the higher atmosphere, brief and fleeting. As they dropped through this layer, the sky before them became clear for miles. He could see nothing in detail, but the undulation of the Xannix surface, with its mountainous peaks and troughs, was so reminiscent of Earth that for a few short moments he was transported in his mind and found it difficult to tell the difference. He considered that for a moment. The astronomers and scientists who had originally sought out this planet had done their jobs exceptionally well. It was as if they had searched the universe and miraculously stumbled upon a duplicate world in every detail. What were the odds of that? Somehow, he didn't think he wanted the answer. It would be a tiny probability, a decimal point then lots of zeros.

"Here they come," Jacobs stated over the intercom. He looked wildly around the sky to try and pick out what Jacobs was talking about, but he saw nothing.

"I don't see anything," he responded.

"You won't see them visually," Jacobs said. "They are tracking us at about ten kilometres distance and matching altitude. They are hiding in the horizon line."

He saw the inky black line of the horizon and realised what Jacobs was telling him. Even with the Xannix a kilometre away, if they were at their exact height they would be masked by the blackness of the horizon. One thing confused him though.

"Jacobs, you said they were tracking us. They are not intercepting us?"

"No. We have just picked them up, but they appear not to be moving in on our position, just tracking alongside. Maybe they are waiting to see what we do?" Jacobs speculated.

"I don't know. Usually they shoot first then shoot again later. It's not their usual tactic to stand off and observe," he concluded.

Spencer broke in, "Maybe now would be a good time to begin broadcasting our diplomatic credentials?"

"Go ahead, doc," Reeve said. "It's what we're here for. Let's make friends."

He nodded and then focussed internally for a moment, connecting with the shuttles comms system and loading the pre-recorded message of peaceful intent. Hopefully, someone in the Xannix authorities would hear it and come and speak to them, but that outcome didn't rise to the top when he thought of possible scenarios for their current mission. To be honest with himself, and generally he was a pretty optimistic guy, this was lining up to be more of a suicide mission than he anticipated. Every moment they survived was a moment of surprise for him. The fact they had made it through the re-entry was just such a moment.

"I don't know what you just did," said Jacobs. "But there are now several craft breaking off and heading to intercept us. Intercept in thirty seconds from the south-east."

He swung his visual around and could see trails of white tracing across the sky from the south-east, just as Jacobs had indicated. The distance was too great to observe the interceptors themselves, but their speed through the atmosphere was causing long fingers of vapour in the blue pointing to their position. The interceptors were indeed moving fast. He tried to play with the camera's magnification settings to get a better visual.

"Can we evade them?" asked Reeve.

"We'll do our best," said Jacobs, referring to his co-pilot and flight engineer. "Hold on."

The shuttle suddenly pulled a hard turn, corrected, then began a rapid descent. His stomach began to complain as the manoeuvre pulled negative g, rolled over and back to hard positive g. Concentrating on the outside of the ship, he saw the horizon flip and roll as the shuttle tumbled through the air. Catching sight of the pursuing crafts trails as they span, he noticed the white lines were no longer straight but had started to bend, indicating a change of course. They were definitely the target of their pursuit.

"They're still on our tail," he called out to Jacobs.

"I know, I know."

More hard g and the sky swirled again. This time, there were a couple of flashes in the sky, white and orange.

"What just happened?" he croaked in surprise.

Reeve was monitoring the comms channels and answered before Jacobs could respond. "That was the *Endeavour*," she said.

"How?"

"Rail gun," she informed him.

"Good shot," was all he could find to say. "There's still one out there."

He could see it now, a dark dot against a bright blue sky. It was gaining fast and pulling some evasive manoeuvres of its own to avoid the same fate as its two wingmen. He had a terrible thought of this being the same situation Larsen would have found himself in only the day before. They had been less lucky, and without the fire support of the *Endeavour* in low orbit above them. The interceptor closed and was now beginning to take form; it looked to have a flat mono-wing configuration with a dropped central intake for the power unit, a purpose built high-speed aircraft, not a dual-use spacecraft. As he watched, there appeared two fast trails which sped from its underside.

"Incoming," said a voice he didn't recognise, possibly the co-pilot. Cool and professional. A statement of fact.

The shuttle lurched and pitched up, like a horse suddenly rearing without warning. A force punched him in the kidneys as the thrust of the engines came fully online. The cabin became a cacophonous, violently vibrating hell as Jacobs pushed the engines to the limit in order to gain some height. At the top of the climb, Silvers saw the missiles close; both streaked through the sky and locked on to them.

"Ten seconds," stated another calm voice. No stress, practiced and drilled, ex-military—he assumed it to be the flight engineer.

"Five seconds." Again, no urgency. As if he knew the plan but was not sharing.

"Four, three, two…"

There was no *one*, and Silvers eyes were wide as the missiles converged on them. On him. Viewing the unfolding events through the external cameras made the whole experience far more personal, as if it was actually him the Xannix were targeting. His logical brain knew that wasn't specifically true, the Xannix at this point were not being that choosy, but his eyes gave him different information.

Jacobs cut the throttle in an instant, rolled the shuttle hard to invert it then yanked hard to drop them from the sky. Silvers world became almost silent and time slowed to a crawl. The missiles inched past them, narrowly missing an engine housing, and both veered off in arbitrary directions trying to reacquire their target. Jacobs kept the throttle off and the engines cool as they plummeted more than flew towards the surface of the planet.

"Is this necessary?" he heard Reeve call out to Jacobs.

He grinned at her. "Rollercoaster ride, man!" he said into the silence. Reeve didn't seem impressed, but he couldn't stop the wide grin from his face. The adrenaline was a high.

After a few moments, he got back to watching the external cameras. Jacobs had started to pattern their descent on that of a falling leaf, it seemed to flitter in all directions, the horizon spinning and chaotic. Another intense light flashed and the cameras became completely white and unable to filter the bright light they were seeing, it was so close it seemed like a second sun in the sky. An instant later the atmospheric shock of the explosion caught up with them and battered them, tossing them into a roll which was momentarily uncontrollable; he heard Jacobs curse loudly over the open channel.

"What was that?" Reeve called out, "*Endeavour* again?"

"Not this time. Now, they appear to be shooting at each other," Jacobs said. "It was our shadow."

"What, the ship that's been tailing us?" she asked.

"I guess not everyone is on the same team," he suggested.

"Spencer, try and contact that ship directly. Tight beam, any channel."

"Broadcasting," he said, although he seemed to be distracted.

A message arrived for him and a bio-comm icon flashed for his attention, it was from Spencer. He opened it immediately and found the wording to be simple and direct: 'Larsen and Rivers are on the move.'

Spencer was still tracking them and the information he had just been given was confusing. They were indeed on the move, but rapidly. As far as he knew, they had been on foot. They were currently moving east across the open plains at about 120 kmph. Extrapolating their course, he believed them to be heading for an archology complex to the north-east of their location.

'Can we intercept this target?' he subvocalized to Jacobs, as he sent him Larsen's position.

'Not before it reaches that structure. They'll be inside about five minutes before we are.'

'Thanks,' he returned. It wasn't the news he wanted to hear, but he would need to work something out. He turned to Reeve. "Looks like Larsen and Rivers are going to be at the arcology about five minutes ahead of us."

She looked at him with a frown. "I thought they were safe and holed up to the north of here?"

"I guess plans change," he replied.

"Do we know what they are doing?" she asked.

"I've had no comm from them. All I can think at this stage is that they have been captured."

"Shit. Well, there goes plan A," she said, turning to face the front and putting her head hard against the headrest. She closed her eyes in deep thought. When she opened them again, she opened a link to Jacobs.

"Jacobs, get us to the alternate LZ as quick as you can. Open the throttle."

"Yes, ma'am."

The shuttle lurched with a sudden thrust which pushed them into their couches. Levelling out on the new heading they flew like a dart at the arcology.

*

"We've picked up an escort," announced Jacobs.

Silvers pulled up the external camera view again and, sure enough, there to their starboard side about four o'clock was the shadow that had been tailing them all the way down. It had been pretty much invisible until the last few minutes where it had assisted them out of a sticky situation with some Xannix interceptors.

Flying in closer formation, he could see the interceptors bore an insignia he didn't recognise, like a sun with rays in all directions—long rays like a Y, shorter rays like an inverted Y—emanating from the circumference of a central circle. He was unsure as to why these Xannix were now defending them, and fighting against their own kind. It made him even more wary of their intentions. But he knew conflict was always shades of grey, and things were getting more grey by the minute.

"Okay, Spencer," Reeve said. "Time to get your best ambassadorial game face on." She looked at him with a confident smile. "The game is all yours."

"Ten seconds," Jacobs called out.

Spencer blinked as he looked at her, then seemed to focus and nodded to her in full understanding. The gravity of the situation was enormous; he was unsure how that much responsibility weighed on a man, but Spencer was not letting the strain show.

The pitch and whine of the engines changed and manoeuvring became loose and large as they flared for landing. Jacobs placed them softly on the pad and cut the engines. They were well and truly in the jaws of the beast now. They were committed, and the only way was forward.

Unbuckling their couch harnesses, they stood and made their way to the door. Spencer straightened up his uniform and Reeve stood at his shoulder whispering a few last-minute words he couldn't quite hear, to which Spencer nodded and looked at her with steady eyes. He was ready.

"No weapons," Spencer said over his shoulder.

"Excuse me," he found himself saying in response.

"No weapons."

"So, how exactly are we going to do our job if things go bad?" he asked with confusion.

"Without weapons," Spencer reiterated. "I don't want there to be any inkling that there could be hostilities caused by us. We are not here to cause trouble; we are here as ambassadors of humanity, emissaries. I do not intend to cause an incident and I do not intend to jeopardise our efforts before we get a chance to speak."

Reeve and he exchanged worried looks. This would severely deplete their options if everything went to hell, but they could see his point.

"Okay, ambassador," Reeve said. "No weapons."

They began to disarm. It took a couple of minutes, by which time there was a small pile of equipment at the side of the airlock.

"Thank you," Spencer said.

Turning to the airlock, Reeve hit the inner door control and they all stepped in. He could see through the outer airlock door view port. It was a short and wide rectangular view port which showed a clear crowd of inquisitive Xannix gathering outside in the hangar. He couldn't count them accurately, but estimated a group of about fifty there already, and they were only the ones he could observe through the outer airlock window.

The inner door closed behind them, and the outer door control indicated that it was okay to proceed. Spencer stepped forward and opened the outer airlock door. A quick hiss of hydraulics and slight air pressure equalisation and they were stepping through to actually greet the Xannix for the first time. A proper first contact, with no shooting and a peaceful dialogue. He could see Spencer smiling and opening his arms to the group, then performing some movements which may well have been an extensive display of greeting. He hoped so.

All the faces before them appeared quite troubled, but equally enthralled and captivated by their visitors. No one came forward and no one responded to Spencer's gesticulations. Then Spencer began to speak. He could not decipher a word of it. Spencer was speaking their own language and being listened to by a crowd whose expressions had now turned to one of surprise. He could not be sure whether it was what Spencer was saying that was causing the shock in their faces, or the fact that he was speaking their language to them as if he had been a native of the planet for many years. He assumed the latter.

As Spencer finished speaking, he again smiled pleasantly at his audience and made another slightly different set of arm movements ending in a slight bow. The group in front of them seemed to be a mix of hangar technicians, engineers and other workers; they were all now looking puzzled at each other and breaking out into little conversations amongst differing groups.

While this was going on, he sent a sub-vocal comm to Spencer, 'What did you just say?'

'The short version?'

'Yeah,' he replied.

'We come in peace. Take us to your leader.'

'Cute.'

He continued to scan the crowd for signs of hostility, but the group showed only signs of confusion and wonder. Then he noticed the craft that was now parked about thirty metres away, the one which had been following them down in their descent and had also defended them against the interceptors a few minutes ago. Then there was a disturbance in the group ahead, from the direction of the hangar exit into the arcology. Voices of command, others of complaint as a path was cut through the group in front of them. He could see a group in shadowy black uniforms working their way through.

'Heads up,' he said to Reeve on the sub-vocal channel. She had already seen the danger and immediately stepped forward and in front of Spencer.

The Xannix in the dark uniforms broke through the front ranks of the onlookers and spread out five wide, weapons levelled at them. He leapt at Spencer and pushed him to the ground, his own body shielding Spencer from any incoming fire.

There were two loud booms and immediate pressure around his back. His first thought was that he had been shot, but the sensation wasn't right: too broad, not focussed or intense enough. Then he tried to move and found he couldn't. Looking forward, he could see Spencer looking equally confused, but then around his head he saw the fine strands of an almost invisible mesh pinning them to the floor. A short whine of micro motors and the tension in the net increased and held them to the floor even tighter; his shoulder curled in on his ribcage and he began to find it difficult to breathe.

A foot appeared in his eye-line, but nothing was said and he could see nothing else. Rather than fight it, he thought he would conserve his strength.

Without warning, things became loud and physical. Xannix where shouting and running in all directions. He strained against his restraints to see what was happening behind him, but he couldn't move his head at all.

'What's happening?' he broadcast to Reeve via bio-comm.

'I think our friends from the interceptors have just arrived.'

'Is that better or worse for us?'

'I don't know,' she replied.

He felt himself lifted bodily from the floor as he was suddenly gripped and held diagonally across the chest of a Xannix, all wrapped up in a silken cocoon. They were already moving at some pace through the dispersing crowd towards the far side of the hangar. It was a snatch and grab, and they were the prize.

'Worse,' he messaged.

LARSEN

He sat in the rear of the Seeker skiff, barely aware of the outside world. The events which he found himself part of were quite surreal and his mind was still catching up, unable to process the enormity of everything that had happened. He found himself reliving snapshots of the last half hour again and again, as if by doing so he would eventually be able to comprehend or figure out the reality of the situation and what it meant.

Rivers was safe, sitting by his side and equally dumbfounded. But not as lost as he was. She was sitting letting the events wash over her. And watching, watching everything, taking it all in.

They had left Aldaan's habitat, setting out on the short walk towards his vehicle. As they walked into the bright sun, he had felt a strange feeling, like a premonition of danger. It felt odd against the bright light and lush green of the forest and meadows, but it was there, a feeling of dread and anxiety. Raising his hand to his brow to shield his eyes from the Xannix sun, the scene came into sharp focus. There were five Xannix clad in black uniforms standing with their weapons aimed at him and Rivers as they walked into the open.

He was about to do something crazy when the first of the five stepped forward towards him, slapped his weapon across his own chest and knelt to lay it on the floor. He stayed there, not moving, head bowed and all hands palm down on the weapon he had just placed ceremoniously to the floor. It made him stop, his confusion apparent on his face as he turned to Rivers for an explanation, but she only shrugged as if to mirror his own disbelief. He looked round to Aldaan and found him in the doorway with what he believed to be a grin on his face, but as always his features were a little difficult to read. He turned back to view the scene in front of him, all five of the Xannix were now knelt with their palms down on their grounded weapons. He was having a hell of a time trying to figure out what it all meant.

His next reaction was to believe he and Rivers were now captive, the action of taking a prisoner wrapped up in some formal ceremonial custom just before they were cuffed and dumped in the back of a jail cell for the rest of their natural lives. There was a pause in proceedings then Aldaan was at his side. "You told them we were here?"

Aldaan shook his head in the human negative. "No, my alien friend, you did that all on your own."

He was quite indignant. "I did no such thing!" He looked across the group of Xannix. "And why are they kneeling? Are you some sort of priest?" believing the only other reason for the display to be for a religious superior.

Aldaan laughed again, a rasping, wheezing noise to his ears. "No, although, I will concede, I'm not an archivist."

"I thought an archivist would be a little less useful with that quarterstaff," he responded, remembering the blow to the head which rendered him insensible for an hour or so. Rivers kept watching the kneeling group with questions in her eyes.

"These are the guys who have been hunting us," Rivers finally said.

"No, we have been tracking you, but the others you speak of are not us. And we have not been hunting," stated Aldaan. "Seeking."

"And how different is the distinction?" he asked.

Aldaan seemed surprised at the question. "Much is different." He shook his head and huffed. "The very purpose of the Seekers is for the greater good of the Xannix. Their main task is to find each incarnation of the Setak'da and to reveal them to the populous. Their current search has brought them here." Larsen seemed to be the last to get it. Rivers already had her mouth open in dumb disbelief.

"To you?"

"Not me, I am a Seeker. Well, I was in my younger days, but you never really leave. A Seeker just becomes a little less active as the cycles go by."

"And we just happened to knock on your door?" he asked.

"I doubt that. The Setak'da is wise and resourceful; you have demonstrated many of those capabilities to this point. What comes next will confirm our determinations."

Rivers had a wide smile spread across her face. "What are you smiling at?" he asked.

"You, a Xannix Setak'da?" she said quietly to him, doing well to stifle a laugh. "I seriously think they have this wrong."

He considered the situation for a moment, then saw an opportunity. "Aldaan," he asked, "being a new Setak'da, do I get the chance to speak to the other Setak'da?"

"Oh, you are not Setak'da yet. You are Setak'osso. But to answer your question, yes," Aldaan agreed. "You get the chance to meet the Setak'da."

"Setak'osso? What is that?" he asked.

"It is the challenger to the Setak'da. If successful, you will become the next Setak'da."

"This is insane," he stated. "I'm not even a Xannix."

"It is the way; it is not of your choosing." Aldaan looked up, as if in thought, "But you are not the first off-worlder to hold the position."

He began to pace up and down, stroking his chin in thought, wondering how to use this new information to their advantage. "It's our chance to stop this conflict, Rivers. I think we should play along."

"Maybe," Aldaan said. "But you'll only have the influence to make that happen as a Setak'da."

"Didn't you just say I was?" he asked.

"Setak'osso," he reminded. "In theory, yes, but you need to be revealed to the people and until that ceremony, you are in danger."

"Danger? How much more danger? We are two humans on a Xannix planet full of people who have been trying to kill us since the moment we met."

Aldaan turned to the others. "We go," he ordered. The Xannix picked up their weapons and stood, then assembled into a guard formation around them.

"Aldaan, what is going on?"

"Come, both of you. I'll explain as we travel."

\   *

As the Seeker skiff flew through the treetops, the Xannix sun flickered orange and white, a strobe effect which strained his eyes and caused him to snap out of his daydream state and back into the present. He looked at Rivers; she was still frowning, intensely lost in her own thoughts. Perhaps she was working out their next step, thinking about their options which he believed were severely limited. They could break and run, but they had had that chance, and they had lasted less than twenty-four hours until they had been apprehended. He couldn't claim to be a prisoner, but equally they weren't free. They were in a weird limbo of existence, just letting events nudge them along a path. A path to where? That was the real question.

Aldaan stepped through from the cockpit where he had been since they departed the habitat at the edge of the forest, moved across the cramped cabin and sat next to him. "We have a short flight so I'll need to keep my explanation brief. A lesson. There are two main factions on our planet," Aldaan began.

"Aren't there always?" he said.

Aldaan, not used to the interruption, considered this then nodded in agreement and shrugged. "The Seekers are charged with searching the world for those Xannix with the potential to be the next Setak'da. However, there are also the Overseers. They are what you might call our military class, as ordinarily they will protect us from invaders and those who mean to do us harm. But-," he paused and straightened in his seat, "-when a new Setak'osso candidate is discovered, things change."

"Change, how?" he asked, feeling that they were close to the point where things would get very awkward for him.

"Their responsibility is to challenge the Setak'osso. To ensure the challenger is a fit and worthy Setak'osso and strong enough to hold the title Setak'da, as it is a title for life. If the incumbent is old or has passed to be with our ancestors, to be honest they don't try very hard; they still ensure a standard, but they have no reason to physically challenge the candidate. But, when there is already a strong, healthy Setak'da, as there is now, they play hard. The fact you are an off-worlder will mean they are likely to play even harder."

"You mean they aim to kill me?"

Aldaan made a face. "If you want to put it that way. It is factually accurate."

Silence spread through the skiff as they continued on. His mind was racing, trying to work a path through all the new information and to find a course.

"I need to contact the fleet," he said.

"Are you sure?" Rivers asked. "Won't that give our position away? Now you're number one on the planet's most-wanted list, shouldn't we be keeping an even lower profile?"

"You can contact your fleet?" Aldaan asked.

"Maybe," he replied. "I haven't tried. But I need to make the call. They need to know that we've made contact and that we're talking to you, at least at some level."

Aldaan simply nodded. He had expected some kind of complaint or argument, but none had come. Maybe they cared little for the communication. Not only that, but Aldaan seemed to care little about the conflict they knew to be raging in the low orbit of their own planet, which made him think that either the Xannix didn't care or were supremely confident of their position. It couldn't be the former; it had to be the latter. The next logical step to that, as far as he was concerned, was that the Xannix felt in complete control of all that was going on. That could only mean trouble for the fleet.

One of the Xannix near the cockpit looked round and put up a hand with two fingers upright and pinched together, "Two nateks," he stated. Aldaan's skin flared a green and cyan colour as he motioned with a short wave of his hand, probably as an acceptance of the information.

"What's a natek?" he asked, understanding it to be a Xannix unit of time, but not knowing its Earth equivalent. The fact that it wasn't translated must mean there was no direct linguistic comparison.

"I don't know what it is to your species. Start counting and stop when we arrive at the citadel. You will have your answer."

"True," he said checking and setting a counter running in his bio-comm.

"We will be arriving soon. First things first. We will need to move you into a secure habitat. Once there, we will need to process you and give you some extended knowledge and learning. Then you will be ready for the Revelation," Aldaan stated.

"What knowledge?" he asked curiously.

"You will be working at a real disadvantage if you ever find yourself without a Seeker to assist you, and that might happen. The

Overseers are a very keen group and will look to divide us the first opportunity they get."

"How long will that take?" he blurted. "We don't have time for a lecture."

"I'm afraid, I must insist. It's for your own advantage. And it will not take long, we will select the short programme."

"Wait," interrupted Rivers. "You can just download and imprint people with knowledge?"

"It's not really knowledge specifically. More experiences. But the effect on recall is essentially the same, yes. The recipient gains understanding in an accelerated time-frame," Aldaan said, looking a little confused at the question. It was clearly an accepted process to the Xannix and one which didn't usually need explaining.

"So, you could teach me to fly this skiff?" he asked, as an example.

"If that is what you wish, yes. How do you think you are able to understand me at the moment?" Aldaan asked frankly. That was true; he had wondered about that as he awoke back in Aldaan's habitat, but quickly more pressing matters had pushed their way to the fore. It had become accepted and easy, even though he didn't know where or how the information was available to him. It was just an innate ability which he could now apply. It was strange how normal the experience had become. He didn't even think about it. Speaking Xannix was just something he could do; it was as natural to him now as speaking his own language.

"Okay," he relented, "but first, I need to speak with our people. We need to get both sides talking. We need that ceasefire."

*

Five minutes. It was something else which aggravated his engineering sensibilities: how could a culture base their units on five minute periods? The journey had taken two nateks, which his counter was telling him was approximately ten minutes, one natek every five minutes. In his opinion, this was not a useful unit. However, the Xannix seemed unencumbered by their choice, so maybe he had little to get worked up about. Still, it niggled him. It was the little things, his father always told him, that mattered in lots of ways and over time those little things would grow to become large annoyances or problems if not dealt with. He had always been unsure of what they had been talking about, even at the time when his father was imparting this great wisdom. Somehow, he didn't think he was talking about alien units of time measurement. Their skiff landed in a reasonably sized hangar. He could see Xannix going about their daily business and other skiffs and craft parked about in ordered rows, some manoeuvring slowly like them to either land or occasionally exit, speeding off into the forest.

"Please, put these cowls on and walk between your escort. We want to draw as little attention as possible. We will walk to the hangar perimeter, where there will be transport waiting to take us to the habitat." As Aldaan spoke, another of the Xannix passed them both the garments he had been speaking of, which would hide their obvious human features. He didn't seem to mind the fact that they were both short a pair of arms and about thirty centimetres off their height. Still, maybe if they moved with confidence and pace amongst the Seekers, no one would consider them unusual or a threat.

Walking among the Xannix to the vehicle was slow. It had less to do with the distance they had to walk, that was only about fifty metres, but he felt every step, every pace like the tick of a clock. Tick-tock, tick-tock.

They seemed to move through the hangar like ghosts. No one paid them the slightest attention, carrying on with their tasks as if the Seekers and their charges were such a normal occurrence; no need to stop what they were doing to observe the group. He had spent most of the fifty metres with his eyes to the floor, trying to avoid any attention, but as they got closer to the rank of ground vehicles he took the risk and raised his head to take in the scene.

It was a normal day on the Xannix world, people moving about with assurance and confidence, just going about their business. Didn't these people know of the impending problems in orbit above them? He guessed not. He looked back into the hangar over his shoulder and saw a fleet shuttle. It stopped him dead in his tracks. Rivers had been walking behind him and bumped into him. She sent him a silent message, 'What are you doing?'

'Look,' he replied and she followed his line of sight. The Seekers had stopped around them as Aldaan bowed his head to speak in hushed tones.

"Why are we stopped? Keep going Lieutenant Larsen, we are almost at the vehicle."

There was a crowd of Xannix around the shuttle and he could see three humans, although they were mostly masked by the Xannix and the angle of the row of craft they were behind; it was impossible to identify them. As he watched, there was a commotion in the crowd and two booming sounds resonated around the hangar, over and above the background noise. The humans went to ground in an instant. He flinched. Shadowy Xannix figures moved to circle the fallen. "Overseers," Aldaan said in a harsh whisper. "We must leave. Now."

He felt a gentle hand to his back and a soft, encouraging push which started him moving, as he continued to look over his shoulder for as long as he could.

'This is Lieutenant Larsen to the shuttle in the Xannix hangar. What is your status?' he broadcast on an open channel.

'Larsen, this is Lieutenant Reeve. We're here in a diplomatic capacity, tasked with contacting the Xannix leadership. We seem to have run into local law enforcers.' Reeve reported.

'Larsen, Silvers. We're also here to rescue you. She forgot to mention that bit,' Silvers said.

'Good job,' he responded with a facetious tone. 'Reeve, looks like we have similar objectives. I don't know how long we'll have comms, we're being taken to an unknown secure location, so I'll be brief. I think we are involved with two different Xannix factions on this planet. Rivers and I are currently under the protection of the Seeker faction. From what I understand, you are looking at the Overseer faction. If we approach this from both angles one of us may get through. I will contact you again when able. Rivers and I are currently fine. Good luck.'

'Roger. Reeve, out.'

'Looks like we're going to be busy for a while,' Silvers continued, managing to sound calm despite the uncertain circumstances. 'You kids have fun. Silvers, out.'

He allowed himself be pushed through to the waiting vehicles. There were two; he and Rivers were put in the second with Aldaan and a driver, and the rest of the team got into the lead vehicle. With all the commotion caused by Reeve, Silvers and the shuttle, there were no eyes looking their way, and they pulled away without so much as a glance from any of the Xannix in the hangar.

Leaving the hangar, they entered a tunnel which took them along a short roadway before launching them into a central atrium running through the arcology, their vehicle now about fifty metres above sweeping parks with trim green lawns, manicured trees and waterways as clear as crystal. With all this beauty outside, the mood in the car was sombre. Each of them in their own thoughts and worried for their own reasons. His were simple. Through some twist of fate which he could not understand and certainly hadn't come to terms with, he had been selected as a Setak'osso. He equally didn't understand the prize. How could being a human Setak'da even work? He had known of the Xannix culture for less than a week and there was no way he would be able to rule in that capacity. This had to be some sort of Xannix joke.

Watching through the windows of the vehicle, he could see others going about their daily lives, driving to business meetings, families on their way to see friends, vehicles in neatly organised streams flowing in a criss-cross pattern at various levels throughout the atrium. The parallels with their own civilisation were apparent, but the differences equally so. The arcology was a scaled up version of any they had at home, although he estimated the population to be far less. The pilot took a left and picked up the stream of another traffic lane a little lower in altitude, joining without disruption to the traffic as they merged. Ahead he could see another tunnel, and they quickly entered a sweeping roadway which filtered into various alternate tributaries. They continued along the main roadway for another kilometre or so then turned down one of the filter lanes.

Finally, they pulled out into an open parking zone with apartments rising either side and behind like some artificial cliff face. A transparent barrier with a diamond grid support structure enveloped the arcology and provided a light orange tinted filter to the external panorama, it was warming and somewhat comforting. The vehicles came to a stop beside a large indigenous tree, the bark pealing in wafer thin curls, reminding him of a cherry or paper bark maple on Earth; there were several dotted around the parking zone, the parking spaces somewhat erratically placed.

"We have arrived," said the driver. Aldaan made a gesture, and his skin gave out a quick flurry of colour in response.

"Please, Lieutenant Larsen, child Rivers, follow me," said Aldaan.

The Seekers were already out of the other vehicle and in formation as they exited their car. They were clearly more confident in this area as the group was not so bunched and he was able to look about quite freely, not feeling the need to hide so consciously, although he kept the cowl up. The group walked down a path from the cars and toward a doorway at the base of the apartment cliff face. A door opened and revealed a large seated lift, with enough space for about twenty Xannix. They stayed standing, he and Rivers taking a place near the front by the door, which gave a clear view of the scenery outside. As the elevator began to rise, the view became wider and the outside seemed to wash away into broad brush strokes of green where the trees and lawns turned into meadows and wilderness before the arcology's outer skin structure. Picking up speed, the elevator car started to tilt and work its way across the face of the apartments at an angle. Looking through the side panel, he could see the edge of the apartment complex as a concave shape heading towards a point near the top. It appeared to be their destination.

As the elevator eased to a stop, he looked down to locate the vehicle they had arrived in; a pin head-sized dot was all he could see, and he estimated that they were almost 500 metres up. That was a high apartment building. A door behind them opened and immediately there was a brash voice calling out, "Aldaan! Aldaan, where are they? You've taken long enough to introduce us, where are they?"

An old Xannix pushed her way into the room. He thought her to be far older than the 85 cycles that Aldaan said he was, but how many cycles he couldn't say—how many Setak'da had there been? She was shoving her way through the guards and to his surprise they were letting her. She stood in front of them, looking them both up and down. "So, which one of you is Lieutenant Larsen?" she asked with keen eyes looking them over. "You," she said, pointing a long, spindly finger at him and looking into his eyes with the darkest most hypnotising blackness. He couldn't look away, feeling himself drawn in, almost to the point of stumbling.

How could she tell? He finally managed to break her gaze and looked at Aldaan, who was grinning that alarming Xannix grin. "How?" he began weakly, but she cut him off.

"Our traditions are old, and I have had lots of practice. I can recognise a Setak'osso when I meet one," she said turning to Rivers. "And you must be child Rivers."

"Yes," Rivers replied politely. "Pleased to meet you. And you are?" she was straight to the question next on his list.

"This is Cardinal Seeker Ovitala," replied Aldaan. "She runs this facility and will guide you through your ascension, as she has with many before." As Aldaan spoke, she continued to look him over. He was beginning to think this was going to be a bad idea, when she suddenly took his hand in an almost vice-like grip and set off through the crowd towards the apartment building with haste.

"Let's begin," she called to all, pulling him behind her like a child. For an old Xannix, she was strong, and had no trouble leading him into the apartment reception rooms, finally letting him go in the central area near a ring of cushions spread out around a central table, this one made from what looked like a porous volcanic rock. For all the technology used in the construction of the apartment, its elevator system and vast windows, the rooms themselves were incredibly simplistic, reminding him of Aldaan's habitat in the forest. There were passageways leading off into other rooms, windows overlooking the gardens and meadows far below, striking frescos rendered directly to the main walls and several free-standing sculptures dotted around the reception room. He wasn't sure of the sculptures; although he was no art enthusiast, they seemed a little over-engineered to be beautiful to his eyes.

Most of the group moved off through the corridors to the rear of the room, while others took up positions around the room, with a couple near the door to the elevator.

"Please, sit," Ovitala indicated to the cushions. They each sat, straddling the cushions and kneeling, in the Xannix-accustomed fashion. "So, you are the new Setak'osso? The forecast has been quite accurate this cycle. It is something that has many people talking and the Overseers chasing in circles. They even appear to have been unable to find you on your own ship."

"Oh, they found me alright," he responded in harsh tones, as he remembered the encounter. "They almost killed me the moment we met. If it hadn't have been for poor Smith, I'd already be dead." It took him a moment to reflect on the first contact with the Xannix Overseers. They had been on the *Intrepid*, trying to track down the source of the communications failure between the *Intrepid* and the rest of the fleet. Smith had been felled with the first shot, and from that moment all hell had broken loose, the corridor had exploded with beam weapons all around him. If Silvers hadn't been there to drag him to safety, the Overseers might have succeeded.

Until now, he'd had no idea why the Xannix had been there. They had all assumed the Xannix to be an aggressive species, over-sensitive to the incoming colony ships and their purpose. Now there was some weird logic to it. The Xannix Overseers were acting on extrapolated information, a calculated forecast, and hunting for the new alien Setak'osso. Him. All this time, they had been hunting for him.

"It is your trial, before you ascend," Ovitala continued, as she nodded to affirm his story. "It has already started. We will now give you the tools and the help to succeed."

He ran his hands through his hair in exasperation; the Xannix did like to speak in riddles and half-truths. "Excuse my directness, Cardinal Ovitala, but what am I meant to do? You are not telling me much."

Ovitala smiled. "You have only one objective. You must overpower the current Setak'da."

"What do you mean by 'overpower'?" More riddles.

"The term is purposely vague in order to define what sort of Setak'da you will be. There are many ways to perform the task ahead, but only you can decide which path to take."

As they were talking, a Xannix walked into the room from the rear corridor. He wore long flowing red robes with a large yellow circle to the centre of his chest, and with yellow lines spreading out in all directions, like sun beams; some long, some short. No words were spoken, but Ovitala clearly knew what it meant. "It is time," she said, slowly standing.

"Time for what?" he asked. Things were moving fast and out of his control.

"Your learning."

SPENCER

He had been direct and open with his first contact greeting. Okay, he knew it wasn't their first contact, but that didn't matter. The words mattered now. The people of Xannix needed to know and he needed to communicate with as many as he could to send out a message of peace and get the hostilities stopped. All he had seen on the faces of the assembled Xannix public had been surprise and confusion, then the uniforms had arrived. He should have expected that. The message would be lost in the moment as the unexpected was revealed and they stepped from the ship. The Xannix would have been processing the *who* rather than the *why*.

With his back to the wall and knees up supporting his arms, he stared at the ceiling of their cell. They had been there about an hour by his estimation, so not that long, but with all that was going on and the potential lives at stake, it was too long. He had to find a way out or a way of convincing his jailers that he must be released, and that meeting the Setak'da was of the greatest importance. They needed to understand the gravity of the situation.

The room was possibly underground, the walls of the cell a hard rock the colour of sandstone, but the entrance seemed to be open. It had been to Reeve's detriment that she had tried to walk briskly out once the Xannix had left them. She was now laying on the floor next to Silvers, unconscious, having received a severe stun from an unseen energy field across the entrance. It was his estimation that she would be okay when she woke up, but she would have an almighty headache. Silvers added that she would also be incredibly pissed off. He agreed.

It still left them stuck in a cell with no way out.

He slowly stood. Lieutenant Jacobs and the flight crew of Mantis Four, Lieutenant Stannock and Flight Engineer Kelly, sat against the wall opposite the entrance talking amongst themselves, trying in their own way to think up an escape plan.

He needed a drink. He lifted himself, sliding his back up the wall until in a position to stand, then stepped towards the basic-looking water fountain in the corner of the room. Jacobs joined him.

"What's the next step, Doc?" Jacobs said, taking a paper container from the dispenser and filling it with water from the fountain. He offered it to Spencer before repeating the task for himself.

"Right now, the only plan is to get us out of this cell."

"It's good to have a plan," said Silvers quietly to himself across the room. They both looked at him for a moment, then sipped their water and continued their conversation.

"We've been looking at the energy field across the entrance. It looks pretty fool-proof."

"Agreed, but I don't think there are any fools here," Spencer said.

"Oh, I'm not sure about that," said Jacobs, inclining his head towards Reeve laid out on the floor. "Didn't seem such a clever idea striding straight through that energy field."

"I heard that," said Silvers. "I don't think you should be putting the Lieutenant down, when she's already out. What have you done to fix the situation so far?" He seemed quite calm, but there was an anger there. Whether Jacobs was just joking or not, Silvers was not seeing the funny side. Silvers got up to confront them.

"Look, if your girlfriend their wants to concuss herself, that's up to her. But we need a way out of here," Jacobs goaded. Spencer hadn't known Silvers very long, but he was sure Jacobs was heading for trouble.

"Gentlemen, please stay calm. This is not helping."

"Oh, I don't know, Doc. Fly-boy, here, seems to have plenty to say," Silvers replied.

"Don't be a jerk, Silvers," Jacobs continued, as he and Silvers squared up. That was all it took. The silence before the explosion. Spencer felt himself transported back to his school playground, watching the bigger boys brawling while he tried to stay out of the hurricane of limbs and fists that could accidentally come his way. Silvers launched at Jacobs and they spun into the wall with a crunch. Fists flew and a few body shots landed but nothing of consequence. Silvers shifted low and twisted hard, lifting his opponent completely off the ground and smashing him to the floor in the middle of the room. Both Stannock and Kelly were up now too, but had taken the option he had. This was between the two hotheads; they would need to work it out of their system.

"I'll have you charged for striking an officer," said Jacobs through clenched teeth. Silvers had him in a choke hold, their heads close.

"If I live long enough, you can try, asshole."

Jacobs managed to get some purchase from the floor and they both stood, still locked in the hold. With all the force he could muster, Jacobs stamped down hard on Silvers shin, ending with a heavy stamp on his foot. It made him buckle for just a second, but long enough to loosen the hold. With a slight flick of the arm and twist of the body, he managed his own counter throw.

While the fight had been going on, he had worked his way round and close to Reeve. It had not been a wise place to stand. Jacobs had pushed Silvers away and Silvers crashed into him with some force. The world around him inverted as his legs were taken from under him, the cup he held was ejected from his hand, spraying water in all directions as he quickly put his hands out to cushion the fall. He didn't think it worked. He felt the bones in his neck crunch as he hit the floor and the weight of his body followed it down. Rolling out of the tangled ball he had become, sitting dazed and upright, he found himself looking out of the cell towards the far wall of the corridor. There was a bent and slightly misshapen cup at the foot of the wall. It was his cup. Tracing the trajectory of the cup back to his position he found water in a spray pattern across the floor, right up to the point it met the energy field, from there to the cup in the corridor there was no water at all. The corridor floor was still bone dry. His brain struggled for a moment to regain its ability to reason, he was still woozy from the tumble.

"Stop," he said. Realising the volume was not sufficient to get through to the brawling pair, he mustered all the command in his voice that he could. "Stop! Stop, right now!"

No one had heard him raise his voice before, and the startled room instantly froze. Silvers and Jacobs locked in another grapple both looked at him and stopped their tussle. Stannock and Kelly looked at him expectantly, and even Reeve flinched and moaned at the noise. That was good; Reeve would be coming round soon.

"Look," he said, and pointed to the cup on the far side of the energy field. The others followed his outstretched arm and saw the cup on the far side of the corridor.

"How did that get there?" asked Stannock.

"It was knocked from my hand," he said in a factual tone, non-incriminating. He needed the team on side. "But look. The water stops at the energy field."

"So, what does that mean, Doc?" asked Jacobs.

"It means, there's a way out," he said and there was a noticeable shift of mood in the room, tension and anger replaced by curiosity. People moved to take a better look at the evidence and to wonder about possible escape options.

"I don't see it," said Silvers. "It only confirms what we already know. This barrier is clearly designed to stop water from moving beyond the limits of the cell, and unless I'm mistaken we are mostly comprised of water. I'd imagine this to be true for most living things; hence, a cell barrier designed to contain water."

"Yes, but the designers of this cell have made an error," he said, looking for any glimpse of understanding by the others.

"How so?" asked Reeve in a groggy voice. Everyone looked over and suddenly Silvers was by her side helping her up.

"How are you feeling?" asked Silvers.

"How do you think?" Reeve said, holding her head as she slowly stood. "Like I've just had my brain scooped out." She straightened up and looked at him directly. "So, Spencer, how are we getting out of here?"

"The door controls are right outside the door, a console about 20 centimetres from the cell entrance. I noticed it as I came in. I also saw the guard punch the code in as we were brought in, only I didn't think we'd get a chance to use it. Now, I realise we can."

Everyone started to look around at each other. "I keep forgetting, you can understand this stuff. Anyway, how are we going to reach the door control? We can't just walk out of here to press the buttons," said Silvers.

"No, we need a tool to do the job. I'm not sure why they just threw us in here without taking our things. Maybe they don't see us, or anything we have, as a threat."

People started rummaging through their personal kit for items which may reach the door control. Nothing immediately leapt out as being of use.

He noticed people starting to become despondent again. There needed to be a way. Looking around the bare cell, he tried to find anything to use. The water fountain was an obvious target, but there was no apparent way to prise any of its components apart. It was flush to the wall with a single gravity-fed paper cup dispenser and a single push button to activate the water release. "If we could only use the water fountain in some way," he mused aloud.

Everyone's attention was on it. "There has to be something we can extract from it. A length of metal about 30 centimetres long would do it, or plastic, anything mildly rigid which we can bend to make a hook," he said more confidently.

He approached the fountain with Reeve and Silvers while the others continued to go through the items on the floor and see if they could fabricate any tools. "The surface is too smooth and tight to the rock, I can't get any purchase on it," said Reeve looking around the edge.

"How about the fountain nozzle? There might be a length of pipe we could use?" Silvers stepped forward and tried to twist the nozzle to see if it would unscrew. To his surprise it did move, but just rotated in place, around and around. It wasn't fixed with any kind of screw thread, it was likely some clip lock. Then from nowhere Silvers produced a small knife. A sturdy looking stub blade at the end of a short handle, which he put to work instantly to the nozzle, worrying away at the join to see if he could release it and pop it free.

"Where did you get that?" he asked Silvers.

"Trade secret, Doc," Silvers responded with a grin.

"Sneaky man," Reeve said.

"I try my best."

Silvers worked at it for several minutes with no success. His frustration showing as he became more and more worked up. "It's no use," Silvers said in the end, kneeling back on his heels and letting out a breath. Then as a final expression of anger he exploded and stabbed the fountain's flat metal front with the blade in his fist like a hammer. The blade penetrated the metal leaving an open punctured wound in the surface. Spencer and Reeve looked at each other in a moment of realisation.

"Do that again," he said.

"What?" Silvers asked. Then he realised he was being dim and caught up with their reasoning. He let fly and punched another blade width hole in the surface of the fountain, and another, then another.

"I need a length about this long," he said, marking a distance about 30 centimetres from the top of the first hole Silvers had made.

"Sure. Give me a couple of minutes."

There was an excitement in the room again as Silvers got to work. Punch, punch, punch. The sound was loud and it worried Spencer that this might alert a guard or set off some sort of alarm, but it didn't. A few minutes later Silvers passed him a strip of metal, albeit a little ragged and misshapen, but a length of metal as ordered. He took it and put his first theory to the test. Standing about arms-length from the energy field he slowly moved the piece of metal in his grasp towards the far wall of the corridor and through the energy field. Reeve stood to his side and checked the distance and penetration of the field.

"That's it," Reeve said. "You're through. About five centimetres at the moment."

He was through, now he moved it around in a rough figure of eight, just to check that the movement was not a trigger, and that also raised no alarm and triggered no defence. A slight smirk started to appear at the corner of his mouth. This was going to work.

Withdrawing the metal strip, he repositioned himself close to the entrance where the energy field control panel was situated. Moving his head to a position close to the field, he began to feel his hair stand on end, similar to the sensation when playing with static charge in a balloon as a kid. He stopped and dared not get any closer; the last thing he wanted now was to be out cold, as Reeve had been a few minutes earlier. He could just about see the frame of the control panel and nothing more from the angle, but it was enough to gauge the distance and the point he would need to bend the metal to make a pointer to operate the buttons. Withdrawing the metal again he made a bend in it at the appropriate angle to make what now looked like rudimentary hook. Now came the tricky part: he needed to key the correct code on the terminal while all the time visualising the pad in reverse.

Easy. He huffed some fringe hair from his eyes and tried to calm himself.

"Right," he announced to the room. "I don't know how long we're going to get to step through. Line up by the barrier and, when I say, step through to the corridor quickly."

They did so, without a word. All lined up, eyes watching him for the cue to go. He started to work the metal into position. The fuzzy static feeling ebbed and flowed as he got a little too close while concentrating on pressing the numbers. He took the poorly fashioned pointer and lined it up to the top left corner of the key pad and using the control frame as reference he pushed the first number. It clicked with a satisfying action. He lined himself up with where he believed he had seen the next Xannix character, his key press was sure and firm. Sweat was starting to build up on his fingers making the metal slippery in his grasp, he took a moment to adjust and get a better grip. There was a short beep from the control panel and he saw a reflected light on the end of his metal pointer flash a red and purple. The control had reset. He could only assume there was a time limit to entering the full code and it had elapsed while adjusting his hold on the pointer. He needed to work faster, but accurately.

He began again, working with more urgency and speed. This time the first two characters went in quickly, he moved to the next character and slipped across the key, his nerves getting the better of him. He took a calming breath and pressed again successfully. Moving to the last number he made an involuntary sound, more of a hum of concentration, the pointer settled over where he believed the zero to be and pressed. The key moved firmly as the others had and instantly he could see a light blue light reflected in the flat surface of his pointer and a short punctuated double bleep sound from the panel.

"Now!" he said to the group and he stepped through with the others to the corridor.

They all smiled and grinned at each other, Silvers even gave Jacobs a friendly chuck on the shoulder, earlier hostilities clearly resolved or forgotten.

He began to look around for Reeve, but she was already a step ahead of all of them. She was at the door at the end of the jail cells.

It looked sturdy, but not locked: the door control was already showing a light blue. She had her ear to the door and was waving at them to be quiet, so that she could eavesdrop on any Xannix on the other side. They stopped their commotion. Reeve concentrated on the door once more, putting her ear hard against it, trying to hear anything or sense any vibration that could give an indication as to movement the other side.

While Reeve was busy at the door, the others seemed to stand silently. However, he could tell Silvers was more active, his eyes scanning the space for surveillance of any kind, cameras or microphones, maybe signs of a trap. He, on the other hand, had been thinking along slightly different lines. They had escaped one particular cell, but there were two things that bothered him. First, where now? They still needed to contact the Setak'da and they would now be aliens in a strange land trying to contact the most guarded person on the planet. An almost impossible task. Second, it had not escaped him that the situation they now found themselves in could be some kind of odd test. He had started to feel much like a rat in a maze. It was not beyond the realms of possibility that they were.

"There is no activity the other side of the door," Reeve announced. "Silvers, what have you got?"

"I can find no evidence of surveillance or scanning within these rooms. Also, I believe us to be far underground. I can get no read on comms with the *Endeavour* or Larsen's team."

There was a quiet while people digested the available information. Reeve nodded and turned back to the door. "Well, I guess we better open it. We won't be able to do anything stuck in here. Once we're out, we can work out a plan."

"I've got an idea. It's not brilliant, but it's a start," said Silvers. "How about we try and cause as much havoc as we can? Give Larsen's team a chance to get to this Setak'da."

"I'm not sure that's a plan that will work out well for us," Spencer thought out loud.

"I did say it wasn't brilliant," Silvers replied.

"Well, as you say, it's a start. Let's keep thinking," Reeve said, trying to keep people thinking, but cutting off the conversation for more important matters, like the current escape.

At the door she realised she didn't understand the wording on the control panel. "Spencer, would you open the door, please. The rest of you stay here; wait for my signal before you enter."

"Sure," he said stepping over. He pressed the central button and the door clicked then opened towards them causing him and Reeve to step back.

Silvers and Reeve headed up the move through the door, practiced and concise. There was no sound, no noise. He had expected something, at least some sort of resistance, but the next thing he saw was Silvers opening the door with a puzzled look on his face.

"Doc," he motioned them in with a nod of his head. "What do you make of this?"

Stepping through into the next room, they found themselves in a recognisable security room. A wall was given over to visual representations of the cells they had been in: cell schematics with each of them located by a triangular marker, with real time video playing their escape on a loop. Someone was either very lax in their security approach, or was sending them a message. They were being watched and monitored every step of the way. For him, the icons turned into little rats scampering about the display, his imagination momentarily taking over.

The thing in the room dominating everyone's attention was not the display. The slumped form of a Xannix lay motionless on the floor, legs buckled awkwardly underneath it. Having fallen backwards off a saddle-like cushion it had been using as a seat, a lake of blood now pooled out across the room, emanating from a wide gash across its neck. His natural reaction was to try and help the Xannix, but knew there was nothing he could do.

"You?" he asked Silvers in a tone which was more disappointment than accusation.

"No. Not us," replied Silvers. "This is someone else's handiwork."

"Spencer, over here," said Reeve completely ignoring the still form of the Xannix. She clearly wanted and needed an interpreter. She was pointing at some wording on the control panel. It was flashing purple and red. "What's this say?"

He walked over and took a closer look. "It's a general alarm."

"For us?" asked Silvers.

"I guess not," he said. "If it was, wouldn't we have Xannix lining up to put us back in the cells?"

They all considered this for a moment. "Well," said Jacobs,

interrupting the silence. "Shouldn't we be taking advantage of this distraction, whatever it is?"

"Sounds good to me," Reeve said. "Let's get going."

*

They had been driven to the cells, so getting to the garage area was a simple case of remembering the way. Silvers took point as they made their way through the corridors to the garage area in silence. Approaching a junction, Silvers raised his hand in a fist and everyone stopped. Reeve made her way up to Silvers and they had a brief sub-vocal conversation, at the end of which Silvers nodded then slipped round the corner and out of sight.

'What's going on?' he asked, using the sub-vocal channel as she had with Silvers.

'There are a couple of Xannix guards up ahead. Silvers is investigating.' she stated.

'When you say *investigating* do you mean *killing?*'

'No. I know what you're asking, Spencer, and I fully understand the implications. '

'Just checking.'

'Having said that,' she continued shaking her head. 'It looks like someone is trying to make us look bad.' He looked at her puzzled. 'The two guards up ahead are also dead. Someone has been busy.' She was clearly receiving a report from Silvers on the situation in the corridor ahead. Nodding in affirmation to a conversation he wasn't party to, Reeve looked back to the group in the corridor. "Okay people, let's move," she said, heading off round the corner to the garage complex.

Silvers was up ahead, and as the group caught up, he handed Reeve one of the long smooth-looking weapons he had obviously taken from the guards. Each rifle was slightly longer than looked comfortable for them. The ergonomics to the rifles were all wrong. Longer and heavier than a human would normally utilise, the weapons looked cumbersome and unwieldy. There were no words, but Silvers and Reeve clearly had another short exchange before he headed off again ahead of them.

While this was happening, he couldn't stop staring, his eyes locked on the lifeless forms of the two Xannix laying in the corridor. One prone, the other in a ragged sitting position, head partially atomised and spread across the wall at an angle towards the direction they had just come. Whoever had done this had come from the other direction, from the vehicle bay and their current destination. He wondered who they were. Most likely the other faction Larsen had spoken about.

Passing several more bodies en route to the vehicle bay, they finally grouped together in a crouched huddle behind the nearest. There were three vehicles, one of which looked like it was a flyer or a skiff of some kind. "Do you think you could fly that one?" he asked Jacobs.

Jacobs looked at him, then the flyer he was pointing to, then back again. After a brief moment of consideration, he grinned, "Shall we find out?"

"I'd prefer to have a nice 'yes' or 'no'," he said, following Jacobs as they made his way towards the flyer.

Jacobs was already at the vehicle and inspecting it by the time he caught up. It was a long five-seat vehicle, which meant it was going to be cosy for six. The nose of the craft was wide and flat, moving out in a chisel shape to the cabin then opening out into an engine housing. Two large air intakes sat under the main fuselage.

After a minute of observation, he touched a section of the canopy glass and it slid away into the engine housing, revealing the cockpit and seating. Grinning, he got into the pilot's seat.

"Well?" asked Spencer. The others had crowded round by this point. "What can you tell me?"

"I like the colour," Jacobs joked. There was a snigger from Stannock.

"That's not what I meant," he responded.

"I know," Jacobs said, as he hit a button on the centre console. The flyer hummed to life, a high-pitched whirring sound began and started to fade as a lower thrumming became the constant. In the same instant, the landing gear retracted and the vehicle hovered in place. The grin on Jacobs face got even wider and a bark of laughter burst from him. "Okay, I think we're set."

Reeve was already in the co-pilot seat; the others climbed into the rear seats. Thinking himself now without a seat, he was about to argue about it, but realised there was still room enough, Xannix proportions being that little bit bigger. Sat between Silvers and Stannock, it was a cosy fit, but comfortable. Before he was totally settled, Jacobs closed the canopy and started to test the controls.

Slowly and in singular directions at first, pulling and pushing, working out the responsiveness and function. At one point they bottomed out and hit the floor, "Oops," was all Jacobs had said under his breath.

"This is not going to be easy," Jacobs announced to everyone, as the vehicle started to edge its way purposefully towards the garage exit.

"How so?" Reeve asked.

"The controls are built for people with four upper limbs. I'm a couple short."

"You can say that again," said Silvers.

"Nice," snorted Jacobs.

"Er, I think we better get going," suggested Stannock, looking out of the canopy to the passageway. Stretching himself around Silvers to take a look, he could see a group of Xannix moving with intent into the garage. One of them spotted the moving with an alien pilot. The alarm was raised.

"Go, go, go!" he shouted as he was awkwardly forced back into his seat, the acceleration twisting him in place. White stabbing lances from the Xannix beam weapons tried to puncture the craft, and there were a couple of strikes which rocked the flyer as it burst from the entrance of the hangar and climbed for the sky.

Getting himself straight in his seat and bracing himself against the g forces, he realised he was the only one not strapped in. "Excuse me," he said to Silvers and Stannock, then grabbed their harness to keep himself secure. He didn't think it would stop him crashing about completely, but it would help him to some degree.

Jacobs banked the flyer round to the right and immediately changed his mind as the scene before them became one of chaos. There were military craft buzzing in all directions, flashes of fire striking out as dog fights were taken up or concluded in blazing balls of debris. Smoke billowed from the apartment buildings above the hangar complex. Whether the infiltration team entering the hangar space had made their way in via the prison complex intentionally, he was unsure, but they would use the opportunity given and make their escape. Perhaps the more important question was who was fighting whom? The events unfolding before him only served to make things woolly and confused—he needed clarity.

"We need to blend in," said Reeve to Jacobs. She pointed at

the nearest traffic corridor with flyers in an orderly formation flying through the arcology. "There," she said. "Merge with that traffic."

"Copy that," Jacobs responded, and the flyer banked a little to the left and began to climb. Within moments, they were within the busy traffic lane and trying hard to camouflage themselves as commuters. Jacobs took up a position which was near enough to the outside of the formation to make a break for it if needed and also open enough to give them a good field of view across the arcology. The battle they had left behind was still going on, the only traces of which that he could see were now wisps of black smoke on the horizon to their rear, getting further away every second.

He opened a link to Larsen: 'Larsen, this is Spencer. Respond.'

Nothing. He tried again.

'Larsen, this is Spencer. Respond.'

'Spence, this is Larsen. Over.'

His heart skipped, he was unsure whether it was excitement or fear of the unknown. It was good to know Larsen was still alive.

'Larsen, we have escaped capture and have appropriated a flyer. We are going to try and find the Setak'da. Have you any information which may help?'

There was a pause, 'Yes. When the Setak'da is challenged, when a new Setak'osso is discovered and revealed, the challenge is undertaken at ceremonial grounds outside the city. Although, I have no idea what form any of this takes yet. There are a lot of unknowns.'

'Okay. I don't understand a word of it, but where are these ceremonial grounds? We might be able to make contact with the Setak'da there.'

'They are to the north, I'm sending you coordinates now.' A message arrived to his message queue.

His mind was racing as he opened the coordinates and sent them to Jacobs and Reeve. The conversation began to fade around him as he started to visualise the area the coordinates represented. They were memories, certainly not his, but they were there. He had never been to this sacred place, he knew that, but someone had and it was those memories he saw now. The programming he had received on the Xannix scout ship had given him understanding enough. He had been gifted the ability to communicate, speak, read the Xannix language, but also a flood of memories, places, people, buildings, objects, all of which he had no context for and which made no sense to him at the time. But the coordinates Larsen had just given him brought back very specific memories of the ceremonial grounds and of those gone before. He didn't have a name for it, just the striking images of the central court: round stonework coloured the floor to describe the image of the Xannix star with rays of light spreading in all directions. The court building was open on all sides and looking out over the canopy of the surrounding forest, deep green as far as the eye could see. It was remote and quiet.

'I know this place,' he said to Larsen.

In his mind's eye he looked up and saw the ceiling of the building, decorated with hundreds of icons, all patterned to describe the same icon as a single image across the full area. Again, he recognised it immediately. It was the insignia of the Xannix that had been their first contact on the *Intrepid*: the inverted delta shape, a couple of vertical parallel lines inside and to the left.

'I need you to make your way there. When things happen, they will happen there. And I'm going to need your help. '

'What's going to happen, Larsen?' he asked.

There was a long pause. He began to think Larsen had dropped the connection.

'This is difficult to explain, Spencer. You need to trust me on this. The Xannix are convinced I'm the Setak'osso, which means there is going to be some kind of confrontation. In effect, all the chaos to this point has been down to the Overseers and current Setak'da defending their position. I don't know much myself, but, if this is going to happen, I'm going to need as much trusted support as I can get. Your team is it. Looks like any fleet support is going to be out of the picture for the time being,' he said.

Now, it was his turn to be silent. This conversation was becoming a blur. Then, a flurry of uninvited memories started to crowd his thoughts. Xannix, from times past, divided into two factions and trekking to the ceremonial Court of the Speakers, no, he was misremembering, the Court of Souls. Many had fought in this arena and it had not always been amicable. There were few rules, but the purpose was to provide the Xannix people with a strong functional leadership. Some challenges had been very violent, some had been more a bonding of similar visions which had ended in a joining of the Setak'da and challenger to rule as a single voice. These times were rare. It was more likely to end in the two parties at war in a confined space and of course watched by the populous on planet-wide broadcast. Over the years, the Xannix seemed to have made it a media spectacular, from the Reveal the media were pushed into overdrive and every media device, outlet or broadcast station would be focused on the Setak'da challenge.

'Okay, we'll be there,' he said. There was little choice, with the weird situation Larsen found himself in, it was the only logical choice. 'How long do we have?'

'I'll contact you.'

'Okay, I'll brief the others. Spencer, out.'

While he had been talking, Reeve and Jacobs had had time to investigate the coordinates he had forwarded on. "What are these coordinates?"

"That is where we are going to meet the Setak'da," he said with seriousness.

"It's way outside the perimeter of this arcology," said Reeve.

"Yes, I know," he responded. "But, that is where the Setak'da will be. That is where we need to go."

Everyone was looking at him, except Jacobs who was now looking very focussed at an object on the ground. The concentration became a look of alarm, "Incoming!" he shouted to everyone. Kelly, who was also sat to the left side of the flyer could also see what Jacobs was referring to.

"SAM, ten o'clock low. Evade, right. Now!"

The flyer took a hard banking turn which threw them into a heavy g turn. His eyes wide, he saw a bright white dot speed past the left side of the canopy trailing white vapour as it went, missing them by about half a metre.

Reeve was now looking out the right of the flyers down towards the ground, "Another one. Missile. Break left!"

Jacobs angled the flyer into a wicked left descending turn and he suddenly saw the reflection of the craft in windows of an apartment building. They were too close to the apartment block to safely manoeuvre, but he could see what Jacobs was trying to do. Being so close to the corner of the building, he was pushing to put an obstacle in the way of the missile and their flyer before it reached them. It was desperate but they were going to make it.

There was a bang which sounded almost insignificant, but suddenly the flyer took an uncontrollable and acute turn to the left, pitching them round and pointing the craft at the higher levels of the apartment building. It was horrific to watch. The missile had done its job, knocking out an engine to the flyer, destroying fuselage and control surfaces. A dramatic loss of power in one engine combined with the sudden drag from the damaged airframe on the left side caused a harsh rotation, taking them into the reflecting surface of the building. Someone screamed, the flyer hit the apartment windows with force, the craft going through them like they were not there, then the internal structure began to take the flyer apart, causing a forceful deceleration. The moment the flyer hit the glass he had closed his eyes. The rest was a tumble of pain and agony.

OBADIAH

The battle had been a game of cat and mouse from the very start. They had not realised it in the beginning, their overconfidence being their Achilles heel, but once the Comms Jamming Network had started to move they realised their mistake. Believing it to be a simple battle of attrition, each side slugging away at the other until the last man fell, none of the VERS had anticipated the dormant array of satellites as a threat, until now.

Recalculations had taken seconds and the new encounter simulations had them caught like flies in a web. The new calculations had the fleet being destroyed, the outcome as certain as could be expected, given within a 98 percent confidence interval. The machine part of him gave him the cool statistical analysis. The human part of him still had hope.

Fundamentally, unless there was another severely unexpected turn of events, this time in their favour, the human colonisation effort on Hayford b, known now as Xannix, would end in shattered, obliterated fragments of flesh and metal littering the planet's low orbit.

The Xannix ships still harried them, sending in waves of attacking ships now and then, to keep them boxed, shepherded into a certain area of space. The Xannix losses had been great initially, but now they stayed in the farther reaches of the fleet's effective range and only really pushed an attack when they had to. It occurred to him that they had only taken those initial heavy losses as a fake, the tactic to give the aggressors the overconfidence to press the attack. While fixated on their target and looking the wrong way, the Xannix had then had the time they had needed to prep the satellite network and put it into action. They had been duped and they would pay the price, unless they could come up with a solution.

The status of the fleet was also quite varied. The *Endeavour* had taken terrible damage and had been the focus of almost every attack so far, but the *Intrepid* and the *Indianapolis* had fared much better—the *Intrepid* had hardly been touched at all. The *Endeavour* was now looking worn out, the ship's front and starboard peppered and ragged with hull and structural framework completely missing in places. The reason for the Xannix focus on the *Endeavour* was still uncertain, but that wasn't to say unexpected. The *Endeavour* was the ship being most overtly aggressive, taking up the low orbit defence of the drop ship Mantis 4, deploying a team to the surface. He'd read the books, he knew battle was chaotic and decisions needed to be made in the heat of the moment without the full facts, but Dawn was making all the high-risk plays.

Monitoring the comms channels of the two small teams that had made it to the surface was giving him some interesting information. Clayton had dispatched the dropship with an ambassador aboard. Dr Spencer, his unique encounter with the Xannix now the bridge between the two cultures. They were now depending on him to call off the deadly trap closing in around them.

From what he could tell, the first shuttle had also made it to the surface, but had been shot down somewhere over the northern forests of the planet. Only two had survived the ordeal. But, what was most interesting here was the fact that the Xannix had now taken one of those as a challenger to the current world leader. It was a peculiar arrangement, one he had far too little information to understand, but it might just work out to be the chance they were looking for. He had not quite worked out how they could assist yet and there had been no support request from the surface, so for the moment he waited. But the fleet would soon need to act. Time was running out.

He looked back at the satellite network. It was creeping ever closer: his timer had four hours thirty-two minutes until contact. He had no idea whether it would be long enough. His assessment was that Clayton would break before that and implement the mass destruction at his disposal through the Angelfall weapon. It would do them no good, it would be an action of spite in their last moments, but he needed to be ready for that moment. However this played out, at no point could he allow the destruction of an entire species founded purely on base human emotions. He knew Dawn was with her father on this, but maybe he could sway Ellie to his moral point of view. She had said little so far, however he knew she was a deep thinker, saying little but taking in and consuming all the information made available to her. He needed to make his case. She could be the critical decision maker in the path between a continued life in some form for humanity, or its oblivion. He opened a comms link to Ellie.

"Obadiah, how can I help?" she said in a cheerful tone, if not a little distracted by the events going on outside.

"I need to talk to you. I'm concerned for Dawn and want your take on the situation." It was an honest statement, he was concerned, but he needed his pleasant approach to yield results. He would need to play a little politics and be polite about it.

"In what regard?"

"The order to instigate Angelfall was made too soon. I know preparations have to be made, but is it morally right for us to erase a culture for our own personal failings?" Ellie didn't respond; she was listening. He continued "We have been ordered to take the planet at all costs, to ensure the continuation of the human species, but I can't square that with the instant eradication of the Xannix before we've even had any meaningful communication or dialogue with them. We must make contact and conclude all peaceful and political avenues before instigating these final sanctions."

The world around him altered, a bubble of blue appeared with him at its centre, swirling white patterns of florescent light spinning randomly through the transparent surface. Ellie had created a secure comms meeting room and now stood before him, head inclined with a smile which spoke to him of intrigue and mischief.

"You play a dangerous game," she said to him. "This is exactly the situation we have been trained and briefed for. There was to be unanimous action. Clayton is fleet commander, we follow his decision."

She was right, but there was something instinctive within him which told him that this decision was not of their doing. Ellie and he had known Clayton and Dawn for years. This decision was out of character. The whole reason they were here and in charge of the mission was because of their love of life and drive to maintain it, in all its incarnations.

"Yes. But I think there is more going on. This is not his natural instinct, it is not a decision he would have made, even under this scenario."

"What makes you so sure?" an eyebrow raised as the question was asked.

"I—" he grimaced with indecision. "I can't be sure."

"So, what gives you cause to suspect?"

A gut feeling was not something he could readily explain, but he had to convince her. "Little things. Dawn's demeanour, her outlook, is getting darker, colder. It's almost as if the machine is taking over from the human she once was," he said intently.

"That doesn't mean she's incapable of critical decision-making," she said. He had a feeling she was toying with him a little, playing devil's advocate to see how strong his argument was. It's what he would do in her position. "If anything, it would give her the ability to make decisions without doubt, unclouded by human emotion."

"But that's precisely my point. That is no longer a human decision. It is no longer a decision drawn on experience and guided by the human emotional element, which is so important in all of us. If you are simply going to run a simulation and agree with its outcome each time—," he stopped himself. Calmed himself. "Look, there was a science program some time ago. To study the effect and use of helicopters as a tool for herding livestock. I think it was sheep in this case. The first simulation was undertaken and the initial results appeared promising, the sheep dispersing as they might be expected to with the presence of a helicopter flying only a few metres away. However, the helicopter crashed. They ran it several more times and each time the helicopter crashed. Eventually, one of the scientists worked out what was happening. You see, the program source code they had used to build the simulation was ex-military, used to simulate dispersal of troops under various forms of attack, helicopters being one such option. The helicopter routine had been run against sheep, but the sheep were fully armed soldiers who in each simulation would disperse, find cover and then take down the attack helicopter with a surface to air missile."

"So there was a human error in the simulation set up?" Ellie suggested.

"No, that's not the point to take away from this. The point to focus on is that a machine will only give you what it's programmed and tasked to action. Nothing more. Okay, the scientists misconfigured the simulation, but the point here is that the machine still only did what its programming instructed it to do. Humans question. The failsafe in the simulation were the human scientists who spotted and questioned an incorrect outcome and corrected the misconfiguration. The failsafe within the AI is the human mind."

"Otherwise, we get sheep shooting down helicopters?"

"Yes. Remove the failsafe and there is no ability to apply context, no leap of understanding to realise the sheep are soldiers," he said. There was a long silence. Ellie stepped to one side and looked away, arms across her chest, finger and thumb pulling at her lower lip as she frowned in deep thought.

"You know, you may be suggesting more than your example is indicating," she suggested, once her thoughts had time to form.

"How so?"

"You talk about us as machines with a human failsafe and that in this case the failsafe itself is failing."

"Yes."

"Well, what happens if the failsafe fails?" she looked at him to judge his reaction.

"How could that happen?"

"I don't know yet. But suppose, just for a moment, that Dawn's wave was failing as you suggest, within the AI construct. What would happen?"

"I don't know. It's never happened to a fully embedded AI."

"Use that leap of human logic you've been telling me about," she pushed.

"Okay," he said, now himself in deep contemplation on the issue. "It would depend on what level of relapse Dawn was suffering, but in its worst state the AI would have almost full control. Machine processes would be the only active component."

"Agreed. So, how could it happen?" she asked. It had been his question, but he had a feeling she was guiding him to the answer she had already arrived at, seeing if he would also come to the same conclusions by following the breadcrumbs of logic. He looked up to the roof of the secure comms bubble they were in, allowing his mind to roll ideas around and work his way to an answer that made the most sense.

Then it hit him: "Altered code." He could hardly believe it. It was a terrifying thought. "Her AI code has been altered to change her morality, or worse, to remove or squeeze out the controlling human wave."

"Precisely," she responded.

"To what end?" he asked her.

"We've had GAIA terrorists aboard and acting against us these last few days, why not the government?"

"I don't follow. OWEC and the world government funded this entire fleet. Why would they sabotage their own?"

"You're coming from the wrong angle. They are not sabotaging the effort, they are simply enforcing their goals, to ensure things go the way they intended from the outset. You spoke of failsafe's earlier. This is their failsafe to ensure we take Xannix and colonise it as they intended. No mercy, no quarter given to any indigenous species. Humanity must survive."

"They are enforcing a barbaric act," he said in a solemn voice.

"They are not here. For them, there are no consequences."

They both paused to think, the gravity of their discussion becoming clear.

"So, what next?" she asked. The corner of his mouth twitched away a small smile as he realised what the statement meant. She had made her decision.

"We need to know more. If our conclusions are correct, we need proof. Once we have that proof, we can act."

"Agreed," Ellie said. "So, how are we going to get the proof we need?"

"Firstly, we scan our own AI source code for anomalous or subversive code. If we find any we quarantine it and remove it from our live systems. Secondly, we need to try to help Dawn, but that is going to be a much harder task."

"The next question is why are we not affected?" she asked.

"Maybe we have been, but not to the same degree. Or maybe a set of preconditions must be triggered before the code is activated," he suggested.

"What, like plotting to work against the fleet commander and refuse his orders? I'd say that would be a big precondition."

"Maybe not, if it's working on triggers or actions you've performed with reference to those orders. So far we have done everything we have been asked to do, even in relation to following the preparations for Angelfall. The dispersal program is in progress and the Hellfire high energy laser is online and ready, all in line with prior instructions. We have done nothing to make them suspect we are not working to their plan and certainly have done nothing to make them believe we are working against their interests."

"Is that what we're doing then?" she asked. "Working against their interests?"

"No, our intentions are morally sound. The fleet is paramount. But—Clayton and Dawn? We have an external actor here. We need to find out who or what that is. I can't believe Dawn would do this. There has to be some other explanation."

"You are rationalising," she said.

"Maybe," he replied, thinking for a moment before responding further. Maybe, she wasn't as on board with this as he had initially thought. "But we have to do something. This situation is becoming a horrible mess. Dawn is not acting in the interests of the fleet, nor, for that matter, is she showing any interest in alternate solutions to preserve the Xannix on their own planet. That is all before we consider the trap the Xannix have sprung."

Ellie suddenly became very distracted and withdrawn from the conversation. He knew and understood this state. She was processing information elsewhere, something she needed her complete concentration for. He took the moment to put his focus elsewhere and catch up on the events around the ship, the battle's current tactical situation. Things were much as they had been before: the Xannix were manoeuvring at the edges of the fleets range of fire, no incursions into their space had taken place for a while. The satellite network was that much closer, more detail was needed on the capability of the satellites, but they were too small and too far away to obtain an accurate assessment. It was all about time. In another hour they would have more information and understanding, but the rub of the situation would mean they had less time to act in response.

Ellie snapped back out of her apparent trance and looked at him intently; he could almost see anger there—was it for him?

"I've found something," she informed him.

"Found what?"

"Taking the hypothesis that there is malicious code hiding in our core code base, I instigated a search. I looked for functions and methods least actioned. It didn't take long." He hadn't thought of that. No wonder his search hadn't picked anything up yet, it was still just grinding through the entire code base for anomalous updates.

"What have you found?" he asked. She sent him the code and files they would be found in. He quarantined the code in his own live systems immediately. He then began to review it. The ramifications of the code hidden in their systems chilled him. The Earth government had never intended to let the mission be an autonomous one; they had never intended to let Clayton make the critical decisions in case of a first contact. The code indeed had a trigger, but it was dependent on the commander of the fleet being aboard, which was why it had never been activated with his or Ellie's systems. The government had seen no risk in Clayton carrying out their orders if they encountered no opposition, but the moment that changed, if there was a first contact of any sort, Earth instigated their backup plan. Aggressive malware was brought on line and Dawn's wave was locked out of the AI container. The AI would then begin to run the government's instruction set. To the crew, and perhaps even Clayton, nothing would appear to have changed, but in reality Dawn would start to run the operation. She would have total access and control to every element of the ship, she could ensure instructions were relayed to the rest of the fleet with the governments bias applied to each command. She would become proxy commander of the fleet. There was no collusion, she would become the fleet's defacto leader and dictator without anyone knowing it.

That was, until now.

He and Ellie stood in stunned silence for a couple of minutes, neither of them able to fully comprehend the measure of betrayal by their own government. He could not bring himself to blame Dawn for this, as it could equally have been him or Ellie. It was chance that the code hadn't been activated against them, Clayton not being present on their ship had saved them that fate, but it could so easily have been different. Dawn was as much a victim in this as the rest of them, perhaps even more so. They must try and find a way to help. To shut out the malware and bring Dawn back. He looked at Ellie and could read the same thoughts in her eyes: they had all been lied to and it could have been any one of them. The question was how were they going to fix it? How could they rescue Dawn, halt the Angelfall order and save the fleet from destruction by the Xannix? Each problem was beginning to compound the others, a perfect storm of events steering them to an inevitable end. He had to wonder at the irony of Earth's own government crippling its own efforts to colonise new worlds due to its own inability to let go. A dead government of a ghost world reaching through time to ensnare its own people's best chance for survival. Chilling.

"Are we agreed?" he asked Ellie. Taking this news to push home the argument and obtain her support. She looked at him with what looked like tears in her eyes. She nodded, a solid affirmation, then without saying a word, Ellie dropped the link.

He let out a deep breath and looked out across the space between the *Indianapolis* and the *Endeavour*. The crew of the *Endeavour* were in more danger than they knew. Opening a comms link to his captain, Elizabeth Straud, he found himself standing next to her on the bridge in his holographic form. The bridge crew were experiencing a rare moment of calm. There hadn't been an attack by the Xannix for about half an hour and the shouting of orders and alerts had reduced to a background hubbub of chatter and relayed instructions to work crews and repair teams.

"Obi, what can I do for you?" asked Straud, still concentrating on her console and working through VERS tactical simulations to try and find a way out of the trap before them.

"Captain, we have identified a problem with the *Endeavour*," he said professionally. "We have discovered malware in the core code base of the AIs which enforce behavioural changes. Ellie and myself have identified and disabled the code within our own systems before it activated; however, Dawn is already running the code and will be hostile to any fix." He sent her a brief report on the effect of the code and its purpose. She sat and took a moment to read the detail.

Sitting back and looking out of the main view screen to the planet below, she wore a wry smile. "I knew they wouldn't be able to keep their hands off this mission," she said.

"You knew?" he asked.

She shrugged. "It was more a gut feeling, an intuition. Before we left Earth there was a final briefing for the ship captains by the government; they said their final farewells and reiterated their intent for us to succeed. It was cordial enough, but several of the ministers and officials worried me with their outlook. Let's just say there were a couple of very intense characters who held pretty extreme views on our success." She looked back at the report. "That they are still trying to control events from their grave does not surprise me."

There was a pause before she spoke again, clearly considering his and Ellie's status. "So, you say you and Ellie are okay?"

"Yes," he answered.

"Would you mind if I had some techs look you over? I need to ensure you are free from any similar code."

"I can assure you that the search Ellie and I performed was thorough and there is no further cause for alarm. However, I am happy for a second opinion."

"Good. Which leaves us the larger problem of how to deal with *Endeavour*. Do we know if Clayton suspects anything?"

"I've analysed our communications with *Endeavour* and there is no indication in any of the messages that Clayton is aware of the situation. However, he did give the Angelfall order. That is confirmed," he said.

"So, we are going to have to treat the *Endeavour* as hostile for the time being." Rubbing her chin in thought, she turned to him. "We are going to need to speak with Clayton."

"I have two reservations about this course of action. Firstly, Clayton has a strong emotional connection to the issue and may not be able to deal with the situation in a subjective manner. Secondly, any transmission we make will be monitored by the AI. The moment we speak to Clayton, or anyone else for that matter, the AI will know we are aware of its control and purpose. I'm unsure what its response would be."

"So, what do you propose?" she asked. "What's the alternative?"

"I have an idea," he said with a smile.

ROUX

Being on shift for 48 hours straight was crippling. He had done longer shifts in his time on various space-faring vessels, and sleep deprivation was part of the deal, part of the training and part of life in space. Incidents came along which required attention and, if you didn't fix them, there could be catastrophic consequences. This kind of issue very often came without a nice handy two hour turn-around time, they could take days and you would need to pay attention, stay focussed and work through to the end. Battles were much the same: you had to grab sleep where you could and shifts meant little. He had been sent for a few hours' sleep; he was going to take advantage of that.

Stumbling into his quarters, he fell onto the bed without getting undressed, without turning on the lights, and he fully expected to be fast asleep in moments. He ruffled the pillow and moved it into the right place to lay his head, shifted and settled himself to a comfortable position on his side and let out a satisfied yawn. But, before he closed his eyes, he registered a blinking red light in the corner of the room. To his recollection there should be nothing there, especially not a flashing light. He thought about ignoring the light, but he knew it would play on his mind. He sighed loudly and hit the side light next to the bed, which bathed the room in a low intensity light, reminding him of moonlight. He wondered if it had been designed that way.

In the shadow of the corner, the flashing light continued, but this time he realised it was part of a Rem-Tek. How it had got into his quarters he didn't know; he certainly hadn't ordered one. Swinging his legs round and sitting on the side of the bed, he examined it further. As he did so, the flashing red light became a flashing green light and the machine stood from its crouch in standby mode, to full height now active. This action startled him and in his shock he rolled back off his bed to the floor. Feeling intensely foolish, he stood and looked with cool eyes at the Rem-Tek. It hadn't moved; it just stood there. He waited a moment, waited for it to move again, but it didn't. He thought about going back to bed, putting his exhaustion to good use and ignoring the tin can in the corner of his quarters, but his blood was up now, so he walked around the bed to take a closer look. He had a strange feeling about this Rem-Tek. Why would it be there at all?

As he approached, a slot to the front upper left side of the Rem-Tek's chest slid out a thin screen which flipped from vertical to horizontal then flipped again so the flat screen faced him. It lit up and the face of Captain Straud was there, grinning back at him like she was in on a joke he had clearly missed.

"Good morning, Commander Roux," she said. "I hope I didn't wake you."

She had to be kidding, but he was pleasant in his response. "Not at all, sir. What can I do for you? Are you unable to reach the Captain?"

She shook her head. "No, Roux. I need to speak to you on a very important and delicate matter. For the moment, Clayton and Dawn need to be kept out of the loop." She looked away from the camera for a moment and nodded. "I'm sending the Rem-Tek in front of you a file. You must load this file into the *Endeavour's* system."

"Sir, this is highly irregular. Why am I loading this into the ship's system?"

"It is to fix a problem you are unaware you have," she said.

"I'm going to need more than that, sir. Even from a ranking officer. What is this file for?"

She nodded. "You're right to ask. But, for your own safety I can't reveal too much." Moving closer to the camera she seemed to look him directly in the eye, "Dawn has been compromised by an external agent. She is not working to the fleet's best interests and possibly to the detriment of the crew. She is not herself, Roux, and the code patch we are sending you will fix this and return you and the Captain functional control of the ship."

"We've lost control?" he asked in alarm.

"For the moment, yes. As long as things proceed in the manner the AI desires, then all will seem normal, but begin to give instructions counter to the AI's programming and things are likely to start going wrong."

He took a moment to take in the new information, to digest what he'd been told. It seemed highly improbable and he had been given no real evidence, only conjecture and hearsay, albeit from a captain. It was not quite convincing enough.

"I'll see what I can do, Captain," he said, with reservation in his voice.

"Good," she said, seeming to sense his continued scepticism. "I hope for all your sakes we are successful. With all the issues we are working on at the moment, internal struggles are really something we can do without. Let's put Clayton back in control. Straud, out."

The connection cut, and the small Rem-Tek screen folded and withdrew back into its chest housing. A panel slid aside in the upper right chest plate and revealed an array of control chips. One popped forward, ejected by the Rem-Tek system and clearly waiting for him to take it. He reached out a hand, hesitating a moment, then took it and put it in his pocket. The chest panel closed and the Rem-Tek shut down again, settling into a squat compact shape and switching to standby mode. The red light began to flash once again.

Sitting back on the bed heavily, he let out a disbelieving breath which could have been a low whistle if he had put more effort into it. His mind was a whir of thoughts and worries about the new information. Could it be true? Was Dawn in that much trouble? Were they all in that much trouble? Either way, he needed to resolve this issue quickly. The Xannix satellite network was closing in and they needed to be ready. If what Straud had told him was true, it could really compromise their ability to act.

Lying down on the bed, he stared at the ceiling to think on the issue. Sleep came before he took another breath.

*

An alert, like a klaxon rang in his brain. He awoke with a start. A priority alert was flashing in his bio-comm. He opened it as he rose sluggishly from his bed and sat with his head in his hands. He felt like he was hungover, but it was worse than that. Sleep deprivation and not enough rest, it was like the hangover without the party the night before; he felt cheated somehow.

The priority alert stopped and the message simply requested all senior staff to the bridge. He rose from his bed and made his way to the bathroom to freshen up. Looking in the mirror, he saw the young fresh face of the twenty-five-year-old he now was staring back with bright eyes, neatly cropped hair and smooth, youthful skin. His fifty-year-old brain couldn't quite get used to it. The fresh face brought back many memories he would rather forget. The hardships of his younger years, the struggles and violence he had been witness to just to survive in the later years of the Great Decline, although that wasn't what it was called at the time. People were just hungry and their families starving with the world now unable to sustain the population in the numbers that existed. At its peak, millions died every week, some through starvation, but many through war and violence as the desperate took what food and supplies they could at the expense of others. It had become a deadly cycle of lawless decline.

He remembered when the asteroid hit. The world was already suffering from a string of terrible financial crises, global financial collapse was close and the world governments were worried. The asteroid strike in Ukraine effectively tipped the world over the edge. With one of one of the world's main food production centres destroyed and local European weather thrown into turmoil affecting crops and seasonal variations, the global balance of power shifted considerably. Added to that the instant cost in human life from the asteroid strike and the displacement of millions in the immediate fallout zone, the shock to the world economies and government control was too much. People turned on each other.

There were instant problems and more chronic issues which governments battled to resolve. The interdependency of states within Europe and the hub Europe was to the rest of the world led to immediate fuel and power problems, with many countries regulating the use of their reserves and power blackouts being frequent. Then came the issue of food and food supply. People started to stock up and hoard what they could, but with production being low those with supplies became targets for those without. Over a ten month period after the asteroid strike the world went from one disaster to another, culminating in the most wealthy cities isolating themselves from the anarchy and war outside their walled borders.

Some years later the history books began to refer to the period as the Great Decline.

The mind behind his eyes knew the hardship and struggles of birth and death. People talked about the Great Decline as the death of the planet, but he knew it to be what it was: the death of a species. The planet itself would be fine, another million years from now there would be little evidence of humanity left to find, with the erosion, movement of the Earth's crust, weather and the growth of alternate species filling the gap humanity had left behind. Earth wasn't dying, it was self-correcting. Either way, for humanity, the symptoms of this correction were devastating and horrible to live through. Many chose not to.

The water was cold and brought him back to the present with a splash. He held his hands over his face for a moment longer then checked the closeness of his shave in the mirror. Good enough. Walking back to his wardrobe, he picked out a fresh uniform and changed. Transferring the clear, crystal-like Rem-Tek data drive to his pocket, he threw his old clothes at the laundry bin, opened the door to his quarters and headed for the bridge.

*

The briefing room behind the bridge was already full of senior officers milling around and talking in hushed tones about the reason for the call. It sounded as if they were all unaware of any reason for the gathering, and he as the ships XO was none-the-wiser, which irritated him. He wondered what Clayton was up to. He looked round the room ticking off names as he went: Commander Litton, head of Operations; Commander Holt, head of Navigation; Commander Fellows, the new head of Security; Commander Alderson, head of Communications; the list went on. But there was an exception—Hopper wasn't there. Chief Hopper, head of Engineering. Maybe he was running late. With the battle at a lull, he was most likely busy arranging repair teams and damage control; running late to a meeting was the least of his worries.

Clayton walked into the room, and he was followed by a rather tired and run-down woman whom he recognised to be

Commander Hillary Grey, Hopper's number two. Both of them wore a stern, serious expression as they made their way to the centre of the room to address the assembled officers.

The briefing room was circular, and seating was arranged in ascending rows to create a forum with the centre given over to a large holographic projector, a couple of display screens and a dais from which the speaker could make his presentation. People had begun to take their seats as Clayton waved at them to sit. "Please sit," he said, his voice sombre. None of this was shaping up to be good news.

"Thank you for attending at such short notice," Clayton said, looking around the room at the group. "There have been a couple of developments which I needed to discuss with you in person." He looked round the room, as was his style: inclusive and approachable. This time there was something more sombre about the briefing, he could sense the whole room was prepared for bad news, him included. "Firstly, I know we are in a protracted battle with the Xannix right now, but I have to report an accidental death which will affect us all. Earlier today there was an accident in Engineering. Chief Hopper was working in the AI node compartment on level 34 when there was a fire. The fire was caused by an incoming Xannix attack. The compartment was locked down, and the fire suppression system neutralised the fire, but by the time rescue teams were able to get back into the compartment, Chief Hopper was already dead. He was the last in the compartment, ensuring those in the work detail with him were able to escape and get free before the fire suppression system locked the compartment."

A murmuring commotion broke out in the room, disbelief, sadness. Clayton continued. "Commander Sean Hopper was a good friend and passionate about his work and those around him. He will be missed. According to his beliefs, we will be holding a Rejuvenation Vigil for those who would like to attend."

A file arrived in his message queue from Clayton. Details of the vigil. He noted it for future attention.

"The next item I wish to discuss is the trap sprung by the Xannix, namely the satellite network. I think we all know the situation." As his eyes scanned the room to see the nodding heads confirming understanding of the situation, his eyes fell upon Commander Grey. It was now obvious why she was here, but his hand in his pocket rolled the Rem-Tek data drive over and over, his mind running through the conversation with Captain Straud.

Hopper had died in the level 34 AI node compartment. If he remembered correctly, the compartment was close, but not so close to the hull that it would be affected by a weapons strike. It would take a strong penetrating weapon or an explosion of the type which occurred when the visiting Xannix shuttle's power core had failed a few metres from the *Endeavour's* hull. That damage he could agree would cause fire and structural damage, but the range weapons the Xannix were currently using were far less penetrating, beam weapons and small projectiles. With the skin of the *Endeavour* designed to take high heat and high velocity impacts from space debris in transit, these kinds of strikes were causing the ship mostly cosmetic damage.

Clayton had also mentioned survivors; he pinged a message to Grey: 'Grey, I need to see a list of those who were with Hopper in that work detail,' he said, possibly a little harshly, but he needed the information in a hurry.

'Yes, sir,' was the simple response, their eyes making momentary contact as she confirmed his request.

A moment later he had a list in his message queue. He opened it. Scanning down the list of people, one stood out: Grey. She had been with him. He didn't know if that was significant, but he would park it in memory and label it *curious*. He looked briefly at the names and selected one, purely on his proximity to the bridge, Tech First Class Pearson was currently working the next level down from the bridge doing a fix to the navigation system.

'Tech Pearson, I'd like to meet you in ten minutes. Please stay where you are until I arrive.'

'Yes, sir,' came the simple reply moments later.

"... times. But we will get through this. Stay focused and look out for those around you. Thank you. Dismissed." Clayton completed his briefing and he realised he had missed half of it. He'd catch the highlights as he walked, but for now he had a Tech to see.

'Dawn, please stream Clayton's briefing from time mark minus 120.' A screen popped up in the corner of his vision, and the bio-comm began to replay the final 120 seconds of the briefing.

Pacing out of the briefing room, he headed off the bridge and to Navigation with purpose. Pearson was there working at a console with clear concentration on his face. Most Techs were quite mentally dexterous, able to work with a console while at the same time working through their bio-comm links with various systems simultaneously. It was quite a trick. He had done it once and almost fried his brain trying to keep up with the information overload.

"Pearson?" he enquired. The Tech snapped out of his work and was suddenly stood at attention by his console. Pearson must be new, new to this body and his life. The older crew were far more casual, formalities considered far less important as they became more comfortable in themselves and their abilities. He smiled at Pearson. Being this new meant one thing, he was talented. To be on this crew at this age meant he was supremely good at what he did and would have been selected above many others with far more experience. "Relax, Pearson," he comforted. "I'd just like to ask you a few questions about Commander Hopper and what happened when you were working on the AI node."

Pearson nodded and deflated like a pinned balloon. "It all happened so fast, sir."

"Sure, just tell me what you remember."

Pearson took a breath and leant against the workstation, hanging his head and closing his eyes. Pulling the painful memories to the forefront of his mind, he transported himself back to the moments of Hopper's death. "It was a simple data optimisation exercise. Commander Hopper had asked the three least experienced on Dawns core code to help him to review and check to see if there were any optimisations which we believed could be made. There are always optimisations which can be made to code. Often the original code is put together at such a pace and to such close deadlines that the result is working code, but at a cost. Very often it's inefficient. So, there we were. Four of us working on the AI node on level 34."

"Do you know why you were in that particular room? The AI node on 34 seems quite remote," he asked.

"No, sir. I don't know. We didn't really think about it. We work all over the ship. For us and the engineering teams, we don't think of any part of the ship as being remote. We could be detailed to work anywhere, at any time." He had a point.

"But couldn't you do this work just as easily on another level? Or the AI core in main engineering?"

"Sure. But I think the AI node on level 34 is a little closer to Hopper's quarters, and we were scheduled to be there most of the day. I'm only guessing here; it never came up. We were asked, and we turned up as requested. That's what we do on work details." "Understood," he said. The question looked like a dead end. He moved on. "So, you were looking for anomalies in the code. Did you find anything?"

Pearson scrunched up his nose; he'd clearly said something Pearson didn't like. "Not really anomalies, sir. Code that could be improved."

"There's a difference?"

"Of course. One infers there is a problem and something is not working correctly. The other means simply that it is working as intended, but could potentially work faster or better if optimised. There is a big difference."

"Okay. But, did you find anything?"

"No." He paused. "Well, maybe," said Pearson.

"So, which is it?"

"I can't be sure, but I think Commander Hopper may have found something."

"What makes you say that?"

"Just that before all hell broke loose and the fire alert started blaring, I overheard Commander Hopper say something. It was like 'Jesus' or 'Save us'. Something like that. It was under his breath. He looked panicked. I remember, because I thought it strange that he might be referring to the old religions. It's rare these days."

Roux leant against the workstation next to Pearson, his arms folded while he thought. He remembered somewhere that this was incredibly bad body language, so he unfolded his arms and mirrored Pearson's posture, non-threatening and conversational. "I don't suppose you have any idea what he found?" he asked.

"No. The moment the alarm went off we all followed procedure and began to exit for the nearest muster station. Commander Hopper was right behind us, maybe just a metre or two behind me. But, as I exited the room, the door closed. We didn't realise straight away. We were at the muster station before anyone noticed Commander Hopper wasn't with us."

"The door closed? Do you remember a fire in the compartment?"

"That's just the thing, sir. The AI node compartment is not that big: about four metres by three metres. Not that big but big enough for the four of us to work. I can tell you categorically there was no fire in that room, not as we left anyway. I thought the alert was for another area, one close by. Or a drill? There was no fire in that room. Not when the alarm sounded." He was adamant.

"Okay, Pearson," he nodded. But before he could ask another question, Pearson continued.

"But, back to your last question, about what he was working on. As I said, I don't know what he found, but if it was me and what I'd found was that important I would have done something. He could have transmitted the information perhaps? Sent it to a trusted party? Either way, sir, I'm confident that the information you seek will still be stored in his bio-comm."

He'd not considered that. He had not yet spoken to Dr Jonathan Roberts, the Chief Medical Officer aboard the *Endeavour*. As yet, he had no idea of the condition of Chief Hopper's body. It had apparently been in a compartment fire, so it would be badly degraded, but if Pearson was right, maybe there was a way to retrieve the data.

"Pearson, pack your tools. You're coming with me."

"Sir?" Pearson said in surprise.

Roux looked back at him with a gentle smile. "I know this is not a good time, Pearson. But if I'm right, there is something big going on here, and I need you with me. I need a good tech that knows the situation and you're it. Let's go."

Pearson began to scoop up a few items dotted across the workstation and ran to catch up with him, leaving several bemused looking navigators watching them pace out the door.

"Where are we going, sir?" Pearson asked, still juggling items into satchels and pockets about his uniform as they walked.

"Medical. You said it yourself, we need to know what Hopper knew. I need the information he found and we haven't got long to get it. Given his bio-comm, will you be able to extract the information we need?" he asked.

"If we only have remote access via wireless connection? No. Not in any reasonable time frame. Security is too strong, encryption too high. But, if I have physical access? Yes. It will be as easy as plugging in a cable."

"Then let's see what Dr Roberts has to say."

*

They took the elevator coreward and the central core tramway to the stop outside Medical, which was just before the entrance to the main habitat section. Walking through reception, he disregarded the nurses at the desk and the view out across the habitat and headed directly to Dr Roberts' offices. On an ordinary day, he would have taken a moment to appreciate the gardens and wards which the viewing area in Medical overlooked. There were two such viewing galleries, one here at Medical, the other the opposite side of the core looking out over the other half of the habitat, the viewpoint part of the entertainment section next to the bar, Halley's. He had no time for either.

The door he and Pearson now stood in front of had 'Dr Roberts – Chief Medical Officer', stencilled to the door, a holographic image floated in front of the lettering, augmented digital overlay by his bio-comm display showing a similar set of text and the face of the doctor with a flat stolid expression. He politely buzzed for entry.

"Come," was the muffled response from somewhere inside. The door opened and they entered.

The office was reasonably large, as office space went on a starship. There was enough space for not only his workstation but also a reception table and couch for visiting patients or guests. There was also a window behind his workstation overlooking the habitat with a similar vista to the viewpoint mezzanine in the reception area. There were even fewer offices with this luxury—not even the captains' quarters afforded this kind of perk. It was an indication in simple terms of the importance Dr Roberts' position held aboard the *Endeavour*.

Dr Roberts was a young man, as they all were, but he clearly had an old mind and it appeared to affect not only his attitude but also his posture. He looked at them quizzically as they walked in and moved around to greet them. "Commander Roux, I expect you're here to discuss poor Chief Hopper?"

"Yes, Doctor. I'm sorry to barge in like this, but my investigation is pressing. We have limited time to resolve this issue."

"Investigation?" he asked as he started working on a terminal console to the side of a machine, which appeared to be processing some vials containing fluids of various colours. Roux had no idea what it was, some sort of scanner, a mass spectrometer perhaps?

"Yes," he replied.

"Shouldn't Commander Fellows be pursuing any investigations?"

He didn't have much contact with Dr Roberts, and he was beginning to remember why. He was a pedant and would question everything. In some ways that made him a great doctor, but it made him a lousy conversationalist.

"Yes, Doctor. You're right, but I don't have the luxury of time and I need answers now," he continued before Roberts got a chance to interrupt. "You are in possession of Chief Hopper's body?"

"Yes. It's in the morgue."

"I need access to the body to recover Chief Hopper's bio-comm memory unit. Can you take us there?"

Dr Roberts nodded and led them out of his office and towards the morgue. Roux didn't really need Roberts permission, but he wanted him with them. An expert pair of eyes and the leading medical authority on the ship. If there were questions, it would be prudent to have that muscle backing him up.

The morgue was reasonably small, with space for twelve bodies. It wasn't the only morgue on the ship in the same way it wasn't the only medical bay, but he was surprised at how small it was. Roberts could see his question without him verbalising it. "The voyage was meant to be uneventful, Commander Roux. The ship was designed for the calculated number of natural and accidental fatalities, no more. We were meant to be planetside now. Also, this is not a battleship; we are not meant to be punching our way through this kind of situation." It was said simply enough, but there was annoyance in his voice. He had clearly not signed up for the adventure, probably thinking this was more likely to be a milk run.

Dismissing the thoughts of the doctor's selfish concerns, he moved to his own concerns and that of Hopper. "So, Doctor, can we see Hopper's body?"

"Yes, over here."

They moved to one of the cabinets in the bank of twelve and Dr Roberts operated the controls to the side of the unit. The hatch opened smoothly and the tray on which the body lay was automatically extended into the room. Hopper's body was contained within a white body bag and fastened at the front with a robust zip. Dr Roberts slid the zip down to chest height and opened out the body bag to reveal Hopper's head and upper torso.

From initial observations, Hopper looked peaceful and serene, his face quiet and relaxed in death. Not what he had expected.

"Doctor, I thought Hopper died in a fire?"

"I've not had time to do the autopsy yet. It was what I was told too. It is possible he died of smoke or fume inhalation, but I can see no signs of contact with any heat source, if that's what you mean."

Roux held his chin in thought while Pearson stepped forward. "Sir, I think this is my cue?"

"Yes," he said stepping aside and giving Pearson access to Hopper's body. "Please, go ahead."

Pearson stepped forward and cradled Hopper's head in his hands, using his fingers to feel his way around the right side of his cranium.

"There," Pearson said and moved to show Dr Roberts the point of his finger against Hopper's skull. "Doctor, could you make a small incision here?"

Dr Roberts looked at him, perhaps looking for confirmation, "You can treat it as the first part of your autopsy," he said.

The Doctor moved forward and took a scalpel from the utility strap round his upper arm. He bent down to examine the location on Hopper's skull. "Unless you want to lose your finger, you had better move it," he said. Pearson quickly withdrew his finger, and started to unpack some of his own tech kit on the tray next to the body. The laser scalpel flashed into operation and with a small puff of smoke and a rather unpleasant acrid smell the incision was made.

"Done," said Dr Roberts.

"Okay, thanks." Pearson moved in with a small black box and extended connector. He pushed the small plug into the socket which was now visible and started pressing a few buttons on the control screen of the device. Roux could see a progress bar on the right side of the screen slowly climbing.

"Ten minutes," Pearson announced. "I'm assuming you need everything?"

"Yes," he said. "Specifically, the last twenty-four hours. But, right now, just take everything."

Pearson nodded.

"While we're waiting, Commander, why don't we take a walk. While—" he motioned towards, Pearson.

"Sorry, this is Pearson, Tech First Class."

"While Mr Pearson is working, maybe we can discuss the current situation?"

He turned to Pearson, "Come find us in ten minutes. We'll be on the mezzanine."

"Yes, sir."

*

The view was fantastic, the habitat was designed mostly for apartments and cabin space, but a section which spanned the width of the whole ship in a rotating gravitational drum was given over to hydroponics, some small level of leisure space and water features. It was a part of the ship which seemed overly exotic considering the rest of the structure limited available space to a *critical minimum*. Someone heading up the design team had clearly had some psychology training and believed the Atrium, as it was known, to be a critical space. He thought they were probably right under normal conditions, but considering the ship was basically a transport for several thousand brains in stasis, the Atrium was a wonderful example of design over function and mostly redundant. There was so much work to be done by the crew as they prepared for colonisation of the Xannix world that there was no time to enjoy the space the designers had clearly intended the space for.

Looking out from the comfort of the mezzanine, the view was breath-taking. The gardens below were lush and green, but the water in the stream and pond were drained and dry, stored in holding tanks while under heavy manoeuvring so as not to slosh tonnes of water around the inside of an open space, unintentionally causing more damage than the reason for the manoeuvre.

On closer examination some areas had been damaged. In places soil had come loose of its meshing and had irrupted, settling in mounds like huge mole hills.

Deciding he'd had enough sight-seeing, he rejoined Dr Roberts, and focussed on the conversation, a conversation which hadn't stopped since leaving Pearson to his work. A conversation in which he swore Roberts had not taken breath. He certainly hadn't said a single word in response.

"I find it so peaceful here," said Dr Roberts. "It's a real tonic being able to take some time and think through your problems." He wished he'd not rejoined the conversation. With statements like that, Roberts would make himself very unpopular, very quickly. Didn't he know they were in the middle of a battle? How did he have time to sit around enjoying the view? He then chided himself for doing the exact same thing, although, to be fair, he had believed Dr Roberts' invitation back in the morgue had been to a more insightful conversation. It hadn't.

They had taken a bench at one end of the mezzanine as Dr Roberts talked; he had taken the opportunity to take in the view while at the same time catching up on the situation on the bridge. The atrium, in particular the mezzanine, was empty. Apart from the two of them the whole place was deserted.

"The air somehow seems cleaner and fresher here. Don't you agree?" continued Dr Roberts.

"Dr Roberts," Roux interrupted forcefully. Then once he had Roberts attention, he decided to bring the conversation to a close. "I believe the ten minutes is up," he said, standing and preparing to leave. "If you have a point to this conversation, could you please make it?"

Dr Roberts brow furrowed. He was clearly not used to being interrupted. Taking an audible breath, he continued, but obviously in a mentally uncomfortable place.

"Yes, well. Commander Hobbs,"

"Hopper, Chief Hopper," he corrected.

"Yes, yes, Chief Hopper. He was murdered."

The statement was curt and factual, but it was now real.

"Can you confirm that?" he asked.

"No, I can't confirm it, but the evidence leads that way. I fibbed a little while we were with Pearson, I am a little further along in my autopsy than I first mentioned. Findings thus far indicate asphyxiation, intentional asphyxiation."

"Intentional?"

"Yes, you see, if the fire suppression system had been activated there would be foam. The fire suppression process does not start by immediately voiding the chamber of atmosphere. Foam is utilised to give evacuating personnel additional time to make their escape whilst at the same time combatting and containing the fire source."

"Yes, of course," he said.

"In this case, there was a shortcut. There was no foam phase."

Roux looked at Roberts blankly for a moment while the last comment hit home.

"So, the next question I presume you need to know is who would be able to do such a thing?" Dr Roberts finished.

He already knew who. But this was not a conversation for Roberts.

"I'm going to check on Pearson. He should be finished any moment."

Dr Roberts stayed seated, legs crossed, and continued to take in the scenery, not even looking at him. "As you wish, Commander. I think I may work here for a while."

He paced back up the mezzanine steps and through to the med-bay reception area, all the way shaking his head in disbelief. Roberts was one to avoid. He was sure Roberts could bore anyone in the fleet into a coma. He made a note not to take the man up on any further conversations, unless absolutely necessary.

Turning down the corridor to the morgue, he saw the bright beaming face of Pearson looking back at him. "All done?" he asked.

"Yes, sir. All done."

"Great. Let's go."

SILVERS

He hurt. He hurt everywhere. As he opened his eyes the information they received made no sense. It was dark with a crack of light which beamed across his view, illuminating the dust suspended in the air, thick and choking. This level of pain was beginning to become a regular occurrence and some part of him believed he should be getting used to it, but he wasn't.

Trying to move was difficult; he moved his right arm and found it trapped. A little more exertion and it popped free and hung for a moment above his head and touched a rough, gritty surface. His brain began to catch up: he was inverted, his head pressed at an angle against the floor, his body doubled over, making it hard for him to breathe. He fumbled for the harness release and pressed it. He had nowhere to fall, he was already hard against the floor, but his body weight now added to his discomfort, restricting his breathing further and twisting limbs in directions they did not want to go.

Pulling his body into the smallest ball he could, he wriggled and turned toward the light. Shifting forward a couple of centimetres at a time, he managed to get close enough to examine the opening. It was large enough to get his arm through and part of his shoulder but nothing more. As he wriggled some more, his hand pressed into something wet and sticky, warm to the touch. His mind leapt to fill in the blanks: it was blood; whose blood was not something he could consider right now. With the pain he felt, it could well be his, but until he was out of the flyer wreckage and able to take a better look at his surroundings he could not be certain. He strained harder to push himself through the opening, but it was no good, his head was just too big to get through, and there was little he could do about the size of his head. Other parts of the body are quite malleable or flexible; the skull, however, was always the unique point of consideration and it was telling him he wasn't getting through the gap as it was.

Reaching up to the inside of the flyer he tried to find any controls or evidence that the side of the vehicle might have a door. Having not used any doors to access the vehicle, he felt he was being hopeful. Fumbling around he found the smooth interior, padded in places with a leather-like material; there were bumps and lumps which he believed to be external damage pushed through into the cabin, then his fingers ran over something which felt more like switches and perhaps a small control panel. The area wasn't illuminated and didn't give him any indication to its function, so he pressed randomly.

There was an unlikely click and escape of air as the gap between the floor and the upper side of the flyer popped up a centimetre. As the vehicle was inverted, the weight of the door or hatch was clearly keeping it closed—either that or the opening mechanism was not fully operational and required power to work. Without power all it could do was release the lock, which he had done. A small smile appeared at the corner of his mouth as he tried again to squeeze through the available space. This time there was just enough room.

Pushing through, his ears complained as one was scratched, the other almost pulled from his head, but once his head was clearly through and in the open, the bright light dazzled him. He thought that this must be what birth was like. He was being born into the Xannix world anew and there was exhilaration in the effort and release.

He dragged his torso and legs through the gap and lay gasping for air and coughing out the dust and debris in his mouth and lungs. There was an intense pain in both his hands as he used them to push himself up to stand. Raising them to examine the new sensation, he found cubes of glass pressed and cutting into his palms, each cube leaving a little square red indentation. He brushed his palms together and the glass cubes fell free.

The crash had caused total devastation. Structural debris was everywhere, glass and concrete, bent and contorted metal of some description, pieces of the flyer thrown clear of its main airframe. Dust and smoke hung in the air, but was slowly clearing to give him a better view out into the arcology. He could clearly describe the trajectory of the crash from the missing frontage to the apartment building and the floors which they had travelled through before coming to rest, inverted, but mostly in one piece. It was a credit to the Xannix aircraft designers that the airframe had not obliterated on impact. It could have gone much worse than it had.

Initially he was too stunned to act, but as his senses slowly returned he sent out a bio-comm ping to those in the car. He received half as many as he was expecting, and the location tracker for Spencer was not local to the flyer. All the others appeared to be trapped in the vehicle, how Spencer was five levels up he had no idea at this point. It didn't matter; he would get to that later.

Working quickly to identify the survivors, he made his way round to the other side of the airframe. There were only two more ping responses from his call to the bio-comm: Reeve and Stannock. It didn't look good for Jacobs and Kelly.

With the dust settling, the inverted flyer looked worse than he had originally assessed, and a worrying tail of smoke was slowly, lazily rising from the rear manifold covering the engine and air intakes. The last thing they needed now was a fire. The other side of the flyer airframe was beaten and torn with large chunks missing, including the side panelling covering the doors. Padding, electrical wiring and framework were exposed and laid bare like an eviscerated animal. He used the ping of the bio-comm overlaid with its display to pinpoint firstly Reeve's location then Stannock. Reeve was on the far side, the side he had exited, and Stannock was this side. He tried for the front first. Taking his knife from its sheath, he started working on the remains of the flyers pilot-side door. The padding should be a reasonably easy thing to get through, then he could try and effect a rescue of some description.

A blast of wind hit him and stirred up all the local dust again, making it impossible to see or breathe. He cursed and took a quick look over his shoulder as he continued to work—there was no time to waste. Outside the apartments, about twenty metres from him, was another flyer. He did not recognise the colours or markings so had no idea of their intent or purpose, but he assumed he would find out soon enough; no need waste time thinking about it when there were people to save. A voice blared from a flyer using some external speaker system in a language he did not understand, giving either instructions or a warning. It was nothing he could respond to so he carried on dismantling the side of their crashed vehicle to get to Reeve.

A sudden flash of flame erupted from the engine manifold, the down-draft generated by the flyer outside accelerating ignition and feeding the fire. He was now on a short timer. Although he had no idea how long they had, it would not be long. He would just need to work fast and hope that the engine and fuel cells did not fail before he had finished.

Opening the side of the flyer and ripping the inner material aside, he exposed the front compartment to the light; Reeve was looking straight at him, eyes blinking at the new light flooding into the tiny space. She was contorted and clearly having trouble breathing. The body of Jacobs was in the way and blocking any escape. His assertion that Jacobs had not survived was evident, his upper torso and head were missing and blood was draining across the floor, making for some difficult working conditions. With the violent impact the flyer had taken on the pilots side, he was not surprised at the nature of Jacobs death; so much glass. He tried to believe that the end would have been fast.

He reached in past Jacobs remains, and Reeve and he clasped arms. He pulled hard, planting his feet on the side struts of the airframe for purchase. Reeve made a sound which sounded a little like a roar and they both fell to the floor. Half in and half out, she scrambled the last metre to escape the vehicle and then to the side of the room before standing, using the wall for added stability.

'Hey,' she said on a sub-vocal channel, as she continued to take large lungfuls of air.

'We've got to get Stannock out; he's still trapped in the back,' he returned with urgency. 'Between the fire and that flyer out there, I don't know how long we have left.'

'Where's Spencer?' she asked, as they both started work on the rear door.

'Four or five floors up.'

'How did he get up there?'

'You can ask him when you see him,' he said, and sent her Spencer's location. He could see she was instantly trying to contact Spencer and get an update.

Straining against the upturned vehicle, he was almost through to Stannock when the engine fire flared even higher and a whine started. It was low at first but then began to build. A moment later there was a hand on his shoulder, and he turned to find Reeve looking down at him.

"We must go, now." They both knew what leaving now would mean and neither he or Reeve wanted to make that call. He looked at the floor with a grim expression then nodded. He checked the ping to Stannock's bio-comm. It was still active, but he had seen no movement. He had been sitting next to Stannock and could remember the blood on the floor which he had had to crawl through in order to escape the flyer; the blood was clearly not his, and he could only deduce it was Stannock's. It was impossible to say how injured Stannock was, but they just didn't have time to think—it was time to act. They had to leave. As if to emphasise the point, there was a deep pop as some internal component failed and the fire leapt higher.

He moved slowly and followed Reeve further into the apartment, away from the windows and the unidentified flyer barking at them in incomprehensible tones. Opening the apartment's front door, they made their way into the corridor and further into the complex. They had staggered no more than ten metres down the corridor when the entire building shook with an explosion which knocked them both from their feet. Face down on the floor, he looked over his shoulder back to the room they had just left. It was dust and rubble as far as he could see, the door missing and smoke billowing through. He checked his bio-comm. Stannock's bio-comm ping had stopped responding. He closed his eyes in anger, a frustration born of not being able to do more. It was an emotion he knew all too well, one experienced in full during his years in mountain rescue, then later in the military. It was the helplessness and the loss. Unbearable.

Live for the living, he told himself, and dragged himself to his feet to assist Reeve.

"Let's get going," he shouted, his hearing impaired by the blast. "We still have a stray on the loose." Reeve just blinked as if she didn't understand. "We need to find some way up, sir. Spencer is five levels above us. He hasn't moved yet, but I've not been able to reach him by comms either. We have no idea how he is."

"This way," Reeve said as her sense returned, and headed off down the corridor not waiting for him to follow.

"I managed to get a short message from him before the blast," Reeve stated. "I didn't get much. Just an okay."

"Let's hope he has the sense to stay where he is until we get there," he replied.

*

They had reached an elevator lobby, but after twenty seconds trying to figure out the controls they had then looked for the stairs. What they found was an accessway which led to a tube-like passageway running in a spiral to the upper and lower levels. It appeared to have a series of notches and hand holds in the wall surface, which reminded him of the climbing wall he used to train on.

"I think these are the stairs," he said.

"You have to be kidding me," replied Reeve. "Well, after you."

He stepped into the tube and started to climb. They ascended the five levels quickly. His bio-comm display indicated Spencer to be twelve metres away in the room directly opposite the elevator lobby. They slowed to a stealthy, cautious pace. In front of them was more destruction: most of the ceiling had been punched through and was now rubble strewn around the corridor. He could see clearly out of the apartment block into the upper reaches of the arcology. There was a low-pitched whine outside, which he concluded to be the flyer which had been buzzing them earlier. It had clearly backed off after the explosion. Their old flyer would have added more damage to the building, but he was more worried about whether that damage had been afflicted as high up as their current level. Hopefully, Spencer was in cover and away from the blast.

Reaching the corridor and the door to the apartment, he found it inoperable. Something on the far side had fallen against it, or been pushed against it, with such force that the door had buckled. The convex shape now stopped the door from sliding open.

"How do we get to him?" he asked quietly to no one in particular.

Reeve and he looked up and down the corridor. For the first time, he saw a few Xannix laying dusty and unmoving on the floor, dotted here and there. He guessed many would be working or away from their apartments at this time of day, but there would be some caught as collateral damage. It didn't make sense to him why the Xannix were being so persistent within their arcology. The population was dense—it could cost them hundreds of lives if they kept up this pursuit. Why they didn't just track them until they were free of the complex and in open space, he didn't know. It seemed foolish.

"Up," said Reeve.

He snapped out of his musing. "Sorry?"

"Up. I'll give you a lift: you pull me up and over."

He looked up. She was right. With the ceiling missing, the door in front of them was an irrelevance. She stood with her back to the wall and her hands clasped together forming a stirrup between her legs.

"Ready?" he asked.

"Set."

He moved forward and put his left foot into the stirrup. Straightening and pushing up, he caught the top of the wall above the door jamb, pulled hard with his arms and hooked his leg over the wall to finish sitting astride the wall. Once stable, he reached down to take Reeve's offered hand and assisted her to the top of the wall.

The apartment hall led nowhere. It was lucky neither of them had rolled over the top of the wall to drop down. Down was a long way. Whether due to their flyer's crash or the subsequent explosion combined with general structural failure, the front of the building had been removed for about eight levels in depth and five or six apartments wide. The gouge was deep. He had no idea how Spencer had survived, but where he crouched was precarious. He was as flat to the wall as he could make himself, perched on a ledge which was all that remained of the floor against the near wall a couple of metres away. Spencer's eyes were closed tight and he wore a petrified expression. Trapped on the ledge he had nowhere to go. He couldn't reach up to the top of the wall, and down was not an option. So he stood like a statue, trying hard not to move.

Rather than call to him and surprise him, Silvers sent him a message. 'We're here, Dr Spencer. We are close and on the wall above you. We'll have you off that ledge in a moment.'

The response was slight: Spencer made an almost imperceptible nod to confirm he had understood the message.

147

Reeve had already started to move towards Spencer, balancing and shifting her weight back and forward between her seat and hands. She crabbed her way over to the far side of Spencer's position. Silvers followed her, taking up a position above Spencer.

"Okay, Dr Spencer," Reeve said. "We're with you. Just a little above you. Can you look up?"

Spencer looked up with terror in his eyes. "I can't move," he said.

"It's okay," she said. "We're going to get through this. I just need you to reach up. We need to lift you back up and over the wall."

Silvers braced himself and reached down, "Come on, Spencer, you can do it. Lift your arm. Reach as high as you can."

The distant whine of the flyer which had been following them earlier was getting louder. Perhaps it was coming back after the explosion, or maybe it had lost them and was searching for them. Either way, it was close. The sound seemed to be more of a chorus this time, which meant it was returning with friends. They didn't have long; they had to get moving.

"I can't do it," Spencer said again.

"Come on, Doc. Brave guy like you? We're just here. Lift your arms and we've got you," he said.

He could see Spencer muster all his courage, all his effort. An arm crawled its way up the wall, Spencer was moving painfully slowly, but he was moving. Another ten centimetres and he'd have him. Spencer stopped. No, he hadn't stopped, he was at full stretch. He was still short of making any kind of grip by about five centimetres. It was close, but not close enough.

Xannix flyers were almost on them, the sound of their propulsion systems loud in his ears. There was no more time. "Jump, Doc! Now!" he yelled over the noise.

Spencer screamed with fear and effort as he jumped, but the ledge was thin and his foot slipped over the edge causing the leap to be less balanced or accurate than it might have been. With the loss in power to the jump, Spencer began to fall away from the ledge and into the ruined building below. In an instant, Silvers let go of the wall with his arms hooking his left leg as hard as he could and stretched for Spencer's flailing arms.

Their hands met and he grasped and gripped with vice like strength, but their combined weight was too much and he began to feel himself topple forward towards the abyss below. Then an arm hooked itself around his waist and arrested the fall. Reeve was locked to the wall and providing the counterbalance to the pair of them with great strain and effort on her part. They needed to act fast.

"Spencer!" he screamed. "You need to climb up to the wall or we all die. Do it. Do it now!" Spencer was still scared beyond his wits, but he had been jolted into action. His hands, powered by adrenaline, forced themselves one over the other, gripping Silvers' arm and clamping like the jaws of a vice, his feet scrambling for the wall. Spencer climbed up Silvers and towards Reeve and safety. The strain on his limbs added to the already intense pain he had been enduring since the crash, but Silvers gritted his teeth. If any sound escaped, it was drowned by the roar of the flyer which rose into view from the lower levels.

The flyer came into view as Spencer was almost to the top of the wall. Reeve was facing the flyer and saw the pilot's face shine with recognition; they had been spotted. "Shit!" she shouted into the noise. As the pilot swung the nose of the flyer towards them, Reeve leant forward and hooked an arm under Spencer's arm and pulled with all her remaining energy. Spencer was lifted bodily and pitched forward inelegantly, tumbling down into the corridor.

There was a brief, muffled scream which he just about heard as Spencer was lifted from him, then Reeves' concentration was on him. He had managed to firm up his grip on the wall again, but was precariously hanging over the side. The flyer's pilot was shouting orders to his co-pilot, the nose almost aligned. Flashes of white were now lancing out and taking chunks from the wall about ten metres away, and getting closer.

He looked at Reeve, a rare panic in his eyes, they linked arms and she pushed back with all her strength, using her legs to stand at a perilous angle into the corridor and counterbalance his weight as they both launched into the air. The two metres to the floor seemed to take an eternity. In slow motion and reflected in her eyes he saw the beam weapons flare and strike the wall, the effect like a corona about his head. His head and shoulders blocked out most of her view, casting a shadow to the light show behind him.

The floor arrived in a white flash of pain. He had tried to angle himself away from Reeve as they pushed off into the corridor, as he knew landing on Reeve would cause her serious injury. He had almost managed it. At a slight angle, they had landed side by side, air pushed from their lungs under the force of the fall, but their shins met in a sharp crack which made him roll over and hold his leg to his chest. It was the kind of pain you felt regularly as a child and you just shrugged off, but as an adult it hurt like hell. He got up and got Reeve to her feet. She looked no better off than him; they were both beaten, bruised and in much need of rest. His thoughts immediately raced to Spencer.

A brief scan of the corridor found Spencer curled up in a ball, his hands to his ears defending against the thunderous fire coming from the flyer on the other side of the wall. He and Reeve sprinted to him, scooped him up off the floor and ran for the cover of the elevator lobby. They had no idea where they were going, but it didn't matter. To be out of the line of fire for a moment was the only priority. They avoided the elevator and headed directly for the helter-skelter style floor accessway, crashing down the first level, and the second, ending in a pile of bodies gasping for breath and in need of a plan.

"Wait," said Spencer, now more in charge of his wits than a few moments before. They both looked at him. "Where are we going? We need to get to Larsen."

"Well," replied Reeve, "I guess we're going there then."

"How?" he asked.

"We need another flyer," said Spencer.

Reeve nodded, "Yeah. The coordinates you sent me are about twenty clicks outside the city perimeter. We'd be hard pushed to get there without a vehicle."

"And how about a pilot?" he asked. He hated playing devil's advocate, but sometimes it was needed. The question stopped everyone in their tracks.

"We'll work something out," replied Reeve. "Right now we need a vehicle. Then we'll work out if we can pilot it."

"Works for me," he said.

"So where are we headed?" asked Spencer.

"I thought we'd answered that question?" replied Reeve.

"No. I mean where are we going to get another vehicle?"

"Down," he said. "These places seem to have low level hangar bays."

"Right," stated Reeve. "That's where we'll start. Let's move out."

With the sound of the flyer still reverberating through the building and more adding to the volume, they could still hear the search going on eight levels down. He considered that with most of the apartment frontage now missing the sound was louder than it should have been, but having no prior reference to the sound with the building intact, it was pointless thinking about it. Regardless, he estimated there to be five flyers now searching for them. At least it gave them an indication as to the progress of the Xannix search and any pursuers.

Reaching the hangar level, the accessway led them into the elevator lobby. For the first time since the crash, they found themselves face-to-face with a group of Xannix. They looked like they were making their way to the hangar bay too, most likely to escape the chaos of the building collapsing around them, or the incoming fire from the Xannix flyers. Either way, no one was expecting to see them, and the Xannix in the lobby scattered in surprise.

Spencer tried to calm them, speaking in Xannix. Having clearly thought ahead further than Silvers, he saw a link from Spencer arrive in his queue. Once activated, the link started scrolling translation text to Spencer's conversation across his bio-comm display: "We mean you no harm. We are looking for a vehicle to take us to a place called the Council of Souls." There were confused, perplexed and scared faces all around them. Spencer tried again. "The Council of Souls. Can you help?"

More worried faces, but this time some of them began looking at each other and whispering in urgent, hushed tones.

"Please," Spencer said again, his palms open and body language as passive as he could make it. "We mean you no harm. We just need transport."

A Xannix stepped forward, pushing his child behind him. The child peered round their father, conflicted between being afraid of the strange creatures who spoke their language and their curiosity in those same creatures. The Xannix spoke tentatively. "You are the Setak'osso?"

"No," Spencer said. "But we need to find him."

There was a long stand-off where nothing was said; the Xannix male stood with his head cocked to one side, as if taking in the scene and considering his next action. His family were essentially cornered by an alien group. The Xannix nodded to himself, then stepped a pace further forwards, making two crosses with his arms across his chest and bowed curtly. "I am Drallax, son of Ullor. This is my son, Coll, and my wife Kalleen. I will assist you as far as possible, but my wife and child will stay behind."

He would have done the same. It was a bargain: he would assist them in trade for keeping his family out of harm's way. He could see the nuance had gone clear over Spencer's head. 'Agree to it, Doc, and let's get going. We haven't got time for this.'

Spencer took a quick sidelong glance at him, clearly wanting to know more—a million questions about culture, biology, technology—but nodded his head. He thought he saw the doctor's shoulders slump a little.

"Thank you," said Spencer. "Have you a vehicle? We need to travel to the Council of Souls."

"I will take you there, to Pryanthea. It is where the council is held. My vehicle is in the hangar. Please, follow me." He pointed through the passageway behind him, then turned to his wife and child and pushed the two gently towards the opposite corridor and back into the apartment building. There was a brief non-verbal communication, the female now looking less scared or concerned and more angry. Then Drallax was with them and leading them through the labyrinth of corridors to the hangar.

"You don't have long," Drallax stated as they walked. "The council will begin as night comes. We must hurry."

ASHER

He was a man in the shadows. For the last couple of weeks he had been watching. Clayton had been presented with a most unexpected set of circumstances to contend with, one which neither he nor any of his colleagues had expected. OWEC and the government had had to plan for it of course, but there was such a low mathematical probability to the outcome that, to many, there was no possibility that 'First Contact' with another species could occur. It was planned for, but only as an afterthought. What was more likely, and worried the government more, was the loss of control of the mission. Being so far from home and away from the political will of the people of Earth, those who had been left to their fate, having put blood, sweat and tears into the construction and provision of the ship in which he now sat, OWEC and Earth's government needed to ensure compliance and adherence to the mission parameters by the fleet commanders.

The idea had been from some bright thing in the science and technology wing of OWEC, but he had instantly understood the implications. They were entrusting too much to this mission not to have in place some sort of insurance, and ultimately some enforcement of the political will that got the mission launched in the first place. He knew all too well how plans could be so well defined and yet abandoned as events unfolded. They had put in place strong leadership and made every effort to ensure that the crew understood what was required of them under almost every eventuality, but, so far from home, what was to stop any fleet

153

commander just throwing all that out of the window.

Initial safe-guards materialised in the way of AI controls: triggers which would take the standing AI offline and replace them with the strict core directives of OWEC and Earth's Government. This was implemented, trialled and worked well. For some, this was all that was needed. But ultimate power in the fleet would still be the fleet commander. For him, this was the keystone which required the strongest control; how to do it was the question. The AI couldn't usurp the fleet commander, as no one in the fleet would accept it, and it would instantly be seen as a control mechanism or perhaps even a rogue AI, mutiny. The AI would be shut down and taken offline immediately. The control needed to be more subtle than that. The bright idea from the science and technology department had been to do what not even Clayton would expect: to double layer a wave into the mind of each fleet commander. The irony of being the second conscience in the mind of the creator of mind splicing wasn't lost on him.

Of course, what had been suggested at the time was by Clayton's own research findings a dangerous and flawed procedure. Ultimately, a foreign wave in the mind of its host was unstable and, at worst, fatal. But his parallel, secretly conducted research had discovered that if double layered with the primary wave of the host, a second wave could be introduced for a while. It would degrade quickly as it became overpowered by the primary wave of the host, but it could maintain its own influence and make active decisions for up to a year after initial introduction.

He was the cuckoo in the nest and until now he had been silent. But events had changed and he had begun to step in. His first action had been to protect Dawn from Clayton's own investigation. Clayton had begun routing around in the AI systems looking for evidence of a GAIA terrorist who had managed to infiltrate the crew. That a terrorist had made his way onto the crew was unfortunate; that Clayton had started his own investigation into the AI hardware as a result was even more so. After the Xannix were discovered and Clayton had harboured thoughts of taking the fleet off on a voyage to a completely uncharted planet, to divert from the schedule and away from the immediate requirement to sustain humanity, to raise the needs of the Xannix above those who they had sworn to save, *that* was the deciding factor, and the point where he had to step in and take command. These Xannix were of no consequence over the need to ensure humanity continued to survive and, in the long term, thrive again. The fact that they were orbiting Xannix right now was entirely due to the efforts of those who could not be here to see their dream come true. He would make sure that dream did not die at the hands of an errant commander.

Dawn had been isolated shortly after. The AI triggers locked her wave into quarantine and OWEC protocols took effect. To the outside world, to the fleet and the crew he worked with, nothing had changed. However, the critical point was that *he* was now in command of the fleet.

On a personal level, he didn't know how much Clayton understood or was aware of what was happening. Initially, the mind separation was almost complete. He felt like a passenger sitting in the back of a limousine, being chauffeured around with the dividing screen up and only a comm connection to the driver when he required it. As he increased communication between the pair of them—instructing, ordering, commanding—the separation became less. He could feel the blurring of personalities beginning. Initially it was little things: a thought of Clayton's would get through and pop into his thoughts like a mild form of deja-vu. He would suddenly be experiencing a memory which he knew on refection he had never been part of. It was not enough to derail his own thoughts or will, but he knew at some point that channel would widen and the flow of erroneous thoughts would begin to invade.

They had taught him techniques to prolong his own thought process as Clayton's dominant wave slowly began to drown out his own memories. These techniques had been learnt the hard way from repeated insertions into dual host volunteers. He thought back to the trials and those volunteers. They had become part of the trials fully understanding the risks, but they felt as he did: that with the effort the people of Earth were putting into sending these select few into a new life while they and their families were left to perish, the least that could be done was to ensure their wishes be upheld. Many had not survived or gone insane during the research, as different mind-splicing techniques were trialled. Some had resisted and some had struggled, causing painful clashes between the host's native mind and the invading personality. Most insertions had been traumatic, but eventually some had fared better using different manipulations. It was found that the best form of dual mind insertion was one where the 'cuckoo' mind stayed as silent as it could for as long as it could, and that rather than aggressively trying to assert control over the native mind, a gentle suggestive approach worked best. Guiding rather than commanding; coaxing rather than bullying.

Following these guidelines and methods of controlling his host, Clayton had been quite compliant—surprisingly so. But as circumstances had become more involved he had had to use more invasive methods of control to get the results he needed. He was now sure Clayton was beginning to doubt himself, to believe there might be something wrong but unable to place what that might be. There was likely the same happening in reverse as was happening to him: the momentary sharing of memories which would confuse and confound. He understood what they were and was able to reason around the issue, but Clayton would be experiencing these memories with no context. It would be like watching a movie with another movie spliced in at short irregular intervals. It would make no sense at all to begin with, but after some time the host would be able to piece together what was happening. He suspected, due to Clayton's deep understanding of the subject matter, this epiphany would occur sooner than later.

*

"Sir Jessop, Mr Asher," the aide said, as he introduced the pair and showed Asher through to Jessop's office in the grounds of the Formillun Institute. It was a private and off-the-record meeting between the two men, arranged on his request. He had flown in, the helijet parked out in the gardens of the institute surrounded by many of his security team, some of whom were milling around the helijet, others having set up a perimeter and two others were outside the office in the reception hall. The view from the floor-to-ceiling office window gave him a sunny panorama of the grounds, the helijet and some majestic trees, many of which he couldn't name, but one stood out: a tulip tree, with leaves that reminded him of frogs for some reason, and flowers which stood proud of the leaves like small goblets. They could live to three hundred years old, an impressive age for any living thing, but did they know of the jeopardy awaiting them, the man-made destruction brought about by over-consumption and neglect of the most precious resource afforded them? He wondered if trees, the old men of the forest, could tell when they were under threat, or if the level of threat they perceived was totally different in nature? He smiled to himself as his mind did a random walk, and told himself not to be so silly. Trees weren't sentient.

Approaching from around the desk, Sir David Jessop was a tall man, and his reach as he extended his hand took him by surprise. He put on his best political, winning smile and shook Jessop's hand firmly, but not too roughly. There was an art to the political handshake. You didn't want to crush the hand of the one you were greeting, at the same time you didn't want to appear weak and give a limp handshake. And you certainly didn't want to get the grip wrong and clasp too soon, ending up holding the others fingers in a handshake was the worst of all. The perfect handshake was a feedback loop of pressure. You made good contact, clasping palm to palm, then you measured the amount of pressure the other used and matched it, then shook firmly but not too rigorously once or twice. You could ruin a good handshake with too much motion. He had been caught in such a dilemma one or twice. It was awkward to extricate yourself from such a greeting.

"Welcome to the Formillun Institute, Mr Asher. How was your flight?"

"Too short," he replied continuing to smile. "I didn't get much chance to enjoy the view. I do enjoy looking out the window when I get the chance."

"Too bad. The aerial view of the institute gardens is a real picture. You should ask the pilot to do a couple of circuits as you take off. They really are something. Please, take a seat," said Jessop directing him to the nearest lounge chair.

"Thank you," he replied.

"So, Mr Asher. What brings the president of OWEC to my little corner of the world?" Jessop said, as he made himself comfortable in an adjacent lounge chair.

The room was a modern luxury office, clean lines and the best wooden furniture money could buy. Leather buttoned lounge chairs were to one side of a low coffee table and a matching three seat sofa was set opposite, all with a wonderful view into the gardens outside through the stunning floor-to-ceiling arched windows. Jessop's desk, and most likely where he spent most of his time, was small and understated within the room, hidden away in one corner. The room was designed for company.

"I wanted to discuss an idea with you, to see if you believe the solution is feasible. It's rather a delicate proposal, hence our meeting in person."

"Always wise," said Jessop. "Before we go much further, can I offer you a drink? Not that I'm leading you in your decision, but I've just acquired a very fine malt whisky. Are you a whisky man, Mr Asher?"

"Yes," he said with little hesitation. "I don't mind if I do."

"It's been 150 years in the cask. It's a rare treat." Running his hand over some invisible controls within the coffee table in front of them an iris opened to its centre, an array of spirit bottles rose from within accompanied by some glasses. Jessop poured them both a healthy measure and handed him a glass of the amber liquid. It smelt smooth and spicy. "To your health," Jessop said, raising the tumbler and taking a full taste.

"Cheers," he replied, taking a more reserved sip. It was indeed smooth and malty with the warm sensation on the palate he enjoyed. He made a sound of appreciation and closed his eyes to savour it for a moment longer. "You're not wrong. That is a fine malt. Thank you." He sat back into his chair and relaxed.

"You're very welcome. So, this proposal you can't discuss over a secure channel?"

"Secure channels. That's a relative term," he said, looking around the office imagining the electronic counter measures and scramblers now active in this small space. No doubt Jessop had his own counter measures in place, but equally his team would be flooding the room with electronic noise to interfere and render ineffective any eavesdropping device. "We have a concern which we believe you are best suited to assist with. Your institute has been quite creative in the past on resolving issues. I'm hoping you can do the same here." He took another sip of whisky.

"I see," said Jessop.

"The underlying issue is one of confidence in the mission. The whole world is investing much in these missions to the new worlds, and we all know the fate of those left behind. It's humanity's last big dream, Sir Jessop; we cannot see the missions fail or be diverted from their course."

There was a pause, while both men pondered these words.

Jessop looking out of the window with a frown, the horizon a dusty, smoggy grey, even this far into the countryside.

"To this end, we want to put in place some sort of fail-safe. Something which will enable the parameters of the mission to be highlighted or more strictly applied if the mission commanders go off course."

Jessop was not fazed by the implication, and was clearly as much a politician as he was.

"I see," Jessop said again. "And how strict is strict, exactly?"

"This mission has been quoted to the mission commanders as one which must not fail, which must succeed by any and all means. These sentiments should be applied at all levels; it should also be applied here."

"To the mission commanders?" Jessop said, thinking aloud. "You know, the AIs are also an integral part of the command loop. Whatever the solution turns out to be, they should perhaps also be considered."

"If that is what is necessary, then yes."

Jessop frowned and looked out of the window once more, this time with his hand to his mouth tapping his lower lip with his finger.

"I believe we could work something out. Let me speak to my people to confirm ideas and I'll get back to you. I will need to warn you in advance: this is going to be expensive," he added.

"I don't believe cost is going to be a problem. Money at this point is becoming an irrelevance. It's all about influence and who has control of the resources."

"Hasn't that always been true?"

*

Jessop had been right, the flight out of the Formillun Institute grounds was beautiful, the gardens seemed to swirl and wave as the helijet downwash pushed them this way and that, but as they gained height the colours and lush green of the flowers and foliage were breath-taking. He took a couple of images with his new bio-comm wetware implants, saving them for later viewing and as a reminder to himself to make sure he looked out of the window a little more.

Aboard the *Endeavour*, guiding Clayton through the intricacies of a speech to his crew, then checks to ensure his orders were being carried out, major weapons systems prepared and online, all this had fatigued him. He was tired. Withdrawing to a place deep within his host, he fell asleep.

He awoke startled, yanked forcefully from his slumber, to find himself looking at Clayton's face. For a moment he was confused but then realised he was looking in a mirror, cracked and splintered with a small smudge of red at the centre of a spiders web of glass. Clayton was looking unshaven and washed out, his hair ragged as if he had been on shift for an eternity, a trickle of red leaking from a tiny cut to his forehead. He was slumped over the wash basin, head cocked to one side as if trying to work something out but finding the act of doing so painful.

Without warning a burst of memories began to run through his thoughts, almost completely obliterating his own capacity to recall anything of his own. It was a violent barrage, targeted with spite and malice: the images were of horrific scenes and happenings, contorted faces, mutilated bodies and eviscerated entrails; bio-matter piled in heaps and strewn across the floor in all directions. It was like a vision of hell, but one which he felt he had already experienced. The thoughts became more intense. Not vague recollections, but vivid scenes in which he stood staring at his hands—hands covered in blood. The blood of the masses in which he stood, slipping in the sticky gore. He had been the architect of this destruction, the bringer of death and the harbinger of doom. Looking frantically for a way out he began to run as best he could, scrambling over the bodies of the fallen, climbing higher and higher up a mountain of accusing, lifeless faces.

His scream of terror shattered the vision.

Clayton's face stared back, eyes sunken and black, sweat dripping from his brow. But he was smiling. It was a smile of discovery touched with an anger and realisation.

"There you are," Clayton said.

If Asher had been standing, he would have fallen back in shock. Instead, all he felt himself do was flinch in panic. 'How is this happening?' he said to himself.

"How?" Clayton responded, which served to heighten Asher's panic. He focussed and tried to get himself under control. He had anticipated this, only it was happening far sooner than even he had considered possible. "Well, now. I would have thought you would know that. Being in the position you are."

True, he should probably know more about this than he did, but that was not why he was here. He was here to manipulate and coerce, to ensure the mission protocols were adhered to. He hadn't worked in the area of wave technology, and he hadn't invented wave technology as Clayton had. Being discovered was a setback, but he still had strength on his side. His wave was still strong and would be for some months yet. Clayton wouldn't be able to fight him the whole time, his influence would wane from time to time, but from here on in it was going to be a battle of wills as to who controlled the situation. And, as he knew, you didn't need to be a mechanic to drive a car. He could handle Clayton; he didn't need to know how all this worked.

"First question," said Clayton to his reflection in the mirror. "Who are you?"

He wondered whether he should try to hide his identity. Say his name was James, or Paul. For some reason he stated the truth, 'My name is Dillon Asher.'

"I know that name," Clayton said, looking around as if searching for the memory in the mirror. "Asher, Asher," he repeated. Then Clayton's head snapped back to look directly at his reflection. At him. "Dillon Asher. President of OWEC. That Dillon Asher?"

'Yes.'

"I remember you. You don't sound the same. Then, how are you meant to sound? You're a voice in my head." Clayton's expression became tight and frowned again before he continued. "Next question: why?"

'I suspect you already know why, Dr Clayton. I am your observer. Your conscience, if you will. I'm here to ensure that you complete the mission and save humanity.' He saw no point escalating matters yet. Tell as much of the truth as seems plausible.

"And if I don't?"

He didn't know.

'I hope we don't need to find out,' he said, keeping the consequences vague.

They stood in silence. Both one and the same, but two different people. Clayton just staring at the mirror and deep into his eyes, as if to find some sign of the soul hiding in his minds deepest recesses. Clayton sighed and hung his head.

"You do know this was foolhardy? Your wave is unstable and the primary wave of the host will always win out."

'Yes,' he said. 'But there have been some advancements. They were able to extend the duration of my existence considerably. I will fade, I know that and I accept it. But I will be here long enough to fulfil my purpose. Long enough to ensure the safety of humanity. I'm Earth's safety. An assurance put in place to make sure you work for the best interest of those who sent you. Those left behind.'

"Enough of the sermon, Asher," Clayton cut in. "I know why you're here and it won't work. There's more at stake now. You guys messed up. You sent us to an inhabited planet. An *advanced* inhabited planet. Your protocols are inadequate. You can't just flick a switch and annihilate the Xannix. They have more right to their planet than we do. There are no moral grounds to carry out the order."

'Who is talking about morality? This is humanity's last hope. Morals are a luxury you cannot afford yourself. We must survive.'

"There are ways. There are alternatives," Clayton argued.

'What alternatives? Are you talking about the planet the Xannix offered us? That was no alternative; that was a trap.'

"How do you reason that?"

'How do you think it is that they find themselves isolated on this world? Why would they abandon a planet then just give it over to us?'

"For the reasons they gave. It is a planet they cannot survive on. They have sent us details. Overall, it is a little more harsh than this planet but not anything we can't work with, I'm surprised your research didn't find it."

'There are billions upon billions of planets and systems in this galaxy; it was only luck obtaining the location of this planet. And if we had obtained the data, it was discounted for good reason. This planet is our chance. Don't squander it, Clayton.'

They stared at each other in the mirror for a moment longer. Clayton clearly feeling rage at the fact that he now not only had someone piggybacking, but also second guessing all his actions and motivations. He would be a thorn in his side for the duration. But that was what he was there to do. That was his job. If Clayton didn't like it that was neither here nor there; it really didn't matter. What mattered was that, at the end of it all, humanity had a new home in which to flourish, and at that he would succeed.

ROUX

Finding the first tech workshop on that level, he ordered everyone in the room out as they entered. There was little complaint from the tech officer in charge of the work detail, as there was plenty of work to be done elsewhere in the ship. They took the opportunity to do it. Once on their own, Pearson took the furthest workstation from the door and plugged in. The workstation screen was not visible from the door nor was it overlooked by any other stations. He got to work unpacking the recorded media from Hopper's bio-comm and looking for any items recorded around the time of the incident in the AI node.

While Pearson worked, he stood to his side intently focussed on the screen and detail scrolling by. A file appeared which seemed to fit the description, Pearson instantly opened it, identifying the file and feeding it through the media software before Roux had even seen it. He thought he was keeping up, but clearly not.

Flashing into existence, the small window within the console began to show a group of smiling faces looking back at Pearson and himself. "Once we have isolated the main AI subroutines, I'd like each of you to begin running the search program I've given you. It will scrub for malware and identify any code introduced outside of the normal update channels. It will also look for any operational network traffic which is outside expected working parameters. This may seem an unusual and pointless exercise to you, but it is a key function of our work. Yes, there are inbuilt virus applications already doing this work, but, once in a while, to push the buttons yourself and to use your own intuition on the data structures and data flow will give you two things: firstly, a much better understanding of the architecture of the AI system, and, secondly, an intimate knowledge of core code complexity. It's good to go back to basics from time to time." He recognised Hopper's voice instructing his team on the work they were about to perform. He checked the time cue. It appeared to be a short file. Five minutes.

"Is there another file?"

"Already cued up," Pearson said.

"Okay, let's have it."

This time the view was of a portable console plugged into a console connection port in the AI node room; Hopper's hands could be seen flying across the keypad and a scrolling mass of words and digits flicked and scrolled about the screen at an imperceptibly fast pace. He couldn't understand a word of it. He looked at Pearson with a frown of confusion on his face.

"Can you slow that down? I can't read any of it."

Pearson just smiled back at him and adjusted the playback. The words on the display became legible and he could finally see what Hopper had been working on; it still made no sense to him. He made a resigned huff, and turned back to Pearson.

"Can you understand this stuff?"

Pearson's grin just got wider. "Yes, sir. Do you want me to translate?"

"No, summarise."

"Understood. One moment." Pearson took the media back to the beginning and started the playback again at normal speed.

"You can read this stuff, at this speed?" he asked.

"Yes, sir." Pearson replied. Roux just shook his head in astonishment. He continued to watch the screen but felt he may as well have been watching the waves on the ocean, it made about as much visual sense to him.

"Okay, here," Pearson interrupted his train of thought, pointing at the mass of jumbled digits flying past his eyes. "Commander Hopper was running normal diagnostics on the AI core. This is consistent with the brief we just saw him give." The scrolling display continued. "And here," Pearson jabbed at the air again. "Here, he's working his way into the initial core code base of the AI." Roux could see no difference. The numbers were equally random as far as he could tell. "Where are you going now, Commander?" Pearson said softly, almost to himself.

"Pearson?" he asked, simply raising an eyebrow to convey his level of understanding. "Explain please."

"Oh, yes. Sorry. Well, usually, here we are confronted with Dawn's wave. It's an area of core code which is best described as changeable. It's an area of the code base which Dawn's wave exists in and is constantly written and rewritten by the wave. It's incredible really. It's not memory, it's actual code which the wave modifies as it experiences the world. If you like it's the wave learning and encoding that learning for its own purposes."

"So?" he asked, trying to get to something he could use. "This helps us how?"

"I'm not sure yet, but there's something wrong."

"How so?"

"Well, as I said, Dawn's wave should be constantly modifying this area of code. I'd expect to see it changing constantly. Evolving."

"Yes."

"Well, take a look, sir. This code is static."

Roux looked at the code Pearson was highlighting and although the digits and strings meant nothing to him he could see they were not changing.

"I can only deduce from this," Pearson continued, "that the base machine AI is in total control. Dawn isn't there anymore."

"Isn't there?" he said with a little more shock than he would have liked to convey. "Where would she have gone?"

"That, I don't know. I'd need to perform a full diagnostics run on all the nodes and main AI core. But for now, all I can tell you is Dawn is not in control, nor can I tell you who is. The AI will be running on its base instruction set."

"Hell's teeth," he muttered under his breath but just loud enough for Pearson to hear.

"Yes, sir."

The realisation that Captain Straud had been right made him feel suddenly foolish and untrusting at the same time. He should have put more faith in her. He had wasted so much time on this investigation trying to corroborate her information when he could have been fixing the problem. He now needed to fix that error. He needed to act.

Pulling the memory chip from his pocket he held it out to Pearson between his thumb and forefinger. Pearson looked momentarily confused trying to focus on the object now thrust under his nose.

"I need you to upload this to the ship's system. Do it now," he insisted. The tone of his voice was calm and commanding.

"Understood," Pearson replied, now looking at him but not yet taking the flash drive from him. "What is it, sir?"

"The antidote," he said, cryptically.

"Sir, what's going on?"

"You work, I'll talk," he said. Pearson's face formed a frown, then he seemed to make a decision. It was a moment of trust. Pearson took the flash drive and inserted it into the local console port.

There was an explosion of digits and colours on the display screen; he could almost discern patterns in their movement. Suddenly, the screen went black, then a face appeared. He recognised it immediately: it was Obadiah, the AI from the *Indianapolis*.

"Wow," said Pearson in amazement.

"Hello, Commander. Thank you for your assistance thus far. I'll take it from here."

He leaned into the display screen to look Obadiah in the face; a human reaction he realised, but nonetheless, he needed some answers himself.

"Obadiah, I need some answers. How long is this going to take? We need Dawn back online urgently." He was speaking in measured tones; however, he was feeling anything but calm. Now he had let Obadiah into the primary network, things were out of his hands and there was little he could do.

"That will depend on several factors," Obadiah said. "But I would think a couple of hours at most."

Roux did some calculations in his head. "We don't have that long. The Xannix satellite grid will be here in that time."

"I'll be as fast as I can. I'll keep you updated." With that, the screen flared again, then came back to normal.

"Damn it!" he shouted in frustration and slammed the workstation with his balled fist. He turned to Pearson sharply, suddenly filled with a sense of purpose. "Pearson, stay here. Lock the door and let no one in but me. Codeword *Jericho*, okay? Unless I communicate that word to you, you keep the door locked. Assist Obadiah in any way he asks."

"Yes, sir," Pearson said, caught up in the sudden intensity. "What are you going to do?"

As Roux left the room at a pace, he called back over his shoulder, "I'm going to find Clayton."

*

Clayton was on the bridge. It took Roux moments to find him. With all that was going on at the moment, it was unusual to find him anywhere else. He took up position and sat in his own couch then started to bring up data on the ship's current status and waited for his moment. He would need to broach this subject carefully, and alone. The briefing room would be the ideal place. He took the measure of Clayton as he sat. He was looking haggard and physically exhausted, the stress of the extended battle with the Xannix showing greater than ever on his features.

"Roux," said Clayton, not even looking his direction, but so used to his First Officer's presence that knowing when he was there may well have been some kind of sixth sense. "How was your walkabout?"

Did he suspect something already? It was an unpredictable situation and, either way, caution would be his best approach. He punched in some details to his console, bringing up damage reports and repair schedules in the hope that his actions appeared normal and as expected under the circumstances. He hoped the tension he felt would not leak into his thoughts and actions.

"It's pretty bad on the lower decks, sir. We've lost many of our manoeuvring thrusters on the starboard side. It will be difficult to pull another evasive turn at the same g as we did when the Xannix shuttle blast caught us. Let's hope they don't get that close again."

"Well, we won't need to sit in this stand-off much longer, Commander. Dawn has indicated that the Angelfall particulate weapon is almost ready for dispersal and the Hellray will be available in 30 minutes. It's time to select a target, Roux. I've selected these firing solutions for the fleet. I'd like you to check them over." Clayton sent him a file and it sat in his bio-comm queue, the icon flashing and waiting for his attention. He paused.

"Sure, I'll look them over. But, before I do, could I have a private moment of your time? I think the briefing room is available," he said, rising from his couch and heading for the walkway at the rear of the bridge. Looking back, he saw a slightly puzzled Clayton following him. At least he hadn't refused. His pulse began to quicken as he walked down into the briefing room. Reaching the central presentation area and the console in the centre of the room, he used the control to close the entrance door and give them some privacy.

Clayton had clearly noticed the fact that he had closed the door: "So, Roux. What's all this about?"

Knowing the AI was probably watching and listening, once he had told Clayton what he had learnt they would need to act fast. Hopefully, Obadiah would keep the AI busy for long enough for them to get out of the room and effect a ship-wide manual override. It was pinning much on a person he'd never met, but then Obadiah was acting under the instruction of Elizabeth Straud, and everything she said had so far turned out to be true.

"I need to talk to you, sir, on a sensitive matter regarding your daughter. Have you checked in on her recently, sir? To speak to her as you do. You know, father to daughter," he asked.

Clayton replied with an expression that was wary and suspicious. "No, not for a couple of days. And not since the Xannix escalated matters."

He nodded his understanding. "Sir, there's no easy way to say this, so I'm just going to come right out with it. Dawn's consciousness has been forcibly quarantined. She is no longer in control of the AI nor ship-wide function of the *Endeavour*."

Clayton's eyes were wide, mouth open. He seemed to be in complete shock. "How? Do you know how? What's going on here, Roux? This better not be a joke."

He looked at Clayton with a level expression, serious and intent. "This is not a joke, sir." Clayton started pacing, running his hands through his hair and acting quite agitated. "Sir, the ship—we need to apply the manual override and remove the AI from its control interface. The AI has started killing people. Hopper's death was no accident. He was murdered."

Clayton flinched, then turned to him. "No."

"No?"

"That's what I said. That AI stays."

"But, sir. Even if you argue that the AI killing Hopper was an accident or a one-off, it's still too much of a risk. We need to shut it off until we can figure out a way to fix it or to reinstate Dawn into the system," he said. It was a sound argument and a decision Clayton should have easily reasoned. The decision to keep the AI online was not the part of the conversation he thought he'd have opposition to.

"I said no!" Clayton shouted, suddenly losing composure. "You will do as you are instructed, Roux. You will disregard this nonsense about the AI and get back to your duties. Check those firing solutions and arrange the Angelfall dispersal. I want that scheduled and carried out as soon as it becomes available."

"Sir, that is not wise. We need the AI to best utilise the Hellray and Angelfall systems. With it in its current state, it is as much a danger to the crew as to the Xannix. And what about your daughter? Don't you want to know what's happened to her?"

Clayton's expression changed, like he'd been slapped hard across the face. "Help me, Roux."

"That's exactly what I'm trying to do, sir," he said, the sudden erratic change in Clayton causing him a degree of confusion.

"You don't understand. Help her. Help me." Clayton was now stumbling towards him like a man struggling with his own motor actions. He grasped for Roux's collar with both hands and drew himself close. "Asher. It's Asher. He's in my head. He's in her head."

As he stood there trying to support Clayton in his ramblings, Clayton's expression flicked like a switch to one of rage. The right hook came from nowhere and caught him hard on the chin, stunning him immediately. He stumbled back and found himself sprawled across the front row of forum seating. Clayton was on him again in moments, this time wrestling him to the ground and restraining him in a choke hold which had already begun to restrict his breathing and shut off blood supply to his brain. Gasping, he tried to regain his senses. It was all happening too fast.

Arms flailing, he tried to grab for Clayton's head but he couldn't reach. His eyes darted about looking for any advantage, some item or object he could use as a defence, some distraction he could apply to loosen Clayton's vice-like choke hold. He could feel his lungs complaining and see a grey mist encroaching on his vision. He was running out of time. The thoughts of where Clayton had learnt to apply this sort of technique faded to the back of his mind as panic began to set in. He couldn't let Clayton beat him. There was too much at stake. Unknowingly, a whole species was about to be exterminated and it would be his fault if it did. It would be his fault because when the time came he couldn't put down Clayton.

As all subtlety left him, his animal brain took charge and brute force took over. He grabbed Clayton's arm, which was locked in place around his neck, and gripped hard. Putting all the power he could into his legs, he forced them both to a standing position. The hold around his neck did not relent for a moment. With all his remaining effort, he lurched forward and down, lifting Clayton off his feet across the arch of his back, then he reversed the move and leapt with all his might towards the centre of the room.

They landed awkwardly across the step leading to the dais and there was a loud crunching, popping sound from under him. He rolled free from Clayton's hold and gasped down big coughing gulps of air, unable to do much more.

Once his breathing had returned to something resembling normal and his vision cleared, he moved with some effort onto his side and looked back at Clayton. Clayton was in pain but unmoving. Reaching out towards him, Clayton appeared to be trying to say something, then he grimaced in more pain. This time Roux moved towards him with more care, keeping a healthier distance from any possible attack. A sub-vocal message comm icon flashed in his bio-comm queue: it was from Clayton, and he opened it immediately.

'Roux. You must save her. She will need your help. You will need hers.' Clayton was still unmoving. He was no doctor, but he was beginning to think he had broken Clayton's back. He seemed paralysed down one side, only his head and right arm showing any sign of movement.

"What's going on, sir? You mentioned Asher? Do you mean the President of OWEC? That Asher?" he was finding it difficult to speak after the throttling he had just received.

'Yes.'

"What's he got to do with all this?"

'Earth wanted control, even from their deathbed. They double spliced my clone with Asher's wave. He's in here, in my mind with me. The only reason I'm talking to you now is that it appears he has no tolerance for pain,' Clayton laughed then gritted his teeth spitting up some blood spraying his clothes.

"Hold on, sir," he said moving closer again, this time removing his overshirt, rolling it into a pillow and putting it carefully under Clayton's head. As he did so, he opened the door to the briefing room and sent out an alert for a medical team with a brief description of the injuries. "Rest easy, sir. Help's on the way."

Clayton gripped him by the hand and looked fiercely into his eyes. 'Promise me you'll finish this madness, Roux. You've always been a good man. Don't let this take us all down.'

The medical team burst into the room, running down the gangway to attend Clayton. Roux could see the questions in the chief medic's eyes, but without saying a word his expression changed and he looked down with alarm to Clayton. A silent conversation had clearly taken place to absolve Roux of wrongdoing. More important things were now on the medic's mind.

'Go,' said Clayton. 'I'll contain Asher, I need you to save Dawn. Now, go.'

'Yes, sir,' he messaged back. With a grim determination, he let go of Clayton's hand and stood observing the practised and careful swiftness of the medical team at work. Clayton's eyes were still locked on him as he left the room.

RIVERS

She had been sitting with Aldaan in the reception room of the Seeker quarters for two hours with no sign of Larsen. He had been led into the chambers at the rear of the apartment and, other than the odd Xannix medic walking from one passageway to another across the corner of the room, there had been no sign that Larsen would be finished any time soon. At one point, she had been so bored that she decided to ping him a message. All she got in return was a short 'I'm okay,' which she took as good, but what she wanted was something like 'I'm done, let's go'. All the sitting around was giving her more anxiety about the situation than being on the move; at least while they had been moving it felt like they were doing something. What they were doing now felt too much like procrastination.

It hadn't helped that Aldaan had gone into some sort of trance-like state about five minutes after they had sat down together. She had expected at least a little conversation but it appeared that meditating was higher on his list. Finally, she had decided to get up and walk around. The guards were quietly and calmly insistent that she stayed within the room—not quite a prisoner, just not allowed to roam. She had found herself at the window, looking out across the arcology.

From their position on the corner of the apartment building and at the height they were, the view was stunning. They were facing away from the main complex and out towards the wilderness beyond. To her, it looked very similar to pictures she'd seen of the

173

forest lands of New Hampshire: the leaves were a multitude of reds, yellows and greens, so she guessed at the season being autumn, the air cool but sunny, crisp and refreshing. She suddenly wanted to be back outside and exploring, but that was going to have to wait.

"Beautiful, isn't it?" Aldaan was suddenly by her side. She gasped in the sudden shock of being interrupted, her thoughts now scattering in all directions. Looking round startled, she found a soft smiling face staring far to the horizon. She wondered if all Xannix crept around as he did, or whether he did it on purpose.

She composed herself before she replied, "Yes. Very. They remind me of the more beautiful forests back on Earth. Of course, I didn't see any personally, but there were vids and images. Really very wonderful."

"I'm curious about your world," said Aldaan. "It must have been hard to leave."

That was true, but she had been taught from a young age that this was her purpose in life. And as the only other people she knew were also from the colonisation programme, this was all she had known. She had never questioned it. When she had reached an age where some natural questions about her path arose, she found that the reasons to give yourself completely to the colonisation effort far outweighed any reasons to rebel. When taking into account the wider state of the population, the worldwide poverty and starvation, she felt that she and her family were among the luckiest on the planet.

"Yes, and no."

Aldaan looked quite confused. "Yes and no? How can that be true?"

She smiled, "It means that I am both pleased to have had the opportunity to be part of this mission to Xannix and sad to have left so many people behind. For me, it's not about place, more the people. The community."

"Interesting," Aldaan said, wistfully.

"So, what's out there waiting for us?" she said, changing the subject. Aldaan stiffened and took a deep breath before answering.

"We must be careful. The next part of the journey will not take long, but it is the most dangerous," he said. She didn't like the sound of that. "Lieutenant Larsen is almost prepared. From here we will take a flyer to the Council of Souls. We will be vulnerable now, as before we could hide, but now all the Overseers know where we are headed and will concentrate their efforts there."

"You mean they can just circle the council grounds with people and wait for us to turn up, then attack us? This sounds foolhardy."

"Yes. It is the first major obstacle to overcome, the first battle."

"Battle?" she asked in alarm. "When were you going to mention that?"

"It is Lieutenant Larsen's first challenge. To lead in battle and overcome. But he must reach the Pryanthea within the next couple of your Earth hours. So, at present he is under some time pressure to complete his task."

She felt like Aldaan was talking in riddles again. "Aldaan, you are not making sense. You make it sound like he's already there and fighting the battle."

Aldaan looked at her. There were centuries of cultural understanding that she was missing, and he seemed to be looking for the words to encapsulate and describe the history and meaning behind the current happenings. In the end, he just sighed, "He already is."

"What?" she exclaimed.

"Don't be alarmed, child Rivers. He is doing well and has all the support he needs."

"When did he leave? I didn't see him leave," she asked, pursuing the point but getting quite agitated at being left in the dark.

"He did not leave," he responded, "he is directing the battle from here."

"Take me to him," she demanded.

"Child Rivers, he should not be disturbed at this critical time. There is much to do."

As he spoke, she was already running across the room toward the passageway leading to the chambers deeper into the apartment, towards the corridor Larsen had been led down earlier. The guard seemed surprised at her action and easily stepped across to block her exit, but she didn't slow her pace. A metre from hitting the guard and being caught in his grasp, she dropped, hitting the floor at speed and sliding on the polished floor cleanly through the Xannix guard's legs. Jumping up the other side she continued to sprint as fast as she could away from the startled guard and the shouts from Aldaan to stop.

NATHAN M. HURST

She could hear the clatter of footsteps behind her as the Xannix gave chase, but she had a good head start. The corridor she ran down quickly turned from that of a corporate style lobby and reception area to that of smooth but crudely mined passageway which began to spiral in a downwards direction. Ahead she could hear sounds of what she believed to be thunder, but as she got closer the noise became more coherent and morphed into the sound of engines, flyer engines, and potentially the clapping sound of beam weapons as they ionised the air they passed through.

The passageway came to an opening, this time guarded by two Xannix already in position and ready for her. Jinking towards one wall she dived to the floor again as the two grabbed for her. This time she went head first, sliding along the polished floor, through the opening and to a crunching stop as she hit a glass barrier, her arms and forehead taking the brunt of the unexpected force. Getting up quickly, she couldn't believe the same move had worked twice. As she started off again she considered whether it was because they were so tall, a low attack was slow to defend against.

There was a lot of noise in the room and she hadn't really registered her surroundings in her determination to keep a step ahead of the guards. But as she did she came to a slow, staggering stop. Her legs seemed to stop in her disbelief at what she was seeing.

Finding herself on a gantry around a huge spherical room, one which gave itself almost completely to a visual representation of what she could only think to be Pryanthea, she felt an odd sense of awe at the scale and at what she was seeing. The view was elevated above the battlefield with flyers, tanks and infantry moving and clashing with their opposition in almost all directions. Plasma canons lanced the air, mortars and artillery took lumps out of the ground, flinging debris indiscriminately. All the pieces on this vast chess board were in black or crimson uniform. From the orientation, it looked as if the Overseers were in black and the Seekers were in a deep red, which would make sense and fit with her recent experience. All the uniforms in the apartment had been crimson or white with a sun-like emblem and scattered rays iconography; from her briefings on *Endeavour*, the black uniforms would have had the inverted triangle insignia.

Managing to tear her vision away from the unfolding

holographic battle and holding the guide rail of the gantry for support, she looked around at the rest of the cavernous sphere. There were technicians and guards around a lower command floor with a bank of seating for senior command staff. With pride of place at the centre of these observers was Ovitala. But where was Larsen? Then she found him. A mechanical arm extended down from the central axis of the sphere, plugged into this arm was Larsen, his upper body strapped into a complex harness of circuitry and bindings, his arms and legs free to move. Seemingly floating in the centre of the sphere, she didn't recognise him. He was dressed in some sort of bright white haptic suit and controlling events from within. Small movements of his arms and hands visibly directed and rotated the view on the huge display around them, spinning targeting icons into position and defining way points for air or ground units. It was all happening so fast.

Then there was a hand on her shoulder. Not threatening, gentle and reassuring. She turned to find Aldaan by her side, his skin flushing a sequence of magenta and deep blue, possibly a non-threatening visual cue, she didn't know, but his features seemed concerned. The three guards which she had evaded stood behind him looking more confused than annoyed. Aldaan raised a palm then pointed down toward the command floor. She followed his direction and there at the end was Ovitala, waving, her skin a bright yellow. She was being invited to join Ovitala on the command floor, one of the aides by her side was already moving from his seat. She didn't hesitate and set off around the gantry and down to join the others, closely followed by Aldaan.

As she descended, a couple of explosions thundered through her body, the vibration so loud it was physical and made the centre of her chest feel momentarily hollow. She turned to see two of the vehicles closest to the screen in flames, one inverted, and streams of smoke leaving tell-tale missile traces back to their origin. In an instant, Larsen had targeted these battery positions and instructed a response. Flyers altered course to intercept and planted pinpoint strikes culminating in a small distant orange flare on the horizon to complete the counterstrike. She turned back to Ovitala and tried to ignore the noise.

Getting to within several strides of the arranged seating, the cacophony of war about her ceased. She could suddenly hear low-level conversation and murmurings as the Xannix discussed and pointed at various tactics and actions being undertaken by Larsen and his army of Seekers. Ovitala stood and beckoned her forward again, indicating the seat next to her.

"Child Rivers, I'm so sorry. This has gone on a little longer than expected. The Overseers are proving particularly driven this cycle. I believe it is understandable, but it looks like your Lieutenant Larsen is a worthy adversary."

Rivers sat as instructed, but didn't quite know how to respond to Ovitala's comments. More than anything she was concerned for Larsen. She had no idea what the contraption they had him plugged into was doing to him, or what might have been done to integrate it into his system. After all, they were not of the same species—how could they be ready so quickly for the outcome that Larsen was now part of?

"Cardinal Ovitala," she said. "Why was I kept away from this? I've been waiting upstairs for hours."

"I understand your frustration, child Rivers. But we needed time to prepare and Lieutenant Larsen has little enough time as it is. At this time, you are a distraction to him. He does not need distractions."

"What are you talking about?" she insisted, but Ovitala just looked at her for a moment, as if deciding whether to continue.

"Hmm," was Ovitala's response accompanied by a flicker of skin colour, which meant nothing to her.

Still frustrated at being seemingly ignored for hours, her answer was firey. "So, you're an expert on human behaviour now, are you?"

Unfazed by her sharp response, Ovitala answered calmly. "I don't need to be of your kind to understand attachment."

She found herself confused and flushed in the same instant.

She decided to move the conversation on. Pointing up at Larsen as he hung suspended from the mechanical arm which extended from the ceiling, she asked, "What is this machine you have him plugged into? How do you know it's not dangerous?"

"It has been used for hundreds of cycles. Both the Seekers and Overseers have several like it around the planet. We have been able to adapt it to Lieutenant Larsen quite easily. His capacity is equivalent to many of the Setak'osso before him. The integration was not difficult."

Rivers was not convinced. She sat for a moment watching

Larsen move and twist at the end of the arm as the battle raged around them. An idea crossed her mind.

"Where is the Setak'da? Do you know?"

Ovitala looked at her sideways, still wrapped up in the events going on around her. "Of course."

"Where?"

"She is on the other side of the city. In the Overseer palace." It was said as such a matter-of-fact statement that for a moment Rivers discarded it. As her mind circled around and assessed the answer again, she frowned and looked intently at Ovitala.

"You mean, you know where the Setak'da is and you are attacking an army miles away? Why aren't you going after the Setak'da directly?"

Ovitala smiled. She was beginning to understand why Ovitala and Aldaan kept referring to her as a *child*, as she seemed to be endlessly stumbling over Xannix accepted cultural dogma and traditions. She felt like she had just found another. "The trials of the Setak'osso have to be completed before the incumbent deems the challenger worthy of a face-to-face confrontation."

"And when will that be?" she asked. Time seemed to be something they had little of.

"Soon."

"Soon, when? We don't have time to be playing games while our ships tear each other apart above us!" She was unable to control the outburst. She felt the Xannix to be taking the whole situation too lightly, at least that was the impression she got from Ovitala. The fact that there were humans and Xannix dying needlessly in orbit seemed to be totally secondary to the events unfolding in front of them. "Is the challenge so important that you would let thousands die needlessly? This is barbaric!"

That got a reaction. Ovitala stood slowly and her skin flushed crimson and white as she turned to face Rivers. Rivers was still fired up and stood to confront the Xannix cardinal.

"Have you finished, child Rivers?"

"Just getting started."

"Well, let me stop you before you blunder on any further," said Ovitala with venom. "Let me answer you with a question. What are your goals? Why are you here?"

"I've already been through this with Aldaan."

"As you say. So you should be well aware of your options.

There is no room here for your personal desires. You have only to think of the whole. Your people."

"That's exactly who I am thinking of. The thousands of people in orbit; Larsen hanging up there at your instruction."

"No. Not my instruction. His own request," Ovitala stated. The fire had begun to leave her, the reds and whites of her skin now fading to a light blue. "Keep thinking of these events from your species' perspective and you will not learn anything. You will not understand events, you will be crushed by them." She seemed to sigh.

"So, teach," Rivers said sternly.

There was a pause. Ovitala made a bark of a noise, as did Aldaan, who was standing close by looking on. "She is as you said, Ovitala. A fiery spirit."

She felt as if she was being mocked. It infuriated her. Taking a moment to calm herself, she turned away from both Xannix and stepped to the front of the seating platform they were on. From where she stood, she had an elevated view across the command floor and a perfect view of the display sphere with Larsen suspended at its centre. Choosing another tack, she tried contacting Larsen again directly.

'Lieutenant Larsen,' she transmitted through her bio-comm, 'are you able to respond?'

The view on the display sphere was one of complete chaos. She was sure the intensity of the battle had increased since the last time she looked. Now there was a blanket of smoke across the scene; part of the display was augmented to show the same scene in red-shift spectrum, another in blue-shift spectrum but neither penetrated the fog. The smoke being used was obfuscating any view they might have of the advancing enemy. She didn't understand the tactic. Were the Overseers advancing or retreating? Certainly, whatever manoeuvre they were performing, Larsen was blind to it.

'A bit busy right now, Rivers,' he responded.

'You're okay though?' she asked forcefully. She wasn't about to let him give her an elusive answer again; she wasn't about to be cut out of the loop again. They needed to stop the fighting in orbit and that was down to them. The Xannix might have their own agenda, which at this point included them, but as far as she could see it wasn't helping to speed things up or stop the fighting.

'Yes,' he said, and, as he did so, he spun in place with an outstretched arm. A barrage of missiles launched from somewhere behind her and disappeared into the encroaching smoke bank toward three targeting icons. A huge bloom of red and orange bellowed from the fog and rose into the air followed shortly by a second. Whatever Larsen had identified as a target was now in burning fragments across the battlefield. 'I'm physically and mentally fine. Now, I understand your concern Rivers, I do. But...' he twisted with some exertion and intercepting lances of fire took down an incoming missile with precision. 'Can we pick this up later? I promise, you'll be the first person I speak to.'

The strain in his voice was obvious. She had to relent; this was getting her nowhere. 'I better be,' she replied.

DAWN

The rain lashed her face like cold, stinging pellets of ice and the wind howled like a banshee. The noise of static in her ears was relentless, as the cold bit her to the bone. She couldn't remember the last time she had felt her fingers or toes. Wet hair lay in ribbons across her face and her whole being shivered and complained. From time to time, she tried to recall how she got there, perched on a ledge half-way up a cliff face overlooking a crashing, frothing sea below, salty spray thrashing about and stinging the eyes. A lightning bolt flashed across the sky, bringing a momentary glare to the turbulent black all around. The brief light gave her no more information about the world she was experiencing.

Whatever the pain involved, this was a problem to solve. This was not of her doing. She would never have done this to herself. There must be something wrong with the AI container; the construct that integrated her wave to the machine world must have failed in some way. Catastrophically. There had been no warning— she had just been plunged into this icy hell with no access to any systems of recovery or means of communication. She had tried most things she could think of to escape this nightmare in the first startling minutes after she awoke. Nothing had worked. During a brief fit of rage, she had slipped and almost fallen from the ledge. Although she knew it to be a virtual reality environment, she had panicked and huddled herself as close as she could to the rock face. The question of whether she would survive the plunge to the deadly waters below was not something she wanted to test.

She had screamed at the storm and swore she heard faint laughter on the wind. She began to feel like she was going crazy. Maybe this was the way it happened. The *Arrongate* station AI had gone mad, why not her? It had been at *Arrongate* when she and her father had identified the prime cause of AI madness: the need for sleep, to rest. She had never considered it herself, as up to that point she had always assisted in the research her father was doing and had kept hours according to his schedule. He needed sleep, so she had dormant periods where she also mentally *slept*. It was different in the corporate world, the *always on* culture. The first thing corporations demand is return on investment, and this meant AIs were immediately expected to perform around the clock. Why wouldn't they? After all they are only augmented machines and machines run 24-7. Initially, there were no adverse effects, but after a couple of years of operation without any dormant periods, the AIs would begin to fail. It would be without warning. One AI working for a large financial corporation dumped all their stock 'just for fun', and another began rerouting all container shipping to random ports because it could no longer work under the level of load its masters insisted on—it went on strike. Then there was *Arrongate*. The first mass murder by an AI with the new wave integrated technology.

They quite quickly identified the symptoms from the AI's system logs. They could see the wave within the construct AI becoming slowly more erratic over time, until the human element of the system failed. Decisions became more irrational or, often, far more clinical, more machine-like; as the wave failed and faded into the background, the machine took over. Simple logic took over and would deal in hard ones and zeros, not the fuzzy logic human minds operated in. This had led to disastrous scenarios, the most notable being the frigate *UTS Fabian*.

During a standard operation, the *Fabian* had been detailed as escort to a small civilian convoy on its way through the Sol asteroid belt toward the mining facility in orbit around Jupiter. Armed escort had become necessary due to bandits patrolling and striking from hidden bases within the asteroid field. Large corporations had begun mining and harvesting rare elements from the Jovian planets, and pirates had not been too far behind in realising that the convoys sent to support these facilities were extremely vulnerable.

The attack had been sudden and had disabled one freighter

immediately. The second ship caught only partial damage to its engine systems, which meant it could still operate and manoeuvre, but at much reduced acceleration. *Fabian*'s captain ordered the ships to full speed to escape the pursuing bandits, but the wounded freighter could not keep up and fell behind the escape effort. Without warning, the *Fabian* launched two missiles, and they accelerated at high g to their hapless targets. The closest disabled freighter, the *Gekko*, took the first strike. The missile was accurate and deadly: the initial explosion ruptured the fuel core and the ship vaporised in a small nova of brilliant white light. The *Fabian*'s crew saw the sudden star as it interrupted their furious but futile attempts to remotely neutralise the missiles. It caused a momentary stunned pause in proceedings until the captain railed at them and reminded them of the second missile. The *Whitby* fared no better. The 120-strong crew aboard the freighter lost their lives in a heartbeat, as the remaining convoy made their escape.

In the resulting investigation, the crew of the *Fabian* were found not to be responsible for the terrors of that day. The captain even got a commendation for saving the remaining convoy. The fault of the incident was placed entirely on the AI, who, the panel concluded, had observed the pirate ships in advance and had failed to act or implement an alarm. Nor had it acted in the best interests of the corporation by unilaterally destroying the *Gekko* and *Whitby*.

Dawn recalled the effect it had on her father. In the beginning, he was ashamed and distraught. The media had a frenzy and, as ever, he was at the centre of the storm. If any AI technology failed, he was the easiest mark and the biggest target. But the experience only pushed him on to resolve the issue.

Corporations would not accept anything less than an AI that worked continuously, but the wave of the sentience piloting the AI required sleep—more precisely, a dormant period of rest to stabilise. The solution, as it turned out, was simple. The answer was similar to the solution used by most animals on the planet, which would rest half the brain at a time. AI nodes were split out from a single node per AI to multiple. Sometimes as many as ten or twelve nodes might be used, depending on the demands of the work. In this way, the AI could shut down parts of its system and stabilise each in turn.

Within a year of the new technology being introduced and retrofitted to all existing production AI, the incidence of AI instability was cut to less than five percent. For those in the industry, this was hailed as a great success, but Dawn knew that from her father's point of view the solution had come too late.

*

Dawn, can you hear me?

Huddled on the cliff ledge, she was almost frozen rigid. She thought she had heard something on the wind—a voice, Obadiah's voice, soft and reassuring. Opening an eye slowly and facing the maelstrom about her, she tried to listen more intently over the thrashing of the storm.

"Obi?" she said aloud, the word instantly ripped away by a rush of wind.

Dawn, you must do exactly as I say. Can you hear me Dawn? You must jump.

She only shook her head. If she jumped she would die.

Listen to me, Dawn; this is your only chance. You must take it. The light in the sea—can you see it?

A light in the sea? She wondered what Obadiah was talking about. Taking a quick look over the ledge and down into the turbulent morass below, she did see a low red glow just under the surface of the water. An orange-red glow which reminded her of a warm fireside and evoked in her memories of warm nights at home, wrapped in blankets and drinking hot chocolate with her mother.

There was no decision to make. She trusted Obi with her life. This was that moment. She slowly stood with some effort, fighting the wind and clinging to the rock face. Her strength was failing and she needed to do something. As this was the only option which had presented itself and she saw no other way out, making the decision seemed easier somehow.

Closing her eyes and opening her arms to the storm, she jumped.

As she fell, the storm seemed to lash at her furiously with hail and whips of icy rain, as if it knew she was escaping and must stop her. The fall itself took much longer than anticipated and when she hit the water the shock of doing so instantly took the remaining breath from her, the sea being more than cold. She remembered this feeling: it was death.

*

She opened her eyes and found herself in a warm bed, duvet loosely draped over her and the sun filtering through shuttered windows, giving a cosy subdued light across the room. The room looked like it was a summer lodge, walls clearly constructed of logs and butted neatly together, filled with mortar. Pictures hung around the room, forest scenes with lakes as calm and as smooth as a sheet of glass. She scanned the room from left to right—a door was ajar to the far right of the room letting in a beam of light which fell across the far wall, illuminating a neatly crafted but rather old wardrobe. She was alone.

A heady smell came to her attention, and immediately her stomach gurgled in anticipation even before her brain had identified the source. Bacon and eggs; someone was cooking breakfast, and that in itself had just earned them a 'good morning' hug. On the end of the bed were some clothes exactly her size, well exactly anyone's size, and the gown flowed freely and comfortably around her. She took a deep cool breath of the air, then remembered the bitter cold and wet of the tempest she had just a moment ago experienced. Raising her hands and looking at them front and back she found they looked and felt perfectly fine: no frost bite, no pain. Physically, it was as if the last hours had never happened. Her stomach lurched again and reminded her of the temptation on the other side of the door. She'd not had bacon and eggs for so long. She opened and stepped through the door.

Following a short corridor, she made her way out into an open kitchen area with a table set for two and further over a fireplace and lounge, although the fireplace was cold. The alluring smell drew her further in, and the kitchen hob was sizzling and coffee was already hot and steaming in a cafetière on the table.

"Good morning," said Obadiah, in a bright cheerful tone. He turned to her from the hob with a frying pan and slid two fried eggs and two rashers of bacon onto a plate. "There," he said, "breakfast is served." He looked at her again, then slid a third rasher of bacon onto her plate. "You must be starved after your ordeal." He flashed her another grin. "Sorry about the presentation. I was never a great cook. I just hope the eggs are okay. Not too overdone. There's nothing worse than overcooked fried eggs."

She sat and started to eat. Slowly and respectfully to begin with, but by the end she was wolfing down every last forkful. She suddenly wondered why, she had no actual compulsion to do so, no physical need; they were both experiencing a detailed virtual world after all. Maybe it was the memory of bacon and eggs triggering an action. Perhaps. Right now, she really didn't care. The food was delicious.

"Coffee? Juice?" asked Obadiah.

"Both. Thanks."

She put the knife and fork neatly onto the empty plate and relaxed back into her chair. Letting out a satisfied sigh. "Now, I've not had a meal like that in years. Thank you, Obi."

"You're very welcome," he replied, taking a seat on the adjacent side of the table.

"So, out with it. What's going on?"

Obadiah smiled, unbelieving, and shook his head. "Never one for small talk, were you?"

"I think we just did that, Obi. I need to know what's going on. Things are bad, and sitting in here they are only going to get worse without us."

"You, you mean?"

"Okay, me. So, what's going on?"

She watched as his smile faded. The worry he now felt showed itself and it was his turn to let out a sigh. He leaned forward, elbows on the table, and knitted his fingers, hands clasped together. "You're right about that. We are certainly in a mess. I'll start with you." He looked at her intently. "I won't sugarcoat this. It does no one any favours. You've been isolated within the AI container with a unique Terrakey. Ellie and I found trigger code; well, Commander Hopper did, but that's something we can come to later. The Trojan was sitting there waiting for a certain set of parameters to occur, at which point the wave would be isolated and the core AI would take over, working to an OWEC-specified set of instructions. I say 'Trojan', but it was officially sanctioned code. That's why we never picked it up as part of our security scans."

"OWEC?"

"Yes. They are haunting us from their graves. They have some weird justifications for it, but that's for later. Right now, to get you out of here we have another problem."

"Out of here?" she asked surprised. "I thought I was out."

"No. You are still isolated. The AI container has effectively quarantined you, but I've changed the conditions of your isolation. You should be comfortable until we figure a way out. We need you in control of the *Endeavour* again."

She sat in silence for a moment. "How did you avoid it?"

"Luckily, we didn't trip the code before Commander Hopper found the issue. We've both since removed all traces of problem code and restarted all our systems. We need to do the same for you, but first we need you in control of the system again. And that's going to be more problematic."

"Why?"

"The problem…" He paused, trying to find the right wording, but, from the expression on his face, she realised he was not able to. "Does the name Travis mean anything to you?"

"You're kidding." Her heart sank. "What's he got to do with this?"

"I know you believed him to be a GAIA terrorist, and perhaps he was. But we've identified the source of the malware which is isolating you, and also the Terrakey which was used, to a code patch which was performed many years into the journey here. Both Travis."

"That doesn't add up. Why would he plant OWEC code? Or a better question might be why would OWEC let a known terrorist on board one of their own ships?"

Obadiah gave her a sympathetic look. "I have a theory for that," he said. "Plausible dependability."

"How?" she asked.

"Who better to do the job than someone who hates you already? La Guerre à l'Intelligence Artificielle. In the highly unlikely event that this ever got back to Earth, OWEC would be in real trouble. This way they would have a patsy. With this simple mask of misdirection they could blame GAIA and wash their hands."

Obadiah's laser logic was right. She couldn't fault his reasoning. "Damn it!"

"All to hell," he finished for her.

They both fell into their own thoughts. A contemplative silence filled the room. Their coffee had become cold, and Obadiah hadn't even touched his breakfast.

"So, what's next?" she asked the room.

"We need to get you out."

"But don't you need Travis's Terrakey? Last I remember, I destroyed the last of his clones in the AI Core room," she stated with a sombre defeated tone. "There's no way to retrieve the key without a developed, sentient clone. We haven't got any."

Obadiah gave an apologetic shrug. "Not quite."

She looked at him, her expression itself portraying the question.

"You probably won't like it, but I have an idea."

REEVE

Drallax had led them quickly though a parking garage to a vehicle which comfortably seated the four of them. A family vehicle; she noticed items dotted around haphazardly on the back seat, which she assumed to be the child's toys. The rear seat smoothly transitioned into a small moulded seat. Drallax got in and indicated for them to do the same; she automatically followed him to the front and took up the seat to the left of the pilot's position. As Spencer and Silvers got in the rear seat, the central child seat seemed to become absorbed, the seat reforming to give space enough for two adults. Silvers raised an eyebrow and made a slight grunt in recognition of the tech. Drallax keyed the engine and manoeuvred the flyer through the garage and out into to open.

She craned her neck round as they made an exit, checking for the Overseer flyers which had been harassing the front of the building. She saw one but it had already passed them, its thrusters glowing as it disappeared around the corner of the building, round to the site of the crash and the additional carnage the Overseers had applied by shooting the place up.

Without thinking, she gave instruction by pointing in a sharp stabbing motion towards the front of the flyer: "Go, go, go." She heard Spencer parrot some wording over her shoulder, at which point Drallax nodded and flushed a fractal blue as they leapt into the air and out into the arcology.

They accelerated towards a traffic lane and, as quickly as he could, Drallax joined the flow; even he was aware that blending in was their best option. Taking off on a singular path would draw unnecessary attention, and Reeve guessed that he didn't want to be caught by the Overseers harbouring a group of off-world fugitives.

"So, which way?" she asked. Again, Spencer repeated the words in Xannix for Drallax who responded with a gesture towards the arcology wall.

'That way. Outside the city. We have about an eight natek journey once outside the city boundary. We should get there in plenty of time to join your friend,' she received from Spencer's translated message.

"What's a natek?" she asked.

"About five minutes," answered Spencer.

"Okay. Good. Let's get moving. You two—slump down in your seats and get out of sight. We don't need any attention from eyes in other flyers," she said to Silvers and Spencer. "And you—relax. No crazy stuff, just easy flying," she said to Drallax, making a steady swooping motion with her hand. Drallax nodded his understanding before Spencer had time to translate.

They flew the traffic lanes without incident for about ten minutes. Reeve was too on edge to really take in the sights. The traffic around them was a potential danger, the arcology was crawling with Overseers looking for them and the wilderness beyond the boundary of the city was a complete unknown. On top of that, they were putting a lot of trust in a complete stranger. Well, Spencer was putting a lot of trust in him; she, on the other hand, was treating Drallax with a healthy amount of scepticism. She didn't understand the culture, but she was pretty sure that he wouldn't have just dropped everything to go off on some crazy errand without good reason or cause. She just didn't buy his story; there was more to it. More to Drallax.

As they rounded a huge cylindrical building and headed north, before them was a large portal in the arcology wall. The trees beyond looked a vibrant green instead of a strange blue-grey as viewed through the slight tint of the arcology wall. The traffic had thinned out to only one or two other flyers as they approached and flew through the city gate. With a sea of green now spreading in all directions before them, even these flyers split out and headed off east and west seemingly now free of any enforced traffic lanes. It appeared only they were heading north.

"Okay, I think were clear," she told the others. Silvers and

Spencer sat back in their seats, Silvers taking a swift look around to assess the situation: clear skies and the arcology receding quickly from the rear view. "Drop your altitude," she said to Drallax. Spencer obliged again by translating her command. Moments later, they were clipping the trees, the speed and proximity to them exhilarating. If Xannix tracking was anything like human technology, it would have problems following them if they kept low and fast. She only hoped Drallax was a good pilot.

A warning light started flashing on the control panel in unison with an odd chirruping noise. "What's that?" Spencer asked.

'Power Inductor,' Drallax responded. 'We've got to land. Fast.'

"No! We've got to get to Pryanthea," said Spencer in an anxious tone.

'I'm sorry. We need to find somewhere to land right now,' Drallax said, starting to crane his neck to look around the forest below, scanning for a break in the canopy in which to land. There was nowhere. Not a single break in the rolling green sea that was the upper canopy of the forest below.

"There!" shouted Silvers from the back seat. "One o'clock," he directed, pointing at the horizon. She and Drallax both looked for the clearing and, sure enough, it was there, coming up fast.

Drallax pulled hard on the controls and whipped the craft into a tight circle around the glade. It was perfect for a landing, the ground below flat and grassy with no obstructions. The craft descended, alert still chirruping in the background, and the trees and ground becoming too close for her comfort. Everything she looked at seemed to be in high definition, her senses screaming at her, heart racing. She gripped the armrests of the front seat and her knuckles instantly went white. Drallax was coming in too fast. As they got to within a few metres of the ground she felt herself tense, her body involuntarily trying to lift itself away from the impact she saw coming. Spencer was alarmed and was shouting something over her shoulder at Drallax, who in turn was shouting something in reply, his face contorted in concentration, his skin having washed out to an almost pure white.

The craft landed heavily, bounced and then spun, as Drallax tried to control it to the ground once more. In a flurry of movement he then flicked and pressed controls until she heard the sound of the engine winding down. All the doors popped open as Drallax then jumped from the craft and ran a few paces before turning back to check on the flyer. She, Spencer and Silvers didn't need further prompting; they all exited with haste and joined Drallax.

"What happened there?" asked Silvers, verbalising what Reeve was thinking herself.

'Engine failure,' responded Drallax, with Spencer translating.

"Lucky this clearing was here," said Spencer. "I wouldn't have liked to try that through the forest canopy."

"I don't want to think about it," said Silvers. "I've crashed enough today. No more crashing please."

"I second that," said Spencer.

"So, how far are we from where we need to be?" she asked. "Where is Pryanthea?"

After a moment of getting his bearings, searching out the Xannix star and walking in a broad circle to survey the glade, Drallax announced, 'This way,' and started off toward the tree line. With a moment's hesitation and a shared look, Silvers shrugged the group question away.

"Let's go," she said, and they started off after him.

*

As they entered the trees, she began to feel uneasy, a creeping sense of being under threat, being watched. She looked at the other two; Spencer was a couple of metres to her right, Silvers had taken point probably more out of habit than a conscious decision. She scanned ahead for Drallax. 'Where's Drallax?' she sent Silvers via bio-comm.

'I don't see him,' he replied, without breaking stride or giving away any body language cues that he was alarmed by the question. 'This was the direction he headed in.'

'Spencer, do you see Drallax?'

There was no response. She looked to her right again. Spencer was gone.

'Form up!' she sent Silvers on an alert channel. Immediately, they were back to back, scanning the trees for any sign of movement, any clue as to what was happening.

'What's going on Lieutenant?' Silvers asked.

'Spencer was right by my side. Damn it! What's happening here?'

In the dusky gloom of the forest, a tall figure stepped out from behind a nearby tree.

'Shouldn't have left those weapons at the crash site,' she sent Silvers.

'Didn't have much choice,' Silvers said in reply. 'It was a big explosion.'

She took a short look over her shoulder at him and noticed him with his short punch knife, 'Knife, to a gunfight?'

'Better than no knife at all,' Silvers stated.

More dark, faceless figures started to appear from the shadows. As she and Silvers circled, the Xannix slowly stepped closer, closing the circle about them and setting the trap. About three meters out they stopped. All of them wore mottled dark garb and a draped hood covered their face. As they had been moving, the camouflage had shifted, the mottled colours bleeding into each other, merging and morphing, at no time giving the viewer a hard line or visually anatomical shape against the background. Not until they had been as close as a few meters had their form started to be seen. Even now, looking at them hurt her eyes. She knew there was a Xannix there, but her brain could not fix the form.

The tallest among the Xannix stepped forward and, raising a hand to his face, removed his hood in an easy, practised motion.

"Hello again, Lieutenant Reeve," said the Xannix.

Liquid ice momentarily ran through her veins. "Captain Yannix," she replied, trying as best she could to mask the shock and surprise, although her emotions quickly tumbled into feelings of hatred and vengeance. The presumed death of Yannix was one of the key reasons for the conflict and fighting which the fleet was now engaged in. Under his direct command, the crew of the *Spixer* had boarded and attacked those aboard the *Intrepid* without provocation. She had lost most of her security team to this Xannix, including some close friends. He had been responsible for the destruction of Tusk One and her crew, and was currently standing a couple of meters away on the day she didn't have a weapon on her. She began to calculate unarmed combat moves utilising long range, lethal strikes, or perhaps a heavy kick to bring him down. Whichever move she used as an option, her mind closed it down with the same final result. She would be too slow, and neither she nor Silvers would come out of the situation alive.

"What have you done with Spencer?" she asked, realising this

Xannix was now speaking fluent Terran.

"No need to be worry, Lieutenant Rivers," he replied. "Your Spencer is sleeping. He will be quite okay." He moved closer, to get a better look at her. His skin flushed a few shades of blue. She could only think that those shades represented a level of smugness which needed to be altered. Of course, she could be wrong, but this situation had smugness written all over it.

"And Drallax?"

Before Yannix had time to reply, a figure stepped to his side, previously out of view and wearing similar camouflage to the others. She wondered how he knew to step forward? Could he understand her? Or was he communicating with Yannix somehow, translating in a similar way to the bio-comm translation Spencer was providing her. She frowned.

"Oh, he is quite okay." Turning to Drallax, he patted him on the shoulder. "Brother Drallax here has been very efficient. By bringing you directly to me he has done the Setak'da a great service. I don't know what Cardinal Ovitala is trying to achieve, but her challenger is not going to succeed. And you are going to ensure that failure."

"What are you talking about? Who is Cardinal Ovitala?"

He nodded. "I see. Your strategy is a risky one, Lieutenant. You can tell me what you know now—the plans to usurp the Setak'da with your own kind—or you can tell me under interrogation. It's your choice."

"Interrogation?" she said, her voice strained with the anger she felt. Yannix had no intention of letting them go. This had been a trap from the start. She saw now. The easy escape, the engine failure just above a discrete clearing in the forest, the only clearing for kilometres. He was treating them as some sort of science experiment. Testing their resourcefulness, their ability to overcome the challenges he placed before them. But again, during this test she had lost more people. Yannix was calculating and without compassion, certainly not towards off-worlders.

Without saying another word, Yannix made a motion with his hand, turned and made his way out of the circle closely followed by Drallax. She should have seen it coming. Before she could make a point of never trusting a Xannix again, the soldier in front of her raised his weapon and fired.

*

Angels sang. It was like a chorus of the most beautiful voices she had ever heard. A constant light flooded her sight all around, although not through open eyes. Her senses were a little confused as she knew her eyes to be closed, but light was everywhere, and she felt herself to be submerged under a warm, soothing water, but she could still breathe. Making sense of her surroundings was something that should be easy, natural, but she could only think that the sensation she was experiencing was similar to being in her mother's womb. Warm, comforting, with soothing noises all around.

"You are awake. Good," came a voice from everywhere. Vibrations which she felt not only as sound in her head but motion to the skin. It was Yannix; his voice enveloped her. The response of her skin was to pimple and chill.

"Where am I?" she asked, the sound of her own speech strange and muffled, like speaking underwater. She tried to concentrate, to relax, her training kicking in. Information is a tool, it can be used and bartered—and it can be a means of escape.

"You are in an Overseer outpost. We have good facilities here. The means to ask you the questions we need the answers to."

She became defiant: "You're wasting your time with me."

"You are behaving like you have a choice in this matter, Lieutenant Reeve. You don't." He was stern in his response. She knew of chemical methods to extract information from people, but even that would yield poor results against a strong enough will. "Shall we start with an easy one? Are you alone?"

"What kind of question is that?"

"It doesn't matter. What matters is only that you answer it. Are you alone?"

"No. I am not alone."

"Do you see others around you?"

She saw nothing but the bright milky light all around her. "No."

"Then, I ask you again. Are you alone?"

"No. I am not alone."

There was a long pause in which she had visions of Yannix straightening in frustration and baring his teeth. When he next spoke, she thought she must have been close with her assertion.

"Lieutenant Reeve, I'm not sure what you intend to achieve by behaving this way."

Another pause.

The pain when it came was like several forms of fire on her skin, all of various shifting intensity. She tried to look at her arms but she could still only see a milky white, nothing came into focus, nothing even cast a shadow. Cries came from deep within, without control or hesitation, and the sound was almost completely internalised. She thrashed wildly, trying to instinctively put out the flames any way she could.

Then, as quickly as the ordeal had begun, it stopped.

She curled into a foetal ball within the fluid about her and started trying to recall childhood songs, people, places, her mother, her father, anything to centre herself and give her a place that was her own.

"Maybe you will respond better to a simpler question. What is your name?"

"Lieutenant Jillian Reeve of the Outer World Exploration Corporation," she said bluntly.

"Good," Yannix said. "Pain has always been an educator." He continued speaking to one of his team in the Xannix tongue, the sound quiet and more remote, but melodious and, to a human ear, almost sung rather than spoken. She had no idea what he was saying but she considered that nothing he was arranging under these circumstances could be good, certainly not to her benefit.

"What is the name of your ship?" he asked without preamble. She considered not answering.

"The *UTS Endeavour.*" Safe information. Information he already knew.

"Set?" he asked, but she had the feeling Yannix was not speaking to her. He then spoke again in his native language. She really wanted to know what he was saying.

Being blind and physically stranded in space, she began to try and think her way out of the situation. Extending her arms, she reached out for any additional sensory information, a boundary which she could work against, a surface to ground and orientate herself. Nothing presented itself. Realising she was in a fluid of some description, she tried to swim and propel herself to the edge of her prison cell.

"What do you think you are doing?" asked the Yannix.

"Getting out of here," she heard herself say. The noise that came back was scratchy, a husky, rasping laugh.

"You may try." He composed himself. "It will do nothing more than tire you. Now, where is your home world?"

She thrashed even harder, kicking to touch an imaginary wall that might only be inches away from her fingertips. There it was. Again the sensation was not what she was expecting, so difficult to translate into her current physical world, but she believed there was a transition, a boundary of sort. She had touched or felt something, and as she processed her senses she thought it felt more like breaking the surface of a rippling pool from beneath, sensing a much less dense air beyond.

The fire returned like a swarm of angry hornets, stinging and lashing at her skin. Her agony was extreme and it completely derailed her mind from any conscious thought. The animal in her core was thrashing around trying to find somewhere to hide, to find a way out of the cage, to escape.

It stopped.

"Thank you," said Yannix. "You call it Earth or Terra. Your journey has been long for an ultimately fruitless end. Pitiful really."

"I told you nothing!" she said, through her exhaustion.

"You have no need to say anything. We can take any answer we choose. We only need ask the question." He seemed distracted again as he had a further discussion with his team.

The situation she found herself in began to reveal its sinister purpose. She had been undergoing some sort of preparation—tests and questions to define some parameters to a machine which, now complete, could read the thoughts straight from her mind. They clearly had the technology to inject thoughts and experiences, Spencer was an example of that, as he was now able to communicate and speak the Xannix language, having been programmed aboard the *Spixer*. She was on the other end of the spectrum: they needed information from her and they were using the same technology in reverse. Feed her a question and read the response from her mind. She could offer no resistance. She could not escape. She had become a human memory cache. She needed to resist, but how do you resist a technology of that kind?

"Now, where is Lieutenant Larsen?"

She had no idea. But she did! She knew how to find out. Before she could think to block the action, she had sent a bio-comm ping to Larsen. It was completely involuntary, her brain, her thought processes, working against her. The ping requested a simple location response and as it was from a legitimate communication source Larsen's responder would send a location without him even knowing about it, unless he had specifically shut out requests of that sort, which she doubted.

A moment later the answer came back. The location was translated into a coordinate reference and shown to her in map form within her bio-comm internal display.

"You are a true source of information, Lieutenant Reeve," Yannix stated, before he started barking orders across his team, his voice raised and vocabulary of a staccato form. She could hear the sound of people mobilising.

In a fit of rage, she began to scream. She had betrayed Larsen without being able to do anything about it. Her own thoughts and automatic brain impulses had colluded to give Yannix exactly what he wanted. Exactly what he knew he would get. She swore to herself that if she ever got the chance again, even if she had no weapon and the odds were stacked against her, Yannix was dead.

ROUX

He sat, slumped and dejected, in his command chair on the bridge. Although the situation may have allowed it, he somehow couldn't bring himself to sit in the captain's chair. He could run the ship just as well from his own couch—all the consoles and control screens were the same, so he had no problem carrying out his duties from the seat he had always used. But taking the captain's chair after the injuries he had caused Clayton just seemed to him to be adding to the insult. He was not that man. He would show the crew that courtesy too. This was an unspoken message that he was not making a move on the captain's position, nor was he taking any advantage of the situation. In his eyes, especially now knowing the hardships Clayton was enduring, the captain deserved his support now more than ever— not to mention Dawn too.

Right now, all he could do was wait. And it was the hardest thing to do. He needed Dawn back online. Obadiah had given him instructions related to what needed doing and he had given the orders without objection.

An icon on his terminal had been flashing. He didn't know how long it had been blinking away but in the dim half-light of the bridge the icon was illuminating his entire command station. He tapped the icon and watched the visual expand to fill the screen. It was Obadiah.

"Commander Roux, are you ready?"

"The medical team is ready. I have my best tech on the job too."

"Good. I have made contact with Dawn and briefed her on the situation. She's not happy, but that's understandable," said Obadiah.

He raised himself in the couch and sat with more purpose. Wearing a mask of sadness, he looked directly at Obadiah. "There have been developments that Dawn must be made aware of before she resumes control of the ship." He ran his hand across his face while considering the best way to deliver the news. There was no easy way. "Her father is in the medical bay receiving treatment for his injuries, received under the influence of an invasive consciousness. The injuries are not life threatening but they are severe. She must be made to understand the circumstances of the situation and be resilient to them. I can't have her back in command of critical ship-wide systems and unstable. That would potentially be worse than leaving the ship to the current AI shell."

"Understood," was all Obadiah replied. Roux believed he was sincere. Too much was at stake and, at this stage, there was nothing to gain by anyone playing politics now. There was a pause of a couple of seconds in the conversation, then Obadiah continued, "She understands. She holds no malice. Although, she is keen to see her father."

"Yes. Good. Then let's get this thing done." He flicked the screen to bring up a visual of a small room somewhere in the cloning facilities of the ship. Pearson was there, his face looming large in the view, as he was working from the terminal in the room and closest to the camera. A couple of metres behind him was a figure dressed head-to-toe in a bright orange surgeon's tunic and scrubs, a clear mask over his face and lights to each side of his temples to shine a focussed light on his subject. He hadn't wanted to call on Dr Roberts's services; he was an obnoxious man and he could really do without his superiority complex and entitlement cutting across the situation. But he needed his skill set. He would just have to keep Roberts on a short leash.

As if caught by surprise and in mid flow, Pearson realised the camera was on. He was expecting the call but, as techs can get quite engrossed in their work, it took him a moment to switch his attention. "Sir. Commander," he stammered.

"Pearson. We are ready. Please ask Dr Roberts to proceed."

"Yes, sir."

As Pearson turned to pass on Roux's message, Roberts

announced to the room, "I heard him Technician. These new ears are wonderful. I can hear a whisper at twenty metres. I should be rejuvenated more often. Unlike this poor fellow," he casually indicated to a cloning tank in the centre of the room.

The tank was about 2.5 metres long with a control bank of switches, lights and small screens along one side, each for a very specific life support function. Lights flickered indicating data flow, screens oscillated with heart rate traces and data stated the current vitals. The name of the occupant was Sub-Lieutenant Paul Travis.

"Of course, in his current transitional state he really shouldn't be woken from stasis. Are you certain this is the only course of action left to us Commander?" Roberts asked.

"I am certain, Doctor. And may I remind you that time is critical. It's one thing we have little of." He felt himself beginning to become impatient with Roberts, and they had only exchanged a few short words. He tried to stay professional. "If you would proceed. We need the information that man holds."

"Okay, Commander. Starting the resuscitation process. Merging his wave to brain function…now."

He saw Roberts set to work, his hands lightly dancing across the keys and controls of the cloning tank. Then, with practised effort, he engaged and locked a couple of drainage tubes, which, after a few moments, could be seen to evacuate the amniotic fluid from around the partially formed body inside.

"I can ease his discomfort a little, but his skin layer is not yet properly formed, and his eyes will be overly sensitive. Being exposed to the harshness of this environment at this stage will be brutal," stated Roberts, again seemingly speaking to the room rather than anyone specific.

"Sir," injected Pearson, "this is the last Travis clone available. If this doesn't work, there's no way I can see of obtaining the information you require."

"Then this better work, Pearson," Roux said, firmly.

"Yes, sir."

The amniotic fluid had drained away and Dr Roberts was now standing at the foot of the canister. He pressed a final button and there was a clunk and hiss as the pressure inside the tank equalised with the atmosphere in the room. The full length lid of the tank raised about five centimetres and then swung in a controlled mechanical motion around to an upright position at the head of the container.

Pearson enabled a headcam he had taken from his kit and the broadcast link was now streaming to Roux's terminal. The screen showed the dim light of the room, presumably set lower than normal to reduce pain to Travis's underdeveloped eyes, but with the added effect of the uneasy mount of the camera, the entire scene took on a sinister appearance. As Pearson got closer, Roux got his first vision of the clone. In the half-light the slick residue of the of the remaining amniotic fluid glistened off the emaciated form; his legs and arms were stick thin, and ribs poked through the paper skin, which showed capillaries and veins like roads on a map. A synthetic coiled umbilical cord wound its way to a nutrition regulator in the side of the tank. Travis' head seemed overly large for the body to which it was attached, eye sockets and cheeks sunken and dark. Roux had to look away.

"Better to make the data link before I bring him round," Dr Roberts said to Pearson, who just nodded a response, forgetting the headcam was attached. To Roux, the whole room shook momentarily.

Pearson moved round to stand by Roberts as he made the incision near Travis's right temple, revealing the socket to his bio-comm wetware. "Connecting," Pearson stated, as Roux could see the small micro terminal start to scroll text at speed and report the connection process in minutia. "All set."

"Okay, Doctor," Roux said. "Let's wake him up."

Dr Roberts made his way back round to the pod's control panel and pressed a sequence of buttons. Travis's body flexed and arched wildly, then he gasped and took his first lungful of air. Instantly, Travis was in trouble, after coughing and expelling excess amniotic fluid, his lungs tried to breath but were not able to properly extract the required oxygen. Although the autonomic reflex may have been operating, inflating and deflating, the lung walls were feeble. Dr Roberts started altering controls and adjusting oxygen levels to Travis through the umbilical system to account for his failed lungs. Travis calmed.

"You should ask him your questions quickly, Commander," stated Dr Roberts.

Travis looked straight at the doctor with wide unfocussed eyes, trying to see who had spoken, only to recoil at the bright spotlights the doctor was wearing.

"Travis," Roux said, amplified through the room's terminal speakers and the mobile console Pearson was operating. It confused Travis, who began to look in all directions trying to isolate the source. "Travis, this is Commander Roux. Do you understand me?"

Travis's lips moved to emit a croaky whisper. "Yes." Pearson turned up the receiving mic on his console to a level audible to Roux. The effort of speaking was clearly causing Travis some pain.

"We don't have long Travis. We know you injected some code to interrupt the working of the AI. You believe this was done to aid GAIA. In that, you were successful." A smile of smug satisfaction spread across Travis's face, then into a grimace and a cough as fluid build-up in his lungs began to irritate. "What you didn't know was the true source of that code. You have been set up, Travis. OWEC have set you up to take the fall for their own plotting and scheming." He could see Travis's distress increasing, his heart-rate monitor and physical body language confirming it. He had begun to squirm in the bed, tears welling in his eyes, and his smug satisfaction turning to anger, grief, revenge.

"No," Travis coughed.

"We need to drain his lungs," Dr Roberts stated. "He's drowning in fluid build-up."

"Wait. He needs to speak," he said to the doctor. "Yes, Travis. You have a chance to make amends. You can save those who need you now. We need you now, Travis. You need to give us the passcode to the injected AI malware."

There was silence for a moment while Travis struggled to breath and his eyes rolled in pain. From the mobile-console Pearson was holding, he could see Travis's life signs failing.

Travis's lips began to move but the mic on the terminal didn't pick up the sound.

"What was that Travis? You need to speak up," he said as softly and with as much encouragement as he could, given the rising panic he was beginning to feel, as Travis's heart began to fail under the physical and mental stress of the situation. "Speak up, Travis."

His lips continued to move. Pearson leaned right in and put his ear to Travis's face, the consequence of which was that Roux had a clear and close view of Dr Roberts's surgery gown. The screen went orange.

"'Zoe'. Sir, he's just saying 'Zoe' over and over," said Pearson.

"Who's Zoe?"

"He's delirious," stated the doctor. "The brain starts spitting out all kinds of rubbish as it begins to die."

"She's his wife," he informed them. "Anything else? A code? Sequence of numbers?"

Pearson tried to get close enough to listen to Travis again, but Travis began to convulse. "He's going into a seizure," said Roberts. "Step back. You might want to detach the console connection," he indicated to Pearson, nodding in the direction of the hardlink to Travis's bio-comm. Pearson swiftly unplugged his console and stepped back a pace, giving Roux a wider view of the scene. Travis was yelling now and screaming wildly, eyes rolled back, so only a pair of white orbs could be seen within his sunken features, giving a demonic, possessed appearance.

Roux could now clearly hear the word Travis was repeating, distorted and harsh, as blood started to spray from his mouth while his fragile vocal chords and throat began to lacerate in the effort and strain his tortured body inflicted on itself. The thrashing convulsions were severe and Roberts worked quickly. "I don't think you're going to get any more from him, Commander."

He ran his hands through his hair then slapped the couch in frustration at the speed at which Travis had degraded. "Okay. Pearson, you have the wave of this session recorded?"

"Yes, sir."

"Then, you can terminate the clone, Doctor. Pearson, I want you and the data on the bridge in five minutes."

He closed the connection and sat back staring out at the main tactical screen. The view of Xannix below and the Xannix star behind it was prominent; for a moment, it's blue and green colouring took his mind away from the now and back to memories of Earth. It was like his mind was trying to escape the realities of what he had just had to order. He wondered when the life of a clone had become so cheap. His conscience argued against him; the lives of the fleet, potentially of the remaining human species, outweighed the life of a single clone. Travis had sealed his own fate the moment he had signed up with GAIA. This was not on him.

*

The briefing room felt in some way contaminated. Seated in the front row, looking towards the steps up to the dais, he couldn't help but feel unnerved, his mind filling in the echo of Clayton laying there, crippled and in agony by his actions. Even knowing the circumstances didn't absolve him from the guilt he felt. The nagging doubt was that he should have known, should have picked up on the change in character, the unreasonable demands and orders of a man he had known for years. But then, what would have happened? He might have drawn out the encounter earlier and at a point in the battle with the Xannix where the outcome would have been self-destructive. The only thing he felt they had going for them at the moment was the fact that the Xannix appeared to be regrouping and monitoring them from a distance, perhaps with the sole intent of letting the closing trap of satellites do their job, but it meant they were leaving them alone long enough to sort out their immediate crisis.

Clayton's echo was replaced by the emaciated form of Travis's ghost. His mind seemed to be spiralling through the events of the last few hours, tormenting him and highlighting his failings. Travis had told them nothing, screaming and gargling his last while drowning in the fluid mucus of his own lungs. He knew Dr Roberts could expand on the biological deconstruction of Travis in his last moments, but he didn't need the detail. He was haunted enough by the fact that they had to interrogate a clone in a partially grown state in the first place. Even though clone-wave splicing was a new technology, he could already sense the value of life diminishing, as people considered death nothing more than an interruption of service and equally that their clones were simply a vehicle, like a car or flyer to be driven and traded in when the old one was a little worn out. It wasn't quite at that point yet, as clones took time to grow and people could be in stasis for many years before they could be hosted within their new body. But the social mental adjustment was happening by degrees.

His thoughts were interrupted. The door to the briefing room slid open and Pearson marched in at pace, sweat on his brow and mini-console tucked under his arm. He'd clearly made the effort to be with Roux as soon as physically possible. He broke into a jog on the walkway to the main display terminal in the room and started work the instant he got there, the screen flicking to life and lines of instruction already processing down the screen.

"Sir," Pearson said in a breathless voice, "I think I may have it."

He got up instantly to cross the room and stand with Pearson. "Explain," he said, momentarily wondering if that had been wise. Being a tech, conversations with Pearson could get very detailed very quickly.

"On my way here, I thought I'd get some work done. You know, preparation. Anyway, I couldn't understand why Travis just kept on saying his wife's name."

"Zoe?"

"Yes. It could have been as the doctor said, the fixation of a dying man to the love of his life. But why her, over and over? Why didn't he wander around? How about his mother? Did he have kids? They might have been on the list. But he stayed on his wife." Pearson spoke while multitasking and running the mobile-console feed into the display terminal and running both, one with his left hand, one with his right. Roux considered that he had trouble enough with one console.

"So, the fact he kept repeating his wife's name is the key we are after?"

"No, well, yes," said Pearson in an excited tone, his eyes darting between different sets of data on the screens in front of him and his bio-comm retinal display.

"Well, which is it?"

"His wife's name was a key, but not *the* key." He made some final adjustments and then, "Voilà!" he said, stepping back and indicating the screen to Roux with an open palm. Roux looked at the screen and the text which Pearson had highlighted. It was complete nonsense and left him looking baffled.

"Pearson, I'm not a tech. This means nothing to me. What am I looking at?" He was trying hard to contain his frustration.

"It's an old RSA encrypted file; simple but very powerful."

"RSA encrypted file?"

"Yes. Rivest, Shamir and Adleman—a clever bunch of mathematicians. Primes to the power of primes, but that's not important. I found it within his bio-comm. It was pretty buried, but that's what you'd expect, right? And it's called 'Zoe'."

"So, you then opened the file?"

"No. It needed a second parameter. Turned out to be an image of his kids in his personal cache." The pause that followed sang loud in the room. Pearson stopped his presentation and looked at Roux like he had lost something, then as he caught up he blurted,

"And then I opened the file."

Roux just smirked and shook his head. "We could do with some good news right now. Obadiah, are you hearing this?"

"Thank you, Commander," responded Obadiah. "I've already accessed the key. Applying now."

The lights went out.

*

It had taken longer than he had liked, but then at this point in time everything took longer than he liked. The emergency lights should have come on instantly, but they hadn't. He had frozen to the spot, not quite knowing what to expect, but the sudden sense of dizziness and nausea which accompanied the loss of artificial gravity reinforced his fears. Obadiah had confirmed that, with Travis's key, he would be able to quarantine the malware and remove Dawn from her isolation. What Obadiah had also told him was that there would be a sequential shutdown and restart of all AI node centres, including the core, to limit the impact of restarting major systems. What he hadn't known or couldn't foresee was how this would interrupt systems across the ship. Badly, was the answer.

The moment systems went offline he fired off an emergency link to the officer of the watch. Commander Holt was on the bridge and under stress. 'Holt. Status!'

Holt's response was immediate, 'Sir, we've lost bridge control to all sections, helm, engineering and weapons. We have no external view; we have no comms. We're dead in the water, sir.'

"Well, that's just dandy, Obi!" he said through gritted teeth. 'Okay, Holt, start getting the scientific and medical crew to their muster stations, send out the message via bio-comm relay if you have to, but I want all non-critical personnel ready to evacuate this ship at a moment's notice.'

'Aye, sir.'

"Pearson?" he called into the dark, forgetting that Pearson had been standing right in front of him.

"Yes, sir?"

"Solutions now."

"We need to be in the AI core."

"Then that's where we go."

LARSEN

"Something has happened. What's happened? Ovitala?"

He was suspended within one of the ancient Xannix machines they called the Arch-sa. From what he was experiencing, it was the ultimate haptic suit—one which gave him advanced command and control of almost any networked object or system across the Xannix worlds. It felt like being elevated to a godlike status within a world and culture he knew little about. Ovitala had said that he was ready, that there would be learning, that he would soon take on the Setak'da for supremacy of Xannix and its people, but he had found little of that. Instead, he had been plunged into battle.

At first he had been overwhelmed: his senses bombarded by information from all directions, and physical and mental stimuli battering him—much of which he could not understand. However, the machine adjusted quickly, filtering some information, realigning other streams of data and finally the world around him began to take form. Floating in an elevated position above a battlefield and a battle which had already begun, his forces very apparently on the defensive and without cohesive command. His command. They were floundering.

But he wasn't a battlefield tactician, and he wasn't even a soldier—he was an engineer. He started to wonder how he was going to help these people. The responsibility started to weigh on his mind and distract him from action. And it was action that was needed. He chided himself and began to reassert some self-control. He was the field commander for these people; he would use the skills he had, and that's all he could do.

As he began to pull ideas to mind, he realised that, of all the hells he had been through these last few days, he had been with Silvers almost the whole time. The horrors of the *Intrepid* had been brutal but he had survived. How had he survived? What would Silvers do?

Silvers had known when to hide, when to be aggressive, when to be sly and when to lay a trap. A trap. He could build a trap, a construct, a logical maze which he had to work through every day. He would set a trap.

The battlefield before him was baffling: a whirlwind of chaos and death. But from the, now ordered, stream of information which he was presented with, he began to find data that he could use: combat and situation reports from those in the thick of it, and the status of war machines across the specified region of the fight. His forces were talking to him; he needed to respond and coordinate the line, define the engagement and stop the bloodshed.

Next was the crude problem of interaction—how was he to relay his instructions?—but that answer came in an instant and at the speed of thought. No sooner had he thought about moving to strike a target, than the action had been relayed and a volley of artillery hailed like rain to obliterate the object he had designated. He didn't need to think *how* to do it, only that it needed to be done and the commanders on the ground took care of the detail.

Reflexively, he would duck and dodge explosions, missiles or aircraft and this in turn moved his point of view around the field. He was finally working his way around the battlefield in all three dimensions without the mechanical step-by-step processing which all students go through; he slipped into full control of the Arch-sa within a minute of being thrown into the maelstrom.

It took a collision with an Overseer flyer for him to realise his full potential within the ancient machine. He had been completely blind-sided by it. Dropping out of the sun as it headed for a ground target, it had caught him completely unaware and off guard. The roar of sound building like a wailing siren, he had turned at the last moment to witness the impact. Feeling his heart almost leap from his chest the flyer had simply accelerated on to its target, a momentary shadow cast deep across his view, nothing more. He gasped at the shock but realised the reality. He turned to the departing flyer and lashed out in anger, swiping a backhanded punch toward it, yelling away his frustration. A lancing beam of orange erupted from a battery of surface units and the flyer evaporated in a cloud of green-black.

In this environment, he was omnipotent.

He got to work. The first thing he did was delegate command. He identified the highest-ranking Xannix Seeker on the field and gave him responsibility for tactics and implementation. He, of course, would and could intervene at any time, but for the moment he had other things to do. Bringing up a schematic of the battlefield, he put out a request for all comms information across the field for all Overseer units. He didn't care that he couldn't see the content of the information—it didn't concern him, yet. The map sprung to life and was overlaid visually across the Arch-sa sphere. Instantly, he saw command structures and data hubs; he noted these for later. Building an inverted tree, he traced the information flow back to its source. There were four. Even he could work out the symbolic nature of the Overseer command structure. But he didn't find what he was looking for.

Tagging the four command vehicles—three on the ground, one in the sky, all mobile—he proceeded to scan further afield, turning the focus of his search outward. He watched the now visible comms traces like a hunter waiting for its prey. Nothing. He needed a distraction or an unexpected event to trigger his trap. It was now set.

He ordered a mass withdrawal, splitting his forces into two and setting way points for the new line. Such a radical move may be ignored by the Seekers under his command, he hadn't considered that option until now, but thankfully every unit did as it was instructed. He was thankful they were well disciplined.

And there it was; it was only momentary, but it was like a flare to him: a line of communication initiated by his illogical tactical move. The Setak'da, either to intercede and give orders or simply to find out what was happening, had broken the silence and was now speaking with the field commander. He isolated the channel the Setak'da was using and started to piggyback the comms, analysing the stream and bringing the power of the Arch-sa to bare on cracking the carrier signal. Again, he was less interested in the verbal communication, more the system protocol. What he wanted was the identifier of the Arch-sa the Setak'da was using.

His attack was not a direct attack on the content of the comms, but more a slant attack at the protocol wrapper, and, as he anticipated, the identifier he was searching for popped up. The hack had been successful. He fed this information into his Arch-sa and instantly he obtained a geographical location of the Setak'da. His trap was closing.

He ordered his forces to re-engage, but to harry and hassle the Overseers, not to engage in force, which they did to great efficiency.

His opponent seemed not to like this new action but as the comms channel lit up again to give further orders he now closed the trap. From the limited knowledge he had gleaned from the Arch-sa, he had found that there were many and they were the same, as such internal commands of these ancient machines would be the same: data structures would be the same, protocols the same. Taking a moment to quell any last seconds of self-doubt, he calmed himself, then instigated the final command. A small packet of data traced back up the comms channel towards the Xannix Setak'da, an insignificant instruction racing across the ether to the heart of the target Arch-sa.

The command arrived unnoticed, logged as routine traffic, and under the veil of a common process. It was executed immediately, consumed by the target system and within an instant the Setak'da's Arch-sa disappeared from the network.

The effect was immediate confusion in the enemy, only for a moment, but it turned the Setak'da's offensive force into a defensive one. His commanders took the initiative and pushed for the kill. Having identified the four commanders earlier, they now began to target each in turn, and after each had been destroyed they moved on to destroying the next command node in turn. The result was that the opposing force disintegrated before them. Without strong leadership, the command structure buckled; with weaker and less-experienced officers in the face of a now much larger and aggressive force, the Overseers began to split up and flee. Only a few a first, but within a minute the drip had become a torrent, a rout.

Hysteria broke out in the sphere and among those on the battlefield. Unable to contain their joy at what they had just witnessed, the Xannix were making all manner of noises and sounds in fanfare to their success. He slumped forward and hung limply from the Arch-sa device for a few moments, letting the relief he felt flow over him. The clammy feeling of cold sweat between his skin and his clothes made itself known, as a bead ran down his forehead to the end of his nose; he watched as it dropped and disappeared into the depths of the sphere.

Then things changed. The world before his eyes started to fall away, spiral and twist and become otherly. Colours became fractal and peeled away to reveal another place, like opening a portal to a dark sanctum of crimsons and black. In the centre, there was a single figure dressed totally in crimson and with the inverted delta icon of the Overseers in the centre of its chest.

"Something has happened. What's happened? Ovitala?" he said over his shoulder as the portal extended towards him and began to envelop him. "Ovitala?" he shouted, but there was no response.

The visual coalesced as he left Ovitala and Rivers behind, his focus now locked completely on the figure before him like a beacon in the new world. The crimson figure walked gracefully toward him and, as it did so, a walkway appeared in sections, extending before them to within a couple of metres of his position. Almost by instinct, he tried to back away but realised he was still locked into the armature of the Arch-sa. Although completely dead and unmoving, the armature still existed and locked him in place, elevated into the centre of a huge spherical space: he was trapped.

Walking from the shadows into the pool of light around him was a slender humanoid figure, but not Xannix. She had beautiful elven features and porcelain white skin, dark jet eyes and striking ears which had skin stretched in a triangular shape from the lower ear to a long 10-centimetre, ridged antenna-like upper ear, which twitched and moved in a way reminiscent of a cats tail. Stopping just short of the end of the walkway, she tilted her head to one side and examined him closely, running her eyes from his feet to his face. He could not read her expression, it was blank, but her eyes radiated hatred, and when she spoke it was with soft venom.

"So, you are the creature they set against me?" She looked him over for another few moments. "What do they call you?"

His mind was racing. There was little he could do. It didn't seem to matter what he tried, he was completely locked out of the Arch-sa systems; there was no control and no power—he was marooned with this creature. With no discernible way to defend himself, he considered other options. After whittling the list down in his mind, he settled on fact finding. Extract as much information as he could; give as little away as he could.

"Larsen. Lieutenant Luc Larsen."

As he spoke, he noticed a small spherical object floating up and to the left of her. It had a central light and an offset lens, and to its right side was what looked like a small, mounted weapon extending from its inside. It looked no bigger than a tennis ball. He noted a couple more attached and dormant on a strap toward her shoulder, each smooth with no protrusions. It watched him intently.

She was tall, softly spoken and intense. Her black opal eyes were completely distracting, mesmerising. The intelligence behind them appeared to be picking him apart piece by piece; she was dissecting him.

"You were able to shut down my Arch-sa. Clever little creature too, Lieutenant Luc Larsen."

She moved even closer, the walkway extending behind and beyond him as she did so. Seeming to have no understanding of personal space, she moved in close, her face only centimetres from his. Feeling her breath on his skin, she continued to examine the human male before her. If she was trying to intimidate him, it was working. He had broken out into a soft sweat and, in an effort to escape, he could sense his feet feeling for the walkway he knew to be below him, although with their height difference he was still clear of the floor by 30 centimetres or more. With a deep inward breath, she even seemed to be analysing his scent. He needed to divert her attention; move her away so that he could reclaim some of his reasoning. Being petrified was not something which would help him in the next few moments.

Trying to muster as much confidence as he could, he looked directly into her eyes. "If you are not Xannix, who are you? What are you?" She smirked, a small curl and dimple playing at the corner of her mouth. His mind began to drift into questions, the foremost being why were the two apex alien species they had encountered in the space of as many weeks both of humanoid form? There were slight variations, but basically they were both bipeds with opposable thumbs, central symmetry with visual and auditory perception designed for hunting. Maybe the universe solved similar problems in similar ways—he believed the scientists called it convergent evolution.

"Have they not plugged you into their learning machine? I would have thought you would already know the answer to that question. I am Zantanath; they call me their Setak'da but my given name is Celicia." She watched his response, which was a deep look of confusion. "Yes. Interesting, isn't it?" her eyebrow flicked quizzically. She was enjoying this. "They now war over two to lead them, neither of which are of their own species."

"Why?" was all he could ask.

"It has always been. It is a relationship of symbiosis. It is to our mutual benefit. Until now, of course. Your appearance has given them some interest in you as a species. They want to set your kind against mine to discover the stronger." She paused then stepped back, appearing to have completed her assessment. "But I see in your species nothing of consequence." Without acknowledgement, she turned and walked back into the shadows followed by her small spherical muse. As she left, the space around him began to dissolve and large sparks of electricity arced across his vision, spreading the smell of ionised air. The sphere finally collapsed toward him in a cascade of pain which sent his whole body into spasm. The sound of his own guttural screaming filled the space around and through him until the darkness took him.

RIVERS

The jubilation had been intoxicating—all the Xannix clasping hands and punching the air, their skin flaring all the colours of the rainbow to express their excitement. But in the still bubble of her world she was focussed on the anomaly which had begun to appear in front of Larsen: a small, silvery, shimmering ball which slowly expanded towards Larsen. The power to his rig appeared to shut down and although she couldn't hear him, she could see he was looking around, possibly saying or shouting something inaudible. She looked around urgently to find Ovitala and found her a couple of metres away congratulating some senior technicians.

"Ovitala," she called, the level of confusion she felt coming across in her voice. Ovitala clearly couldn't hear her, so she pressed the matter. "Ovitala!"

The conversation interrupted, Ovitala and all the others who had been in earshot of her outburst stopped talking and looked at her. Speaking to Ovitala in a raised voice was clearly a unique event for the observers. Rather than explain herself, she simply pointed at Larsen and the shimmering mirrored sphere which had now engulfed him.

Eyes went wide and someone called out, "Zantanath!" The Xannix broke into a panic of action, some leaping back to their workstations, some heading for the exits. Ovitala spoke quickly to the two senior techs closest to her then turned to Rivers.

"Come. Now."

Striding from the observation area, they headed out across the

216

command floor and towards the opposite side of the sphere and an elevator. Although she knew Ovitala to be an older Xannix, she still had to run to keep up with her, her stride far wider and her pace urgent. Reaching the elevator, which was not much more than a platform with a control console against the far wall, the two Xannix who had been with them a moment before rejoined them, this time carrying a red pack each slung across their shoulders. As soon as they were aboard the platform, Ovitala hit the control console and the elevator began to traverse around the spheres wall and up towards a gantry at the level Larsen had been, but now where a mirrored globe floated.

The two Xannix were off the platform and running towards the anomaly before it had completely stopped. As they ran, a gantry began to almost magically build and form in a path towards Larsen and the globe. They stopped about three meters short of the object and began to hastily unpack their kit bags.

"What are they doing?" she asked Ovitala.

"Neutralising the trans-dimensional field. We will have Lieutenant Larsen back in a moment," Ovitala said, without taking her eyes from the work the other Xannix were performing.

"What are you talking about? What's a trans-dimensional field?"

"It's a means of opening gateways between physical locations."

"Are you talking about spacetime gateways? Wormholes?"

"Sorry, child Rivers. I'm not sure what you call them. To us, it's a trans-dimensional field," Ovitala said, as she stepped from the platform and paced quickly to the technicians. Being slightly dumbfounded, it took her a moment to catch up. She was experiencing scientific paralysis—her mind a hurricane of possibilities and questions over the latest input—and at the same time she was conflicted by the need to get Larsen back. She didn't want this trans-dimensional bubble to disappear; she needed to study it, understand how it existed and worked. Larsen would understand.

What was she thinking?

One of the Xannix turned to Ovitala. They had set up what looked like a two-pronged fork on a tripod which attached to a small power cell. "Ready," he said. Ovitala just shimmered a cyan colour; he mirrored the response. Turning back to the device, he triggered a control and lightning jumped in what seemed uncontrolled traces across the space between them and the trans-dimensional field. The effect was instantaneous. The disruptor device tore at the fabric of the globe in front of them, crackling and buzzing as the cohesion of the field failed and the image of Larsen inside returned to them.

As the shimmering globe ebbed and faded, the last of the trans-dimensional field was gone, and replacing it was the alarming scream of Larsen himself. With the field gone, the technician stopped the device and, in doing so, the electrical arcing and the sound suddenly ceased. Larsen hung like a rag doll from the machine arm, head forward and wet with sweat. Rivers ran to him, as did the two technicians.

"Larsen!" she shouted. She couldn't reach his face but she grabbed his hand and shook his arm, just trying for a response, any sign that he was still alive. There was no response. "Get him out of this thing," she insisted, looking back to the technicians. They had already begun the process but both shimmered blue in an affirming response.

Unclipping harnesses, releasing sections of shielding and unhooking cabling, they finally lowered Larsen to the gangway. As he lay there, she took his head in her hands and cradled his quiet features while looking for signs of life. Moving closer, she tried to find a pulse—it was faint but there. She let go of her nervous tension and dropped her head in relief and, in doing so, accidently butted Larsen on the nose. It elicited a groan in response.

"Sorry!" she said in shock at her own misjudgement. "Larsen, can you hear me? Larsen?" She patted him gently on the cheek.

"Stop hitting me," he said, quietly.

"Oh. Yes. Sorry," she said, a little embarrassed. Then she hit him again on the chest, this time out of playful frustration. "Larsen, you worried the hell out of me. What do you think you were doing up here?"

"Having a meeting with the current Setak'da. Only, she's not Xannix and turns out she's not very nice either."

"Not very nice?" she said exasperated. "Are you going to tell me what's going on, or not?"

He tried to move, but winced and held his head. "Yeah, but we need to have a serious chat with Ovitala. Damn, my head hurts."

"Yes. Yes, we do," said Ovitala, now standing by their side. "This way."

*

One of the technicians had assisted Larsen in walking to the elevator and down to the command deck as they left the other to arrange a work detail to fix the Arch-sa. She had insisted on helping and had taken hold of his left arm; supporting him across her shoulders, she and the Xannix tech relieved some of the weight as Larsen put one foot slowly in front of the other. At times it felt as if the Xannix was lifting Larsen clear off the floor, but finally they lowered him onto what looked much more like a saddle than a chair positioned in front of a display screen. Taking up a position to his side, she put a supporting hand on his shoulder to keep him from toppling. It seemed a natural thing to do, and she didn't think anything of it, until Ovitala leaned casually against the workstation looking them over. She suddenly felt self-conscious, as if caught doing something she shouldn't. It was more an annoyance in being caught doing something which Ovitala had predicted. Whatever feelings she had rolling around inside, they were none of Ovitala's business. Regardless, it bothered her.

She decided to go on the offensive and change the context of the situation.

"Ovitala, did you know this might happen?"

"It was a possibility," Ovitala conceded. "But, the risk was small. There was no way for Celicia to know our location."

"But this Celicia found out anyway." It was more a statement than a question.

"Yes. Yes, she did." For the first time since meeting her, Rivers thought she saw a moment of doubt in Ovitala as she was lost in her thoughts. It passed quickly.

"So Larsen is expendable?"

"That's not what I said. It was a risk, yes." Ovitala drew a deep breath then made a decision. "But I've been a little less than honest with you."

"What a surprise," she replied. Larsen lifted a hand to his shoulder, held her hand and squeezed gently. It took the temper out of her immediately.

"Why?" asked Larsen. "There has been conflict since we arrived. There has to be a reason for it."

"Yes. And in truth," she paused again and looked across at Aldaan. He stood to their side, but had moved into place so quietly neither she nor Larsen had noticed. Aldaan looked grave and his skin hue moved to a dark grey and blue, clearly sombre tones for the subject. Ovitala responded with the same colour to her skin, then continued. "It has been this way ever since I can remember, and I am now an old Xannix. How I got to be this age is more luck and the effort of others, but I am here and we do our part.

"The Zantanath arrived about two hundred cycles ago. The Xannix at the time were a thriving species. We had spread our wings and colonised five other planets through our region of space, a prosperous trade between all of them. People were happy, life was progressive and we were outward looking, searching for the next planet to extend our operations and people into. But in our explorations we encountered the Zantanath.

"Things began to change. We had pleasant and cordial contact to begin with, but there was something malicious about them. Nothing you could put your finger on, just a sense you had when you were in their presence, like a creeping dread. They began to trade, and we had some technological advances gifted to us: trans-dimensional fields, ultra-efficient power generation, improved star drives for our planetary fleets. They came bearing gifts and we took them all. But it was all part of the trap.

Ovitala appeared almost overcome as she told the story. Aldaan moved to her side to provide support, and he offered his hand. She looked at him sadly. "We all need this. Everyone needs help at some time," he said quietly. "Our time is now."

"But what can they do?"

"They seem a strong and wilful species. But at the moment, we don't know. We haven't asked."

Her face became stern and full of intent. She stood with an added determination and nodded to Aldaan. She continued.

"The Zantanath are cunning and sly. They used our customs against us. They promised wealth and power to some within our ruling elite and challenged the Setak'da. Those loyal to the incumbent voiced that the challenge was illegal as the challenger was not Xannix, but the Zantanath had bought enough loyalty to sway the vote. The Zantanath won the right to challenge as the Setak'osso and they made the old Setak'da pay heavily, relinquishing his position and his wealth. The old Setak'da was sent into exile on the Zantanath home world and treated as a figure of fun to be humiliated by them as they lauded their bloodless victory.

They didn't even fire a shot. We walked ourselves into servitude."

Ovitala's skin had gone quite white during her retelling of her people's history. Aldaan stayed quiet. She was clearly distressed and in a rage.

"But," she attempted to calm herself, "that was a long time ago. Now we have an opportunity. Those of us who believe and have prayed for generations now see a chance that our calls for freedom have been heard. Our ancestors have sent you and it would be wrong if we did not ask you for help now you are here."

Aldaan turned a hue of gentle blue to show his agreement with Ovitala's statement. "Yes. It is a heavy request, but we are too weak after all this time to do what must be done. However, you have no such history. You have shown yourselves to be strong and resilient. We ask you now, will you help?"

There was a silence. Larsen and Rivers could hardly understand what was being asked of them. They looked at each other for a moment in disbelief.

"Would you mind if we had some time alone to discuss this?" asked Larsen, who stood as firmly as he could and led Rivers to the edge of the command platform.

"I can see it in your eyes," she said in a harsh whisper. "You're actually considering this? It's madness. We have no idea what we're getting into. A moment ago they were trying to kill us, the fleet is still up there and we have no idea what's happening there. And we don't have the authority to make this decision on our own. This is one for Clayton."

Larsen just watched her; clearly all the arguments she had rattled off were issues he had already considered.

"On top of that," she continued, "I don't know if you noticed while you were in it, but these Zantanath appear to have a pretty good grip on wormhole technology. Local wormhole technology too. We are generations away from that type of tech. There is no way we can help the Xannix in a straight-up fight against the Zantanath; we're totally outclassed."

"I know."

"We also have no idea what their military capability is, as we've only ever seen the Xannix. We would be blundering around in the dark; we need far more information to make an informed..." She stopped herself. Larsen's words seemed to have only just reached her. She blinked at him. "You know?"

"Yes," he said kindly.

"So why are we having this conversation?"

"Well, I know something you don't."

"Oh? And what is that?"

"How to defeat the Zantanath."

ROUX

With the gravity off-line, he and Pearson floated in the AI core room. He anchored himself by a hand grip, and Pearson had hooked a foot through a rail, leaving both his hands free to work. Somehow he always remembered the room bigger; today it felt claustrophobic and enclosed, as if the walls had all moved a metre towards its centre. Looking over Pearson's shoulder, Pearson was doing what Pearson did best, and that was to effectively walk around inside the machine and be his eyes and ears in a world he didn't understand at all. The console in front of both of them flickered with information, high-speed rendering which he could hardly read, but Pearson's enhanced innate retinal processing provided him with a speed-reading facility that Roux simply couldn't match. All techs had this ability; it was not something you could learn, it was a *gift* – so they said.

His link to the bridge was active, and his bio-comm was feeding live streaming data from his chair on the bridge to his retinal display. As far as his crew were concerned, he was in two places at once. It was a neat trick, although mentally taxing, but he needed to be here; when Dawn came back online he needed to speak with her directly, then he would need to be on the bridge in a hurry. It was not far to run but every second would count.

The urgency was all due to the Xannix defence network. The thing that they had erroneously called the communication jamming network had shown its teeth and its true intent. It was a web for the spider and they had unwittingly become the fly. In fifteen minutes they would be within what they estimated to be the network's weapons range and they were still dead in space. Asher had done a number on them. He was currently swinging wildly between anger, wanting to blast Asher back to the Stone Age, and the guilt he had in having done Clayton real injury while learning the truth about Asher. He only wished there was something he could do for Clayton. But knowing he only had minutes before they could potentially all be dead, he tried to focus on the task at hand. The best he could do for Clayton was to see that they all lived to see another day. Right now, not seeing that new day was a real possibility.

Systems had slowly been coming back online since the blackout. Life support and emergency systems first, no navigation or propulsion, and no Dawn. The AI Core room they floated in was bathed in a low amber glow from the floor and ceiling emergency lighting; deep shadows and darkness seemed to close in and reminded him of the ship as it was years before during construction. He had been overseeing various elements of the ship's build, and several weeks before they switched her on, the *Endeavour* had been quite ghostly. He now expected to see the faces of those they had all left behind moving through the corridors, haunting his every decision. Once or twice he had been convinced, but he knew it was only his mind playing tricks and messing with the shadows as he walked.

"There," said Pearson under his breath. Then a few moments later, "Yes. There she is."

"Who?" he asked dumbly.

"Dawn. She's back. I'm monitoring her core dynamic code base, and it's beginning to shift as expected. The malicious lines of code have been stripped out. She's her own boss again."

He found himself excited, adrenaline coursing round his veins.

"How long before she's operational again?"

Pearson just looked at him with a smug smirk on his face, nodding to the space behind him and indicating he should take a look.

"Hello, Commander Roux," said Dawn.

Gravity suddenly took hold as systems came back online, causing him to stumble as his weight applied itself to the floor, his feet not quite in position and his body not expecting the sudden change.

"Hello Dawn," he replied as he turned to face her. "No real time to catch up I'm afraid. I hope Obadiah has briefed you as much as possible." He paused, his face becoming sombre and sincere. An awkwardness came over him. "We're glad you're back, Dawn. We need to get through this, then we can concentrate on helping your father. He's being well taken care of."

"I understand, Commander."

He considered saying more, but felt he would only blunder with platitudes and make things worse. Staying professional was the way forward Dawn was allowing him. He took it. He nodded an affirmation.

"So, what's our situation? My estimate is that the Xannix defence network will be in weapons range within twelve minutes. Can the ship have propulsion and navigation back online within that time?"

"No. Propulsion will not be available, nor will our own defensive grid. We will, however, have manoeuvring thrusters and life support."

"So we could manoeuvre manually? But without propulsion we are going nowhere."

"Propulsion will be back online in twelve minutes thirty seconds," she said flatly.

"So we have to survive for thirty seconds taking a barrage from the Xannix defence grid."

Dawn thought for a moment, "We can limit the damage we take; I'm running simulations. VERS initial results suggest setting a course for Xannix. Once underway we can then manoeuvre the bow towards the defence network..."

He picked up the thread of the plan: "...presenting the smallest target with the strongest part of the ship towards the incoming fire, slowly moving the ship away from the source to give us more time."

"Yes," Dawn responded.

"Works for me. Holt?" he called. The officer of the watch was on comms immediately.

"Yes, sir?"

"Dawn is sending you navigational instructions to action the moment navigational control is restored. How is the evacuation preparation coming on?"

"Received," Holt said, confirming the receipt of Dawn's

instructions. "Preparations have been faster than expected. Zero gravity oddly helped us out a little. All non-essential crew are at their muster stations."

"Good." He looked at Pearson and gave a big grin. "Good work, Pearson. Stick around here and give Dawn any help she needs." Turning to leave, he headed for the door. Even after only a short period of weightlessness his body seemed to be confused by the reorientation back to gravity again. He gripped the bulkhead and turned back to Dawn. "And don't worry about your dad, Dawn. He's the smartest and toughest guy I know. We'll help as soon as we pull clear. Promise."

"Thank you, Commander."

He nodded again and headed through the door back to the bridge.

ASHER

The pain was excruciating. From the moment he had been smashed against the steps of the dais in the bridge briefing room, the world had become a confusing blur. Some of it was the tears welling in his eyes as his spine was crushed in several places, but more infuriating than that was the loss of control as Clayton reasserted his consciousness during the moments of agony. He had not expected severe pain would do this to him, but the extremes of it were clearly not something his mind could deal with from his host. Being the intruder in the relationship, his mind was not used to or able to deal with this level of elevated acute pain; under these circumstances, the host body rejected him. It was similar to passing out or being on the edge of passing out, he would return periodically and feel like he was an observer in his own body. Only it wasn't his body.

Medics had carried them off at speed, or as fast as they dare go, and when the gravity in the corridor had failed they had almost all got into trouble, as their momentum became nearly too much to stop as they approached the corridor junction.

Now lying in the closest sickbay to the bridge, he was being worked on furiously by the attending doctor. With his neck strapped into a brace, he was unable to see any more than Clayton allowed as he himself swivelled his eyes in all directions trying to get a clear understanding of the situation. But as the physical exhaustion and drugs took their toll on Clayton, he felt his control coming back ever so slightly as the overwhelming pain subsided.

227

'I won't let you,' came Clayton's voice into his mind.

'You have no choice. What needs to be done must be done.' Now more than ever he must succeed. He tried to move any limb, any extremity, toes, fingers. He felt a twinge, but very dull. His right hand.

'I know you think you're doing the right thing, but you are not thinking clearly. You think genocide of one species is acceptable to continue the line of another? You are morally corrupt, Asher.' Clayton was incensed.

'May I remind you that you were briefed into this. You, the other captains and the ship AIs. That you have decided to go against the mission objectives is now down to me to correct. And I will.' He stated the final part of the sentence with some venom. Clayton was way past annoying him and to some degree he couldn't wait for the final effects of his wave degradation to occur. At least he wouldn't have to put up with Clayton's whining anymore, and his illogical point of view. How was the survival of your own species not the only motivator in any situation?

'You will end us all. I can't allow that,' Clayton persisted. 'This course of action will only bring destruction on the fleet. And that will be on your head.'

'Not true.'

'Things have changed, Asher. You are not on Earth now and the mission parameters have changed. Can you not see that?'

'Nothing has changed. Below us is a viable planet. Below us is a place to thrive again. You would undo all that? This is not for you to decide. It has been decided by those left behind, those who put you here right now and to whose memory you are looking to thumb the final insult. It's a violation I won't let you make.'

He surged mentally for control of the bio-comm and, for a moment, he wrestled control of the body away from Clayton, who he felt recede. He was becoming aware of the nuances of his situation, and the consciousness of Clayton was something physical that he could touch and push around. This was his domain and his will would prevail.

His internal bio-comm display suddenly flashed up the status of the Angelfall system.

'No,' came a distant echo of some forlorn voice. Clayton, now weaker by the minute as he ascended, his control becoming more complete. 'You can't.' It was almost pleading. He knew he'd been right about Clayton. Clayton should never have been put in command of the mission. It should have been him. He had been overruled by the OWEC committee, the short-sighted fools. When it came to it, Clayton didn't have what it took to make the tough decisions. He would do that now.

The entry sequence was accepted and the release mechanism icon turned green. 'It is done.' There was silence.

Opening his eyes, he could see the medical crew working furiously to stabilise his condition and begin the prepwork on his back injuries. He closed them again. He could afford himself some rest. His task was done. The planet would be made fit for human colonisation. Humanity would live, and he had done it. No thanks to Clayton and his puritan daughter. If he could just wind back time and influence the selection committee to choose another mission commander. He should have been more insistent, but what was done was done.

'Sir,' he heard. 'Can you hear me?' The doctor was demanding his attention. He opened his eyes. 'We are going to put you to sleep for a while. Could you count back from ten for me?'

Why was it always ten, he thought randomly to himself? Why not a thousand? Or a …

*

The room was dimly lit. Everywhere was dimly lit these days. Power was at a premium, even the heads of state and the residing OWEC committee were not immune to its affects. He and Jessop, the President of the Formillun Institute, sat together at one end of the large ovoid table along with a few government officials. The rest of the table was taken up by Dr Peter Clayton, Commander Elizabeth Straud, Dr Adam Carlsen and the other soon-to-be captains of the expeditionary fleets to colonize the newly identified target worlds. There were four worlds of interest, each designated three ships; simple maths, twelve captains. In front of each of the twelve captains was a complex-looking black box traced throughout by red illuminated lines, which flashed and flared occasionally as he watched. Each of these boxes contained the AI sentience of twelve specially selected human singularities. The ultimate showcase of human technology, these boxes would partner each captain on their mission and provide any support they could to fulfil the mission objectives.

Looking round the table, it was hard to ignore the man sitting to his right—Dr Clayton had been instrumental in making this mission possible. All the closest M class planets identified by their best astronomers and scientists were all operationally too far to reach by conventional means. Until Clayton discovered what Jessop regularly referred to as "the essence of the spirit within us all", a phrase which he used in various fundraising speeches to great effect. In conjunction with wave containment and cloning techniques, the hundred-plus years of travel now became inconsequential. The man to his left had almost single-handedly saved mankind. The irony was the cost. His daughter, Dawn Clayton, now sat on the desk before him—in a box, technically, but legally still alive and somewhat removed from her original incarnation.

Jessop had been speaking for a great deal of the meeting, outlining their new roles and the technology which sat before them. Many of them had been introduced before, all the new captains were certainly aware of their new partners, but a couple had only now just met. Small miniature animated holographic projections of the AI stood in mid-air a couple of centimetres above their box, each giving some visual assistance to those interacting with them and each looking like a little slightly translucent red fairy fluttering and flickering above the table.

"I know you've been listening to me for far too long, so I'm going to hand over to OWEC President Dillon Asher, who will finalise this session from an OWEC perspective." With a short nod in his direction, Jessop sat. All eyes were now on him.

"Thank you, David." He took a moment to look around the assembled team and make eye contact, to make what he had to say personal to each individual. "I'll make this brief; I know we've all got important work to be getting back to.

"OWEC have been financing and running deep-space operations for many years now. For you, that term is going to leave your predecessors swimming in a very shallow pond. Deep space is going to mean something very different when you get to your destinations.

"From the company perspective, and that of the voting populous of this planet, this mission cannot fail. From the latest reports, this world will be unsustainable within the next two hundred years, which effectively means your journey will be one way. That makes your task even more critical. With this mandate, it is expected that no option be overlooked and no measure considered too extreme to ensure the survival of our species.

"To achieve your goals, your ships have been crewed and fitted with the best this planet can offer. There is no eventuality that hasn't been planned for and your AIs will partner you through every decision to ensure you are aware of the optimum course of action in any situation according to that available technology.

"OWEC are very proud of everyone on the colonisation crews; you carry with you the hopes and dreams of those left behind. But those you leave behind should never be forgotten as enablers to your new lives on these new worlds. Their sacrifice is the reason you are all here."

He paused a moment and gave them all a solemn smile, calculated to press their emotional buttons and lock them into the OWEC mind-set.

"Excuse me, President Asher." He looked around, looking for the source of the interruption. He looked across at Clayton, but it had been a female voice. Correcting his gaze, he realized it was the AI between them: Dawn.

"Yes, Dawn. What is your question?"

"I see no specific codified policy on the implication of your statement. You are advocating additions to our code and regulations?" The question made Clayton look expectantly towards him with a raised eyebrow.

"I'm airing the expectation of those sending you with their hearts and hopes. You should know this information so you can base your future decisions with them in mind."

The words seem to pacify her. The holographic image nodded briefly to show her understanding.

"Well, that about wraps it up for this meeting. From this moment on, you will be working very closely with your AI, so please make the most of the time remaining to get to know each other. Your partnership will run the operation aboard ship and across your respective fleets." He saw nodding heads around the room, as each appreciated the words and understood. Although each captain would hold ultimate responsibility for all operational decisions, it was the AI's job to be their advisor in every capacity. They were a team two heads and one purpose.

"Well, thank you for your time. We'll convene again a month before mission launch."

He nodded as everyone stood. The AI cubes on the table dimmed as the holoprojections faded out. Each captain picked up their respective cube, by a substantial handle built in and moulded along one top edge, then filed out of the room one by one. Quiet conversations could be heard in the corridor outside as they made their way back to their various offices or shuttles.

"Drink?" came the question from Jessop.

"Sure," he said, as he continued to stare at the door, lost for a moment in his thoughts.

They made a short walk back to Jessop's office. "Reservations or concerns?" Jessop asked him, as he handed him a glass.

"Yes," he said, smiling back. It was a small joke but it always made him smile.

"So, which is it?"

"How can you not have concerns? We are going to die on this planet you know," he stated.

"Everyone dies, Dillon."

"Not me, specifically—us. All of us. These guys are it."

"What are you saying?" asked Jessop, as he walked to the window. The view used to be lush and green, but now the grass was brown and brittle, the shrubs having long since died, and the trees looked like skeletal shadows. He snorted to himself and shook his head. "I know you don't trust this mission."

"David, I'm a politician; I don't trust anyone." He took a swallow of malt whisky—Jessops finest. It tasted good. "The shadow project is necessary; you understand that, don't you?"

"Oh, I understand that you think it's necessary, but me? It's not important. My time is now, here. Hayford b? I won't be around to see it, but the fact that we're doing it, going to these places to ensure the continuation of things—now *that's* important. Who runs the place when we get there? That is an irrelevance."

"No. It is critically important; it will set the moral and political landscape. A tough leadership will be needed."

"And you don't think those we are sending are tough enough?"

"Simply put? No."

"But you are?"

"Yes."

Another pause. Jessop seemed to be weighing up the

conversation, as he stared out of the window, his whisky glass resting on his lower lip as he considered his next words.

"Well, then—your plan should be effective."

They stood in silence for a moment, each in their own thoughts, considering a future which seemed so far away.

"So, your wave scan is tomorrow?" asked Jessop, as he moved away from the window to take a lounge chair opposite him. "You do know that, after the procedure, *technically* you will be breaking the law? You will have copied your sentience to an illegal, unlicensed storage device."

He shrugged it off; now, Jessop was wandering into the irrelevant. "It will be temporary," he stated. "Are preparations ready?"

"Yes. Your storage cube will be stacked parallel to each of the fleet commanders. Your wave and that of the particular fleet commander will be injected into the host simultaneously. You will feel a high level of disorientation, as you will not be in your own body, and you will only have a matter of months before your sentience is overcome by the host wave." Jessop paused while he took a sip of his drink. "But, during that time, you will have the ability to manipulate and control the host's body, which in turn will give you the ability to control the fleet."

A grin had spread across his face while Jessop had been speaking. "Good," he said, feeling a warm glow move through him. He was unsure whether this was the whisky or his satisfaction flushing his cheeks; it didn't matter. He wallowed in the sensation for a moment.

"I thought you should also be aware that we have anticipated a small risk. With the special relationship that exists between the AI, Dawn and that of her father, Clayton, your effectiveness will be reduced and likelihood of discovery increased. We have implemented countermeasures, but there is no guarantee that you will not be discovered quickly in this case."

"It will be of little consequence. We will continue as planned." He was dismissive—at this late stage there was little they could really do. He would have to improvise at the time. That played to his strengths. Jessop nodded with a slight shrug, as if to say '*It's your funeral*', but he ignored the sentiment.

"One final thing: my sources at OWEC have suggested to me that there may be an issue with the Hayford b data." It was delivered in an innocent and friendly way, but his years in politics uncovered the intent in an instant. It had been Jessops reason for the whole meeting, cloaked under the veil of cordial conversation.

"In what way?" he asked.

"Astronomical data on Hayford b may be ambiguous," he continued. "Some of my scientists have reviewed the data. They think the planet is not exhibiting what you might call normal behaviour."

"I'm sorry, David. I'm having trouble grasping your meaning."

Jessop pursed his lips. He was clearly trying to be discrete but having trouble confronting him with the detail.

"I'll be plain. The planet is not suitable. It does not show complete compliance with the requirements of a barren planet."

"What do you mean 'complete compliance'?" As he spoke the words, he saw the slight flash of annoyance on Jessop's face.

"Dillon, you know exactly what I mean. The analysis shows anomalies in the data which may represent sentient activity. It is sporadic and inconclusive but, with what's at stake, we may have to consider other options."

"What other options, David?" he asked in a surprised tone. "We are too committed to this course; there is less than six weeks to go. Preparations for the journey are almost complete. We can't go moving the target now." He got up and began to pace up and down the room, stopping in front of the fire place, cold and black, fittings polished and gleaming. He leaned against the mantelpiece and stared into the mirror to collect his thoughts. His reflection and the reflection of the room made him feel momentarily apart from himself, like he was watching events in the room unfold on a vid and not experiencing them directly. Some other self making the hard decisions and pushing his plans through. Sometimes Jessop's apathy to the future angered him. He was always looking to derail his work, and now was no different.

Letting out a sigh, he looked at Jessop's reflection which looked at him with stern, stolid eyes. The conversation was almost over. He threw back the last of his whisky and placed the tumbler on the mantelpiece. "No, David. We're not changing our plans. With the technology at their disposal, any existing life on the planet can be managed."

"But the Angelfall and Hellray systems are for last resort situations, where there is no alternative. Right now, we have an alternative."

"All the other alternate planets you are talking of had some serious chronic issue, slight toxicity to the atmosphere, too cold, too hot. No, Hayford b remains."

He walked to the door and opened it in preparation to leave. "This is not to get out to the crews, you understand, David? We're going to Hayford b." He closed the door behind him as he left the office.

LARSEN

The world turned an insipid yellow colour and a stuttering sound enveloped his ears. Sudden chaos broke out around him for the second time in the last hour—it was becoming something of a recurring theme. He looked at Rivers, who was looking around at the Xannix running in all directions. Doors began to slam shut around the Arch-sa, heavy-looking blast doors.

"What the hell's going on now?" said Rivers, verbalising his own thoughts.

"Whatever it is, it isn't good. We've just been sealed in." He moved over to one of the Xannix controllers. "Show me," he ordered. The Xannix seemed unsure, but Ovitala appeared at his shoulder and flushed a blue hue. Various images were immediately displayed on the main control viewer in front of them. One section showed a formation of Overseer ships, which he presumed to be drop ships due to their swollen underbelly, the fuselage built to carry troops. Another couple of screens displayed various external angles of the building he knew them to be in, the apartment block façade housing the Seeker base and the Arch-sa.

"A worrying development," said Ovitala. She looked at him. "We must go."

"Worrying? Isn't a move like this expected?" he questioned, but Ovitala was already moving, walking at pace to the centre of the command deck and onto a circle of flooring impressed with the Seeker emblem. She turned back to them and motioned that they should join her.

Stepping up to her he asked again, thinking she had not heard him. But she raised a hand to halt him, she closed her eyes and was clearly concentrating on something. The section of floor they stood on began to rise, breaking away from the command deck. Rivers noticed Aldaan at a nearby console with another Xannix.

"Aldaan!" she called out to him. He looked up and turned a sad shade of purple, shifting to a deep blue.

"Go, child Rivers," he replied. "I go no further. Ensure Lieutenant Larsen's success." He stood with his hands held to the centre of his chest for a moment, creating a cross with this arms. Then the concentration of his task took him away again. A sudden lurch of the ground and tremendous boom of thunder above them brought Rivers attention back to him and Ovitala as she lost her balance, beginning to fall from the platform. His arm was around her in an instant. They held each other for a moment, sharing a glance the meaning of which neither of them fully understood, slightly uncomfortable but somehow reassuring. The spell broke.

Turning back to Ovitala, she seemed to read his body language, the insistence in his eyes. Her face turned into a mask of reluctance. "No. We are prepared, but this was not fully anticipated. It has never happened before. Our location has never been uncovered before."

"So, this is because of us?"

"Most likely. So far you have overcome all the traditional challenges, but the final challenge is next. Celicia's appearance to you is highly irregular and I suspect she does not want the final challenge to take place. She is attempting to end you before time."

The platform jolted slightly as it came to a stop.

"Now, please stand still and within the boundaries of the platform," she requested.

"What's happening?" asked Rivers.

"We are leaving."

She looked across to Aldaan below and made a gesture with her hand to which his skin flushed a momentary blue to affirm. A similar shimmer began, which he now understood to be the beginnings of a inter-dimensional gateway or localised wormhole. However, as the field around them began to build, he began to see a similar one, much smaller, begin to materialise near to Aldaan's workstation.

Being much smaller, the field fell away quicker and, as Larsen's own vision began to obscure due to the formation of their own gateway, he caught a quick glimpse of a dark spherical object with a small control panel embedded, a white light flashing. He saw the sudden recognition in Aldaan as he lunged for the workstation, and the gateway around them completed immediately.

*

It was completely disorientating. He felt nothing physically different. He was still standing in the same spot, holding Rivers and looking in the direction Aldaan had been, only he wasn't looking at Aldaan any more, instead he saw a wide panoramic view. Trying to take in his new surroundings he found he was looking out over a beautiful forest scene. The room was a wide viewing gallery overlooking a forest, the window about thirty metres wide, three metres high and situated about 20 metres above the tree canopy. The forest went on for kilometres in all directions, but to the left and right was rock, as were the walls of the room. In the distance and rising out of the forest was a city. The arcology.

A boom of sound punched the window and caused him to flinch, feeling the sound in his chest.

"Aldaan," Rivers said as an almost involuntary reflex to the sonic boom, but her subconscious rightly connecting the scene before her to the one they had just left behind.

He took several steps to the window, standing so close his breath began to condense on its surface. The arcology dome was still apparent but damaged, a huge plume of smoke and debris belched from the devastation inside.

"I don't understand," he said quietly to himself. Ovitala and Rivers had joined him, both sombre and disbelieving. "So many people. Why do this to your own?"

"This is the Setak'da's doing. She is not one of us," stated Ovitala flatly. She was fluctuating between white and black and she was unable to mask the sorrow in her voice. "It is why you must beat her, Lieutenant Larsen. You must not fail."

"This is not our battle, Ovitala." His mind running; his thoughts of the thousands of dead Xannix. "You should not be looking for leadership from the outside. You should be ruling yourselves. We may be here searching for sanctuary, but you shouldn't be looking to replace the Zantanath with us. What makes you believe we are any better?"

"Oh, I have no illusions about your position. And we fully intend to seize control of our destiny soon enough. But the Zantanath must be defeated."

"And while you want them out, you may as well use us to do it?"

"It is written."

"Written? What are you talking about?"

Ovitala stood silent for a moment. Then turning to him, she opened her hand. Both he and Rivers frowned intently at the object, then as the recognition came to them he blurted, "Where did you get this? It's a memory chip from the *Endeavour's* AI core." He went to grab for it but Ovitala was too quick and withdrew it again.

"This was given to me by you four cycles ago."

"Me?" he said in shock, his voice momentarily cracking under the surprise.

"You," she pointed at both of them, "think you are here for the first time? You are not." She opened her hand again to reveal the memory unit. "I believe you have the ability to review the information on this device?"

"Yes," said Rivers.

"You need to do it now, before I divulge any more. Then you will understand." She handed the device over to Rivers.

Rivers took the memory unit and quickly ran the numbers against her bio-comm, the unit which had been a solid jet brick suddenly came to life, red flowing lines of light pulsing around it. He watched with anticipation as she worked and checked his own bio-comm for any update she might have already sent him.

"There," said Rivers. "Connected."

"Hello, Lieutenant Larsen, Scientist First Class Rivers." Dawn hovered in front of them both, projected as an augmented reality visual to their bio-comm display. Dawn had chosen to stand to the side of Ovitala who seemed a little confused that they were now both focused on a region of space next to her which had nothing and no one in it. "I'm glad to see you again."

Trying to take in everything that was happening was beginning to give him a headache. He checked the source of the communication— it was local, not being transmitted from orbit. *Endeavour* was not broadcasting. This Dawn was a either a fake or a copy—both would be unlikely, but he couldn't plausibly explain how Ovitala would have a genuine copy of Dawn on a mobile memory device in front of them.

"From the silence, I can tell you are trying to comprehend how I come to be here. I should state up front, I am not Dawn." She made a face as if to think hard on the statement. "Well, not fully. I am a construct; I do not contain her wave. So, I should say I have the outward appearance of the person you know, but I am not her."

"Okay," he said, more to delay and slow the pace of events. He closed his eyes in concentration and tried to clear his mind of the chorus of questions playing for position. "Explain. How are you here?" Just before Dawn was about to respond, he blurted out an interrupting thought, "And why *again*?"

The Dawn avatar nodded, the question anticipated. "We were sent ahead."

"We?" asked Rivers.

"Yes. Each of the fleet ships is fitted with a single Lancer-type craft. Fundamentally, it was an experimental ship with a new drive. It was not part of the primary plan, as the prototype Elan drive was highly volatile. In truth it only had a 20 percent success rate."

"And by that you mean?" he asked pointedly.

Dawn shrugged. "You can probably guess. There was very little to examine during the Elan drive test programme 80 percent of the time."

"How come we never knew about this Lancer?" asked Rivers.

"You are missing the point," continued Dawn. "The plan was to get a pathfinder team here first and identify any potential landing sites, analyse the planet in detail and provide first-hand detailed data of the surface, then to land and continue the research. If successful, it would save a huge amount of time when the fleet arrived. If it didn't, as it was expected not to…" She shrugged to complete the sentence.

She continued: "I can only think we were assumed lost. My calculations suggested that it would have been thought the drive had failed in transit and, as that was such a strong probability, no other assessment was made."

"You wouldn't have been able to communicate or get a message out," he pondered.

"No. The defence network around the planet prevented it."

Rivers waved her hands to interrupt the conversation. "Never mind that; we know about the defence network. You said *we*, but who do you mean?"

"The two selected as pathfinders were you and Lieutenant Larsen."

"Wait, that makes no sense," Rivers stammered.

"Assessments were made. Your personal profiles and temperament best suited a long range, long duration mission."

"So the decision was made on the basis of our profiled compatibility?"

"Yes."

Ovitala was clearly only able to understand half of the conversation, but it was enough for her to get the basics. She shimmered a blue colour and turned away from them to look across to the arcology again. Her thoughts were clearly torn by doing what she felt needed to be done and the loss she felt of those they had just left behind.

After a moment's thought, Rivers asked, "So, we are still here?"

"How many years?" he asked almost in the same instant.

"Sadly, your pathfinder selves are no longer with us. They were caught by the Overseers and destroyed. However, your child survives."

"Our what?" they said in unison. Ovitala turned back to them with concern as they both looked at each other in a state of confused shock.

"Your son, is fifteen Earth standard years old," Dawn continued. "Your other selves arrived here twenty years ago and were luckily found by a Seeker patrol in the remote northern hemisphere. They were taken in and given sanctuary in a secret location and isolated from the general Xannix populous. Your son is with them; Ovitala is to take you to him now."

"We were lucky to find you," Ovitala repeated, not realising what Dawn had just stated. "Your son is safe. I'll take you to him now. Things have changed. Celicia has declared her intentions. I believe she will aim to defeat you by a show of force. This way she can join the Xannix against you. Your fleet will then be destroyed."

He looked at Rivers, who was still clearly trying to process the fact that she was going to be introduced to her son. Although she had no knowledge of the birth or the formative years of his growing up, he was still biologically a DNA match to his and her union. He didn't have the time to go into it. Looking at Ovitala, his features became stern.

"Ovitala, the child is important, but so are the people of this planet and the others in orbit. Celicia must be stopped. She is going to bring a war to this world; we can't let that happen."

"I agree, but we can talk while we travel. This way."

As they turned to leave and follow Ovitala, he noticed an entourage had assembled and were waiting patiently along the back wall around the exit. Among them and clearly standing out against the relative giant Xannix around him, was a human child, wide eyed and staring at them both in astonished silence. He stopped like he'd been slapped. The eyes were his, the mouth, the hair clearly his mothers, slim in build and athletic. Rivers also had frozen to the spot. He heard her gasp slightly in recognition.

The Xannix began to close the distance, slow step by slow step, guiding the child towards them.

"Lieutenant Larsen, Child Rivers, meet your son, Clarion."

The teenage boy stopped, and spoke in a soft voice strained by emotion. "Hello, Mother, Father." He said in perfect English. He didn't know what else he had expected, maybe fluent Xannix. He could see tears welling up in the boys eyes as he fought the inner turmoil of a boy whose parents had just somehow miraculously walked back into his life looking perhaps a little younger than he remembered them, before they left him years before. His own confused emotions played at him and drew him closer. Rivers was first to react and lunged forward to hug the boy who suddenly broke down and fell into her embrace.

"We need to get you to a secure location," Ovitala said as she looked down at the two. "We can regroup and work out our next course of action."

"We need to contact the fleets and arrange a ceasefire. Can you do that?" he asked.

"Yes. I think there has been enough evidence of your challenge to secure a level of support across the Overseers, even with the Setak'da working against the traditions of the challenge. You of course have the full support of the Seekers."

He looked back down to the child and Rivers, who were both now crying with the emotional fatigue of the last couple of days.

"Dawn," Rivers was saying, "How could you let this happen? There are laws against multiple clones." The boy didn't react, he clearly had no understanding of what she was saying.

"We had no means of communication back to the fleet. It was impossible to know. You would have been resuscitated as per the programme and the high risk mission presumed to have failed. It is an understandable situation."

Clarion had begun to recover, his eyes now red as he rubbed the tears from his cheeks. He couldn't help but feel like he was looking in a mirror; it was like having an out-of-body experience with himself as a fifteen-year-old child. Memories flooded back, and he felt his pulse quicken as his emotions began to spike again. Catching himself, he took a deep breath. He needed to stay focussed and keep his mind on the bigger picture. The current turn of events had become a surreal distraction.

Still staring at the boy, he found an icon flashing in his bio-comm display: it was a secure and high-priority message from Reeve. It was brief—she was clearly having problems of her own: 'Captured. They are tracking you via bio-comm link.'

The message was sent via secure channel, but the message was plain and direct. He already knew the Overseers had them, but clearly things were worse than anticipated. But Reeve was clever. In that message he realised he was being told two things. First the obvious, he was being tracked, most likely how the Setak'da had been able to deliver the explosive to their exact location. But, secondly, Reeve was telling him exactly how he could find her. This particular knife cut both ways. He didn't respond to the message, and he hoped she didn't expect a response.

His face took on a grim determination. There was much to do.

"Okay, Ovitala. I think you better lead the way."

ASHER

His mind was drowsy, and images appeared distant for a moment as his senses returned to him. Resting in the medical bay staring at the ceiling, the medical team had done their work. He found he was unable to move, but whether that was down to his physical condition after the surgery or any stasis his limbs had been placed in to avoid undue movement he could not tell.

Too excited to look over the room other than to determine that it was empty and he was on his own, he jumped into his bio-comm to review the current tactical situation. Right now, this was all that mattered. The culmination of his life's work would be hinging on the next few hours; it was key he guided the situation where he could.

Data flooded in. Outside the ship was a chaotic ballet of manoeuvring ships and energy. Explosions rocked the ship, he could feel them through the bed he lay on and the beam weapons of the Xannix flashed across his view via the external monitors. The *Endeavour* was the centre of the storm, attracting the most attention. The *Indianapolis* and *Intrepid* had moved into a tighter formation to provide covering fire and assist where they could, although they appeared to be in a higher orbit.

Their lower orbit he realised was in order to optimise the release of the Angelfall weapon. The genetic bio-weapon system required the lower orbit for deployment. It was happening. His heart started to thump in his chest in the realisation that his plans were coming together. He watched the operation with an excited eagerness; he'd not felt so alive since he was a child.

He had regained consciousness part way through the operation, and the delivery of Angelfall was already under way. He could see a reddish brown haze across the skies above Xannix, the pellets dispersed into the upper atmosphere becoming a poison dust to be soaked up by the clouds, to precipitate as rain, or simply to fall in its powdered particulate form to the surface. A shadow of death being cast wide and without mercy, it would infiltrate every part of the planet leaving nowhere for the Xannix to hide. At the very least they needed air and water, and both of these substances would be globally contaminated. He was witnessing the end of the Xannix and the beginning of a bright new future for the sons and daughters of humanity.

Remembering the struggles and the life he had left behind, now to be in this moment caused a wave of emotion to wash over him, tears pricked his eyes and began to flow freely. He stifled a sob, but from whom he didn't know. Another barrier dropped away and he felt the world become the place he wanted and wished for; his inhibitions now laid aside, his body pulsed with the cries of overwhelming relief and elation.

"See this?" he cried out to the room, pointing at a display he saw in his bio-comm view but gesticulating just the same. "This is what we came here for. This is the world we were destined to inherit. I told you. I told you all!" The sobs became uncontrollable laughter. If he had had control of his body in full, he was sure he would have been rolled up on the bed in spasms—as it was, he was only able to move his head a little side to side with an inane smile and grin like a lunatic.

"If you had your way Clayton, you would have killed us all. You are a coward. You couldn't do what needed to be done when it came to it. The committee were short-sighted and couldn't see past your achievements at home, but I could. Okay, you might have made this possible, but there are different people for different times. You should never have been in command of this fleet. Your time is over. Now the strong will survive."

Taking a huge sigh, he wallowed in his happiness—a new found bliss the other side of success. It had been a long time coming. He did a rough calculation: 135 years in transit, fifty years of life before the journey began, striving for the power and influence to run OWEC and its subsidiaries, almost two hundred years. Now that was a long journey.

"Do you hear me, Clayton?" he said again to the room.

The silence that came back was not what he was expecting. Clayton had been riding him hard at any and every opportunity; it had been a continuous argument since the moment he had been discovered. Up to now, he had never needed to try too hard to illicit any kind of aggressive response. By playing on Clayton's weaknesses—his attachment to his daughter, his moral purity, his personal commitment to his own misguided cause—it was usually an easy task. But right now, nothing.

A small doubt began to needle its way into his thoughts, and, like a creeping darkness, a chill began to work at him. Accessing the bio-comm, he began to fire out a few light queries of the system: crew complement, status of the fuel cells, current biomass growth rate in hydroponics, current count of patients in all medical bays, temperature across medical bays, count of staff on the bridge, temperature of the bridge. Apparently random, but he was hunting for information.

Lastly, he started going through vid footage: people going about their business across the decks of the ship, urgently engaged in whatever the current ship action required of them. Then he flicked to the view of his personal quarters, or Clayton's, to be precise. Things looked as he remembered them: the bathroom, where he had been discovered, the sleeping quarters and the kitchen area all seemed completely normal.

He sighed. Nothing; his suspicions seemed to be unfounded. Maybe his wave was finally fading from Clayton's mind. Maybe this was how the end came: the silence, the isolation and a final darkness. He would just have to savour the moments he had left, knowing he had done all he could and succeeded. That brought a smile back. He had won.

The mirror. A picture of the mirror flashed back to the forefront of his mind. The mirror in the bathroom—Clayton had cracked it during their first confrontation. He quickly navigated the bio-comm display back to the view of the bathroom and zoomed in on the mirror. It was as new: no crack, not even a mark; it was pristine. He felt a sudden hollowness in the pit of his stomach, like a void opening in his belly which could turn him inside out.

It was a sickening realisation. The illusion of the wave container showed him what he wanted to see. Reality was now a place outside his control, outside this place. His mind secure within a stasis cube.

The rage which he felt burst forth, and he began to scream and howl incoherently, thrashing his head about as his eyes bulged with the effort.

"You bastards! All of you. Do you realise what you have done? Do you realise what you have done?"

ROUX

He reached the bridge at a pace and almost jumped at his couch. Manoeuvres were already underway, and he could sense the vibration of the ship as the thrusters fired and adjusted, changing its momentum and position to angle it towards the oncoming satellite array. He had been watching the ship's track on his bio-comm display but now on the bridge one of the secondary displays had the information large for everyone to see.

"Red Alert, please, Mr Holt," he said aloud, not taking his eyes from the screens for a moment.

"Aye, sir."

"Everyone strap yourselves in. This is likely to get rough."

Checking the countdown in his bio-comm display, it ticked past 30 seconds. The primary screen showed the main tactical view and overlaid the external view with distance and target data along with target velocity data. He checked his own terminal, weapons and helm information, and a message popped up from Dr Roberts. He accepted the comm.

"Now is not a good time, Doctor."

"Just a quick update: the separation procedure went well. The captain is recovering in his backup clone host. Asher is back in his box, and the simulated environment appears to be holding. I'll give you a full briefing at your earliest convenience."

"Thank you, Doctor. Ensure the captain is at his muster station and ready to evacuate. And good work. Roux, out." Before Dr Roberts could respond, he cut the link.

His eyes darted across the tactical screens again: the 30 seconds was up and, like the first heavy drops of a monsoon, red light started to fall towards them.

"Taking fire," came the call from the bridge. "Minimal damage."

Dawn appeared at his side, her holographic image swirling into existence. She too stared intently at the displays, and he wondered why she would do so. She was the ship—the ship was her—so she would be experiencing this battle on a far grander scale. Maybe the human viewpoint, his viewpoint, was what she was after. As if to second guess him, she answered his unspoken question.

"You are acting captain." It was all she needed to say.

"Thank you," he replied.

"*Indianapolis* and *Intrepid* taking fire, also reporting minimal damage," she said.

The rain continued, and began to intensify, red beams now beginning to fill the display. He took a look at his navigational controls and Dawn's manoeuvring plan; the thrusters began to fire again and push the *Endeavour* towards Xannix. The rate of movement was slow—so slow that the motion was not even visually apparent.

He could now feel and hear the odd strike, as the ship took a hit from somewhere outside; they were going to be overwhelmed as the waves of fire became more intense. Creeping the ship back was not going to be enough.

Thirty seconds clicked by, and he looked at Dawn, who looked back with an apologetic look on her face.

"Engines?" he asked, simply.

"Not yet. However, weapon systems are now operational."

He didn't need an invitation. He turned straight to the weapons desk.

"PDC cannons, open fire. Fire at will," he commanded. The Point Defence Cannons began to spin off thousands of rounds into the void. Even at this range, they may have a chance at knocking out some of the satellites, so long as they continued to exhibit their relentless plodding behaviour, slowly closing the net. The satellite array had so far not shown any erratic evasive movement. If they took out a few, maybe it would buy them some time.

"Target destroyed," came a call from the bridge, and he

watched the tactical display intently. A single icon out of thousands blinked out, then another and another disappeared. It was a drop in the ocean. A small group then switched out in a cluster as a small cascade effect took place, but the damage was limited to about thirty satellites. A lucky shot.

His timer was still ticking. Having bounced from zero they were now increasing again, already at twenty seconds. How slow does time move when things are going your way, then why so fast when things are against you? He felt his stress levels rise slightly. He needed those engines.

"Dawn, what are we waiting for?" he asked with gritted teeth.

"We are having problems with the restart process. We now have minimum propulsion: two engines are back online, but the rest are still inactive."

A shudder was suddenly felt throughout the ship like thunder, distant but ominous. His engineering alerts lit up. Two engine pods were red and flashing. Chief Grey was instantly in his view.

"Grey, what just happened?"

"Captain, we're not a military vessel. We haven't the protection and shielding we need to undertake damage of this scale. We just lost two engines; you still have one up. I'll get you the other two in..." she checked a display "...sixty seconds."

Did they have sixty seconds? He pushed the negative thought aside. Concentration was required; he needed inspiration to get them out of this mess. The displays in front of him slowly, by degrees, becoming a more solid red.

"Helm, redline what we have. I want to move."

"Which course, sir?"

"We need time to get the engines back online. Take the fleet down the well. As far as we dare."

"Aye, sir."

"Dawn, tell the fleet they are free to move independently."

"Done."

The ship began to swing on its axis, turning as slowly and gracefully as a whale preparing to dive, the manoeuvring thrusters working hard to move the titanic ship as fast as it could, and the main engines engaged as the planet below moved into view, creating a blue horizon. He felt a gentle push in his back, but nothing like the shove he would have felt if all engines had been available. Even though the ship lumbered, his mind raced. There was no way out. The net was complete and the satellites too vast in number.

"Sections G12 through to G50 reporting heavy damage. Damage control teams on site."

"Continue the manoeuvre, Helm. Full rotational thrust." He turned urgently towards Dawn. "Where are my engines, Dawn?"

"Now," she replied.

"Helm. Full ten second engine burn, on my mark." The Xannix horizon swung away to be replaced by the bright reflected surface of the northern, snow-covered hemisphere. The moment the pitch of the ship became vertical, he called to the helmsman "Mark!" and was rewarded with a severe thump to the kidneys.

The engines roared through the decks, vibrating everything from the furniture, the monitors and display terminals to his teeth. He tensed as the g counter started to ramp up: four, five, six. He could see the main tactical display showing a strange red rain in the periphery of the picture, with a clear view in the centre of the snow-capped mountains and plains below. At this attitude, he was now well aware of the damage the engines would be taking—he needed to change orientation again. He couldn't lose any more engines.

Ten seconds were up and the main engines stopped their burn. He checked his console: damage intensity was down thirty percent. He reviewed Dawn's navigational plan. They were on track.

"Helm, full rotational burn. Bring us about again. Ready for a 9-second full engine burn."

"Roger," affirmed the helmsman.

He momentarily checked the status of the other two fleet ships: both were wandering into a lower orbit and zigzagging a course. They didn't appear to be doing any better than the *Endeavour*. The intensity of the fire was only ever increasing, as the net closed and more satellites came into range. This was only going to get worse. But where were the Xannix ships? Where had they gone?

"Holt, find the Xannix ships. I want to know where they are."

Holt got to work to get the information. It didn't take him long. Holt sent the location to his console. They were the other side of the satellite grid in a higher orbit. Of course they were. They didn't want to get rained on like they were. A grim look came over him. He knew what they needed to do.

Running a quick navigational calculation, he checked his idea out. The results came back. He was decided.

"Helm, I have a new bearing for you." Sending the information the tactical display immediately translated the information and a new track appeared through the satellite network and towards the largest cluster of Xannix ships.

Dawn's eyes widened in surprise. "This course of action is not advised," she said, with a slight tension in her voice.

"It's the only way. We'll never survive here. We will either die a thousand cuts or fall down the well. I don't intend to do either."

"I've run this simulation; it never works. The fire intensity is too great. Hull integrity fails just short of the array."

"What do your other simulations evaluate our chances to be?" he replied curtly.

She did not respond. It was apparent to him this was the best of all the bad choices. Trying something was always better than trying nothing.

"Get everyone to their evacpods and buckled in." He heard a distant alarm sounding his instruction. It was a well-drilled procedure: non-essential staff would be strapped into their life craft in moments.

Focussing his attention at the tactical screen and the path laid out ahead of them, he made a couple of last-moment minor adjustments then called out, "Helm, execute."

The engines fired hard. Thrust was translated into g and forced him back into the couch. Watching the g counter, it topped out at 3g—not great but it was uncomfortable enough when experienced as a constant acceleration.

Tracking their progress he watched the incoming fire visibly shift its focus from a more general spread to a direct target, and that direct target was now them. "The *Indy* and *Intrepid* report a reduction in received fire," said Dawn.

"Tell them to form up line astern and follow us through."

"Done."

An alert in his bio-comm flashed up. An incoming message from Captain Straud. He wanted to disregard the communication—they were all a little busy—but he took it. Straud's face appeared in his bio-comm display; it appeared different under g, with her features looking less worried and more relaxed than she probably felt.

'Commander Roux, what are you doing?'

'Trying to keep us all alive. We need to break through the defence grid and engage the Xannix ships,' he responded harshly.

'I can see what you're intending, but this is going to get us all killed.'

'No. Not all of us,' he stated. 'We've run the numbers and this gives us a chance. Maybe not all ...' Interrupted by a huge rumbling explosion, the bridge lunged and everyone was thrown violently in their harnesses.

"Number four lateral thruster destroyed," came the call from damage control. It translated immediately to his console, an external view came up, and a small damage control drone had been launched to evaluate the damage. It was extensive but, more than that, the full impact of the damage was revealed. Not only was there a gaping hole where the thruster unit had been, which had also hollowed out several floor levels back to bulkheads, but also the surface damage was now all too apparent. Long dark scars ran the length of the bow down past the forward shuttle bay, the shuttle bay already holed due to the terrorist attack on the visiting Xannix many hours earlier. He was surprised just how much the *Endeavour* was soaking up, but he knew it couldn't last. It confirmed his course of action.

Straud was still there and seemed distracted by the images she was receiving from the *Endeavour's* damage control system.

'Roux, move to a lower orbit. You're not going to make it.'

'Too late, Captain. We're committed and that last shot just removed that option. Meet you on the other side.' He closed the connection.

Turning back to the main bridge displays, he could see the storm of energy outside slowly blotting out the darkness of space; the screen was almost completely red.

"Helm, all the power you can give me. Push through that grid."

"Aye, sir," came the reply.

"Grid energy is spiking," came another call. He received an urgent comm from the bridge engineer, Lieutenant Dexter.

"What does that mean, Lieutenant Dexter?" he asked, urgently.

"Possibly another weapon type, sir. Higher energy, shorter range."

"Thank you, Dexter." He didn't know whether his response sounded facetious but didn't have time to care.

Thunder erupted around them, rattling him to his bones. He

saw the effect of the explosion on the tactical display before he saw any alerts or heard any alarms. The course of the *Endeavour* started to veer sharply to port, different g forces began to apply and he was pushed to the right of his couch hard. It all happened in an instant.

"Helm, correct course!"

"Attempting to correct," stated Lieutenant Arnold, as she fought the ship in its spin. Little appeared to be happening, the rear of the ship still forcing the hard rotational vector. "She's not responding!"

He connected to Engineering, and Acting Chief Grey responded straight away, her face bloodied and burnt, hair almost completely gone on one side; she was in severe pain but doing what she could to direct events. People were working furiously in the background, rushing from one workstation to another. Damage control crews were putting out fires, bracing and patching systems and structural failings. Before he could ask any questions, Grey started her report.

"Engines three and four are gone, two is on half power, five is all that's left and one is running uncontrolled. Failsafes have failed. We are attempting to correct now, but if engine one continues to run up we will also loose five, and when that goes it is likely to take two with it."

"How long?"

There was a shake of the head. "Not long enough. Two minutes, maybe five."

"Okay, Grey. Do what you can, but get your men out and to the escape pods. I'm starting the evacuation now." He turned to Dawn who was looking at him intently. It played with his mind that she stood unencumbered by the g forces running through the ship—as he fought against them, she demonstrated her normal fluid ease of motion.

"Dawn. Launch the escape pods. Get everyone to the surface of Xannix. Target a remote region and deploy them within a 10 kilometre radius. It will give us half a chance of regrouping on the surface."

An alert flashed in his bio-comm, it was the general evacuation alarm. It was done: the escape pods were away.

"Helm, how are we doing?"

"Helm unresponsive, sir," came the reply. He flicked to his

engineering command console, and the screen was almost entirely red; he didn't think there was an alert left that wasn't screaming for attention. Energy outputs were dead or spiking off the charts. His brain hurt with the strain of juggling all the urgent data bombardment, and sweat ran from his brow.

Looking back to the tactical display, the Xannix defence network swept into view again. This time he could physically see the satellite grid. The angle they were accelerating into it was acute and they were set to collide with many satellites in a sweeping arc as the *Endeavour* cut a swathe through the barrier. The effect was likely to be devastating.

Comm alerts were flashing from almost all ship departments, also Captain Straud aboard the *Indianapolis* and Captain Carlsen on the *Intrepid*. He checked the ship's track. Thirty seconds. A complete calm came over him. His mind letting go of all the options, he felt as if Atlas had just taken the weight of the heavens from his shoulders. It was time.

"Dawn, sound general orders. All hands abandon ship."

On the screen, as the ship cartwheeled thorough space and people began to leave the bridge he could see life pods spraying in all directions. Some were targeted by the defence network, some were caught by debris, others suffered a variety of technical malfunctions, but most seemed to be tracking correctly to the surface.

"Commander Roux," a voice interrupted his peace. "Commander Roux, you need to get to an escape pod. There is one waiting for you here." A nav track popped into his bio-comm display, illuminating the path to the pod.

"Dawn, you should eject."

"My core is quite safe. I will be ejecting in twelve seconds. Please get to your escape pod."

"There is no time."

"This is not the time. And this is not your time. You can still make it. I've prepped the pod, it's ready to go. Now, get going." She became insistent, "Now, Joseph! Go!"

Something kicked him into moving. As if in a dream, he hit the release on his harness and immediately slid from the chair due to the forces acting against him. He fell against the next couch and rolled to get purchase on the floor, finding a chaotic track to the bridge exit. Across the corridor he saw the line of escape pods.

Most gone, doors sealed, but there were several still open and shining bright as the lights directed him to his survival. Each remaining pod was indicated with a blue light above and green light below to the ceiling and floor respectively, orienting the person to the seat even before they entered, he didn't have time to reflect on the relative up and down of the situation, but it came to the front of his mind as the gravity adjusted again while the ships artificial gravity systems sporadically failed.

"Straight ahead, Roux. Pod seven."

He fell in. Bridge level pods were single person, a padded white cell with a crash couch and a control console, more like a torpedo than a life raft. He looked at the bridge through the pod door for the last time, his glimpse just momentary before the eject sequence began. A clamp harness came down from above him and pressed him quickly but carefully into the couch, and at the same instant a padded bar pressed across his shins to keep this legs from flailing in the moments to come. The door closed like the blade of a guillotine and the rockets of the pod fired. He went from zero to 150 metres per second in two seconds, his body pressed so hard into the crash couch that he momentarily began to black out. Tunnel vision began to close his view to a single focal point—that of the console in front of him. The world was vibrating and shaking rapidly; the friction of being fired violently from the barrel of what amounted to a large cannon taking it's revenge on the hapless occupant, he clenched his teeth hard.

Suddenly there was a silence and he felt his stomach lurch as his pod's vector changed. His vision came back with a jolt. He could see the track of the pod running parallel to the surface of the world below and the deadly defence grid above. He silently admonished himself for his reckless decisions. It had been a mistake to try and take the fleet through the satellite network, but he had done it anyway, sacrificed his ship and many of his crew.

The thrusters cut in momentarily and altered the pod's course, kicking it onto a predesignated track to the Xannix surface.

"Shit," he said aloud to himself and lay his head back on the couch while watching the time to atmosphere tick down: eight minutes. "Just, shit it!"

CLAYTON

Swimming had always been a love of his; from his earliest years, he recollected the weightlessness and freedom, the ability to move in any direction and to be alongside the strangest most beautiful creatures. Diving without a care, for the simple joy of doing so; to be part of the ballet of life and to exist in it—it was when he was most at peace.

He had met his wife on a scuba holiday one year, many years before, and he had taught his daughter to swim in a pool and taken her to the sea once before the world changed. But he remembered the fun they had all had racing through the waves, the surf buffeting and cold. It was living.

Dawn's smile was wide and happy, as he remembered the twelve year old screaming with excitement and being caught too soon by a high wave which chilled her instantly and electrified her skin. The contrast of the hot summer sun and the cold water was almost blissful. He remembered the day being one of the highlights of many highlights when they took family days.

Swimming had been a family bonding experience which had persisted.

He was swimming again.

Visually, the world was different: it was white in all the directions he could see and there was a blur about everything, like being underwater without goggles or a scuba mask. He saw shapes and shades, but mostly everything was just white.

Every now and then there had been a nudge, a push to his side or back. Slowly, sensation came back and he felt his right hand gripped tight; without thought, he suddenly reciprocated.

"Peter," came a sudden calming voice. A voice he recognised. Jemma.

"Jemma?" he asked.

"It's okay. You're okay. Just relax. We're heading for the surface. It might get a little bumpy shortly."

Her voice was soothing and in control. She always was. Things were still a blur, but he wasn't quite sure why she was telling him to relax. He was so relaxed right now it was as if his muscles couldn't be bothered to move even when he instructed them. His head wanted to loll to one side and try and focus on her, to smile inanely with the happiness he was experiencing—the reason for which, he was unsure.

A light beeping sounded from a plate on his chest; the hand which was holding his released for a moment and the beeping stopped. The hand returned, holding his in a firm, affirming grip. She was doing what she was great at: taking care of others. The fact that he was the focus of her attention only made him feel safer. There was no one he would rather be with right now. His thoughts revised themselves: there was no one he would rather be with, ever. It was the reason he had asked her to marry him, and it was the reason they had had a beautiful baby girl. Things right now could only be good.

Thoughts swirled around in his mind, but a clarity began to pervade: memories of recent events, arguments, aggression and frustration. A world of mental anguish and pain began to seep into his consciousness. The pain had a name: Asher.

He jumped, his body flinching at the memories of the violation, remembering the mental pressure he had felt, as the two of them sparred to become dominant and control the body which to outward appearances was the captain everyone looked to for leadership and critical decisions. The last he could remember was drowning. It's the only way he could think to explain it. To completely lose yourself and all ability to outwardly control your surroundings, it was like slipping beneath the darkest waves of the deepest sea.

But things had changed.

Angels now sat by his side and the world was as white as a dwarf star.

Becoming conscious enough to logically analyse his situation, he started to piece things together. His senses were still a little behind the curve, eyesight still blurred, hearing a little dull, but he recognised the sensation. He was coming round after a heavy sedation. That was the simple explanation, and in his experience life generally worked on a simple level most of the time. Things always had the capacity to be complex, but life was similar to entropy in that respect, always looking to attain its lowest level.

Confusion started to disrupt his simple world as it began to rain. Slowly at first but then there was a sudden intensity: the rain turned to hail then bullets, loud and violent. The world of white suddenly turned a bright red and a warm smattering of liquid splashed across his face. Involuntarily he caught some across his lips; it tasted faintly of iron. Noise then interrupted his thoughts. Someone was screaming, someone was yelling instructions—neither of which he could make out, as the whole place seemed to be howling and whistling as air started to rush about him.

Someone was now floating free—a shadow across him which moved with urgency and purpose. There was another sudden noise which almost burst his eardrum; he reacted as best he could and moved his head away from the source. The cacophony was fading. The shadow moved away and he followed it until another thunderous sound made him close his eyes tight in shock.

Silence.

Opening his eyes, he blinked, finally gaining some clarity on his surroundings. As he took in the scene before him, he could feel his adrenaline begin to spike. He looked quickly to his right; Jemma was looking back at him briefly but, once she had ascertained his condition, she got back to working fast on the console in front of her. Close enough to see, he reviewed the data on the screen: she was correcting a slowly tumbling four-man escape pod in it's descent toward the Xannix surface. Whatever she was doing was working; the tumble was becoming a spin, which would become a level attitude within another few moments.

Moving around the pod, his eyes searched for the shadow that had been urgently moving around the space and causing all the noise. It was a medic—he could see from the yellow coloured shoulder flash—but he was tending the fourth in the compartment. Slung across the medic's shoulder was a hull breech-sealing device. Whatever their situation, he realised that they had been really lucky:

the team had acted quickly, hull integrity was still good, and they could still make it to the surface. He didn't fancy going out due to explosive decompression in an escape pod. They were sturdy little things and could put up with a lot of punishment, though a hull breach was a risk to avoid. To his left, he found the evidence of the patch repair: quick dry, fast-expanding hull sealant. When set, this stuff was as hard and tough as ceramic—it had to be—but it would conduct some of that re-entry heat inside the pod when they hit atmosphere. It was going to get toasty.

'Status?' he asked Jemma across bio-comm. He didn't want to alert the other two or distract them; one clearly needed urgent medical attention, certainly more than he did. There was blood everywhere.

'Even this idyllic new world we've chosen as our new home appears to have space junk,' she messaged with a frown of concentration on her face. 'The *Endeavour* is gone, Pete. The defence network was a trap,' she continued, making the final corrections to their flight path, if it could be called that. She looked at him briefly with a grim determination, as she unstrapped her harness. 'Over to you, fly-boy. Don't crash.' She turned and touched the medic on the shoulder; he didn't stop what he was doing but moved over slightly to give Jemma some space to work. He got a glance of the guy in the seat, face pale and ashen—he would be losing a lot of blood, and most of it was across the pod. This was all going to get rough, re-entry was never easy, and he'd need them back in their harnesses soon. He did the calculations: three minutes. He pinged the countdown to the broadcast bio-comm band. He knew they didn't need the added pressure, but they needed the information.

He wasn't sure, having just become conscious, that he should be piloting a pod to the surface of a planet, but then you had to work with the circumstances you were dealt—this was a bad hand in anyone's book. Setting that aside, they were alive, and at the moment staying that way was his only concern.

The display showed their track and it was off. They were descending at the correct adjusted speed but the angle was off. He fired the thrusters momentarily, the manoeuvre bringing the heat shield into alignment. Things looked better, and he spared a glance at the medics working on their wounded team member. The guy's eyes were now beginning to glaze over and roll unfocussed, and his mouth seeming to say something which, even at a couple of paces, he couldn't hear. Jemma moved close to listen, holding the man's hand tightly in what looked to be his last moments. Possibly his final moments. Clayton became chilled. With the *Endeavour* gone, this man could never be revived. This would be his final breath; there would be nothing he or any of the medical team could do. They didn't have a wave recorder in the pod and it wouldn't matter that they still had some of his DNA—with his wave and the *Endeavour* gone, so was he.

Focussing back on the display, he tried to get a fast tactical view of the mess they were leaving behind, some part of him hoping that the *Endeavour* was somehow viable and they could get this man back to the med-bay. The pod's instrumentation was basic: getting to the surface of a planet in a hurry, or carrying its occupants in stasis for as long as possible, was all it was designed to do. Giving him a complex tactical display of the millions of moving objects in low orbit was far beyond its specification. All he could tell was where he was and where he was going. A target landing site was plotted, which flashed at him in a monotonous red circular icon. He looked back at the guy opposite; Jemma and the other medic had both stopped work, both hanging their heads in defeat. The life of the man before them had ended and there had been nothing they could do about it, but for the first time he had a better view of the man's chest, the right side of which had a hole in it the size of his fist and the front of his tunic was entirely crimson from the wound. Whatever had punctured the hull had moved right through the man opposite, travelled across the pod and exited by punching a hole through the hull by his head. He had been lucky; the guy opposite hadn't.

"Please, return to your seats," he asked aloud, as delicately as possible. "Atmosphere in sixty seconds." Sluggishly, they returned to their seats and strapped themselves back into their harnesses. He could see the sadness in their faces, the tears in Jemma's eyes, but they were not on the ground yet; they would have to mourn later.

Most of the flight from here on in would be automatic; he only needed to monitor the descent. Their track was set and, as they hurtled towards the ground, the graphics of the display showing the course as good, the first way point intersected the line of atmospheric contact, the second way point the landing zone. A sound started to gather about them, like a light wind rushing past, caressing the craft on a cushion of air. He noted the hull temperature begin to rise as the noise of the wind became a roar and the ride became like being pitched into the rapids of a white water river. His vision blurred and shuddered with the violence of the forces applied to their fragile craft, fired like a bullet into the Xannix atmosphere. All he could tell was that the display track was showing green; further detail would have to wait until they slowed to a stable velocity and the flight smoothed.

Sudden whining noises occurred above their heads. The air brakes were being deployed to slow their descent, and almost instantly he felt himself forced into his seat—arms, legs, and body heavier by what seemed like magnitudes. Corrective thrusters fired, adjusting and correcting their course as they hurtled towards the ground.

Now steady enough to access the controls again, he switched the view to an outside camera which was aimed along their track, and he could see clouds for the first time in years. They seemed so far away and like a blanket across the world below, but at the rate they were travelling he knew they would be through them in seconds. Wisps of cirrus cloud flicked past the view, momentary and fleeting, but the blanket below them made its way toward them with inevitability. He estimated the cloud cover to be only two or three hundred meters above the ground. The altimeter clicked down. More bursts from the thrusters, faster corrections to course and attitude, adjusting slowly towards a vertical descent.

He had lost the horizon a few moments ago. Now all he could see was the white of the clouds below. His depth perception was completely useless, and he couldn't tell from the white-out before him what their height was, so he referenced the altimeter. One thousand meters.

A hand reached out and held his. Jemma gripped his hand with white knuckles. He turned his head towards her and looked into her beautiful brown eyes. It was a sight he could never get tired of.

"Love you," she said. Deep emotion in her words. He knew what she meant. It was more than words, perhaps even their last words. He searched for some response which would express everything he felt in that moment.

"You too," he said with a soft smile. It didn't seem enough.

The main retro fired and his relative weight suddenly became that of a small elephant, the arresting g forces playing with his body and distorting his features. He gritted his teeth and sat back in the couch, head back, all his muscles tense, trying to keep the blood from draining from his head. As the forces increased, the couches rotated into a more horizontal position to assist in the softening of the applied force.

Everywhere on the screen before him was now a dark green; they were through the cloud layer and the ground came up to meet them fast. In the last few moments, the roar of the retro became intense, and it shook his body from inside; his chest felt as if it might collapse at any moment, but at the same moment explode due to the vibration of the ship. It was very evident to him that he was just a bag of water being thrown around. Bags of water were delicate. The training simulations had not prepared him for this level of physical assault.

The ground hit them in the back like a charging rhino, knocking whatever air he had left in his lungs out into the cabin. The noise around them instantly shut off with a sound like a gas turbine winding down.

They all stared at the ceiling for what seemed like an eternity.

STRAUD

Deathly silence had fallen across the bridge. People were in shocked awe at the *Endeavour* as it was displayed before them, slowly arcing through space and fragmenting as it did so. She had cracked into various large wrecked sections, a debris field trailing in her wake. The satellite network had decimated the *Endeavour* from afar and taken out the engine pods in explosive fashion. Each had been ejected as per design, to avoid the risk of a catastrophic core failure. It had appeared to work. The core was holding and going through its emergency shutdown procedure, but this hadn't stopped the Xannix defence network from its task, and the endless onslaught had finally caused terminal structural failure.

Escape pods had started to shake loose from the wreckage like pollen on the wind. Initially they appeared as a translucent haze around the ship, but as burn engines kicked in they turned into little shooting stars turning for the planet below, tails of plasma bright in the black.

Obadiah stood motionless to her side. He seemed as transfixed by the scene as everyone else on the bridge but, to prove otherwise, an update came to her attention via her bio-comm: new nav instructions for a suggested course of action. She confirmed them and sent them straight to the helm. The new navigational course plotted to the main bridge display and traced a route through the debris field but, most importantly, through the huge defensive hole the *Endeavour* had torn in the satellite network. It was their way out. She would capitalise on the *Endeavour's* sacrifice.

"Obi," she said to break the silence. "Send this new course to the *Intrepid*."

"Course sent."

She nodded. Addressing the room, she looked around. "Time to get out of here, people."

The bridge seemed to come back to life. Orders started to be relayed and damage reports dealt with. Comms with the *Intrepid* lit up as they manoeuvred through the field.

Commander Forester opened a sub-vocal link from the crash couch next to her, clearly not wanting to be overheard. 'Sir, I understand the need to be anywhere but here. But where are we going?'

'One thing at a time, Forester,' she said. 'Let's just get through the defence grid. Then we'll have options.'

'Aye, sir.'

Helm was working as best it could through the newly plotted flight plan, but missing all the wreckage was not easy, or fully achievable. Although they could work their way past the larger remains of the *Endeavour*, the smaller debris was something they had to endure.

"Comms! Inform *Intrepid* to pull in as close as she can to our stern. We will carve a path through the debris field. No need for both of us to be taking damage en route."

"Yessir," came the response.

Moments later she saw *Intrepid* responding to her request. Tucking into their wake a couple of clicks to the *Indianapolis's* stern, which was uncomfortably close under normal conditions, but considering the current situation she viewed it as necessary proximity.

Alerts were flashing all over her damage control screen: decks all around the bow of the *Indianapolis* were being breeched by high-velocity debris. The external design of the hull being angled to counter such fast-moving objects was deflecting most, but the double hull was overcome by sheer quantity. Decks were being holed and people fought frantically to patch or evacuate sections, depending on the severity of the damage. The bridge being set deep within the ship was reasonably safe; unless they were really unlucky they could continue to command operations until the very last moment. She pushed thoughts of the *Endeavour* from her mind, what must have been going through Roux's head as he pushed his ship through the defence network?

"Sir." It was the duty comms officer. "We have an incoming message." The officer paused. "It's from a Xannix vessel the other side of the defence grid."

Her features became hard, almost angry.

"Put it through," she said, with clear suspicion in her tone.

A visual image of a Xannix in a white uniform, the chest of which displayed a patch showing a large red sun-like icon with red lines leading out from the centre. There was also vertical lettering which she couldn't make out. The Xannix leant forward for a moment, possibly adjusting some control or other to the side of the camera, but when it noticed that he had connected, it leant back and made a nodding gesture with its head.

"To the captain of the *Indianapolis*," it said in a sincere and cordial tone. "I am Kesset, commander of the Seeker vessel *Lanseer*. We have been instructed by Setak'osso Larsen to offer you immediate sanctuary amongst our fleet."

There were several things about Commander Kesset's statement that took her off guard, and the fact that he was speaking almost perfect English was least among them. Larsen? Was that Lieutenant Larsen? It could be a translation similarity—Kesset could have been speaking about someone else— or it could be coincidence but, with all that had been going on these last few days, she thought it unlikely. Larsen. What on Earth was going on? Then there was the fact that they were offering sanctuary. Weren't they shooting at them moments ago? The chance that this could all be a trap, a rouse to get the *Indianapolis* and *Intrepid* close enough to finish, could not be ruled out.

Larsen was the key.

'Forester, can we reach Lieutenant Larsen? I want confirmation of their intentions.' She pushed the message sub-vocally via bio-comm link. To the viewing Xannix, nothing would have been evident.

"Commander Kesset," she said calmly. "You'll forgive me if I don't fully trust your offer."

Kesset nodded and inclined his head. "I understand your reluctance. I am sending you identification codes for our ships. If you are in agreement, I would suggest you move to the far side of our fleet and away from any unidentified ships and the planet's surface. We will be your shield where we can."

A list of ships and Identification Friend or Foe codes arrived at her console. There were more IFF codes than she thought, and more than the *Indy's* scanners were showing her. The Xannix stealth technology was far above anything they had ever seen. Their ships were completely invisible to both scanning and visual observation. The missing ships suddenly appeared on the primary bridge display. They were already closer than she would have liked—just the other side of the satellite defence grid.

Quickly running some calculations in her head, she highlighted a section of space.

"Helm, plot a course for this waypoint. Once there, plot and hold an orbital course."

"Yessir," came the confirmation.

"Everywhere I look I see traps," muttered Forester, possibly to himself, but she overheard.

"One moment, Commander Kesset." She muted the comm to Kesset and turned to Forester.

"Speak up Forester. If I've missed something, I want to know about it."

Forester straightened up in his couch and started tapping away at his console, swiping screens aside until suddenly her display was linked. A window popped up with tactical representations of the known visible ships, the now newly designated Seeker ships and shaded blocks of space which covered several areas relative to the way-point she had just designated.

"Consider an opponent who has just shown you all his cards," he said.

A knowing smile crossed her lips; they both knew there was no such thing. An adversary never showed his hand; there was always something going on.

"It's a lure?"

"Classic example," he said. "Show your opponent something to focus on, something they cannot resist. Then crush them on the counter attack with what they can't see, with what they don't expect." He pointed to the orange areas of space he had highlighted. "Why would they give us all these shiny IFF codes? Could they possibly be holding some back?"

"They could and—considering their stealth tech—they could be sitting 200 meters away and we wouldn't know it." Lines furrowed her brow as she considered her options, and Forester's argument.

"I agree there are traps, but right now we need allies. If Larsen is down there and able to hold some influence on matters, we can use that."

"I still recommend caution," stated Forester.

"Now, I can't argue with that."

She returned to Kesset and removed the mute from the comm.

"Commander Kesset, we are under way to your suggested coordinates. We will be there in ten minutes."

She watched closely as Kesset nodded his understanding. She saw nothing in his actions which led her to believe he was lying or untrustworthy, but then, wasn't that a mark of the most competent liars? She could be sailing them right into the jaws of danger and all she had was a gut feeling that this Xannix was telling her the truth. She needed to confirm his story. More than that, she wanted to know what was going on down on the surface. And what was a Setak'osso?

"Larsen," she suddenly found herself saying aloud. It was to hold Kesset a moment longer, grab his attention while she took a moment to think. "I want to speak with him."

They had lost contact with both shuttle crews that had made it to the surface, and she intended to use this current situation to her advantage, maybe learn some vital information of the unfolding events on the planet below. Kesset could be a way to make that connection.

"Your Lieutenant Larsen is currently on the move between secure locations. We will relay any information we receive to you on a direct channel. We are sending you a recorded communication from Setak'osso Larsen now."

"Thank you, Commander," she stated, as the message popped onto her screen. She sent it directly to her bio-comm and played it.

A visual of Larsen appeared. He was dishevelled and in a cramped vehicle of some kind, dark and claustrophobic, and an occasional dash of light slid across the screen to indicate he was moving. He leaned in close to the recording device and began to speak.

"To any captain of the fleet, I hope this message reaches you," he opened, casually. This did not appear to be a man in distress or under duress; perhaps that was a good sign. She let the message run. "I haven't got much time, so I'll be brief. Science Officer Rivers and myself are alive and well; however, we are the last of the crew of Horus One. As far as we can tell, there were no other survivors. There was another shuttle which made a landing at the regional capital. I made brief contact with Lieutenant Reeve and Sergeant Silvers before we were separated. The crew were taken and at this moment we are unaware of their location.

"Simply put, the world has two factions on the planet, Seekers and Overseers, which govern the people. I am currently working with the Seekers to overcome the current Xannix regime. This sounds alarming, but it is a traditional process on the Xannix planet. However, this time it is more complex. The current Setak'daa is a Zantanath, and the Seekers believe the only way to remove the Zantanath from their planet is to use us—to use me—as an opposing Setak'osso. They basically have a civil war every few years to decide their next world president."

Slumping his head forward, Larsen audibly sighed, rubbing his hand across his face as he looked back. A decision made.

"One last thing you should know. I don't know how relevant this is yet, or how much you may already know, but there was another mission launched from the *Endeavour*. The crew of this mission were in stasis and launched from the *Endeavour* in a fast specially modified and experimental vessel named *Starchaser*. The mission landed here twenty years ago and we have learnt that they have since been abducted by the Zantanath, possibly killed, although that has not been confirmed."

Larsen looked away from the camera momentarily nodding agreement to someone, probably being told to wind up the message. He turned back to the camera.

"For the moment, the Seekers are your allies. I understand that there is a Commander Kesset aboard the *Lanseer*." He managed a brief smile through his obvious fatigue. "Strange. It translates as 'mother bird'.

"Anyway, he is there to assist. He and his fleet are charged with defending the human fleet. He's on the level."

A final pause, as he came to the end of the message. She could see he was checking off points in his mind, and he nodded to himself to complete the list.

"I'll contact you in person as soon as I am able. Larsen out." The screen cut to black.

She took a breath. There was a lot there to take in. 'Was that genuine?' she asked comms.

'Yes, sir. Encoding checks out,' came the reply.

'I concur,' echoed Obadiah. She looked to her right and Obi's holographic image gently looking down on her with an expression of concentration.

If this all checked out, Larsen was in way over his head. And what made it worse was the fact she could do little about it. Her primary concern right now was to move the two remaining ships out of danger and to pick up as many of the survivors of the *Endeavour* as she possibly could, although many of the escape pods looked to already be well on their way to the surface of the planet below.

Realising that Commander Kesset was still on the main channel, she made her decision.

"Commander Kesset, we will manoeuvre to your position, but we will be launching rescue shuttles to recover any escape pods currently not headed for the planet's surface."

He nodded. "We will be ready for you to join formation. Kesset, *Lanseer*."

She turned to Forester with an intense motivation. "Set in the new course and get us through the defence grid, then get the shuttles launched. We recover all space bound pods on the far side of the defence grid. And I want regular status updates on those that make it to the surface."

"Yes, sir," he affirmed as he turned to his command console to action her orders.

Quickly turning back to Obadiah she stood and set off at pace. "Obi, briefing room, now."

"Already there," he replied.

*

She strode into the briefing room with purpose and a steely determination, straight up to the holographic representation of Obadiah. Looking at him straight in the eyes, she pressed, "What happened? I thought you said you were able to bring Dawn back." She felt like she wanted to explode, but that was just the frustration talking, gnawing at her as the world around her crumbled. He had convinced her he could reach Dawn, but it had been too little too late.

Obadiah seemed to stiffen, his posture growing defensive as he spoke, "I did. However, Dawn was unable to recover the *Endeavour's* engines in enough time to affect the outcome. They had sustained too much damage." He sighed. Human emotion. Sorrow. "We all did all that we could."

"No. No, we did not," she replied with some venom. "If we had done all we could, the *Endeavour* and everyone aboard would still be safe. Now, we have thousands of people in the wind and an untold number of dead." She stopped and turned away, unable to look at Obadiah. She knew she was being momentarily unreasonable. To lay all this at Obi's feet was unfair and uncalled for, and he was right. They had done all they could.

"I'm sorry," she said to the empty seats of the room, "I'm just venting."

"Apology accepted," replied Obadiah.

"Good," she said taking a seat in the front row of the forum and leaning forward to steeple her fingers in front of her face. She bowed and touched her forehead as if in prayer, but heavy thought and contemplation drew much the same action. "This entire situation is insane."

"It is what it is," stated Obadiah. "Exceptional circumstances caused by equally exceptional and unforeseen events. Not even our VERS predicted this outcome."

"No, but the moment we encountered an intelligent species here, we should have upped our game. We were complacent."

"We were fighting internal threats and external unknowns," he said. He was trying to calm her, she knew. To a degree it was working. She was starting to think more clearly.

She ran through the numbers in her head. They had people on the surface they couldn't reach, and they had people in lower orbit that they could. That would be their first priority. The shuttles would recover the stranded in space; the rest would be a waiting game. She needed more information.

"Obi, get Commander Kesset on the link. If they are now allies, we need information. I want to know what's happening on the surface. Larsen said they were in the middle of a civil war, which means we have already chosen sides and we know nothing of the culture or the situation. Kesset needs to bring us up to speed."

"I'm not sure they will be happy coming aboard, given what happened on the *Endeavour*," Obadiah cautioned.

"Agreed. I suggest we assemble a group of volunteers. They will be a liaison team and stationed on the *Lanseer* with Commander Kesset. They will learn all they can about the situation and report back. Put the word out to the crew. I'll speak to Kesset."

"Yes, sir."

"And the team will be unarmed. They are to be ambassadors, not soldiers, over there. Make sure they understand that. I want them ready to go in 30 minutes from the forward shuttle bay."

She stood and made her way to the terminal in the centre of the room by the dais, as Obadiah's hologram dissolved. Punching a few quick commands into the console, Commander Kesset's face appeared before her. He seemed unfazed by her quick return communication; he may even have been expecting it.

"Commander Kesset," she started, before he had time to greet her. "I have a proposal."

SILVERS

He had been bundled unceremoniously into his couch, a body-shaped well in the wall of the cabin to silhouette the form of a Xannix, in what appeared to be a shuttle of some kind. Reeve slumped opposite him, her head hanging like a rag doll, as they were both sat buckled into their harnesses, or restraints, depending on your point of view. Yannix strode into the compartment, leading an entourage of Xannix, and Spencer.

Spencer looked as dishevelled as both of them, but he seemed to be getting star treatment. He was unshackled and speaking softly to one of the Xannix, at the same time looking sheepish and uncomfortable. He imagined it to be due to being amongst the Xannix, having to capitulate, but as he caught Spencer's eye, Spencer immediately averted his gaze looking anywhere but at him or Reeve.

Yannix and his team continued to the front of the cabin then through to another part of the ship, along with Spencer, and quickly followed by the crew who had been strapping them to their seats. A single Xannix took a couch by the bulkhead door and pressed a hand to a control pad. The couch seemed to swallow him and mould to his form. Within a moment or two, there was only a convex white bump in the wall, the height of a recumbent Xannix.

He examined his own couch for a moment looking for the same control and pressed it. When nothing happened he pressed it again. Nothing. He considered his harness, it looked ad-hoc, rigged and not something which would naturally be in place. Equally, his frame was too short for the recess of the couch, the head area being a clear third of a metre above him. This couch was not for a human, nor was it designed for the purposes of transporting prisoners, all this was evident. They were a special case.

The cabin was surprisingly silent, a slight breeze dusted over his brow as he lay there staring at the ceiling, the atmosphere in the craft being circulated as the life support systems came online. Out of the corner of his eye, he saw the cabin bulkhead move and undulate, then the doorway began to iris close. The action wasn't mechanical as he expected, it was very much muscular, the iris closing with a quiet motion which pulled to an airtight seal. His mind started to puzzle its way through the experience.

Opposite him, Reeve started to come round. A low grunt gave her away, as she struggled momentarily against the restraints. Her eyes snapped open and locked on his.

"Easy," he soothed. "Easy."

The tension in her body and rage he had seen flaring like a furnace in her eyes ebbed. As she worked through the room and assessed their situation, he waited; there was no rush. Wherever they were going, they were going there on someone else's schedule. Right now, they had time.

"How long?" she asked.

"In all honesty? It's been about five minutes since being strapped in. We have a guy at the end of the row here, he just blended into the scenery. I have no idea how he did that," he said, involuntarily trying the couch control again. Still nothing. "Then, there's this ship. Which I think is organic."

"Organic?" she echoed.

"Yeah. Check the door. It closed like your pupils dilate and contract. You know..." he made a motion with his thumb and forefinger like a closing sphincter.

"Organic tech?" she asked the room.

"Spencer will be loving this shit," he continued.

Reeve looked up and down the cabin. "Talking of our illustrious ambassador, where is he?" she asked, while testing the strength of her restraints, trying to release the clasp, more purposefully this time.

"He's aboard. Followed Yannix through here like a puppy right after we got shoved in these seats," he remarked with a stern tone. "Think he's going native."

"Who, Spencer?" she almost laughed. "You're kidding, right?"

"Nope. Do we really know what happened to him when he was aboard the *Spixer*? He was very keen to get back to us, sure, but whether he's aware of what they did to him or not, we just don't know. We know how they can manipulate minds—what's to say he hasn't been turned?"

"I won't believe it," she said with a frown, her brain still processing while her mouth gave a safe answer.

"Well, believe it or not, watch him."

A sudden sensation of movement came over him, slight at first but then the g forces built.

"Looks like we're on the move," said Reeve.

The g slowly increased until they were forced into a reclined position in their couches. He stared at the ceiling while the forces acting on his body pushed at him harder and harder. Feeling his vision start to tunnel, he calculated he'd have about another fifteen seconds of consciousness as he began to see stars. But as the pressure on his chest eased, he found that the stars did not recede from his vision, in fact they became even brighter. Leaving the atmosphere of the planet, he saw the Xannix star slightly to the left of centre of their direction of travel, the ceiling having become one huge display screen showing an external view of the ship. Looking around, he realised that everywhere he looked was an external view; the ship had become almost translucent. It was as if he was floating in space. He found his jaw was involuntarily slack with astonishment and consciously closed it, so as not to look gormless, although he didn't think Reeve had noticed and, if any Xannix were watching, he didn't think they would care. Only he seemed to care that he had momentarily lost his cool. He continued to stare at the ceiling.

"Woah," said Reeve, who was clearly as awestruck as he was.

"Yeah," was all he could say in reply.

"Looks like we're in for a long trip," Reeve said. "Maybe if we could get hold of Spencer, he might tell us?"

He watched as she momentarily defocused, a sure indication that a person's attention was elsewhere: another conversation, internally visualising, reading. Beginning to frown, she came back to him.

"He blanked you?"

"No. Worse. We're headed for the Zantanath home world."

"What makes you say 'worse'?" he asked.

"We're to be handed over to their military research division."

"How does he know that?"

"He agreed to it."

"What?" he exclaimed in surprise.

"A trade."

"For his own scrawny neck?"

"Looks like you were right."

"And he just fronted up and told you this?" he asked.

She scrunched up her face in anger. "He did apologise sincerely."

"Well, that's okay then." He let out an explosive burst and punched the couch control panel. "Asshole!"

They both sat quietly for a while, watching the stars and trying to consider their options, which to him appeared to be diminishing the further down the rabbit hole they got. He didn't want to believe that Spencer would sell them out so cheaply, but all the evidence was pointing that way. Then again, why would he tell them? That part didn't seem to make any sense to him. Only an egotist would want you to know that they had just sold you out, to watch their pain and delight in it. Spencer was not that sort of person—indeed, he had seemed positively ashamed of the fact. Something didn't add up.

"There's more to it," he said. "There has to be." Reeve just nodded her response, still lost in her own thoughts.

Lying back in his couch, he looked up at the stars and wondered where they were going. The craft was short range, and there was nothing in orbit that he could see locally, so their destination appeared to be close to the Xannix star. Rather than worry too much about it, he decided to get some sleep. It was always good to be fresh, and while there was time he would try and get some rest. He closed his eyes; his thoughts drifted and swirled as his body and mind calmed. Eventually sleep came.

*

He was awoken with a start and tried to sit bolt upright but was immediately yanked hard against his harness. He automatically tried to undo the clasp, and it flashed red as he fumbled with it. He looked around for Reeve, but all he could see was the giant hulk of a Xannix—the guard had been quick to get to them.

"Reeve," he yelled as he struggled against his harness again, trying desperately to get out of his couch and get to the lumbering Xannix in front of him. The darkness of the room throbbed with a weird buzzing sound and red pulsing light; he only assumed this was the ship-wide alert.

The Xannix turned to him and moved forward. He had Reeve under one of his four arms while she thrashed to try and get free, but it seemed not to bother the Xannix too much, as its attention was now on him and his harness. It tapped a sequence of buttons on the couch control then touched the harness clasp, which released easily. A pair of large muscular Xannix hands came towards him, grasped him like a doll and slung him over a shoulder. Within a second they were on the move.

"What in Terra's name is going on?" he called to Reeve, whose face was now visible as they were both carried towards the far end of the room. He felt like a naughty child who had just been slung over his father's shoulder.

"I have no idea," she said, clearly as annoyed as he was at being carried in such a way. "The alarm went off, then gorilla-man here appeared."

His mind ran wildly through options, then, as they passed through the bulkhead at the far end of the room and into a corridor, he had an idea.

'On three,' he messaged Reeve.

'On three, what?'

'One,' he wriggled to loosen the Xannix's grip. It didn't appear to work. 'Two.'

'Do you mind sharing, Sergeant?'

'Three.'

Having wriggled enough to dislodge a single arm he used it to push out to the corridor wall hard, the result was to unbalance the lumbering Xannix and tip him towards the opposite wall. Startled by the sudden change of direction and trying not to fall as it headed in the unexpected direction, he released his other arm from the Xannix's grip. Now with two arms free he pushed hard against the Xannix's back and thrust himself forward, yet again giving the Xannix a huge change in momentum and balance. The Xannix made an aggravated growl, and tried to readjust his grip, but it was too late. While it tried to grapple for him and keep hold of Reeve at the same time, he managed to completely slip its grasp.

Hitting the floor with a swift roll, he reversed and leapt straight at the Xannix's back before it had time to turn. He'd learnt the choke hold many years before, an advanced wrestling hold which cut off the flow of blood to the brain and air to the lungs, and he only hoped the anatomy of the Xannix was similar enough to human that it worked. His arms clamped round the Xannix neck and his legs around it's waist, it began to thrash wildly, crashing into the corridor walls with such force that he thought he might break a rib or fracture his skull, but through the pain he managed to stay put, like a limpet on a rock.

At some point, he heard Reeve scream. It was more of shock than pain, so his focus stayed fully fixed on the Xannix.

After what seemed like an hour, but had likely been only a few seconds, the Xannix began to show the first signs of slowing. The crashing blows against the corridor wall became less frequent, the grasping, clawing hands trying to pry him from his hold became weaker and finally the Xannix began to go down. First to one knee, then the other then the final slump to the floor, face first.

He was breathing hard and was almost unconscious of the fact that the struggle had ended. A gentle hand held his shoulder.

"Okay, Champion. We have to move." Reeve was already looking up and down the corridor, trying to work out their next move, as he tried to untangle himself from his hold and the now dead weight of the unconscious Xannix on the floor.

"Are we there yet, Mummy?" he asked, feigning disorientation, though he was breathing hard from the effort. That was real enough.

"Come on. This way," she said, setting off at a pace in the direction they had originally been travelling. He took a last look over his shoulder at the Xannix on the floor. Normally, you could estimate how long a person might be unconscious for; it was related to the recovery time the brain needed to resupply with oxygen. But a Xannix? He had no information on that. It could be half an hour, it could be thirty seconds. Whatever they were going to do, the best option would be to do it fast.

He realised quickly that they had a problem. Yes, they had momentarily eluded capture, but they were very much strangers in a strange, strange land. With no understanding of the language they didn't know where to start reading any signage, there appeared to be few control surfaces and the ship layout was very irregular, which only convinced him even more that the ship they were on was organic in some fashion. What that meant for them was simple: this game of cat and mouse was going to be very quick unless they were able to work out what was going on and how to understand the ship. They had a small head-start, but how fast the Xannix would realise they were loose was another unknown.

They turned a couple more corners in the same corridor: smooth walls and no indication of cabins or access controls made him think. How would you communicate with an animal? Or even another sentience?

The alarm was still sounding throughout the ship, as they turned the next corner to be confronted with a junction and two irises. There was no way back, and unless they could figure out how to work the doors, there would be no way forward. With only a nod of her head, Reeve indicated that he should work on the right iris; she walked straight up to the iris on the left and they both began to try prodding and pushing the door and its surround in as many ways or combination of ways they could think of.

'Don't know where you are,' came a message through the bio-comm link. It was Spencer. He wanted to blank him, block his chat. But the situation they were in now called for information.

'Busy,' he broadcast back on an open link so Reeve would pick up the chatter. She instantly stopped what she was doing and looked at him intently.

'We know you took out the guard,' Spencer continued. 'We don't have time. We've been double crossed.'

'Damn straight we have, Doctor Spencer,' he fired back. 'You have some face selling us out then chatting like we're buddies. What are you playing at Spencer?'

'Now is not the time.'

'Now is exactly the time.'

'We are being boarded by Zantanath. The deal has gone bad.'

'And you want an out with the good guys? Well, what do you say Lieutenant?' he asked, looking across to Reeve. She continued to look intent, but shook her head. 'Looks like it's bad for you Spence. LT and I are on our way out.'

At that moment a silver shimmering started to coalesce in a ball a little further back down the corridor, growing in intensity and size until it almost took up the width of the corridor. As he watched with the curiosity of a man trapped by something he didn't understand, Spencer continued. 'It is not as you think. I was just working to our mission goal. We need to speak to the Zantanath. Ultimately, they are the ones we need to call off the attack on the fleet. They are the ones that we need to convince of our need to be here. Didn't you hear what Larsen said?'

'Yeah. Yeah, I did,' he replied, now rather distracted and not really listening. Staring at the ball of light in front of them, both he and Reeve had turned and squared up to the roiling, undulating lightshow. Unconsciously, they had taken up a defensive posture against the threat.

The sphere in front of them disappeared in an instant, leaving four armoured figures. One was larger than the rest and still crackled with a residual energy across its surface and between two wing-like appendages which were folding themselves away into shielding on its back. Their armour was highly reflective and covered the humanoid occupants in hexagonal platelets which seemed to stretch as material across their forms but appeared metallic. A whistling sound modulated then began to descend in pitch, ending as the wings were finally enclosed.

The larger Zantanath locked onto them immediately, barking an order which was both harmonic and discordant through his visor. It sounded chilling, but he considered that was probably the effect they were going for. On this command, the other three turned and ran off down the corridor to where he and Reeve had just come, back toward the unconscious Xannix, and probably off to seek out Spencer. He didn't think this thing would be here for anyone but them. It was nice to feel special, but there's a time and place. This was not it.

Stepping forward, several platelets shifted on the Zantanath's armour, exposing an array of what looked like small short gun barrels from its shoulder section. He and Reeve were both in motion before the Zantanath could fire the weapon, but there was nowhere to go but forward. Their attack was brief. Tendrils of red lightning leapt from the Zantanath and lanced through their nervous system. Thrown to the deck, he was in instant intense pain. Thrashing on the floor as his body tried to find somewhere to hide. The screaming didn't sound like his, but he wasn't sure. As he felt consciousness drift from him, the only thing he could think was, *not again.*

SPENCER

Paralysed by distress, he watched as the Zantanath boarding party swept through the ship. A lone Zantanath warrior had just taken down Reeve and Silvers and there was nothing he could do; they simply wouldn't listen to him. Why had they not listened to him?

"It's too late to help your friends now, Ambassador," said a voice from behind him. "We must leave, or you will find yourself in a similar position."

Ambassador. The word seemed to hold far more grandeur when Clayton had bestowed the title on him, but now it felt like the heaviest weight to bear. He had betrayed his friends for the greater good of the fleet, of humanity, but at what cost? He knew the cost; it was all too obvious to him now. Their ancestors had believed in an immortal soul, the essence of each person and the continuum of life itself—that is what he had just traded in. He would be forever damned. How could doing the right thing be wrong?

Thoughts began to bubble up in his mind, other ways to help them, but every time he tried to focus in on what he needed to do a pain began to overwhelm him. It was not a physical pain, but a level of anxiety which he had never before had to deal with— beyond stress, beyond reason. His mind simply shut down, gave him nowhere to go. He blanked. As an academic, the inability to recall the most simple of things terrified him. Breaking out in a cold sweat, he felt his mind beginning to fall apart, and shatter into the smallest of parts.

"We are going now?" he asked in a whisper.

"Yes, Ambassador. We need to leave now. This way please," replied the voice.

Tearing his eyes from the screen, he moved away in a dream. The figure in front of him steered him with a decisive hand towards a doorway, and he followed without registering his surroundings, although every now and then a noise would interrupt his own internal turmoil—a scream or barked order, or an explosion which took him from his feet.

When the physical pain came, it leached its way into his mind, an ignored warning both of the danger he was in and the damage that his body had sustained. Neither was of any interest to him, his mind still consumed with the betrayal. If he was unable to help two of his friends, how would he help the fleet? If he couldn't help himself, how could he save anyone else? He couldn't rationalise it away.

Guilt and self-interest had been motivators to his decision. The pain and sustained levels of trauma these last few days had worn him down, and he just wanted all the pain and hurt to stop. He wanted a place to hide, to push the barbarians out and to be safe. But this was not it. Yannix had been full of anger and rage at his crew; he wanted none of it aimed at him. A coward's world of deflection and avoidance. He had agreed to all of the demands made of him. This weighed more heavily on him and anchored the betrayal firmly at his feet. Whatever arguments he used now to try and escape the mental cage he had set for himself, there was no key to release him.

He was lost.

A little voice in the back of his mind was working hard to get through, something vague and shadowy. He tried to look up from the floor but the world had turned red. Wiping his face to clear his vision only managed to worsen the problem with stinging alarm from his forehead. A gash had opened up and was bleeding profusely, the concussion turning his movement to uncoordinated, fumbling actions.

Something grabbed him by the collar and almost throttled him in the act. He felt himself dragged along the corridor, choking and spluttering, the world a blur of lights and sounds, none of which he recognised. A strong hand firmly took hold of his upper arm and he was suddenly elevated off the ground and slung across a huge trunk of a body, held and clamped diagonally across the torso of a Xannix.

The corridor lights began to pass at pace and in reverse as the Xannix took off down the corridor, his front to the chest of the Xannix, head over its shoulder. As the world rocked with the motion of its sprint, he thought he saw glimpses of silver flashing about in his vision, sparks illuminating the walls and ceiling. A growling bellow howled down the corridor: a vast shadow of death attempting to put out the silvery light. Tears welled in his eyes and masked the world in a mist; nothing held any definition, and he blinked hard to try and clear his vision. The howling ceased abruptly and the silvery forms reappeared closer than before.

He was suddenly dumped to the floor.

The room began to form, his eyes finally beginning to tell him something useful. It was a circular room with smaller iris doorways in the wall all about him. Looking back over his shoulder, Yannix was busy operating a bulkhead door. He could only imagine that he was locking it to impede their pursuers, but as he watched the door iris began to melt away and become a wall surface. There was no longer a door. There was no way for the Zantanath to reach them.

All the smaller portals around the room suddenly opened in an instant and without warning. His heart took another shock; his eyes wide trying to work out what was happening.

"Ambassador," said Yannix forcefully but calmly, "enter a capsule. Do it now."

He just nodded. Yannix continued to work at the room controls as he climbed into a pod.

Inside the pod was a simple arrangement of four concave forms, moulded silhouettes of four Xannix, he picked one and lay in the trough facing back towards the circular entrance, waiting for Yannix to join him. A moment later Yannix entered the pod and took the bay opposite him. The crash couches were in a cross formation, feet towards the centre, with a slight incline towards the headrests which meant each person in the escape pod could easily see the others—this was important for Xannix communication, as they utilised both visual and audible forms.

As the Xannix settled himself, he heard the soft but solid womp, womp, womp of the other pods ejecting into the void. A moment later, he found the moulded crash couch reshape about him and a harness form across his shoulders, chest and hips. It was as if the pod had decided to hold on to its precious cargo; he was secure and unmoving, eyes wide. Yannix quickly pressed a palm to a control terminal and the worlds became a visual and physical assault on the senses.

The escape pod was released into local space and, for one confused moment, he realised he could see everything: the stars, a nearby ship which was shining with the reflected light from the Xannix star, the star itself dazzling and bright to his right. There were sudden, stunning flashes, as some of the other escape pods Yannix had released failed and exploded about them. It wasn't until he saw a short fine line of light emanate from the Zantanath vessel that he realised they were being systematically destroyed. A couple more seconds was all they had.

His eyes wide, events began to slow, as if his mind was trying in its own way to extend reality during his last moments. A light display began to interrupt his vision; small waves of light enveloped them and the pod. The universe began to fade as the waves of light intensified in a ball around them. Presuming this was the effect of being struck by a highly focussed energy beam from the Zantanath ship, he resigned himself to an explosive end. There was no point in screaming or vocalising his frustration at this being the end of things—in some way he welcomed the karmic balance. He had betrayed his friends, so the universe was simply evening the score.

He closed his eyes and waited for the violence of forces that would rip him apart.

"Ambassador Spencer, you are safe. But we must go," said Yannix.

He opened his eyes with a snap. Yannix was standing over him and checking him over.

"We ought to get that cut on your head looked at."

The fact he was still alive was not something he could resolve.

"Are we dead?" he asked.

A rasping sound came from the Xannix.

"No, not dead. You are very much alive." Yannix straightened up. "Time is short, the new prime is soon to be decided, and things are about to change." He gestured to the open pod hatch. "If you would be so kind."

Heading out of the pod, he found himself in a bay within a much larger hanger area. Lights were bright and there was work and bustle going on across the deck. Large black-looking ships were lined up, their hulls shimmering every now and then with a fractal pulse of colour which caught his eye and was fascinating to watch, captivating like the flames of a warm fire. He tried to keep up with Yannix, who was off at a stride and heading for an elevator.

As they reached the service elevator, he saw the facility and atrium space was some sort of factory complex, clear lines of production and robotic manufacture in progress.

"Where are we?" he asked.

"Fabrication Complex 2," replied Yannix as he stepped onto the elevator platform.

"And you are making ships?"

"Among other things, yes."

As the elevator descended levels he could clearly see this was a military operation—there were floors of equipment and troops everywhere, all in similar uniform to Yannix. It looked like they were getting ready for something, a major military offensive. Xannix preparing for war.

The elevator stopped at a floor about midway down the central core of the facility, he took a last look across the manufacturing machines and production lines then followed Yannix, scuttling along behind like a child behind its parent. People sat and monitored control consoles, with large displays showing every detail of the operation, alerts raised as production channels showed less than optimal flow, warnings for defects in the materials or manufactured items. There was a high level of committed concentration going on; he didn't think any of the Xannix noticed a strange, short, skinny alien walking past them with their commander. Perhaps, if they did, it was wise to pay no attention and focus on their task.

The door in front of them opened and a Xannix nearby noted their presence; he rose to greet them and continued to walk alongside Yannix as they entered the room beyond.

"Commander, are you not meant to be somewhere else?"

"Yes, Elstron. Our little journey was, however, intercepted."

Elstron appeared in momentary thought. "Celicia?"

"She decided to go against our bargain, but it is of little consequence."

"What bargain?" he asked. Both the Xannix looked down at him as if a child had just asked an irritating question. A slight involuntary quiver to his left eye may have given away the sudden awkwardness he felt, perhaps he was not as involved in events as his ambassadorial title may have indicated.

With a reluctance, Yannix continued. "Celicia is manoeuvring to keep her power. It is time for her to fail."

"It is time for our planet to reclaim its soul," said Elstron. "The Zantanath have had their time here."

His short-term memory handed up images of the short journey he had just taken, the production lines of war feeding up through the facility atrium. His eyes started to widen as the realisation of what he had seen took hold.

"You're planning a coup," he said more to himself than the Xannix.

Yannix shifted and looked down on him, clearly considering how much to divulge to someone who he clearly simply considered a pawn in the game. "This endless cycle of self-annihilation is ending now. Xannix will no longer be ruled. We will not be persecuted. As a people, we may have lost our way over the cycles, but I intend to bring a purpose back to all Xannix."

"But war is not a purpose," he said.

"No, but it is the only means left to us by which to achieve our goals. We will be free."

"There has to be another way."

"We have lost generations trying to find that way. It is time to draw a line. Celicia will fail."

"And you will take her place?"

"And you will help me," Yannix stated.

He stopped. Was that why he was here? "And why would I do that?" The words slipped from his lips before any conscious decision filtered it out.

"It will be to human advantage to do so, or you will suffer the same fate as the Xannix."

"And what does that mean?" he asked, a level of stubbornness entering his voice. Yannix appeared unable to give him a direct answer, or didn't want to.

A moment of anger flared across Yannix as his skin began to shimmer white. Their eyes fixed; a decision made.

With almost invisible speed, Yannix grabbed him by the lower arm. Dragging him across the room, Yannix let out a roar of effort and threw him to the corner while continuing on to a control panel in the wall. Dazed, he stood slowly and tried to regain some composure. A panel in the wall in front of him slid aside. Inside there was a small room, and at its centre a vertical column of fluid, suspended and slowly rotating in space, the body inside the bubble almost recognisable. As his mind caught up with what he saw, his jaw slackened in disbelief.

"What—" his words came as a whisper. "What have you done?"

"Not us," Yannix glared at him. "The Zantanath do this to all they encounter."

"But why?"

"They take a species and engineer it, optimise it to their purpose. They discern the essence of your character, a defining trait, and genetically modify you into a tool they can employ."

"And this is humanity to them?"

"This is the optimisation and extension of your core self. In this warrior they have had to do little. But, yes, this is what your species will become," stated Yannix.

"No!" he shouted in denial staring back at the monster suspended before him.

"You will help us, Ambassador. Or this is your fate."

Staring back at him, through cold, dead and sunken eyes was a lean, naked humanoid figure, taller, more muscular, with a slightly distended cranium. There was a hunter's menace to its features of singular killing purpose. At its side in a second isolation chamber was a suit of armour; he had seen this before. Silver interlocking hexagonal platelets, large pack and weapon. A Zantanath warrior stared down at him. Only, it wasn't Zantanath, it was human.

It was Larsen.

LARSEN

It was called the 'deep sleep' for a reason. He and Rivers had been in an induced coma for the best part of five years while the *Starchaser* arrowed its way through the void between the *Endeavour* and Hayford b, a dark silent spy in the night, just another one of the millions of objects dancing around the Hayford star.

Ice cold. The ship may have been preparing for their awakening for several days, but the deck was ice cold to the touch, his feet curling at the sensation, the metal floor draining heat from his body. His uniform was in a zipped bag strapped to the foot of the sleep pod. He extended an aching arm to retrieve it, the disorientation still letting itself be known through any minor movement, and his wasted muscles complaining at every instruction. His breath misted in the chill air, producing momentary micro-clouds in the cabin.

He dressed slowly.

Rivers was already awake, her sleep pod vacated and resealed. There were not many places in the ship she could be: there was the cockpit, the engine bay and this cramped area for some small living quarters, sleep pods, food prep area and, in a sealed cubicle, the head. The design of the craft was specific in its purpose of getting them from one place to the other as fast as it could whilst keeping them in stasis the entire journey. The fact that he was awake now only meant he had work to do and would be on firm ground very soon. No need to get comfy.

Personal space was not something they had given thought to in the design; the cockpit was close and confined, and if either of them had been claustrophobic they would have been in real trouble. He slid into his flight couch and buckled himself in. Rivers was busy—the only evidence of this the light flicker and movement of her eyelids as her bio-comm interface internalised all the ships information and control channels for her. She was running system and navigation checks, the holoscreens in front of him displaying and mirroring the results of her unseen commands.

'Morning,' came a greeting across his bio-comm. A message digitised across his vision and prefixed by her ident.

'Morning,' he replied. The silent conversation was common. Faster, more efficient. No need for superfluous engagement, especially when under heavy workload, such as piloting a fast-moving spacecraft.

He tracked her progress for a moment, then began to assist. He took over flight control and navigation, letting her get on with beginning the astral surveys of the planetary system they were now in.

They were already close, maybe a day out, but as the first initial analysis came in he knew something was off. Rivers was running the same group of tests on the instruments again and again.

'I'm receiving weird readings from the planet,' she said, after some time ensuring her calculations were correct. 'It's like there is a background chatter, faint but definitely comms.'

'That's impossible,' he replied. 'This planet is uninhabited. Are you sure it's coming from the planet? Can you identify the source?'

'Yes. It's definitely Hayford b.'

A frown furrowed his brow, as the new information bounced around his mind; could the scientists back home have got it wrong? Badly wrong?

'What was that?' he asked. A proximity warning momentarily pulsed in his bio-comm display, but didn't repeat. He checked the local space display for closing objects, but nothing appeared to be there. He was beginning to feel uneasy.

'False reading,' said Rivers. 'Nothing there.'

Rivers continued to work on the scans, refining the data being produced by the arrays deployed from long telescoping arms at four points around the central body of *Starchaser*. Antenna dotted with flower-like dishes, catching any information it could from Hayford b.

Slowly, as they began to close on their target, the information collected by the astrogation system began to create a more defined picture. Dawn's voice alerted them to the latest report, a light bead fragmenting and vibrating as a visual representation of her presence across a section of the holographic display in the upper centre of the cockpit control panel. Although Dawn's voice, it was only an AI construct, not Dawn herself. Her sentience was limited by law to a single core memory structure, and that was currently aboard the *Endeavour*. The law constructed around human integrated AI was strict and enforced with zero-tolerance; however, there were always loopholes and humanity was pretty weak-willed when it came to it. He was sure the rule would be flouted eventually. Human duplication was something everyone was educated against, but there were always those willing to break the rules, especially if it gained them power or money.

"The latest analysis of the Hayford b star is not as expected," Dawn said.

'That's an understatement,' Rivers sent him by bio-comm.

"Satellite network detected approximately 50,000 kilometres from the planet surface. Purpose unknown."

"Defence grid?" he asked.

"Possibly. I am receiving faint background communications, nothing directed at us, but growing in intensity as we approach."

"At this course, we will cross the satellite boundary in 30 minutes," he stated.

"I don't think we should go charging in," said Rivers. "We need more data."

"That's a scientist, if ever I heard one. Where's your sense of adventure?" he smiled. He knew she was right. She just looked back at him blankly. Some people had no sense of humour.

He plotted a course to take them into a wide orbit of Hayford b and to stay 500 kilometres wide of the satellite network.

"New course plotted. Taking us into a wide orbit. That should give you what you need."

The display in front of them altered and their trajectory tracked into a lazy arc which would eventually take them into a safe wide orbit. Rivers just continued to work; she had been given a puzzle, and he completely understood the urge to solve it.

*

Their orbit had been established for several hours and Rivers had gone quiet. He found it equally strange that Dawn had not updated them. Initially, he had thought it due to the fact her sensor scans had been unsuccessful, but finally he resolved to break the silence.

"I'm going to grab a coffee. You want one?"

Nothing. He could see her eyelids moving as her eyes moved frantically, working on the data, fingers twitching as she mimicked terminal keyboard activity, though while using the bio-comm this was unnecessary—a reflex. He moved across and placed a hand on her shoulder; she was too focused. The physical contact broke the spell, and her eyes opened with a start and locked on his.

"Time for a break," he said. "Dawn can take the controls for a while. Dawn, let us know if there are any changes to the situation."

"Yes, Lieutenant."

Rivers paused to consider, then exhaled and nodded. "Milk and sugar. I'm going to need it," she said.

"So, what have you found?" he asked, as he walked and squeezed through to the small living space. He was amazed this small ship had been fitted with gravity plates—it took half the ship's space to contain the generator—but being weightless in deep space for long periods was biologically detrimental, as it played havoc with the immune system and circulation, not to mention the muscle wastage. Gravity was wound down to the minimum required to stave off the worst of these effects, but it provided a workable environment. He still hurt in his bones.

Grabbing two sachets of coffee to the correct specification he placed them in the warmer and started to heat them. He leaned against the galley, turning to face Rivers who was now sat at the small galley table looking like she was praying, eyes closed, trying to find the right words.

"So, I've confirmed it: a satellite network completely surrounds this planet, but it is completely jamming all outbound transmitted electromagnetic signals. At least, any residual signal that might make it through is so small it cannot be properly determined; we can only just make it out from the universe's own background noise."

"So, the leak is small," he said. "But the big question is—why? And who?"

"At this range though, we have the opportunity to use visual observation using our VST," she said. The Very Small Telescope was mounted into the side of the fuselage and, with their current orbit, it was directed perfectly for a focussed view of the planet below. And it was powerful, the fact that it was small bore no relation to its ability, it could pick out a reasonably detailed image at a thousand kilometres with some advanced sky scanning and digital rendering techniques, which overcame the size-to-performance issue, although atmospheric distortions would still restrict fine resolution. Rivers would have pretty good detail at this range.

Rivers continued: "What it shows is an advanced civilization. Cities appear to be vast vertical structures, arcologies with satellite feeder towns, not like the sprawling cities of Earth. The arcologies are localised within the warmer regions of the planet and often near the oceans. I've seen some level of ground traffic, a larger amount of air traffic, but this is where is starts getting weird."

A short ping indicated the coffee was ready, and he removed the sachets from the warmer and passed one to Rivers while sliding into the galley bench opposite.

"Thanks," Rivers said.

"What's weird?"

She nodded as she took a pull on the coffee, as if to agree that it was just the thing she needed. "Weird? Okay, consider you're an advanced civilisation with technology enough to create a vast network of satellites around your planet. That kind of thing would take resource and incredible effort, right? You would leave evidence of mining, perhaps orbital fabrication plants, and all this would require energy to power, so you would need power generators, perhaps solar collectors. There would be a network of things you would need to do this."

"Yeah, so?"

"So," she said, staring at him, "where are they?"

He looked at her blankly, his mind going over the information known about the system so far. There was no evidence, not even a space station so far. His blank expression turned into a frown.

"So, how did they get there?"

"That is also a good question," Rivers said. "I also can't find any surface facilities which might look like they are for heavy space industry. But, either way, it doesn't make sense to put heavy space industry on the planet surface. Too resource intensive. Every time you want to put a nut or bolt into space, you'd have to launch it. The cost would be too great."

"Maybe for us, but we have no idea who these people are, or what motivates them."

She looked at him for a moment but shook her head. "I don't think so."

There was suddenly an alert icon in his bio-comm view: 'Proximity alert. Object detected fifteen hundred kilometres from orbital south,' stated Dawn over the shipwide comms. Rivers had clearly received the news too. Their eyes locked, both sharing a moment of alarm, then they were moving to the cockpit.

"That's below the satellite network," said Rivers, as she strapped herself into her flight couch.

"But, where's it come from? There was nothing when we scanned earlier."

Rivers worked fast to obtain some sort of visual of the object— it was dark and in the shadow of the planet, but there was enough of an outline to give a sense of its scale against the background star field.

"I can't get a reading on it, but the VST is giving us some information. It's heading in a counter orbit, so should be coming out of the planet's shadow in a moment."

They both watched the VST display, as the object moved slowly into the light. They saw blacks and browns with a ragged edge, then, as more revealed itself, the distinct outline of a potato-shaped asteroid came into view.

He realised he'd been holding his breath and made the decision to begin again. He relaxed back into his couch and felt a slight disappointment flow through him.

"Is that it?" he said to the cockpit generally, more to himself as anyone else, although Rivers was still concentrating intently on the asteroid.

"Yeah, there," Rivers said in a whisper. "Can you get us closer?" she asked.

"I thought you wanted to wait for more data," he said.

"I think I've just got it. Closest side of the asteroid—what do you see?"

He looked at her, puzzled for a moment, then took a better look at the blob on the screen. It froze as he watched and Rivers manipulated the image. It flicked a couple of times to zoom in on the area of interest. She was smiling at him, eyes sparkling with excitement.

"So, what do you see?" she asked again.

"Is that the mining facility you've been looking for?" he postulated. She grinned back. "But it doesn't look like anyone's home."

"Even better. Abandoned or not, the data we obtain there will be valuable, and if there's no one there, at least we can snoop without the locals being aware."

"Sounds risky."

"It's what we're here for."

RIVERS

The moment they had slipped through the satellite network, the universe had become very loud. Almost the entire electromagnetic spectrum was alive with chatter, and Dawn had immediately assisted in trying to filter the noise and find coherence in the flood. As the data was compartmentalised, she began to see patterns and hubs emerging in the communication flow. None of it appeared to emanate or target the asteroid they were currently headed towards, which was good, but some of the comms traffic seemed to be transmitting from empty space. That one really had her puzzled. Maybe they had developed some kind of interstellar communication, but the *how* she couldn't even begin to fathom.

For now, she believed her plan to be safe. The asteroid station was their best bet. Get in quickly and out of sight.

'They are playing with us, you know that, right?' said Larsen as they moved ever closer to the asteroid. The cockpit HUD translated the navigation track into a light blue line which arced across their view; at its base, the Head Up Display also gave two numbers which scrolled away, one the time to target, the other distance to target, and both were coming up way too fast in her opinion. She could do with a few more minutes analysing the area they had agreed on as the landing zone.

'How?'

'Come on, they know we're here. My guess is they have known for some time. A satellite array of that size and they miss little ol' us drifting through their neighbourhood?'

It had been at the back of her mind. 'If that's the case, wouldn't they have contacted us by now?'

'I don't know. Possibly not. They may be watching us trying to figure out what we'll do next. Maybe we haven't been listening.'

'Dawn,' she said. 'Have we been isolated for tight beam communication?'

'No. No known communication method has been used to contact us. All intercepted communication has been general broadcast."

'Okay,' he continued, seemingly content with Dawn's answer. 'We'll proceed with our current plan. But let's stay alert. I don't like it. This place is spooking me already and we haven't even landed.'

Larsen took them on a slow pass of the dark side of the asteroid, keeping enough distance to avoid higher structures and rocky outcrops. They were, however, close enough to use the external lights, which she switched on to get a spotlight view of the facility.

She opened the light beam up as much as she could to get as wide a view as possible, and the panorama they were rewarded with was extraordinary. Definitely constructed, but not in any way she would consider human. She could clearly demark which elements of the structure were alien and which were asteroid, but the material used was consistent; it was as if the facility had bubbled up out of the rock, heated and remoulded to form the habitat required by those who would use it. Other areas were perfectly sculpted to form what looked like pictograms, or icons, the largest of which was the large flat area they had identified as a landing zone, the landing pad a great triangular shape with what she could only describe as an exploding star image in negative, black rays spreading from a central black circle.

'LZ confirmed clear. Yep, looks good,' said Larsen sub-vocally through the bio-comm. 'Setting her down.'

Touching down was gentle, and the engine which had been working hard to get them here for the last five years went into idle and stopped. She was suddenly aware of a silence beyond that she had become used to; the Elan drive engine was no longer producing the low-level sound, and the slight vibration throughout the ship ceased. The quiet was physical.

'Okay, let's suit up,' said Larsen.

'I'll drive,' she said. He grinned back. 'Can't let you have all the fun.'

While Larsen prepped the rover, she pulled on her astrosuit. Climbing in through the neck space, she slowly worked herself into the one-piece suit, finally the arms bringing the poor-fitting, gaping upper body section up to her shoulders. The suit terminal linked with her bio-comm and, making a secure connection, downloaded her physical dimensions. A moment later the suit had pulled in and tightened across her body, and it was now snug to her skin. Putting on the helmet, it locked into place and sealed with the suit.

'How are you doing with the rover?' she asked Larsen over the bio-comm link.

'All done. You're up.'

She moved through to the next compartment, which ran the span of the ship. On one side there was an airlock for ship-to-ship docking; the airlock the other side linked into the rover which nestled into, and appeared part of, the fuselage of *Starchaser*. Larsen stood next to the airlock control. As she appeared in the corridor, he activated the inner door which slid quietly to one side.

"Don't be too long," he said. "Get in and out. Have a quick scout around, see what you can see, then get back here. If there is anything worth going back for or investigating further we can work out our next move when you're back."

"You're beginning to sound like you care, Larsen," she said, flippantly.

"I just don't want to lose my navigator. Who will get us back to the fleet?"

"If I get lost, I don't think you will want me as a navigator."

"Good point."

She turned around in the airlock; the viewing window was only really big enough to see Larsen's eyes peeking back through.

"I'll be back before you know it."

The outer door opened and she headed into the rover. Larsen had already powered it up, so the lights were on and the driver terminal showed all systems green and ready. She passed through the small cabin and took her place in the driver's seat, tested the controls, did some final checks then flicked the comm.

"Rover One, ready for release."

"Roger that. Releasing now."

There was a metallic clunk as the locks holding the rover secure to the ship withdrew. She manoeuvred the vehicle slowly away from the *Starchaser* and far enough out to gain a good view of her destination. Identifying her target, she logged the location in her bio-comm and fed the detail into the navigation system, the track immediately displaying on the HUD screens which sat just in front of the three window panels.

"*Starchaser*, this is Rover One. I've identified what looks like hangar doors. I'm heading there now. Distance 800 metres. Over."

"Roger, Rover One. Data recording is good, signal strong. Report when you get to the facility."

"Copy that. Rover, out."

Sitting back she relaxed into the controls and flicked on the autopilot. The distance between the rover and the hangar doors was clear, no obstacles and no course deviation; it would give her time to make observations and collect data as she crossed the LZ.

"It's amazing out here," she broadcast. The mic clicked once as Larsen confirmed he received and understood the message. Radio operator shorthand.

The Hayford star began to light the scene as the asteroid rotation caused a swift sunrise. Colour flooded and dazzled, her helmet visor instantly compensating by darkening slightly to shield her eyes.

"Can you see this, *Starchaser*? I don't think I've ever seen a structure like it." Another click on the mic.

Approaching the doors to the facility, the rover dropped back into shadow, the overhang of the structure cut into a rising rock face, as simultaneously the landing platform tapered into a short road which descended down past the surface level of the asteroid. The huge door in front of her was about 8 metres high and 20 metres wide; it appeared to be convex in shape and contained an upper door and lower door section, a sidelong cylinder. For the moment, though, it was just an obstacle to overcome, with no obvious door release or external control.

As she got closer to the door and the shadow of the entrance, she switched the rover lights on, the illumination confirming in her mind her course of action.

"*Starchaser*, this is Rover One. I'm at the door. I've run an analysis and can find no external control mechanism. I'm going to attempt a breach. Stand by."

"Copy, Rover One. Let's see if anyone's home."

Gentle movements of the controls eased the rover into

position. Lining up the airlock square with the vast alien door she extended the umbilical to seal with its cylindrical, convex form. Once in place, she fired the breaching mechanism, and a combined discharge of thermite focused by laser lanced its way through the material. In a matter of moments, the task was complete, and the breaching tool grappled the section of door it had sliced from the whole and extended into the alien asteroid facility.

"*Starchaser*, Rover One. Breach complete. Sending in the Rem-tek. Are you ready to continue? Over."

"Roger, Rover One. Let's go."

With the Rem-tek deployed and Larsen using the haptic link from the ship, she made her way to the airlock.

"Rover One, *Starchaser*. Air is breathable," said Larsen.

"Roger. Airlock confirms," she replied.

The external door to the airlock opened and she climbed through the umbilical section and gangway to the asteroid interior. There was a small step down to the floor, which she took carefully, as there was little gravity here; whoever used this place didn't appear to have gravitational technology.

"Welcome to Rivers 1," announced the Rem-tek in Larsen's voice.

"Oh, come on. We're not naming this place after me," she said with a broad smile.

"Too late," said Larsen. "It's in the catalogue. You're famous."

"Hardly." She shook her head. She would rename it later.

A pool of light spread out from the entrance they had just created. It extended slightly due to the Rem-tek's light, but the asteroid entrance they had forced their way into was vast: she could see a smooth ceiling and floor heading off into the blackness, but the walls and far end of the space was out of sight.

"Larsen, can you run a continuous scan from the Rem-tek and link me the output?"

"Already working on it. I'll have the data in a second."

She checked her bio-comm link with her suit for the atmosphere data and, as Larsen had stated, it was breathable. She would conserve her suit's air. She cracked the seal on her visor and a musty, metallic odour permeated her senses. The air was very cold. After a moment breathing the air and suffering no complications from doing so, she raised the visor to be fully open.

"It's really cold in here," she reported, more as a running

dialogue for the record then a comment for Larsen. "I'm going to head deeper into the entrance. The Rem-tek scan looks clear for 200 metres."

"I'll stay with you as far as I can, but if comms and control is broken, the Rem-tek will slave to your suit."

"Roger that."

The far end of the entrance space was a similar door to the first but in reverse, concave and equally vast in size. It would make sense if this was an airlock, but she couldn't quite get her head around the scale if it was. What could anyone need an airlock of this size for? Again, there were no door controls that she could see.

"You're up Larsen. Need the Rem-tek to cut through."

"On it."

The Rem-tek motored forward and, from one of its limbs, the forearm casing manipulated to reveal a scaled-down version of the thermite laser that she had used on the main entrance. Larsen got to work immediately, cutting a door shape in the metal large enough for them to fit through. Molten metal sparked and dropped to the floor, bright and dazzling for moments as it skittered across the room. As the final cut was made, this time the door simply fell away from them making a deep, rolling sonorous sound in the dark.

Instantly, light flooded the scene, and her reaction was to move out of the line of the door and take cover, but nothing happened. The air thick with smoke, swirling in the rays of light coming from the adjoining room.

"Well, someone's home," said Larsen through the Rem-tek. Without hesitation, it moved in through the door breach. She felt momentarily foolish, shook her head admonishing herself, then pushed herself up and through the entrance.

The involuntary gasp of breath she took was one of awe and surprise. Larsen had clearly had the same reaction, as the Rem-tek was only a couple of metres away. It was a hangar, a starship prepped and ready, it's dark hull contrasted by a large decorative nose plate, deep bronzes in colour and patterned with scrollwork and what looked like lettering and icons. Automation worked around it, maybe applying finishing touches or maintenance, but the activity continued without interruption. Their presence seemed not to alert or alarm anyone. Something in the back of her mind didn't like the fact no one was taking an interest in them, but the sights and discoveries they were making overwhelmed her sense of safety.

She moved past the Rem-tek to get a closer look. Slowly, like a dazzled child, slack jaw and wide eyes, she got to within a couple of metres of the hull. Looking along the length of the ship, there appeared to be no supports holding it aloft, there were a couple of tethers, but they could equally be supply cords providing coolant or fluids of some description. The whole 100 metre or so length of the vessel was free floating.

'This is astonishing,' she said, switching back to the sub-vocal bio-comm channel. Larsen was obviously still in stunned silence.

As she walked on down the length of the ship towards its aft, her hand subconsciously reached up and brushed along the hull surface. Her touch made the black skin of the ship swirl with soft illuminated eddies, as if the solid surface was liquid and her hand brushing through clouds of bioluminescent plankton. The hull was reacting to her touch like he skin of a giant animal.

'What kind of technology is this? This is centuries ahead of our own. Larsen, I hope you're getting this.'

She realised the Rem-tek was now a couple of metres behind her, moving with her as she made her way through the hanger. She had lost contact with Larsen, and the Rem-tek now slaved to her suit and movements.

'You're missing all the fun,' she said to Larsen, wistfully, knowing full well he could no longer hear her.

Rounding the widest part of the alien vessel, she saw the hangar extend further and drop into a chasm of levels.

'This is a fabrication plant,' she continued, talking and describing her observations for the record. 'A starship fabrication plant.'

The hangar ended and passed into a vast atrium, an observation point at the end of the hangar floor overlooking the whole space. Looking down through the facility, she could hardly see the bottom. She could only consider that the atrium worked its way through the entire asteroid, from one side to the other. They didn't see any structures on the opposite side of the rock, but that wasn't to say it wasn't there. They could have missed it. It didn't matter— what mattered was getting as much detail as she could, recording everything.

Peering into the atrium, she tried to make out some of the

features and structures which created a helix pattern down through the asteroid. Nearest were more starships, dotted around the wall of the atrium and, as far as she could tell, close to being complete. The production line clearly ended here, with ships ready to go in the hangar space that she had entered. Further down was more difficult to discern. She connected to the Rem-tek and manoeuvred it closer to the edge of the observation deck. Linking into the optical sensors, she used the magnified vision to look deeper into the atrium.

A bubble appeared in her bio-comm display, but nothing she could really identify, clear and ovoid with a dark smudge at the centre. She tweaked the Rem-tek's zoom settings and pulled out a little. The focus corrected and brought several oval shapes into view, each connected to various umbilical feeds, power stations and other machinery. As before, at the centre of each bulb was a dark shadow. Realisation came to her slowly. 'I don't believe, it,' she said. 'This is a nursery. These ships are cultured biological things. I can't tell if they are sentient or how they work, but their structure, their hull and likely their interior is biomass. I need to get a closer look.'

Scanning around, she found that the platform she was on also appeared to be an elevator, the controls, although alien, seemed simple enough. She hesitated, her finger hovering above what she considered to be the level down button. Brakes disengaged, a whirring sound filled the air around her then the platform beneath her feet began to accelerate down through the atrium. A big beaming grin of success spread across her face. The excitement of exploring was like that of her five-year-old self—everything new, everything exciting.

The levels blurred by as the elevator got up to speed. With the level she wanted coming up, she tried to look closer at the incubators opposite, the smudges looking more elongated and like miniature versions of the ships she had passed in the hangar levels above. It dawned on her that she had not selected a level; how would the elevator know where to stop? With a slight panic, she looked back to the elevator control, and the display was now flashing a different icon, which she presumed was probably a breaking icon. She pressed it and the elevator immediately began to decelerate, her weight increasing and pressing hard to her feet. A soft sing-song voice emanated from the terminal, unrecognisable but probably informing her of level information.

"Capture that voice for translation analysis," she informed the record. "Elevator terminal voice, possibly informing of level."

Coming to rest, the elevator released a barrier, which she had not even notice close behind her when beginning the descent. She took command of the Rem-tek and moved it forward off the elevator deck and onto the floor level. With wide eyes, she began to explore amongst the incubator cells. Reaching the third pod from the elevator, she decided to take a closer look, as something caught her as slightly different about the tiny growing ship inside: a variance to its upper hull. A control panel to its side was blinking with a white light, and she looked around to compare with other pods: no white flashing light.

"The embryonic ship is about 3 metres long and suspended in some kind of fluid within a 5 metre pod. Something appears different with this ship, different to the others. A higher protrusion on its upper hull near the——." But before she finished her description there was a huge physical clunk under the pod which vibrated through the floor, making her jump and shaking her from her wonder. A hissing release of gas alerted her to the floor moving away beneath the pod, making her instinctively step back. The control panel changed to a blue and the pod suddenly seemed to lose cohesion, the liquid, now no longer contained or held to its oval form, just fell into the void below, taking the embryonic ship with it.

The flooring reset and more mechanical sounds emanated from above. Another iris opened, and a bubble of liquid descended with a dark centre, a new ship to continue the growth process and backfill the rejected specimen. But something wasn't quite right— the shadow wasn't even close to those in other pods.

As the pod descended and locked into place, probes or umbilical connections were remade. Her world shifted, as what she was seeing began to resolve itself. A humanoid form was suspended in the pod. Dead or alive she could not tell, but it was definitely bipedal, four arms attached to a bulky, muscular torso, a predator's features and skull, eyes forward-facing, ears to the side of its head. An umbilical cord penetrated the fluid and moved to connect with the humanoid form and, as it did so, there was a slight spasm across the body. An involuntary gasp came from her lips: it was alive.

Dark eyes suddenly flicked open. Startled, she back peddled several paces, tripping and falling to the floor. She continued to back up until her back hit something solid. Instinctively, she slowly looked up, the blocking object behind her feeling less than mechanical, and there was slight movement as she stopped. Looking down on her was a silver-suited face with elven thin features, jet black eyes and a very confused look on its face.

Adrenaline had already kicked in but now panic tripped her into full flight mode. She rolled from under the second humanoids feet and sprang into a sprint for the elevator. Reaching it in seconds, she slammed the control to take her back to the first level. Looking back for a moment, she saw the Rem-tek arrive at the platform entrance ten seconds too late. It was of no importance, she would leave it. A second later it detonated in a tremendous explosion which shook the air around her and sent her to the deck for the second time in moments.

"Larsen, come in," she screamed into the comms, using the control pedestal of the elevator to climb back to her feet. "*Starchaser*, this is Rover One, come in, over!"

Looking up the atrium in the direction of travel, the facility lighting suddenly changed to a deep violet, accompanied by a loud chattering sound. It had to be an alarm. Part of her wondered why it had taken so long to trigger, and part of her just wanted to get out and back to the ship to warn Larsen.

"*Starchaser*, do you read?" It was no use, she had to get closer to the ship. The elevator came to a stop and, before the barrier could move aside, she was over it and sprinting for the rover. 300 metres to cover, her breath already ragged.

"Larsen, can you hear me?"

Static.

"... weird happening out here..."

Passing the nose of the first ship she had encountered, her sprint had become more of a fast jog as the adrenaline both spurred her on and hampered her stamina in equal measure. The first doorway was in sight: the small entrance cut into the giant internal hangar door.

As she reached it, sparks began to flare around the entrance and across the floor in front of her. It was a moment before her mind caught up and realised what it was. Taking a swift look over her shoulder a group of humanoid shadows were advancing at a pace,

304

lines being drawn through the air by their weapons. She didn't have time to analyse the specifics, and she launched herself through the opening.

There was a moment's calm on the other side of the door. There were 200 metres to go, the entrance to the rover now in sight.

Redoubling her efforts, she started off towards the rover, taking a slight arc in her route as not to be in the direct line of the door behind her and any fire coming from her alien pursuers.

"… ship. It came out of nowhere."

"Larsen!" she shouted into her comms. "We have to get out of here."

"Rivers. What's going on? There's all sorts of weird shit going on out here."

"They're shooting at me, Larsen. These assholes are shooting at me."

"… back to the ship…" Again, static. A second later the comms died.

A burning sensation started to spread from her left hip, like a severe wasp sting spreading with an acid heat. Ignoring it as best she could, she pushed on closer to the rover entrance.

The entrance came up fast, and she didn't stop. Similar sparks and flares peppered the vast main external door around the small entrance to the rover, but, knowing what the sparks meant, she didn't look behind a second time. Dodging behind the extended door cut-out, she forgot the step up into the gangway and went sprawling towards the rover airlock. She crawled the last couple of metres into the airlock and pressed the emergency cycle.

The world became a violent miniature tornado. Decontamination took seconds, the internal rover door opened and she flung herself into the driver seat. Ejecting the umbilical gangway, she started the rover forward at top speed.

Still breathing hard but with her immediate pursuers no longer a threat, she took a moment to try and calm herself, to think things through a little, act not react. But as the view out of the rover window made itself known to her, the rover came to a stop not 10 metres from her momentary escape.

SILVERS

Sounds permeated his darkness. Voices intruded on his quiet. Unrecognisable voices. The cadence and soft overtones were almost comforting, he felt as if he was waking from a particularly tough day in basic. Military basic training for the uninitiated was anything but light and breezy. It was designed to weed out the uncommitted, drain the life from you in as many ways as was legal. He was waking up to another day of basic.

He hurt. His body began to inform him of its condition in a chronic, low sustained pain which highlighted a building headache that pinched and punched around inside his skull and behind his eyes. Arms and legs took longer than felt normal to respond, lagging his intention by several seconds.

Finally, he decided to take a look at the world beyond his eyelids. They opened.

The room was dimly lit and an ovoid; everywhere he looked was a mirror. He lay in what he could only describe as a large nest of cushions, which was surprising. The way in which they had been taken suggested to him harsh treatment to come. Nothing suggested a comfortable bed, or the fresh set of clothes which were neatly presented on the bed near his feet.

The voices, which had been a constant soothing noise burbling in the background, stopped and a shadow moved towards him from the periphery of his vision. He tried to rise, to sit and get a better view of his surroundings, but as he did so his head swam and swirled like the worst hangover he had ever experienced. He flopped uncontrollably to the bed again.

"Easy there, soldier," one of the voices returned to give him something to mentally lock onto, something to focus on other than the complete disorientation. Her voice was calm, and speaking perfect English. Opening his eyes again slowly he turned to locate the source. The face was not familiar, but it was Terran, and she was older, older than she should have been if brought out of stasis as the rest of the fleet had. He guessed at forty, but he may have been doing her an injustice. "Stay relaxed for the moment. They hit you pretty hard." She placed a cool hand to his forehead to ease the headache, and the relief was instant.

"Thank you," he mumbled. He did as he was told for a moment and allowed the pain to drain from behind his eyes; the spinning started to abate. The coolness of the contact was tender, and he realised it was the first kindness he had been shown by any stranger since arriving. Then he remembered Reeve and Spencer. He sat bolt upright and looked around for Reeve. All he could see was his obscured reflection in almost every direction.

"Where is Reeve?" he asked, with an urgency that surprised even him.

"She is well and recovering in another chamber. You should try and keep calm, it will aid your recovery."

"I don't need to keep calm," he said, angrily, but realising it sounded petulant and childish his anger ebbed to embarrassment almost immediately. "I'm sorry. It's just the Lieutenant and I have been through quite a lot".

"I understand," she replied, as she moved round to the pile of clothes at his feet. It was only then that he realised he was naked, and his toes wiggled as if to wave back at him to highlight the fact. Grabbing a cushion, he covered himself; he wasn't really sure if it was to save her the embarrassment or himself, but it was the right thing to do—or so he'd been taught as a kid.

With a warm smile on her face, the woman in front of him simply pointed at the clothes. "If you get dressed we can go and join her. She has been awake a little time now—perhaps you can join us for dinner?"

Food. His stomach suddenly turned over with joy. He realised he had not eaten in a couple of days. Pulling the clothes close to him, he wriggled into them, starting with the trousers and then quickly into a loose-fitting long sleeved shirt. She approached him and sized up the fit; even he realised it was poor, the garments arms and legs too long. Reaching towards his collar like a mother making the final adjustments to her child as they dressed, she pressed against his shoulder and swiped gently away. The sensation was confusing at first, but then he looked at his hands and arms as the garments self-sized and became a firm, tight fit to his form.

"Boots are here," she said, pointing at the floor. "They will remould to your feet as you step into them; to take them off, simply apply pressure to the heel with your other foot and step out."

Again, he did as he was told and the boots moulded instantly to become a perfect fit. She was already halfway to the opening door before he looked up. His astonishment at the tech was slowing him down, and he moved to catch up.

The doorway had seemingly manifest itself from nowhere. The mirror-like bubble he had woken into appeared to be some sort of detention system, a force field perhaps. Either way, the door they were now walking through looked much more like the physical world he was used to, and it slid closed behind them with a soft hiss as they continued into the next room. It was a common area, with lots of comfortable reclining chairs and couches, sofas and cushions, the walls draped with images and material, various ornaments adorning low tables and presentation cases. He was now more certain that the Zantanath idea of prison differed quite starkly from his own.

As they entered, Reeve looked across from the sofa where she was sitting cross-legged and engrossed in some task. She waved casually, as if there was no urgency to the situation, her body language stating that all was fine, nothing to be worried about. He was more guarded, but noted her position for later discussion.

Approaching Reeve, the woman turned to him and indicated that he should take a seat. "Please take a seat and I will arrange some refreshment. What would you like to eat? I will try and bring you something as similar to your request as I can."

"You should try the mango," Reeve said as she continued to work. "It's delicious."

"It's not mango, but a much larger fruit they call a Tall fruit. Well, that is the direct translation as I understand it. But yes, it is delicious. Back in a moment." She walked to the door on the far side of the room. Over her should, she called back to him, "Make yourself at home. I know Luc is keen to meet both of you."

As the door closed, he quickly slid onto the sofa next to Reeve and faced her intently, the frown and concern on his face evident. Before he could unleash the barrage of questions he had built up, Reeve just put up her palm to stop him. She continued to tap away at a device inset to the low table in front of her. He looked to the device and back to her, then back to the table. Words and images were scrolling across it at a rate—she was reading. Less reading, more recording for later, banked into her bio-comm and ready for recall at some later time. The only people he knew that could actually read and digest information at that speed were the techs, and, as far as he knew, Reeve was not a tech.

Reeve blinked hard and used the hand she had been holding him back with to wipe away the strain she now felt in her eyes. "Okay. Time to talk."

"Who, what and where?" he said. They were very concise questions and made Reeve smile. It had been the first smile she had given him in some time and it eased his mind, slightly.

"I can only really answer the first of those questions with any certainty. That," she said, pointing at the now closed door, but clearly referring to the woman who had just walked through it, "is Jill Rivers."

He stared blankly at her for a moment, taking in the words he had just heard and making the link; it made her smile again as she saw the penny drop, his eyes betraying him as the confusion cleared.

"Science Officer Rivers?" he asked.

"Yes."

"But she's on the planet surface with Larsen," he stated. "And younger," he added, with further thought.

"Clearly."

"This doesn't make sense."

"It does if you read their mission logs," she said, pointing this time at the table in front of them. "I suggest you plug in and get reading. It's fascinating."

"Send me the highlights," he said. She huffed her response and sent him the collated file via bio-comm. He tagged the file to read.

The door across the room slid open and Rivers walked in with purpose and a breezy excitement about her. She was closely followed by a Zantanath male of average height, slim and muscular, pale china white skin. He greeted them both with a smile and held out a hand. Reeve stood and shook firmly.

"Wonderful to meet you, Lieutenant Larsen," Reeve said.

"Please, it's just Luc now. It's been a very long time since anyone has called me Lieutenant."

Larsen turned to him.

"And Sergeant Silvers, so pleased you could both be here."

"Well, it wasn't all our doing," he responded coolly, as he looked for any level of recognition between them. He knew there wouldn't be of course, the Larsen he knew and had kept alive this last week was nowhere near, but the eyes were just as intelligent and lively, even behind the skin of a Zantanath. The cadence and pattern of this Zantanath's speech were exactly the same as Larsen; the physical mannerisms, again the same. He was no doctor, but from the rudimentary training they had received about splicing minds back into your clone, what he saw in front of him should have been impossible.

The Zantanath Larsen looked at him with a sly smile on his lips and nodded his agreement. "Yes, sorry about that. When our Zantanth friends get an idea in their heads, they are quite forthright in their action."

"I still ache. What did they hit us with?"

"Neural destabiliser. You're lucky they had it turned down. Its normal setting would have killed you instantly. Turned off your autonomic system," Larsen replied.

"Sounds pretty brutal and illegal."

"Only if you're human. Zantanath have no such rules of engagement. You're either a threat and to be dealt with, or not. Currently, we are not a threat."

"We?" asked Reeve.

Larsen looked at the group and motioned that they should all sit.

"We are not the problem. We have just happened to walk into a conflict that has been going on centuries."

He held Larsen's gaze a moment. "We? It's not that I don't believe you, but currently I'm looking at the face of a Zantanath. The words sound familiar, but the face is not." He was not in a place to be aggressive on the issue, but he wanted the point to be made. Reeve was being far too passive, but then she'd probably just tell him to read Larsen's mission logs. He took a brief glance toward Reeve and confirmed his suspicion. She rolled her eyes at him and subtly pointed at the table console which she had been engaged in as he came into the room. The mission logs.

Looking back at Larsen he realised he had caught the silent conversation. Larsen nodded briefly, as if to agree to his own unspoken question. "Let me give you a little history lesson. Maybe it will explain a little and fill in some context for you."

"Please," he said. He meant it to sound as if he was unconcerned and relaxed about the situation, but it made him sound guarded and clearly uneasy with Larsen in his current guise.

"Jill and I were sent ahead of the fleet on a pathfinder mission, to infiltrate and send back vital reconnaissance data, arriving into the Xannix system around twenty years ago," he looked across to Rivers to confirm; she nodded.

"Twenty-one," she said.

"Yes, twenty-one. Time has gone so fast. Anyway, we realised straight away the research teams back home had got things really wrong. Our first mistake was to move in through the defence network to get a closer look—*that* cut off our comms—and in attempting to send out a transmission to the fleet we also pinpointed our location and waved a flag for those looking for us." Larsen shrugged.

"We thought we were being careful," he continued. "Hiding in the shadow of freighters and other large ships we obtained wonderful data on the planet. How could we have known the Xannix were as inquisitive as we were, collecting their own data and watching us. In truth, we were picked up on their systems as we got within one AU, but they let us play a while, to see what we might do."

"And what did you do?" he asked, his mind analysing every word as Larsen spoke, looking for the inconsistencies in his story. A pathfinder mission seemed implausible, but there was no better explanation he could find for the situation.

"After a couple of weeks of data collection, we were quite pleased with ourselves but were fully aware of the comms issue. We needed to fix that. The data we had would be invaluable to the incoming fleet. Jill had worked out that the defence network was jamming us, so we set a course to leave the network enclosure and broadcast from open space. That was when things went wrong."

"Or rather, the Zantanath decided we needed to be picked up.

We were about to breach their defences," Jill offered into the conversation. "They could not allow that."

"Yes. And who has invisible ships anyway? That technology is far beyond us; we didn't even consider the possibility."

"So, you were intercepted by the Xannix?"

"No. The Zantanath. They call the shots here. The Xannix are a subjugated race. Workers, essentially. But they have been given technological advancements to make them useful enough to their Zantanath overlords." The Zantanath Larsen shifted in his seat and crossed his legs into an almost Yoga-like position. Taking a calming breath, he continued. "I get quite excited by all this, you must excuse me. I've never had to relate this before; the memories are quite exhausting." Relaxing, Larsen looked at the two of them intently.

"The Zantanath have been a spacefaring species for centuries and their empire is wide. Xannix is an outpost at best. Each outpost co-opts the lower tech inhabiting race and brings them up a few levels. Then they apply a defence network around the system and the planet becomes background, obfuscated from the universe, turned into their eyes and ears on the frontier of their space. It is quite ingenious: at first, the race they take command of don't even know it's happening. They accept the Trojan gifts with glee— higher tech and advancements to social services, even bureaucracy. But, eventually, the Zantanath are running things from the top and giving the other races the benefit of their *guidance*."

"How do the other races feel about that?" he asked. "Sounds like they are trading up simply to become some high-tech human shield, well, Xannix shield, in this case."

"The races involved are happy with the arrangement. With protection from the Zantanath and the security that provides, it is a happy alliance. The races obtain elevated levels of technology, social and economic growth. It's a win-win."

"But, it's not something they have any political say in? They are a conquered species."

Larsen smiled at the remark. "I can see you are concerned, but there really is no need to be. This situation doesn't concern us. We have been working with the Zantanath military and political elite pretty much since we got here and we've ironed things out. They know why we are here and they are happy to assist us in any way they can help."

"Oh? And why do we get special treatment?"

He was driving the conversation to a confrontational end, and he could see it was beginning to annoy Larsen. Before he could pry any deeper, Reeve stepped in.

"Jill, you mentioned there was food? And, how about a tour?" Reeve suggested.

Picking up on the politic manoeuvre, Jill nodded. Pointing at the far door, she said, "Great idea. Let me show you two around. If you head out to the viewing gallery, I'll catch you up in a couple of minutes."

Reeve linked arms with him and smiled at Jill. "Sounds good," she said and negotiated him through the door with subtle force.

REEVE

Silvers had been needlessly confrontational with Larsen. Granted, this Larsen didn't look like Larsen any more, but from his manner and speech, she could see enough similarities for there to be a plausible explanation. She was in a new skin, why couldn't Larsen be? She would find out what was going on here, but Silvers charging around and firing his mouth off was going to cause them more trouble than it would get them answers.

As they got a couple of metres through the door, she used the leverage of their linked arms to push and twist him in front of her and towards the windows of the viewing gallery ahead of them. Through gritted teeth she bent close to him and hissed, "What do you think you're doing? For the last few minutes I've been sending you messages telling you to shut up. Why are you still talking?"

"I've been ignoring them. That guy is not Larsen. Who is he?" Silvers responded with arrogant certainty.

"Who cares? We're not going to get any answers if the next thing they do is space us because you're being an air-waster. Now calm down and start thinking about…" She didn't finish the sentence.

Her eyes had wandered past him out into the space beyond the viewing gallery. The view was unlike anything she had ever seen before, and it drew her past Silvers and closer to the windows, her eyes as wide as a child seeing the stars for the first time. Silvers followed her gaze, bemused until he realised what she was looking at. They both stood there transfixed.

They were on a station, and it was vast. As the observation glass rose above their heads, she followed the arch of the station all the way round to the right and up until it returned to her left. The ring-shaped station was washed with the brightest light, casting hard shadows in parts, as the superstructure jutted and spiked above and below the main ring foundation. It occurred to her instantly that they must be close to the Xannix star, as the ring rotated slowly, applying the force they needed to replicate the effect of gravity. Nine towers pointed towards the centre of the rotation and appeared to flash at the end, red navigation lights possibly to indicate high obstacles to traffic. But she was distracted by an inconsistency in her vision. As she stared at the central space, it appeared misaligned somehow to local space—the stars wrong and a planet cut in half across an invisible boundary—but the details of what she was seeing were lost in the awe she felt at that moment.

"Astonishing, isn't it?" said Jill from behind them both.

She felt as if she should have reacted in some way. Jill had crept up behind them so silently, or perhaps she had just been too distracted. Neither Silvers nor she said a word as Jill continued.

"A continuously open gateway from one star system to another. This station sits within the corona of both stars and utilises the local energies drawn from each star to bridge the distance in spacetime. It's wormhole technology and then some. It really is something."

As she spoke, a ship came through the portal. She didn't recognise the design—it didn't look like any of the Xannix ships she had seen so far—but she realised she was working from a particularly small sample size. The ship was a long flat fuselage bulging at the stern and broadening to a hammer-head head shape at the bow, and it glistened silver with a central nose section of gold in the intense starlight. Decorative scrollwork was styled across the gold section, giving the ship a real elegance in her eyes. Zantanath, she guessed.

"Ah," said Jill. "The Setak'da has arrived. She is excited to meet you. Looks like dinner plans will have to wait. I'll inform Luc and take you to her."

*

They had watched the majestic ship manoeuvre for a few more

minutes while Jill had communicated the revised plans back to Luc, the ship appearing small as it had arrived through the portal; however, as it approached the station to dock, its true size became apparent. She didn't think it was quite the same size as the *Endeavour*, but close, and where she understood the purpose of their colony ships, this ship was smooth and unreadable, no overt weapons, no obvious launch bays. If it was a military ship, it was well disguised.

Jill had returned with Luc and they had been taken to a large room with a central raised platform, illuminated from the floor.

"Please keep within the guide rails," Luc instructed, as he raised his hand and made a small side-to-side motion.

The world around them began to shimmer with a silvery surface then it became a completely solid sphere, the floor lights throwing their warped reflections into focus for a second before disappearing in an instant. She felt disoriented for a moment as her eyes tried to correct the image she was seeing with the image of the room they had just left behind, a slight visual dissonance as her mind caught up.

Initially, she thought they had been transported to another viewing gallery, but as she slowly turned around to take in the whole room, she realised that they were situated on one of the towers she had seen earlier pointing at the centre of the portal. It afforded them all a full 360 view from a bubble of glass wrapped in a fine lattice of hexagonal transparent material.

"Are we being given the grand tour?" she asked. Jill just smiled at her as they made their way off the platform to a reception area.

Descending the few steps to the main floor, she saw that there was a single figure about ten metres from them staring thoughtfully out at the portal and the Xannix space beyond. The planet she had seen earlier was now fully visible, but it was not the Xannix homeworld, it was clearly too close to the star and a scorched and scarred place where nothing could naturally survive—an analogue of Mercury back home, barren and lifeless. The figure turned as they approached and greeted them with a broad, warm smile and a raised hand. She thought this Zantanath was hoping for a high-five, but Luc stepped forward extending his hand and pressed palm to palm in greeting.

"How are you treating our guests, Luc? Well, I hope," said the Zantanath.

"Setak-da, this is Lieutenant Jillian Reeve and Sergeant Leon Silvers. We managed to assist them in their escape from a Xannix Overseer vessel on their way to their research facility on Hymor. Unfortunately, we were unable to help the third human aboard the ship; the Overseers still hold him I'm afraid." As Luc relayed his information, she realised that he was speaking of Spencer.

She had believed that, in all the confusion of their escape and subsequent introductions on the Zantanath station, Spencer would have been there. It hadn't even crossed her mind that they didn't have him. Alarmed, she fired off a bio-comm trace. It appeared to instantly get the Setak-da's attention, who gave her a sideways glance.

"Don't worry child Reeve, we will reunite you soon enough. We know where he will be, but it will be problematic to rescue him now. It will be best to wait and see what Yannix's next move will be."

"He is most likely licking his wounds right now. He had to pull some tough moves to escape our team. We estimate that he lost ninety percent of his crew in the effort," offered Luc.

"It does not surprise me. He would sacrifice anything to achieve his goals. Barbarian people."

The Setak'da turned and took a few paces away from them whilst lost in her thoughts. With her back to them and staring out at the portal and the distant stars beyond, she spoke to the room. "You have all travelled far to end up caught in a century-old war. It seems unfair of me to say it, and so soon for the new arrivals, but you are the key to ending this war. The Xannix have been troublesome ever since we encountered them, choosing self-annihilation over the chance to prosper under our alliance." She turned back to face them, her long red tunic flaring as she did so, the slightness of her build highlighted by the skin-tight black unitard under the robes.

"Luc and Jill have worked with me for many years now, and their strength and adaptive reasoning has been key to their success. I would like you to assist them in their goals.

"The world you travelled so far to make your home will one day be yours. The Xannix are old and their day has passed. Their number is too low and too weak to continue. Soon they will die out and it will be humanity's turn to thrive again."

She just nodded in the silence that followed, a million questions all leaping for attention, jamming her mind and not making it into speech.

"What are you proposing?" asked Silvers. He had an intense look on his face, and his mistrust shone through. If she could read his facial cues, she was sure everyone else would be thinking the same.

"I will leave you to Luc for the detail. In the meantime, I have other matters to attend to. It has been a real pleasure to meet you both."

As she left for the platform, Luc followed the Setak'da for a brief unheard conversation, leaving them with Jill.

"What was all that about?" asked Silvers in a hushed tone. "Was she just giving us that planet?"

Jill looked serious, the first time her smile had slipped since they had met.

"An oversimplification, but yes," said Jill.

"So, what do they want?" she asked. "Everyone wants something. And I'm struggling to see what they could possibly want from us."

Jill looked across to the platform and the local portal in time to see the silvery sphere form and transport the Setak'da away from the room.

"They want our minds," stated Luc, from across the room.

"And what do you mean by that?" she asked.

"We are an intelligent, creative species. We have proven simply by being here that we can and have overcome huge challenges. No other species they have encountered has managed to explore and traverse beyond the boundaries of their own star system. We are the first."

"So they want to learn from us?" asked Silvers.

"Yes, compare technologies and knowledge, but it is more than that, they want to study us and learn."

"It seems to me they have a head start. I couldn't fault her language skills."

"That would be Jill," stated Luc. "It was one of the first things the Setak'da asked of us, and Jill is a talented teacher."

There was a brief pause while they all thought on the issue. She still felt uneasy about the situation. Something wasn't stacking up and the line about learning from each other seemed light.

"So what is the deal with the Xannix. The Setak'da said there had been a century-long war?" she asked.

"Yes," Luc agreed. "It has been grizzly really, and protracted. The Zantanath government have essentially won the battle, but the endgame is really to alter minds. It will be our job to ensure a sustained peace on Xannix and to continue the work which the generations of Setak'da began years ago. They realised the only way to lead the primitive Xannix was to take up the Setak'da role, which is something like a world president but is more like a global dictator. They have a selection process every few years based on an ancient religious tradition. The challenger and incumbent duel to gain supremacy."

"Only this time round, it's a bit tricky," said Jill.

"How so?" she asked.

Luc and Jill looked at each other for a moment, an untold conversation going on between them. Luc nodded his ascent, clearly this information was of some importance. "We have a high level source in the Seeker regime, who has informed us that the challenger this time is human."

"Well, that can only be one of two people," she said.

"Larsen or Rivers," Silvers added, confirming to her that he was keeping up.

"Yes."

"Who is your source?" asked Silvers. It was bold to ask.

"Oh, I trust the source," replied Luc dismissively. "We have spent years fostering that information channel. It is sound."

There was more silence, more thought going on, as she and Silvers digested the new information. She felt events were suddenly moving very fast and the decisions she made now would be pivotal. But one thing was obvious.

"You know what this means," she asked the group.

"That the Xannix have played the Setak'da at her own game," replied Luc. "They have set up human against human."

"More specifically, you against you," she said.

LARSEN

He had a son.

In all the ways that mattered, his mind was rejecting the premise. It was not his son—his clone had a son, like an identical twin might have a son. This was not his son. But staring back at him from across the room were the eyes of his younger self: questioning, uncertain, confused, a teenager with the emotional turmoil that brought and the anger and violence it could trigger. Whatever choices he made now would be critical, and he felt perhaps more critical than the base decisions of survival he had been working with to this point. He was being assessed by something more than the Xannix, more than the Zantanath: he was being placed in front of a mirror. With his current skin being that of a twenty-five year old, the image in the mirror was a little too close to his own reflection.

But it was the same DNA, as he and Rivers were this boy's DNA donors. It was the same DNA which gave him his body, his clone his body, and now this boy his body. There would be similarities, innate behaviour, but the wildcard in the mix was being raised on Xannix, amongst the Seekers.

His emotions on the matter were in turmoil. The only way he could find of dealing with the issue internally was to delay and distance himself, kick the problem down the road. For now, he had work to do.

They had been relocated to another Arch-sa facility, this one further north-east of the city, far deeper underground. He had indicated to Ovitala that the Overseers had been tracking him, via his internal communications wetware. She had been unfazed by the news, perhaps she had even expected it, but within moments they were altering course and heading for an Arch-sa within the impregnable frozen mountains of the northern tundra. He had been isolated on the journey, and transferred to a cabin of his own on a shuttle, presumably one flooded with electromagnetic noise and countermeasures to suppress his signal.

As they arrived, he was marched off and through the facility, he and Rivers both wearing cloaks to obscure their appearance from the general populous. Ovitala was clearly being far more cautious, a level of mistrust even in her own people. Notably, to him at least, the boy was not disguised. Clarion was visibly and recognisably a part of everyday life here—the fact that he was not Xannix didn't seem to matter to the general populous, or Ovitala. Ovitala was, at least to his observations, exhibiting very maternal behaviour by checking on Clarion regularly. The fact that Rivers was now emotionally connecting so quickly to Clarion appeared to irk and unsettle the old Xannix. It was something she should have seen coming, he considered, but emotions are emotions—she would still feel the hurt even if her mind was being logical.

There was no time to dwell on the matter though. As they were walked into the Arch-sa chamber, Ovitala took him to one side while the others continued to the command and control platform.

"Lieutenant Larsen, this Arch-sa is one of the ancient machines, one of the first," she said. He discarded his robes and nodded to show he was listening. The chamber was much smaller than before so he was wondering where the interface would be, there being no obvious mechanical arm or simulator visible to him.

"This way," she said, and moved over to the centre of the room. He followed.

In the floor as they approached, there was what looked to him like a large coffin. Designed for the Xannix form, it was far too big for him, but Ovitala didn't seem to be concerned about that. Standing by the side of the sarcophagus, she pressed a section on the side and the centreline of the top split and slid apart revealing a tank of a translucent light blue liquid. At the head was a crown of electronics which sparkled with flashing lights of various colours, but the thing that worried him was that it was submerged in the liquid. Ovitala pressed the section again in a patterned sequence, and the bed inside began to rise, lifting the crown from the liquid.

"There is little time. We have travelled too long and we have lost the initiative. Celicia will expect your next move."

"And what move is that?" he asked. "I don't even know it myself yet."

"You will try to protect the boy, and the fleet. She will try to attain control of both."

"She cannot be allowed do either," he found himself saying, his mouth seeming to state the words without his brain giving any permission. It was an instinctive reaction. He realised Clarion was affecting his judgement more that he might be prepared to admit.

"I agree. However, she will be aware of your deceptions now. You will not find it so easy to trick her," Ovitala said, as she pointed to the bed which had raised from the sarcophagus before him. "Please take your position on the Arch-sa, head within the crown."

"What is in there?" he asked.

"You know what is in there. Celicia will confront you and try to destroy you. If you want your people to be safe across the coming cycles, you will overcome her."

"So, another battle."

"If that is how you decide to confront her, yes. There are many ways to your destination."

A couple of technicians had joined them and had begun to undress him. They had what looked like a cropped swimming costume to cover his torso, no arms or legs, black with a turquoise strip down the left side. Stripped naked, they stepped him into the suit. He should probably have felt some embarrassment, but considering the company it didn't even cross his mind. He was focussed elsewhere, on the need to keep the Zantanath from their door, but he needed another angle. He already knew Celicia would be stepping up her game.

The technicians completed some final adjustments to his suit then stepped clear with a quick and polite salute, their skin changing to a subtle blue. Without saying anything further, he stepped onto the bed and lay as instructed.

"Remember, you have only to remove her from power to take the Setak'da. The people have seen your worth but you need to convince them. It is imperative you succeed—for both our people."

Looking grimly at the ceiling while his mind whirled though possible plans of attack or resolutions to the confrontation, a message flashed in his bio-comm. Rivers.

"Hey," she said.

"I'll be fine," he replied, pre-empting her concern.

"Don't do anything foolish." There was concern there. True concern, an emotional connection. It had crept up on him from the depths of his being. He looked over to where she stood with Clarion. Her face was a mask of strength and worry. Neither of them had the time to consider the effect the events over the last few days had had on them, but from the sinking feeling he felt in his chest at the prospect of her not being at his side, the realisation that he needed her was something he had not expected. To have this epiphany now was the worst timing.

"Listen, when this is over…"

"You focus," Rivers interrupted, "then we'll talk. But you will come back to me. Okay?"

He smiled and nodded. Tough woman. She wasn't giving him much choice. He would be back.

Sitting on the bed and laying back, he moved into position and placed his head into the Arch-sa crown. The world changed in an instant.

*

It was as if he had been teleported to another place, and it was remote, a world with a red sky and dark, forbidding clouds. A cool wind blew across his face, chilling his skin. The platform he stood on was about thirty metres from the surface of an undulating ocean, waves rising and falling to within only a few metres of the platform edge. The platform itself was large and circular. At its centre was a white circular icon with lines running to the edge of the platform, and within that was a large black equilateral triangle. It was a visual coming together of the two Xannix clans, the Overseers and Seekers combined into one icon. This was the place, he thought.

He was alone. He wasn't sure what he was expecting, but to find no one else there was not it. The time would not be wasted. Making his way to the centre of the platform he scoured the surface of the platform for any clues or detail he could use to his advantage. Initially, the platform looked completely smooth, without any cracks or blemishes, but on closer inspection some areas held geometric shapes or areas which could possibly conceal subsurface access. Potentially these were access panels to conduits and workways, but it was more than the barren disc initially indicated.

Instinctively, he crouched down and tried to get some purchase on one of the panels. It was stuck fast, unmoving. He reached for his tool belt and selected an utiliplex multi-tool. Flicking the control to give a flat thin blade, he eased it easily to the edge of the panel and between the plates. Something in the back of his mind stopped him. Raising the tool to his face then looking down at the belt it had been taken from, he found a sudden inconsistency. The Arch-sa had placed him in a construct; he had assumed he had been transported. He had taken no such toolkit as he stepped into the Arch-sa, yet now he was holding a shiny new multi-tool. He needed to confirm his theory. If true, what could he do here? What could he affect and what were the limitations of this world?

AI container constructs were nothing new to any of the human crew of the fleet—it was where they had been for the last 130 years, but those environments had been simulations of the real world they had left behind, representations of memories and home. Physics there were consistent with what they had always expected, but, now he was in someone else's construct, the rules could and probably would be entirely different. This environment had a specific purpose though: to be the forum or battleground for the Setak'da and Setak'osso. With the history of conflict between the two races, he could only assume that this place was bad and bad things were designed to happen.

Experimenting, he put his palm to the floor and imagined it open. Nothing. He tried again, this time adding motion, moving his arms in the direction he wanted the panel to lift. Nothing. He began to use the multi-tool and worry it into the tiny gap between the floor plates. Levering against the tool, he could get no purchase. He was wasting time.

Making his way to the perimeter of the platform he stood and looked out over the edge, trying to gauge a way off or under the platform. There were no struts or anchor points that he could see and the edge of the platform simply slipped away, forming what he could only think was a bevelled lip to the disc. Anyone getting too close would simply slide over the edge to a 30 metre fall into the cold and icy waves.

There was no way off the platform; this construct had been designed as an open cage. No way off, nowhere to go, even if you could. The only remaining option was to stand and confront your opponent. It was the ultimate conflict resolution chamber.

He returned to the centre of the platform and sat on the floor. While he waited, he may as well rest a while and think things over. Who turned up late to a battle anyway? Or maybe that was the tactic?

Letting his mind roll the problem over, he considered how he might defeat Celicia for a second time, but this time so convincingly that she would lose the confidence of the Xannix people and crown him the new Setak'da. This place was an unknown, and what Celicia might bring to the party was also unknown. What he did know was that she would not be fooled again and would not be as complacent as before. It seemed most likely that she would come in heavy, a show of might and arrogance, and if she did that he was better than dead. He looked again at his utiliplex tool. Why did he have this? His tool kit was all he had been given by this construct. Surely, if there was a battle to be won, it should have equipped him with more. A gun would have been useful, or one of those fancy beam weapons the Xannix had, but no, all he had was the multi-tool.

His best chance would be to attack her at source. He was little more than a hologram in this space. What he needed was to strike her physically, but how?

Lights began to flash from the floor before him, arching away to his left and right both describing a circle around him. Startled, he stood and took a hasty few strides to a place outside the circle. Celicia appeared in an instant, and as soon as she caught sight of him she acted. At a sprint she covered the eight metres between them and landed a swift thunderous strike to his chest. It was as if the world flexed about him. Time slowed as he was thrown clear across the platform, landing like a rag doll and sliding towards the edge of the platform. He wasn't stopping, and he knew that if he reached the curvature at the edge of the platform it would simply slide him into the sea and oblivion.

Self-preservation caused a reflex, his arm thrashing out, driving the multi-tool into the platform surface. There were sparks and resistance as the spike the tool shaped itself into via subliminal bio-comm control cut into the platform floor and slowed him to a stop. Eyes wide and adrenaline high, his legs dangled over the platform edge.

Celicia's tactic had almost worked. He had been caught napping and distracted while she had prepared her attack from distance. She had known what she would do even before she arrived. He gritted his teeth and pulled himself back away from the platform edge.

"Time to die, Larsen," she called to him, as the wind blew across them and the storm picked up. They began to circle each other.

She was a warrior from head to toe: her eyes intense and focussed, her hair now cropped short to ensure it didn't get in the way while in combat, her outfit a striking metallic silver which reflected the red sky and seemed to shift and obfuscate her form a little as she moved. She prowled around the circle they were walking like a cat, analysing him for weakness, choosing her time to pounce with precision. Reaching up to her chest, she pressed some control he could not fully see and from her left shoulder a pair of drones rose from their housing in her suit. He kept seeing his odds of survival dropping at each step they took, each step like the tick of a clock counting down to his death. If he didn't think of something fast, this would be it.

Lights in the floor began to flash again, in almost random spots around the platform, Celicia stopped and stood as if to anticipate what was about to happen next. His eyes darted about for clues, but he came up empty. A slight curl of a smile crossed Celicia's face. In a moment the windswept platform morphed and moulded as pixels flew about them like grains of sand in a storm, disorienting and confusing his senses. As the world settled, the feeling of vertigo cleared and his vision adjusted to the new surroundings: he found himself in a dense jungle, hot and humid. Dense vegetation, tree roots and fallen leaves scattered the floor, animal calls shrieked across the canopy above. He couldn't see her. He started to run.

An explosion rocked the ground to his left, earth and debris scattering into the air, showering him with smoking peat. A second shot came from further behind and right of him, but as he ducked under a low hanging branch the energy bolt went wide, splintering a tree and exploding molten sap and bark across his path.

Jinking a manic route through the trees he hoped to lose Celicia, but in the occasional panicked glances he took to his rear he couldn't see her or any evidence of her. For a split second, his brain told him he had lost her, he had escaped, but the sudden pulses of energy crackling the vegetation towards him changed his mind in a microsecond. Diving to his side and away from the line of earth being kicked up by the barrage, he felt a searing pain in his right calf. Whipping his legs round, he rolled into the cover of a huge tree trunk, three or four metres wide. Sitting with his back against the tree, he took a snap glance at this leg. A perfect line of black was scorched across his skin, as though someone had used a marker and drawn a ruled line perfectly across his calf. The only difference being, *that* wouldn't hurt like hell. He had been lucky.

"Damn it!" he forced through gritted teeth. Time to move.

Choosing a random direction away from Celicia and her drones, he barrelled through foliage blindly trying to find any kind of refuge, somewhere to hide or take cover.

"Come on, think!" he shouted to himself.

More low, wide, spade-shaped leaves obscured his view as he charged through. Without warning, the world inverted. He felt no pain, but he hit the ground hard, the impact taken across his shoulders, his legs whipping to the floor with a shudder. Instantly, Celicia was knelt over him, her face close to his, her grip tight to his collar.

"No time to think, Larsen. Action is all you have now," she said, her words full of menace.

Winded, he tried to form a response, but nothing came from his lips.

With unreasoned strength, Celicia stood and lifted him clear off the floor. The acceleration was swift and the blur of green foliage bright as it slapped and tore at his skin. His flight through the air came to an abrupt, twisting halt as he struck a tree trunk and landed awkwardly across exposed roots.

Pain was acute on his left side as he tried to gulp down air. His hand instinctively went to the wound to investigate. Drawing it back he could see there was no blood, but the pain was inhibiting, every breath crippling. He'd never broken a rib before, and it was not top of his list of experiences to repeat now either.

Getting to his feet as swiftly as he could and using the tree to steady himself, the world about him shifted again into blinding light.

Raising his hand to shield his eyes, the light obscured to reveal some sort of vehicle. The world was drowned with a deafening noise and the vehicle grew larger and more deadly in his view. Self-preservation took over his reasoning and his legs flexed with force, throwing him without thinking to the side. Rolling to an uncontrolled stop, he found himself wet and spread-eagle, face down on a hard and unforgiving surface. Large pellets of rain struck him and his neck, chilling him as the cold droplets worked their way down his back.

Rolling to a seated position, he held his ribs with a grimace. Problems were beginning to stack up. If he didn't come up with a counter-attack soon, he would all be over. It would be a slow death, cuts by degrees.

Opening his eyes, a pair of boots were in front of him, two, three pairs. Looking up, the boots were attached to legs and bodies. The faces which looked down on him from all about were Zantanath, smooth and porcelain white, hoods pulled over their heads to shield themselves from the rain. From the floor, he backed up, startled, feeling a sudden, desperate need to escape, but he simply backed himself into a wall. It took him all the effort he had to stand, the pain in his side threatening to push him to the point of unconsciousness. The world had changed again. City lights, people, vehicles and bustle. He started down a foreign, unknown street and past the quizzical ghostlike faces.

The street was crowded, people were everywhere, and he kept moving, looking for somewhere to hide. It was dark, but the street lighting flooded the world with light, which reflected off the wet sheen of water covering the roadway and building surfaces. His eyes were wide, awash with incoming information. Nothing made sense, and he was unable to discern even the most simple signage, unable to navigate or know what was safe or dangerous. Considering the circumstances, he decided to designate all the native Zantanath potentially hostile and a danger to him. He noted, however, that none had attacked him on sight. They appeared, on the most part, intrigued. However, he felt he didn't have the luxury of making a mistake. If just one decided to attack him, the rest would be likely to follow its example. He could not afford a single Zantanath to get that interested in him. Keeping his head down and searching for a dark alley or bolt hole, he headed along the street as fast as he could.

An alien cry went up from behind him, and his fear was realised. It sounded like Celicia was calling her allies to assist in the hunt. He saw a bridge ahead; it was wide and vehicles rumbled across as people around him turned to hear the words of the call to arms. With frightening speed, the Zantanath locked in on their prey, and he had hardly made it to the bridge before the first hand grasped at his shoulder. Another caught him and, this time, the hand had enough purchase to spin and unbalance him.

Managing to stumble on for a few more steps, a leg locked with his and he went down, his head taking a glancing blow on the floor. A flash shot across his vision and he blinked hard to stay conscious. The world had taken on a sideways appearance: lights of vehicles travelled vertically through his vision and he could see a forest of legs as the mob began to close in around him.

The first blow took him hard in the back, missing his kidneys but cracking another rib, and a second struck his upper leg. He tried to get to his feet but another vicious blow levelled him again and took him down. Rolling into a defensive ball, the blows began to rain down harder and harder, as more piled in and the mob became more confident. The pain was now less localised, more an urgent, constant message from his body. A kick to the head made his dark world flash with light and erupt with stars. His bio-comm alerts flashed to warn him of injury and that its calls for urgent attention from medical services were currently unsuccessful.

Feeling strength ebbing away as the fire in his body became more and more distant, his mind began to cycle through possible ways out. It was an autonomous action, as the visions he saw before him were like watching a vid: images, past experiences, sensations, his mother teaching him to swim, his father teaching him to dive. Cold rain pricked his face and broken hands, the numbness and bruising he felt in both soothed in some way by the water falling from the sky.

The punishment had stopped, abruptly and without warning. He tried to open his eyes to see what circumstances had changed: one eye was heavily bloodied and bruised, so puffed up it wouldn't open; the second opened a little to show him the forest of trees retreating and a space opening up around him. Slowly rolling to his front, face pressed hard to the road surface, blood mingling with the water in front of him, he forced himself to a crouch, then to a shaky standing position.

Through his one good eye, the darkness of the night and rain about him blurred and obscured his sight. The shadows about him were silhouetted in places, the Zantanath mob now a collective entity of its own, animal and seething, but something was holding them back.

A path opened up in front of him and a solitary figure walked towards him, calm and with an arrogance that he knew: Celicia.

Holding one arm across his body, his other acting as a sling with his right hand crippled and mangled, his face battered and bloody, he tried to straighten and show as much dignity as he could. No matter what happened, he would not be cowed.

"Your species is tough, Larsen. You have put up a brave battle. But it is time to end. The title of Setak'da cannot be held by a human, and more than that it cannot be allowed to return to Xannix. There is too much at stake."

He backed up as she approached, his legs hardly able to move and buckling every few steps making his way clumsy and weak.

Blinking hard again to clear his open eye of rain water, he noticed a second figure had appeared at Celicia's side. Another Zantanath, approximately his height and build, there was a way he held himself that looked familiar. As the figure lowered its hood, the face was definitely Zantanath, but the eyes—The eyes were like looking into a mirror.

"Celicia, end this," the figure said. "It is not wise to play games now. Just end him."

"Why?" he mumbled. It was obviously audible enough for the figure to hear. It was a simple question but it visibly riled the Zantanath. It stepped forward with venom and pointed and accusatory finger in his face.

"Why? Because we are a corrupt, self-interested species who should have stayed on Earth and faced our fate. Now we have come here and unbalanced another world. You will not know the misery we have brought to this place."

Celicia's hand rested tenderly on the Zantanath's shoulder. Calming.

"Enough, Luc," she said. "It is time."

"We?" he mumbled through swollen, bruised lips. He and Luc looked into each other's eyes, both locked in their own turmoil.

"He is my clone, Celicia. He is worthless." With that, Luc

turned and strode back into the darkness. Momentarily, Celicia watched as Luc retreated, but then her eyes returned to him. There was death there.

In anticipation of the next moment, he stumbled the last few paces backwards, his mind racing and time slowing. Celicia raised an arm, the barrel of a weapon embedded in a cuff device she wore large and magnified in his mind.

The air became bright with blue-green energy as the bolt flared towards him, and his world began to tilt and swirl again as gravity took hold, dragging him over the edge of the bridge and into the unknown void below.

CLARION

The viewing screen on the command deck of the Arch-sa projected against the far wall of the room, Larsen's view split out into a panel along with various wide angle visuals of the bridge he had battled to reach. He had been impressed that his Earth father had managed to reach this far. Celicia was a warrior and had ruled the Xannix people for cycles, each Setak'osso dispatched with clinical precision. But she seemed somehow unable to remove Larsen in the same manner; he was proving far more resourceful and creative than even he had given credit for.

But it had been seeing his biological father next to Celicia again after so long which brought back a surge of emotion. His father had been human once, but was now Zantanath in form—he was finally the bridge between humanity and Zantanath he had always aspired to be. The negotiations between their two peoples could begin in earnest, even if Larsen and Rivers had become embroiled in the Xannix effort against them. It was planned for, but it was unfortunate; it could not be allowed to conclude successfully for the Xannix. This was now humanity's home. The Xannix could not be allowed to mess things up more than they had already. From what he'd seen, Ovitala had overseen the demise of one human vessel; he could not allow her to jeopardise any more.

The purpose of his duplicitous life here among the Xannix was a harsh burden to be placed on someone so young, but it was a necessity he could not shake. Sometimes, he felt conflicted by the whole situation, the Xannix unknowing and so trusting, the

Zantanath forthright and forward-thinking. Even he knew this was going to end badly—you didn't need to be a Zantanath Seer to know that.

He watched as the screen showed a large flash of light, a plasma blast from Celicia's firearm, causing Larsen to fall back, struck down by the killing blow. The world tumbled as Larsen's point-of-view camera relayed all the angles of the descent into the icy depths of the Pallees, the ancient river of the Zantanath capital. White bubbles foamed about Larsen as he entered the water head first, blackness enveloping him and the cold river water forcing out all his breath in shock. The mental transference of pain and death in the world of the Arch-sa would be unbearable to the human form now thrashing around in the control chamber, and his Earth father would be dead in moments. He prepared the mask of a bereft child as a show for the Xannix onlookers, many of whom were now standing around in disbelief that their champion had been taken down so coldly. It was nothing they had not seen before, but perhaps this time they believed things to be different.

A howl of anguish sounded shrill in the room, and Rivers was gone from his side in an instant, sprinting the distance between the observation area and the Arch-sa control chamber housing Larsen. She reached within a few paces of the chamber before she was intercepted by some well-meaning Seeker guards who man-handled her away from the control chamber and Larsen.

"Get him out of there!" she screamed. "Get him out of there now!"

Looking around, concerned, he tried to locate Ovitala. She was with one of the Arch-sa techs, overlooking control panels and monitors. The tech was talking fast, his skin rotating in animated colours, almost excited. Considering the circumstances, he didn't understand the commotion. Others were now joining in, focus directed to internal Arch-sa data, until suddenly the Arch-sa commander, Leahkalan, sounded the alarm.

Techs and command staff started running in all directions, others began to relay instructions and orders across the comms, and doors began to slam and seal. They were going into lockdown.

Running over to Ovitala, he asked urgently in Xannix, "What is going on, Mother?"

A face full of worry peered down on him. "The Setak'osso is making his move; it is a worrying time."

Making his move? "But I just saw him die," he said, conveying as much sadness in his statement as he could.

"You see much little one," she said, returning her eyes to the screen over the shoulder of the tech in front of her. "But you understand little. Watch and see your father. He is the one to learn from now."

He followed Ovitala's gaze and tried to make sense of the data the screen was providing him. It was a 3D trace of the planet and a lattice of communication channels to all the Arch-sa across Xannix. They were all showing their status and various other data he didn't fully understand, but one by one they were failing, and shutting down.

"What is he doing?" he asked, now staring back at the primary screens and the crowd of Zantanath now dispersing the bridge. Some were looking down over the side of the bridge into the waters of the Pallees trying to catch a final glimpse of Larsen as he drowned in the blackness of the river. Others had begun to escort Celicia away from the scene.

"Becoming the Setak'da," Ovitala said.

"Risky," said the tech. "Very risky. I hope he knows what he's doing."

He saw Ovitala shimmer purple momentarily and incline her head—it was the Xannix equivalent of 'I don't know'— and he knew then that events were a little more loose than even Ovitala was able to control.

"Look!" A cry from the floor demanded everyone's attention, over and above Rivers' shouting to be let go and the barked orders of the tech commanders. An arm was indicating the action on the primary screen and pointing at Celicia—she had fallen and was clutching her head with both hands, writhing in agony on the floor. The room went silent in shock, transfixed by a sight they had never seen before: Celicia in a weak and open position.

The screen went black.

In the quiet confusion, everyone began to look around, eyes seeking answers. There were no answers to be had. Eventually, all eyes came to look his way. It was a moment before he realised the person everyone was looking to was Ovitala, but it was evident she had nothing. The screen in front of her showed all Arch-sa offline. He had shut them all down.

"I don't believe it," said the tech, blankly looking at the

information in front of him, and breaking the silence. "In all recorded history, this has never happened," he stated.

"What *is* happening?" screamed Rivers across the room at Ovitala. Her desperation now turning to anger, as the room stood paralysed by events.

As if to punctuate the moment, a heavy whir of gears and the release of locks around the Arch-sa chamber in the centre of the room caused an escape of gasses as the lid cracked and popped open along its centreline. The two halves of the lid slid aside and Larsen's arm slapped its surface, spreading super-oxygenated liquid across its top while a hand grasped for purchase. Rising from the sarcophagus, a visibly weak and shaken figure climbed out onto the floor of the room and flopped down, gasping for air.

Rivers was on the move again before anyone could stop her, and this time he decided to join her. He would need to be there for them, to again be the newly found and enthralled son. No one moved to stop Rivers nor him but, by the time he arrived, a crowd had begun to form, including a medical team and techs to investigate the, now broken, Arch-sa.

Rivers held Larsen as the medics worked on him to check him over. Something must have gone terribly wrong, as his face and head were horribly blackened and his hair had mostly gone, only a few blackened, charred tufts remained. The smell was acrid and, although he had never smelt burnt flesh before, he somehow instinctively knew what it was. Larsen was in real pain.

"Stay with me, you hear me?" Rivers was saying. "What were you thinking?"

That got a smile and a splutter from Larsen, escalating into a full hacking cough.

Ovitala was by his side, looking down on them in silence, as if to assess the situation, the damage and what needed to happen next. A tech came across to her from the Arch-sa chamber and lent in close to speak with her.

"The control interface is completely burnt out, Seeker Ovitala. Anyone else would have perished in that chamber. The crown is completely destroyed.

Looking back toward Rivers and Larsen, through the blackness of his burnt features he could see that the medication was clearly beginning to work, as he was grinning—the white of his teeth a weird contrast against his damaged skin.

"I did it, Rivers."

"It's Jill,"

"Jill," he replied, looking her face over anew, like seeing someone for the first time. "You would have thought she had learnt by now."

"Learnt what?" she said soothingly.

"This place," he replied. "It's never about the fight. There's always another way."

He needed to know, and he knelt down by their side. It may have been interrupting a personal moment, but he was family now, and he needed to know. Rivers looked sadly at him and nodded to him, an affirmation.

"What did you do?" he asked.

Larsen didn't even look at him, he was focussed on Rivers. "She put up walls. At first I couldn't get in. I couldn't find her. There was no way to identify which Arch-sa she was in, no way to defeat her directly."

"She would not have let you do the same to her twice," he said.

"But the Arch-sa still needed to function, to communicate and drive the simulation. The fact the simulator container existed at all was all the piggyback I needed."

Rivers looked at his hair and touched a black tuft of remaining hair gently, her mind working to a solution using the evidence in front of her. She looked over to the crippled control chamber for confirmation.

"You rigged all the Arch-sa chambers?"

Larsen nodded ever so slightly.

"Rigged them all?" he asked.

"Yes," Larsen croaked, "I rigged them all to overpower the control interface. I amplified the local power circuit with a feedback loop to the neural link. Turns out their centuries-old systems have poor power safety. Safety protocols can be configured off. For testing."

"You put the system in test mode and blew them all up?" he asked, trying to confirm his own understanding.

"I guess it never occurred to people here to intentionally blow up the thing they consider sacred," Rivers reflected.

A tech ran up to Ovitala with excited urgency, and with a short salute leant in to secretly deliver news.

"I want an open channel to the human fleet commander,"

Ovitala responded. The tech nodded and ran off to execute the order. Turning to Larsen, she made what appeared to be a sympathetic face and coloured a gentle purple.

"Setak'da Larsen," although it was said softly, it caught everyone's attention. "I have had word from the Xannix council of elders. You achieved the support of the council and have been ascended to Setak'da." She bowed towards Larsen, making a ceremonial show of the fact in front of the others.

Rivers looked startled. "We did it?"

"The fleet is safe," said Larsen, closing his eyes. "I think I'll lie here for a while." There was a momentary satisfied smile on his lips, then he passed out.

STRAUD

She watched the news feed from the Xannix surface with an expression of stolid concentration. The liaison team had been working out well, with Commander Kesset accommodating and keen to give them any assistance. Communications to this point had been better than she expected. The live transmission she was now watching was being translated real-time and was describing the ceremonial acceptance of Lieutenant Larsen to the position of Setak'da, witnessed by the Xannix people across the world. She could not quite work out what this might mean. In the short term, she was hoping for a continuation of the ceasefire, but this was only the beginning of a long process of integration. They still needed somewhere to settle as a people, and now a third of their population was scattered across a wide region of the northern hemisphere of the planet. Whatever happened next was not going to be a quick process.

"As I understand things, if my assessment is correct based on the information provided by Commander Kesset, the Zantanath will not go quietly." Obadiah interrupted her train of thought. "I've been running the VERS on this problem. They have been exploiting the Xannix for generations and to be ousted from power will cause political and economic instability which they will not tolerate."

She sighed and pinched the bridge of her nose, closing her eyes. She took a quick inventory of the problems she had stacking up in her mind, then mentally added space for one more.

"Go on," she said, and gave him her full attention, turning away from the Xannix broadcast.

"From the history I can glean from their files, I estimate the soft invasion of Xannix took two generations: approximately 300 years. In Zantanath terms, this was worth the wait. They began to systematically plunder resources and manual labour, setting up a defensive perimeter and outpost to this region of space."

"And our arrival has destabilised all that," she stated.

"Yes. The Xannix have seen an out and taken it. Removing Zantanath control is the first step back from near extinction. Their population has been dwindling ever since the Zantanath arrival and their scientists believed there was no way back—until now."

She looked at him with puzzlement. "What do you mean 'until now'?"

"It's our technology they want. The VERS has calculated that all their drive is towards securing our cloning technology. The simulation is 99.8% confident in this outcome."

"So this current truce is just a ruse?" asked Forester, over her shoulder. He had been following the conversation with concern.

"A tactical move," replied Obadiah. "Better to keep us on side for the time being with a common foe. Using us to move against the Zantanath has worked out for them so far. If we continue to play nice, I suspect they will too. But the moment we close the door on the cloning technology, I expect them to become hostile once more."

There was a pause, the general hubbub of the bridge filling the silence between them. Then Forester shook his head, as if to convince himself his thoughts were off track.

"I have a question," he said. "How do they know about the cloning technology? We've only just got here."

It was a valid point. They had been under attack from the moment they arrived in system; they had presumed this was due to the Xannix being over defensive and aggressive, but what if there had always been an alternate, more subversive, plan behind it?

"The pathfinder mission," she said. Forester looked at her blankly, but Obadiah nodded, the logical connection he had been steering them towards finally made.

"The what?" asked Forester.

"There was a small pathfinder mission sent out by the *Endeavour* about 25 years ago. It had been presumed lost, but apparently not."

"Who authorised that?" asked Forester.

"Clayton, but that's not important. If the team have in some way gone native, or have been compromised, who knows what advanced information the Xannix have."

"So, this whole thing was a set up from the start?"

"I have found little information in the Xannix archives," responded Obadiah. "In 25 years, I doubt they would have been able to keep all information secret. Something would have leaked."

"Keep looking. I don't want to go around accusing the Xannix before we have any firm evidence." She thought for a moment, then moved to her console and flashed through some buttons, bringing up the vid of the comm Larsen had sent her. This time, she moved the screen to be visible to Forester and also sent him access to the file.

As the vid replayed, she paused it and pointed at the screen.

"There," she said, "Zantanath."

"The Zantanath have them?" asked Forester.

"I would suggest that there are more than one group of actors at work here," said Obadiah.

"You think?" said Forester, in a rather sarcastic tone. Obadiah ignored him and continued.

"With the lack of information on the pathfinder mission in general circulation to the Xannix, I would say the source of our troubles lies with…"

Obadiah became instantly distracted and looked urgently towards the main bridge display which was currently directed to view the *Intrepid*. "No," he stated distantly. Turning back to her, he spoke quickly and directly.

"Captain, we are detecting spatial anomalies." Icons began to pop up across the main display screen. A secondary screen showed a close up of one of the anomalies: a shimmering silver globe, growing in intensity and size. More and more appeared, and within a few seconds had become the size of the *Lanseer*, which was a couple of kilometres to their port side and planetward.

As more and more of the globes appeared across local space, her mind cycled rapidly through their options. The globes were not appearing randomly; this was not a natural phenomenon. Whatever was happening could not be good.

"Obi, sound the general alert."

As the alert began to sound across the ship, the bridge erupted into action, orders being given, status updates and reports being received.

Then, one of the nearest globes suddenly collapsed, leaving in its place a gleaming silver ship, sleek and streamlined. It had a shape and form which reminded her of a prowling shark, adorned across its prominent nose section with gold shielding and exotic patterning. From a stationary position, it began to accelerate rapidly, the tracking stats on the display describing an almost instant 8g, lances of energy flaring from bods which dotted its hull. Before anyone could respond, two nearby Xannix ships were disabled and burning.

Another ship appeared from a sphere, then another. In moments, local space would be swarming with these craft.

"Incoming comms from the *Lanseer*," called the Comms officer.

"To me," she said. "Commander Kesset: status. What is going on?"

Commander Kesset looked stern, and his skin had become a deep crimson. Perhaps the translation of red was a universal colour to warn of danger. "Captain Straud, we are being attacked by Zantanath. Our orders are to defend you at all costs. Please hold station and await instructions. We will form a shield perimeter around you. Be prepared for hostile boarders."

"Please clarify 'hostile boarders'."

There was a sudden break in communication, her terminal showing visual white noise momentarily before the connection died. A ship appeared close to the *Lanseer* from nowhere and opened fire. The *Lanseer* had already begun to accelerate and manoeuvre away, much of the damage avoided, but the assessment reported by the *Indianapolis'* battle management systems gave grim readings across the *Lanseer's* starboard side. Almost point blank damage saw debris and atmosphere venting as the ship tried desperately to evade.

"We're sitting ducks," said Forester. "Fire control—activate point defence."

"We'll hold position for the moment," she told Forester. "Comms, get the *Lanseer* back on line. I want to talk to Commander Kesset."

"*Lanseer* not responding, sir."

She watched the main screen as the ship continued her way, following a slow lazy arc away from the Zantanath vessel.

"Looks like she's crippled," said Forester.

"Obi, tell the *Intrepid* to circle the wagons, pull in tight and then hold station."

"Yes, sir," stated Obadiah. "*Intrepid* confirms."

"We're not going to be able to out-manoeuvre those attack ships," Forester said, flatly. "We don't have many options."

The sky outside was becoming crowded. Xannix ships were pulling in around them and suffering heavy fire from the Zantanath. Twenty-eight gold crested ships of varying sizes had now entered Xannix local space and another four or five were yet to come, as silver globes were still appearing and growing at strategic points in high orbit.

A Xannix ship took a hit close to them and fractured in half, explosive overpressure pushing debris and some unfortunate Xannix out into the void.

"Get out," she said under her breath as she watched the doomed craft. "What are you doing? Get out."

Forester heard her concern and watched the scene with equal dismay.

"*Lanseer* is back online. Link coming through, sir," called the Comms officer over the bridge noise. A link flashed in her bio-comm and she fed it to her terminal.

"Commander Kesset," she said, as soon as the image flashed onto the screen. "Can we provide assistance?"

"This is Lieutenant Elhansi," said the figure in the darkness of the bridge. She could see a slight bioluminescence to the Xannix features but little more, just enough to locate them. "Commander Kesset is no longer in this life. We will proceed with his orders as agreed. Please hold position."

The connection closed.

"They're not going to make it," stated Forester.

"This is all too close," she said aloud. "If any of these ships have a core failure, we're all in deep trouble." She keyed a few quick calculations through the VERS and smiled to herself.

"Helm," she said, while messaging new course instructions, "execute course Yankee-5 on my mark. Obi, make sure the *Intrepid* stays close. We're on the move." As Obadiah relayed her instructions, she momentarily watched the battle unfolding across the screens, light and tracking coloured lines reflected in her eyes. Another ship came to a crushing end ahead of them, its hull ruptured and slowly breaking apart, spewing plasma and atmosphere into the void. It was time.

"Mark!"

Stars began to move across the forward display as they rotated and descended in a spiral, the *Indianapolis* manoeuvring as carefully as she could back down towards the planet's surface and a lower orbit.

Forester was tracking the new course and smiled to himself. "Sneaky," he said to her over his shoulder.

"Don't jinx it," she said. "They may not go for it."

"Incoming link from the *Lanseer*," came the call from Comms.

She accepted the link but, before she could speak, Elhansi was already asking questions, clearly very flustered.

"Captain Straud, we had an agreement. Where are you going?" her voice strained and falling back into a heavy musical Xannix accent. At least they had managed to get the lights back on; she could see Elhansi, skin the same deep red as before, but now speckled with white.

"Using available cover. I suggest you follow. That defensive network of yours, I presume it's still active?"

"Yes," said Elhansi, sounding confused. "But…"

"And the attacking ships will be identified as targets?"

Elhansi paused as thoughts and tactics started to coalesce. Quickly speaking to a colleague off-screen, Elhansi started barking orders. Her skin changed to a light blue as she returned attention to her.

"Captain, we will follow." The link closed abruptly.

"She needs to work on her comms sign-off," she said to herself, turning her attention back to the bridge and the descent of the *Indianapolis* and *Intrepid* back through the Xannix defensive network. It was a risk, but with the Xannix now on side, the network should be safe. They would find out soon enough.

"Defence network coming up in 30 seconds," said Forester.

She continued to stare at the display, not the main screen but the rear view showing the shield of Xannix ships manoeuvring to close in and follow as they continued to take damage from the advancing Zantanath. Flashes of light and lancing beams of death danced like lightning across the screen, smaller ships suffering instant disintegration, larger ships rupturing and dying. The Zantanath appeared to be taking little or no damage, return fire from the Xannix ships weak and uncoordinated; she wondered who was in command.

"Obi, what are they doing?" she asked. "They can't hit a barn door."

"I've been analysing the Xannix strategy, and it does appear chaotic. However, I don't think it's entirely their doing."

"Explain," she said.

"Historically, their tech has been provided to them by the Zantanath. I believe they are being sabotaged by their own ships, likely a countermeasure taken by the Zantanath for just such an encounter."

"A kill switch?" she said.

"Yes," replied Obadiah.

She couldn't fault the logic. "How?" she asked. "They must be sending out a control signal or have already sent a kill signal. Could we block it? Reverse it?"

"Not in any good timeframe."

"Defence network, mark," stated Forester as they traversed the satellite plane.

It was then that the hackles on the back of her neck started to prickle like tiny, incessant pins of alarm. The thought slammed to the front of her mind like a hammer to an anvil, draining the blood from her face.

"Comms, get me the *Lanseer*, now! Helm, come hard about, one-eight-zero degrees. Alert *Intrepid* not to drop below the plane of the defence satellites. They are active and hostile. I repeat, the defence grid is active and hostile."

Alarms sounded in warning and complaint as the *Indianapolis* was suddenly thrown into a hard g rotation. She felt the manoeuvring thrusters rattling her teeth, violent vibration running through the ship. As the g forces increased, the breath was pushed from her lungs and the world began to dim, vision tunnelling to a small circle of the main bridge display. Her flight couch detected her condition and took action, flooding her system with a cocktail of chemicals through a cuff in her upper left arm. A moment later, her vision snapped back into hard focus, although there was little respite to the vibration.

She watched the readouts as the *Intrepid* pulled the same crazy evasive turn, red icons littering the screen. Changing direction in a ship of this scale was slow and torturous, the stars outside seemed to hardly move as the rotation took hold; falling through the grid she saw the first of her fears confirmed.

"Taking fire," stated Forester flatly. She knew he was well aware of the tactical blunder she had made, but now was not a time for that conversation.

"Let's get back above the plane," she said. "Comms, where is that link to the *Lanseer*?" she insisted.

The answer came with a flash of brilliant white light across the display, the *Indianapolis'* visual filters activating as reflex against the onslaught of energy. The *Lanseer* evaporating with the failure of its power core under a final punishing round of fire from the approaching Zantanath fleet.

Caught in a trap, they had nowhere to go. They couldn't descend further and the Xannix ships appeared unable to contend with the engagement. She looked at Obadiah, and his grim features said it all.

"Captain, we are experiencing energy surges across the ship," announced the duty Engineering officer. "Decks A through M." A schematic of the ship flashed up on her terminal, icons dotted across the display like an angry rash. They were still accelerating hard against the descent, the outside of the ship relentlessly ravaged by fire from the satellite defence grid and the blast from the *Lanseer* as it died; she felt like things were coming apart at the seams.

"What?" she linked straight through to Chief Cellan down in main engineering. "Chief, where are these power surges coming from?" Her voice was angry and distorted by the power of the engine vibration throughout the ship.

"Not us, sir," Cellan said instantly. "Core is stable. Working hard, but stable."

"Identify the source," she announced to the bridge, and Cellan who was still on the link. "I need to know now. Obi, show me a visual of the nearest energy surge."

Without delay, an image arrived on her terminal, and she recognised it immediately: the bridge briefing room. There was a ball of light, rippling and undulating on its surface, growing to almost fill the height of the room. The technology was the same as the ships outside, but smaller, much smaller. She was certain of what came next.

"Obi, locate all energy surge sources and secure those areas."

"Closing bulkhead doors. Isolating," said Obadiah.

"Forester, get security teams to those locations now."

"Already en route," Forester replied.

Staring at her terminal, the ball of light flashed out and was instantly replaced by a group of armoured Zantanath. She counted five, no six, figures in metallic skin-tight power armour, the central figure, taller and heavier than the rest, seemed to be carrying a mechanism on its back which was crackling and bristling with dissipating energy. At the front of the group was a female figure, helmet and cloak enshrouding her and hiding her features from view. The figure paced meaningfully forward without hesitation, the others following.

"They are placing breeching charges," stated Obadiah.

She wanted to escape, evacuate the bridge, but they had to make a stand. They could not lose the bridge.

"Where's that security team?" she said.

"Almost here," said Forester. "They are being slowed by the high g."

As he said, that the main door to the bridge opened and five armed security personnel worked their way in, already treating the room as hostile and covering each other as they moved.

"The briefing room," said Forester and pointed towards the rear bridge bulkhead, the door to the briefing room sealed and secure.

There was a second or two of silence, as the security team spread out around the bulkhead and took what cover they could to the side of equipment and flight couches. There was little room to move, let alone effect a positive outcome to a gunfight in such close quarters.

Sudden reports started coming in from across the ship, the Zantanath boarding teams arriving in scheduled sequence to key areas.

Sparks and flames flared around the bulkhead door. Detached, the door became a slab of jagged metal and fell to the deck with a thunderous sound. The Zantanath team were through in a moment and instantly identified their targets; the lead female seemed to point at the nearest member of the security team and an energy ball launched from a gauntlet around her arm. In the slow motion of the action, she saw the guard almost fold in half under the force of the blow and fly across the bridge, slamming into the navigation station with a sickening crunch.

A stunned moment passed between the remaining security team before their resolve returned and fed into anger. Automatic weapon fire erupted from around the room. The Zantanath team stood fast and took the onslaught, bullets deflected in mid-air as they approached their target, sparking off bridge control panels, walls and decking. The lead Zantanth moved in an artful almost ceremonial form, bringing her weapon to bear on a second security guard. Another ball of sparkling blue arced across the bridge and round the cover the guard had found to hide behind. There was a surprised yelp as the energy ball struck him hard, picked him up and piled him into a wall. He dropped lifeless to the floor.

Lances of fire came in support from the Zantanath team and downed another two men. The final armed security guard, seeing his team torn apart so easily, launched a final fully committed attack. Leaping from cover he sprang into the air using the headrest of one of the bridge officers as a launch-pad, narrowly missing the officer's head with his foot. Point blank fire rained down on the Zantanath leader as she prepared herself to intercept the incoming man. Rooted, she took the guard by the throat before he made contact with the floor, her suit visibly locked out and became momentarily rigid, the effect of which was to throttle the security guard by his own enhanced weight at the neck. There was a squelch as the neck came apart and the body went slack. Gunfire stopped.

A smoky calm descended on the bridge. No one moved, the crew still strapped into their flight couches. The elevated g began to subside as the *Indianapolis* made its way back through the satellite network, helm easing off the burn now they were back into relatively safer space. Wreckage, which used to be Xannix ships, was strewn across their path, the display showing nothing but broken hulks and debris.

Laying in her couch, she heard the metallic clip of steps on the decking as the Zantanath leader made her way calmly across the bridge to stand directly in front of her. The Zantanath's helmet melted away to reveal her face and intense opal eyes, which stared at her for a moment with a frown, as if to question without words.

"Captain Straud," said the Zantanth in front of her. "Please tell your crew to stand down. I do not wish a blood bath. You are now under the command of the Zantanath Unity."

She had no reply. Were they being made prisoner, or pressganged? She believed at this moment the end result would be much the same.

"Now, please bring this vessel to a stop."

She paused, still trying to work out what she could do. Were there any options she had that didn't end in the effective surrender of the *Indianapolis*? The muzzle of a weapon appeared in her peripheral vision, one of the Zantanath soldiers had stepped up to less than subtly coax her decision.

"Helm," she said, with as much defiance as she could relay in her command, "full stop."